Flight into Terror

Fasten Your Seatbelt!

By
E. K. Barber

E. K. Barber

PublishAmerica
Baltimore

ISBN: 1-4241-2852-8
PUBLISHED BY PUBLISHAMERICA, LLLP
www.publishamerica.com
Baltimore

Printed in the United States of America

To Ken
My real life hero
To Fran
You would have loved this book

Acknowledgements: Thanks to the readers who will recognize in the following pages their suggestions: Kim, Carol, Maureen, Marlane, Judy, Erin, Hazel, Michelle, JoAnne, Eric, John, and Terri. Initial edits were completed by Ms. Barb Estervig and Ms. Kristen Beach

Read the first in the Flight Series:

Read *Flight Into Danger*...the first book in the Flight Series featuring Alexander Springfield and Skyler Madison. (ISBN# 1413709729)

Visit our Website: Go to www.ekbarber.com for updates on further sequels.

Who is E. K. Barber? E. K. Barber is the pseudonym of Professor Elaine Estervig Beaubien (**www.elainetrain.com**) Elaine is an award winning educator, an experienced corporate trainer, an accomplished speaker, a published writer and a successful entrepreneur. She is a member of the tenured business faculty of Edgewood College and writes nonfiction for business publications. As a corporate trainer and CEO of Management Training Seminars, she travels around the world delivering high energy, high content presentations. Her clients have been as diverse as Harley Davidson, the Peabody Hotel, St. Mary's Hospital, the State of Wisconsin, Bayer, Oscar Mayer, Goodyear, Rayovac, and First Tennessee Bank.

Having met all of her personal and professional goals, she semi-retired and moved into other areas of interest. Some would say Elaine completely jumped the track when shed her briefcase, PowerPoint presentations, and class notes and became...E. K. Barber, writer of romantic fiction. Professor Beaubien continues to teach business to graduate and undergraduate students and consult with corporate clients by day...and by night she sits tapping on her laptop. By day, marketing, supply and demand, leadership, employee retention, communication and team building...and by night love, lust and intrigue. From the corporate boardroom and college classroom to the world of romance and suspense...from the pragmatic and practical to the provocative and romantic. Now that is a paradigm shift!

If you are planning a large event, bring E.K. Barber or Elaine Beaubien in to speak, inspire, entertain, train, or just tell her story. Visit her websites for further information, fees, and biographies.

CHAPTER 1

"Love is perhaps the only glimpse we are permitted of eternity."
~ Helen Hayes ~

Alexander Springfield waited outside the gates of the International Terminal at Dulles Airport. He knew Captain Skyler Madison would soon be shooting through the doors leading from the security checkpoint area and into her new career, her new life, and the arms of her future husband. Husband. God, he liked the sound of that. They were going to be married and he wanted her to set the date by the end of the evening. She'd been skittish for the last few weeks, committed to the idea, but not without doubts. It made him edgy that she had the whole Atlantic to fly over with all that time to think. On the other hand, even though she might not admit it, tonight she'd be feeling sentimental because this was her last flight for International Airlines.

Glancing up at the board, he saw that Skye was due to land in a few minutes. Her departure from International was going to be bittersweet. She was the youngest pilot ever to sit in the left seat of an aircraft for a major airline and one of only a handful of women. It was something she was proud of and had worked hard to achieve. Becoming captain was all about skill, experience, talent, training, and the total number of hours logged in the air.

Skye had it all and even though she was young, she was far from inexperienced. Her father, an avid private pilot, had her in the cockpit from the time she could toddle to the plane, and she soloed cross-country before she went on her first date. It was a passion that helped her cope with her parent's tragic death when she was fifteen. Flying was the only thing that could fill the wrenching void, so she racked up an incredible number of hours throughout her teenage years. In addition to her flight experience, she held a degree in Aeronautical Engineering from Embry

Riddle Aeronautical University, one of the finest aviation schools in the country. She could not only fly a jet, she could take one apart and put it back together.

Carter and Bill, two of her best friends and diehard party animals, had everyone at his townhouse waiting to celebrate her new career. Within the next few weeks she would be piloting a Gulfstream for Skyward Corporation, his newly formed consolidated company. Her dream machine. Hopefully that would put her in a soft and happy state of mind. He would pull out the calendar and make a few suggestions.

If her sentimentality didn't work, then the amount of champagne the guys had ordered might. He was an attorney and knew about diminished capacity, but what the hell. Whatever worked. Maybe he could talk her into eloping. Smiling, he let that thought develop. By this time tomorrow night she could be his wife. Quick, spontaneous, hot. Just like their courtship. The woman lived for high speed and risk. It could work.

Alex looked out the window and up into the deep blue sky. A perfect day for flying. His mind conjured up a picture of his beautiful fiancée as she would look coming through that door. She was tall, slender, and an absolute knockout in her tailored captain's uniform. She'd be wearing her professional look since she was just getting out of the cockpit of the Boeing 767. With her captain's hat pulled down over her forehead and her regal, confident way of walking, she always created quite a stir as she strode through the terminal. She never seemed to notice the appreciative stares, but Alex was once assigned to shadow her, so he saw the impact of her captivating charisma while following in her wake. He smiled. He'd been immediately caught up in that incredibly intense wake. He'd lost his heart the minute he saw her. And now she was his.

Alex impatiently looked at his watch again. On the seat beside him was a bouquet of her favorite white gardenias and in his pocket was a small jewelry box from Tiffany's. Since Skye had accepted his proposal a few weeks earlier, he was determined to put a ring on her finger…to tie it up and make it official. It was his plan to have her wearing it when they arrived home.

He looked out the window again and decided to change the slide in his mind to Skye as he'd last seen her. She wasn't an early riser, hated waking up in fact, so she'd still been in bed when he'd left for the office two days before. She'd been warm and naked, her beautiful, well-muscled shoulders exposed, those hands tucked under her cheek as she lay on her good side. Because she'd been recovering from an injury to her ribs, she still favored that side.

Both he and her doctor thought she was pushing it by flying so soon, but she was determined. Alex was anxious for her to complete this last flight so she could concentrate on full recovery while outfitting the new corporate Gulfstream to her specifications. A flash of concern fingered through the pleasant feeling. Would she be fatigued and in any pain from her long flight? Her chest still bore the scars of her brush with death.

Frowning, tensing, Alex shook that part of the picture out of his mind. This was his daydream and he wasn't going to revisit his anxiety over her injuries and recovery. Instead he concentrated on her lovely face surrounded by long, wheat colored curly hair in complete disarray from a night of making love. He couldn't get enough of her most nights and that night he'd known she would be away from him for a few days. He'd spent the time drinking her in so he would have a reserve for the dry spell.

Alex could feel the desire run through his body. Maybe he should move to the next slide. No. He relaxed and enjoyed the feelings the replay treated him to. She was a tireless lover. Her physical conditioning, her passion, her love all fueled her. Okay, he thought as he shifted in his seat. Time to move on. He could feel his pulse accelerating and his lower body dancing to its beat. The people around him may not be able to read his mind, but they would soon be able to read his body if he continued this hot, steamy mental slide show.

Checking his watch again he was surprised to see little time had passed. The minutes were now crawling by. He looked around at the other people waiting for passengers. His eyes traveled over the faces, many of them smiling in anticipation of seeing someone special come into view. His eyes stopped and rested on an attractive, older woman with her nose in a book. He looked in amusement at the cover. It had a man and a woman in a full body embrace, both of them with a look of rapture on their faces. Shifting again, his eyes traveled up and he smiled broadly when he saw whose nose it was buried in the book. Staring and grinning, he waited for her to look up.

Amanda Mitchell was an agile, alert, beautiful woman of 70. She was absolutely hooked on romance novels ever since her retirement and brought one with her to the airport to read while waiting for her grandson. She was getting to the really good part, where the hero and the heroine finally discover they couldn't live without each other. It was the pay-off for reading thirty-five pages of wonderfully tense dialog. Come on. Come on. Just snatch her and plant one on her, boy. Or in this case, because this series was a bit racier, plant one *in* her, boy. When they finally embraced in a passionate kiss and he carried her to his bed, she sighed. Now that was satisfying. Not that she didn't get satisfaction at home, but when she dove into one of these especially hot novels, well...she might be 70, but all her parts were completely functional and could be turned on full.

Closing the book and checking her watch, she saw she had successfully passed the half-hour wait. Her eyes roamed to the cover of the book, onto the fabulous face of the hero. He had a look about him that could melt glass. She always thought heroes in the romance genre were just a bit over the top. Too tall, too dark, too handsome. She blew out a puff of air.

Amanda did remember one man, though...a lawyer she met on a flight from London a few months back. He had beautiful blue eyes and a wonderful, hypnotic voice. Actually it was her little secret, but whenever she read a romance novel now, it was his face she saw. They had a very pleasant evening and slept together after only a few hours acquaintance...fully clothed of course and strapped into first class seats of a Boeing 767. The dreams she had that night...my goodness. Hot and steamy. And it had nothing to do with hormone deficiency or hot flashes. She'd blush right now if she were the blushing kind. She remembered that he played football for the University of Wisconsin and could see that he was still fit and obviously successful. She was a trained observer and he was an eyeful.

Adding up the clues, she knew he was completely smitten with the female pilot of the craft...actually the captain. Amanda had often wondered what happened to that little affair. The captain had come back to use the lavatory that night while dreamboat was sleeping. She just stood looking at him with such tenderness and affection on her face that it made Amanda's romantic heart soar like the metal bird she was in. The captain was tall and trim and striking in her uniform, but it was the look on her face that made her so compelling. In that unguarded moment, her face reflected her timeless love for the sleeping man.

Needless to say, the man the captain stood drinking in with her eyes was dazzling...his handsome face was caught in the soft illumination of the plane's night lighting. He'd taken off his jacket and tie, and rolled up the sleeves to reveal beautifully muscled arms. They were folded over his broad chest and the steady, deep breathing of slumber made them move slightly up and down. God, what a picture he made. The pilot's eyes softened as she lingered and indulged herself in the best show in the air.

The lawyer and the pilot. Now that was a title for a romance novel. She sighed again, looked up and stared into the smiling blue eyes of her daydream. At first she thought she had conjured him up from her mind. Then she thought she might be hallucinating, but her mind wasn't *that* feeble. When she focused on his smiling lips and look of recognition, she realized it *was* the lawyer. She smiled back, absolutely delighted.

"Hello Seat 6A...are the flowers for your pilot?" she asked gaily. He was more casual than the last time she saw him when he had been dressed in business attire. Today, he was wearing jeans and a light cotton v-neck sweater, giving her just a peek at the strong neck and shoulders lying beneath the bulky fabric. He looked absolutely edible.

"Hi 6B." He was pleased to see her. The night he rode in the passenger section of his future wife's aircraft was special to him and Amanda was a part of that. They got a little tipsy on some fine Scotch and shared war stories. She was a retired Washington D.C. private investigator. The tales of some of her cases were captivating and so was she.

"How good to see you." She took his offered hand. "And from the look of you, I bet there's something more for your pilot in your pocket." She gave him a little wink.

He laughed with pure pleasure. "You're spooky, Amanda."

"Not spooky, my dear. Years and years of investigative work has given me the sight. Let's see." Amanda tapped her chin and smiled broadly. She began ticking off her observations. "Even though you're trying to project casual nonchalance, your body is a bit tense...a positive tension but on the edge. Anticipatory. You have white gardenias—her favorite as I recall. Your captain flies the London corridor and it's probably her plane coming in. Of course, there is also the fact that the heat you two put out the last time I saw you nearly caused the fuselage to melt and is probably still roaring in your fireplace. Also there's a slight bulge in your pocket, too slight to be...well." She looked down at her romance novel. "To be the obvious affirmation of your manly desire."

"You must have been really good at your job before you retired."

"That I was, young man."

Pulling the box out of his pocket, he handed it to her.

"I can also see why you were dying to show it off," she said as she opened the box and saw a brilliant princess cut diamond set in what looked like tiny wings. "Oh Alex, I'm nearly 70. You have to prepare someone with an antique heart before you spring this kind of thing on her." She fanned herself vigorously.

"Her sister helped me with the design…do you think she'll like it?"

"It's perfect…a dream. She'll love it. Elegant, strong, one of a kind. Just like her. As my grandson would say, you're going to blow her away."

She reluctantly closed the box and handed it back. "Does she know?"

"About the ring, no. About her status as my future wife, yes."

"That's so wonderful." And romantic, her inner voice whispered. So perfectly, beautifully romantic. "A great deal must have happened since I saw you last."

She had no idea, he thought. "Waiting for someone special?" he asked, taking the ring and changing the subject.

"Sure am." Her eyes twinkled. "As handsome as you, I would say. Not quite as tall, but smart as a whip."

"He's a lucky man."

"Actually, he's only fifteen. My grandson is coming home from an advanced-study program at Oxford University."

"Wow. I'm impressed. Must take after his grandma."

"I'd like to think so. Anyway, fill me in on your romance while we wait, huh?"

He gave her a version that was heavily edited, but she was more than satisfied. His eyes kept traveling to the sign near the door. Even though the plane should have been on the ground ten minutes before, it was still listed in transit.

Why hadn't she landed? He wouldn't have given it a second thought if he weren't so eager to see Skye. It was amazing to him how much he missed her. Four months ago, he didn't even know she existed. Now it seemed he'd been waiting for her his whole life. When they met, there was an immediate, powerful, undeniable attraction. Skye's problems with making a commitment were daunting and it had taken a relentless campaign before she agreed to make their relationship permanent. But there had been no denying the perfection of the chemistry or its combustible quality. He needed every bit of the heat to melt the steel she had constructed around her heart and now he was determined to get the ring on her finger before she changed her mind.

When he looked at his watch again, she laughed. "The passing of time is relative, isn't it? I'll try not to take offense with your obsession for moving time along."

"I just want to get this ring on her finger before she comes to her senses," said Alex.

"I'm surprised that after all these months with you she has any senses left," Amanda laughed.

They smiled at each other and Alex was about to respond when they both felt the chill. Their smiles froze, then faded. There was an unease edging through the space around them and it rippled through them at the same moment. Tension edged with fear.

Had Alex not been so engaged in conversation with Amanda, he would have seen the uniformed officials from International Airlines enter the waiting area a few minutes earlier. Now both Amanda and Alex turned to look at them. Alex's instincts made him suddenly alert. Immediately attentive. Amanda's intuition wasn't far behind. Something was wrong. Very, very wrong.

The officials were whispering with a few of the security guards and were about to make an important announcement. An announcement that was the nightmare of every airline official in the industry...and every friend, family member, and associate waiting for an anticipated landing. The gathered assortment of people stopped talking, turned, and stared at the grim-faced pair.

"Excuse me, ladies and gentlemen. My name is Paula Frost and this is Charles Bushman. We would appreciate it if you're waiting for passengers and crew from Flight 127, to please come with us. We would like to talk with you about the status of the flight."

Alex could see the anxiety around the eyes and mouth of Frost and Bushman. He knew what was coming and so did the people around them. They had seen this kind of thing acted out several times on television. It was the first step in the devastation of families and friends. The preliminary announcement leading to the horrific collective grief of a plane crash.

Both Alex and Amanda shot out of their chairs as the people began to press forward.

"Did the plane crash?" asked a hysterical woman standing next to the counter. "My husband was aboard that flight! Oh my God! Oh my God!"

She started screaming his name, which set off a cacophony of sound, emotion, and panic. Frost and Bushman tried to reassure the horrified crowd of men, women, and children...all bonded now by a common fear.

"Please, please, remain calm. We will share with you all the information we have on this flight. Come with us while we wait for more data. Ladies and gentlemen, we can't deal with all your questions here. Everything in the sky is in excellent hands. Captain Madison is one of our most experienced pilots and she has a first rate crew. We're simply listing this flight as overdue at this time. Please follow us."

Several more officials from the airline obviously placed in charge of crowd control and keeping the people relatively calm, joined them. They worked as a team to gather the terrified people into a private room in the terminal.

Amanda turned her stricken eyes to Alex but he had vanished. She looked around. The white gardenias were sitting forgotten on the chair. Right next to the romance novel...symbols of what now seemed so remote and extraneous. Her grandson's name came out as a whisper...then as a prayer. "Fisher...oh God...."

Alex refused to let in the panic that was attacking him from all sides. He knew as well as everyone else sitting there what this protocol meant. The plane was not overdue, it was missing. Conclusion: there was a high probability it was down. In the ocean. His brain wanted to scream crash, but he ruthlessly tuned out the ugly, treacherous voice.

He had to move. Move. Now. It was the only way he could control the terror that was threatening to fold in on him. He didn't know what happened, but he did know how he could start getting answers and it was not from the trained spokesperson at the airlines. Nothing from official sources. Flipping open his cell phone, he called the townhouse. When his housekeeper Cynthia answered he could hear sounds of the party in the background.

"Springfield residence. Make that Springfield and Madison residence," she said gaily. Alex swallowed hard. His breathing was coming in shallow gasps and a sharp pain was beginning to work its way up his chest.

"Cynthia," he started.

"Mr. Springfield! Everything is set here. If I can just keep Hazel out of the kitchen and Jason and Al out of the candy dish, I think we have it all under control. Just a minute, I can't hear you, everyone is shouting at me. They want to know if you're on your way home. Let me get to another phone. Here Jason, talk to Uncle Alex while I get to the extension in the library. I'll tell you when to hang up."

"Hi Uncle Alex," said 10-year-old Jason. He and his brother Al were down from New York for a visit. "Aunt Hazel is teaching me card tricks. Mrs. Cleveland said Aunt Hazel has to stay fifty feet away from the kitchen and she has to deal from the top of the deck only." Hazel was Skye's great aunt. She and Cynthia had become fast friends and allies, but Hazel's disastrous forays into cooking were legendary, and whenever possible they found other things for the 80-year-old former Las Vegas dealer to do. "Do you have Aunt Skye with you? She promised to buy me a Scotland Yard T-shirt. I wanna be a cop…just like Dad and she…she said she could get me one. Is she there? Can I talk to her?"

Alex was nearly brought to his knees with the poignancy of this child's eager desire to talk with Skye.

"Hang up, Jason," said Cynthia breathlessly as she came back on the line.

"Okay, Mrs. Cleveland. Tell Aunt Skye I have kisses to trade." The phone line went quieter as he hung up his extension. They always did what Mrs. Cleveland said. She was the keeper of the cookies.

"Whew!" said Cynthia. "It's been hard to contain those boys. It's a good thing you didn't take them with you."

"Cynthia." He couldn't get it out clearly on the first try, so he cleared his pulsating throat and took a deeper breath. "Cynthia."

She heard it in his voice and the vibration of it moved straight from him to her. Through her.

"What is it? Did Captain Madison overdo it? I knew she should have taken a few more weeks to convalesce. Is she ill?"

"No…no. I don't know." The enormity of what he had to tell her thudded through him, making him hesitate…as if stalling would make the reality dissolve and blow away.

"What?" Her confused voice was now edged with fear. "Mr. Springfield? What is it? Alex?"

He couldn't just let her stand there tortured by his silence so he forced the words past his constricted throat. "Cynthia, listen to me. Skye's plane has been listed as overdue."

"She's late?" asked Cynthia, hopefully. Desperately.

"No. I get the impression it's far more serious than that. I want you to find Jim Stryker for me."

"Oh, God." Her voice was small and was starting to shake. "What's happening?"

"I don't know, but I'm going to find out."

Jim Stryker was Skye's godfather. He was also Alex and Skye's boss. Alex was indeed an extremely successful corporate attorney and businessman and Skye was a captain piloting for International Airlines, but in addition to their 'day jobs,' they were both highly trained special agents for the Intelligence Branch of the Justice Department. Now Alex needed Jim, not Skye's godfather and surrogate dad, but Jim Stryker,

Director of Intelligence. Together they would cut through the red tape and get to the inside information he needed. Information that would either put him into immediate action or plunge him into instant, absolute, bottomless despair.

"Alex? What is it? Cynthia is as white as a sheet." Jim's voice was brusque and concerned. "Did Skyler change her mind again? That girl is going to kill me. Let me talk with her."

"Jim, she's not...it's not...," Alex began, then shook himself into a straight line, calling up his training and forcing his mind to remain focused. "I'm still at the airport. Skye's plane has been officially listed as overdue. They're taking the families and friends to a special room now."

It took only a few beats for Jim to reign in his shock and play his role. "This is serious. I'll inform the people here and tell them to stay put until they hear from us. Then meet me at the entrance to the control tower. I'll make a few phone calls on the way and gain entry." His voice was steady although Alex's trained ear could hear the anxiety in the outer edges of his tone.

"Hurry," was all Alex could say before he punched off. He leaned against the wall and put his head back for a minute. He needed to get his heartbeat and breathing under control. Closing his eyes against the unrelenting tightness around them, the terminal faded and he saw images.

Skye, his mind whispered...Skye. He saw her. Skye smiling and laughing. Skye sleeping in his arms. Skye filled with fury kicking out and subduing an adversary. Skye over him, inflamed with passion. Skye as she might be right now...was right now...captain of her craft...her eyes alert and sharp, her hands steady and competent, her mind flying spontaneously to every possible alternative. Polished, professional, driven. No panic, steady, focused, determined.

The very best person to have in an emergency, he thought. His fearless fiancée and professional partner...as hard and multi-faceted as the diamond in his pocket. Alex's heart pounded so painfully, he had to rub his chest. She had to be all right. She had to be alive. They'd come through too much for it to be over.

"Skye." The sound came out softly through his lips. "Skye." His need for her was a powerful and tangible force throbbing through him in rhythm with his heartbeat. His love. His life.

Then he felt it. A faint, unmistakable current of electricity. It flowed through him, giving him a jolt. Starting in his chest, capturing his heart, his soul, then pounding into his brain. It went from red-hot to a fabulous soothing warmth…touching him, blanketing him with a comforting undertone of incredible relief. It was Skye. He could feel her…then he heard her voice in his head.

"Alex. J'ai bosoin de vous. Venir pair moi. J'taime. I need you. Come for me. I love you."

His eyes flew open. It was her voice…not just a memory or echo. He was sure of it. Looking around he half expected to see her standing next to him. Containing the disappointment, he concentrated on the voice. He could still hear the sounds of the airport, the incessant intercom, the passengers calling their greetings, the people talking on their cell phones, the bustle…but beneath it, in a breath of air, in the silence beneath the sounds, he heard it again.

"J'ai bosoin de vous. Venir pair moi. J'taime."

Imagination? Not a chance. It was a voice. Her voice. A whisper in his head. A message just for him. Skye spoke five languages fluently but she usually saved her French for love…for him. When she used the melody and pulse of the language, the words didn't matter. Their sound and sensuality always made his heart melt and his temperature flare. He felt the connection, heard her voice, felt her heart beating. Strong. Alive. In trouble. But alive.

His certainty completely overpowered the dread, controlled the shock, and made the terror manageable. It cleared his head and that was what he needed to get through this. To get to Skye.

Come for me. It was the call from the hunter to her guardian. He narrowed his eyes and pushed himself off the wall with renewed energy and resolve. He was going to find her. Alex Springfield, successful corporate attorney and real estate investor no longer looked like a millionaire or a lawyer, he looked like a soldier ready for battle. All Special Agent Springfield needed now was information and a plan.

Less than twenty minutes later he met a serious and subdued Jim at the doorway to the control tower. Jim already had clearance passes, keys, and identification. He worked fast and efficiently. "We'll be meeting with the team in the tower. They're waiting for us. I saw Duncan outside, filled him in and sent him home." Duncan was Alex's driver. He'd been waiting to drive his boss and the captain to the party.

"Sloane, Hazel, the rest?" asked Alex. As concerned as he was, he also realized the tremendous blow it must have been to Skye's friends and family.

"They've all agreed to wait at the house. They want to be together anyway. It's become its own command center. Sloane is on the computer working to gain access into the manifest."

Sloane Madison was Skye's fourteen-year-old sister with a genius IQ off any known intelligence chart. One of her interests and areas of expertise was computer science. She could hack into any computer in the country and would if she thought it could help her sister.

"Carter and Bill are using all their contacts in the company to find out what they can." Carter was the Marketing Director for International Airlines and Bill had been Skye's copilot on many occasions. He would have been by her side on this flight, but he left the company the week before to take a vacation before becoming her copilot on the Gulfstream.

"They're tapping every one of their friends and colleagues," Jim continued. "Alex, I'm sorry, but none of it is good so far. International wants to keep a tight lid on it, feeding the information out to the families and friends first, then to the media. They never want to give out the whole story right away. They prefer to mete out the data in progressive reports. Usually progressively bleak and unfavorable reports in situations like this."

"Okay. Will they call you here with any additional information?"

"Yes. And Alex…" Jim had to take a deep breath.

"I know," said Alex, bracing himself. "It's bad. It's very bad. Tell me."

Jim nodded. "According to Carter, it doesn't get much worse." He put his hands on Alex's broad shoulders and looked compassionately into his eyes. Eyes that were now blue chips of ice.

"The plane is gone…missing. At approximately 1400 hours, when the flight was an hour out, the plane disappeared from radar. Repeated attempts to contact Skye and her crew have been unsuccessful." Jim delivered the report as he would behind his desk…direct, concise, and with no prevarication or deception. A slight shake of Jim's hands was the only sign of the incredible emotional toll his statements were taking on him. He'd helped raise Skye after her parents had been killed. Outside the office she was like a daughter to him. In the department, he was her mentor and she was his pride and joy.

Alex and Jim stood and looked at each other. Two strong, powerful men having to deal with dreadful news. Jim had to clear his throat before he could continue.

"All right…now let's go and see if there's anything new since this last report."

As Alex looked into the agonized eyes of his boss, he forced himself to hold on to the memory of the voice he'd heard in his head and felt in his heart. *J'ai bosoin de vous. Venir pair moi. J'taime.* She was sending him her love and strength…*through* her love and strength. What he was feeling was something critical to retaining his sanity at the moment. Hope.

"There's one thing I have to do first. I need to call Sloane," he said to Jim, who nodded and went on ahead. He took his cell phone and speed dialed her number. She answered on the first ring.

"Alex?" Her voice was breathless with anticipation. "Any news?"

"Nothing yet, sweetheart. I just wanted to tell you." He hesitated. Was it fair to share this with her? Was it fair not to? Trusting his instincts, he went on. "She's alive," he said simply. "I don't know where she is, or in what condition. But I know she's alive."

"Heard her or felt her?" asked Sloane simply.

"Heard her."

"Tight. That's pure gold, Alex." No questions. No skepticism. Her relief was obvious in the soft sigh. "Thanks for calling. I felt her…only felt her. Wasn't really sure, so I didn't call. I was afraid it might be wishful thinking. Find her, Alex. Find her and bring her home."

"I will," answered Alex. Sloane's confirmation, her unwavering belief brought additional relief and his terror took another step back.

"I'm into the passenger manifest right now. I thought I might cross reference it to known terrorists and general wackos," said Sloane.

"Call if you find anything."

"Will do," answered Sloane. "And Alex?"

"Yeah?"

"Thanks."

"I love you, kid."

"To Pluto and back, Alex."

When he met up with Jim at the entrance to the control tower they heard footsteps behind them. They both turned. Amanda Mitchell stood there, her lovely face stricken but set with resolve.

"Amanda," said Alex kindly, but firmly. "You can't be here."

"You know each other?" asked Jim.

Amanda looked from Jim to Alex. "We met on a flight from London a few months back."

Alex just stared. Amanda stood in the corridor. Or at least the woman resembled Amanda. The spry grandma and kindly private detective faded into the background behind a stiff-backed, commanding attitude that radiated personal power. It was an amazing transformation.

"Amanda?" Alex's face registered his confusion.

"Clearance?" snapped Amanda in an authoritative voice, looking at Jim.

"Level Three."

Amanda's eyebrows went up with new appreciation as she looked at Alex. Then she nodded slightly at Jim.

"Alex, I think you have probably met Amanda Mitchell the retired grandmother. Now, I would like you to meet Amanda Lambert. The woman who trained me and a legend at Langley, Virginia." The headquarters of the CIA.

"I'm not just spooky, Alex," said Amanda. "I'm a former spook. And it appears there's more to you than meets the eye as well."

Then she looked straight into Jim's eyes, her green gaze sharp and shrewd. "My grandson is on that flight, James. Please report."

Jim's reaction was swift and automatic. Amanda Lambert was a woman who demanded and received both respect and unquestioning allegiance.

"First of all, the pilot is Perry Madison's daughter." Perry Madison had been Jim's best friend and Amanda had trained him too. He'd been one of the Justice Department's best agents until he and his wife Angelina, the U.S. Ambassador to Italy, had been killed by a car bomb fourteen years before. "Secondly, and most importantly, Captain Skyler Madison is one of mine."

Amanda nodded, her well-trained face remaining stoic even as the surprise of the revelation sunk in. "Well then, for the first time since those officials tried to herd us into a room with their platitudes and clichés, I think I can breathe again. Fill me in."

CHAPTER 2

Captain Skyler Madison stirred slightly in her seat as her breathing changed. A switch deep in her brain clicked on as she spun slowly toward consciousness. On a higher level of awareness, her instincts were sending insistent messages to pick up the pace. Voices inside her head were screaming danger. Urging her to surface.

Prepare for action. Now!

What action? Why? What happened? Good God. Why couldn't she think? What was this cloud and why was it inside her mind?

Danger! Red Alert! Shields up! Red Alert! Red Alert!

Was she on the bridge of the Starship Enterprise? Danger? Where? Who? Klingons? No. Nope. Not Klingons. They're on *our* side now. Couldn't be them.

Her brain was spinning too fast, circling in and out of coherent thought. Danger. Was it real? It felt real.

An unruly mob of thoughts started pushing and shoving at her to get attention…all wanting airtime. Each determined to be acknowledged…screaming all at once. Her plane. Her passengers. Men. Last flight. Alex. The ocean. The cockpit. The instruments. Men talking. Gas. Get up. Fight. Contact Jim. Stuart. No. Going under.

Stop, her inner voice screamed. Think, Skye. Think! Focus! Hazel always said if you chase two rabbits, they're both going to get away. Focus!

Skye forced her thoughts to stop jumping around. Slowly, the voices of confusion in her head stopped shouting for attention and started to fade.

Fighting a nearly irresistible urge to go back under the cloud, she went in to retrieve her last conscious thought. Her brain maneuvered a free fall until she hooked onto the memory she wanted. It seemed like just minutes ago.

She'd been flying. Okay. Good. Solid. Elaborate. She'd been flying a plane. And? She'd been flying on a plane going over the Atlantic. All right. This was working...but why was she so stupid and slow? This would take forever to reconstruct. Right. Start again and faster.

She'd been in the cockpit thinking about Alex and the fact that this was her last flight. Alex...she could feel her mind floating away from its task...drawn by its infatuation with the new target. Alex. A wonderful thought. Stopping its linear journey and digressing into the new image, her mind's discipline began to dissolve. She smiled. Alex. So beautiful...so hot...so wonderful. She sighed.

Wait. This wasn't her assignment. She had a job to do. Slap on some discipline, Skyler. First things first. Fine. She would get back to Alex when she could. She'd been in the cockpit thinking about him and feeling a bit nostalgic about her last flight...doing okay with the lump in her throat when...bam. The image surged into her mind sharp and fully formed. She'd looked over at Stuart and he'd been going under. Smiling like an idiot and falling asleep. What the hell?

Stuart was down. Something happened to him. Something was happening to her! Her brain had a split second to register a faint berry odor and her training kicked in. Recognizing the smell, she'd instantly stopped breathing and held her breath. Her mind raced as quickly as her reaction. Gas. Sterohydroxophene. Fast acting. Fairly long lasting. Not deadly, but it would be if there was no one in the cockpit who could land the plane. She could feel herself fading fast. Damn. She got too much in her system before she closed it down. Scanning all the controls, she took in all the readings. They were on automatic pilot. Safe for the moment.

She was going under. Couldn't raise her arms, couldn't get to her oxygen mask. Was going under. Under. Didn't care. Had to care. Her job to care. It took all of her will, her last bit of strength, to press the button on the yoke and open the radio to the tower. "Sterohydroxophene," she whispered as she struggled against the darkness and the intense desire to giggle. Then she couldn't speak, couldn't move. She'd left the tower a clue. It was all she could do. The last thing she could do.

Then she'd been floating out among the clouds. Who needed a plane? She had wings. Beautiful. *Alex, Venir pair moi. Come for me,* she'd thought as she drifted out into the clear blue sky...the color of his eyes. Her favorite color. She swallowed a giggle. What was the matter with her? On some level, she knew she was in deep trouble but the drug made her very, very light. *Alex. I need you. Something is wrong. Come for me. I love you.*

Feeling the leather seat under her, she realized she must have landed back inside the plane. But not in the cockpit. In a first class seat? The leather felt soft and warm. Nice. She sighed. Maybe it was time for another nap. Sterohydroxophene. What a gas.

Drifting again, she could hear her father's voice. *Airspeed, altitude, or brains; you always need at least two.* How could she hear him? He was dead. Dead for years. Wait. Was it possible? Was she dead, too? Was he there to escort her to the big aircraft in the sky?

Gravity; it's not just a good idea, it's the law. Ha. That was a good one...she could barely suppress another giggle. Dad. It's so good to hear your voice, but I don't want to be dead. I want to wear a white dress and get married and live with Alex. Alex. Alex. His name sounded like a sweet distant echo in the blur of her mind.

Young lady, was that a landing or were we shot down? Dad, stop. I love you, but I would really rather not be dead.

The only thing that scares me about flying is the drive to the airport. There came that urge to laugh again...like the prelude to a sneeze. What was so amusing? Answer? Nothing...not a goddamn thing. Stop. Dad. Please. Something is wrong. I think someone has messed with my plane. That thought brought her closer to the surface. Bye Dad. I love you. Say hi to Mom. I have to go.

She sighed and riding on the extra oxygen that brought into her brain, she crossed through the edge of consciousness...into some superficial awareness of her situation. They'd been gassed. That meant trouble. Serious, nasty, and real. She sniffed. No more gas in the cabin. That was good. From the vibration, she knew the plane was still in the air. Even better. On the other hand, someone else must be in the cockpit. Her cockpit!

She could feel her temper flare and burn away more of the fog. Her last flight and someone else was flying her plane. The temper she usually worked so hard to control was fueling her resolve so she let it out to do battle against the drug, still powerful and alluring. Get a grip, Skyler! Someone else is flying your plane! She breathed more deeply, deliberately using the oxygen flooding into her system to stonewall the pull of the gas.

Feeling mostly conscious now, she slowly, cautiously, opened one eye, just barely, and tried to focus. Everything was fuzzy and there was a floating feeling swimming through her arms and legs. Swallowing a little nausea, she found her throat was dry. Parched. Arid.

Would someone get her a Diet Pepsi if she could get to the call button? With lots of ice? Sure would go down nice right now. Wonder if one of those hijackers would mind serving? If they were going to take her plane, they had to understand it came with responsibilities. There surged the urge to giggle again...the seduction of the euphoria the gas offered. Good God. She swallowed the giggle and recalled her temper to the front lines.

Hijackers. The word chilled her and sobered her up. Terrorists. This wasn't a dream, it was a nightmare. Were they now flying her plane? Somebody was. Feeling the banking and pulse of the engines, she knew they were no longer in autopilot. She needed to get to the cockpit and assess.

She moved her fingers and made a fist. No restraints. They must have thought she would be out for quite some time. Fooled them. Chalk one up for our side.

Hot damn, she had to pee. Could she get to a bathroom without being seen? Uncertain. Reconnaissance was needed before action could be taken. On the other hand, some things were worth risking your life over. Yup, getting to the bathroom right now would be one of those things. It wouldn't do to have one of those hijackers scare the piss out of her. Now that was funny. This time a little giggle did escape. Shut up Skye, she shouted silently to herself. You're in some bad ass trouble here and you have to get serious.

She really, really had to lose this urge to giggle. Moving her head slowly, she did a visual scan. Passengers. Her passengers. That got through the last of the fog. First comes the safety of the passengers. Shifting in her seat, she turned to look back. There they were...all of them. Sleeping, not dead. She was sure of it. She could see several breathing and there wasn't the smell of death in the cabin. Relief flooded through her.

The combination of time, adrenalin, re-circulated air, and her iron will fought the last stubborn pull of the drug. She looked down at the first class satellite phone nested in the arm at her right. Great. Communication device at hand. Damn. Did you need a credit card? She had a few of her credit card numbers memorized, but she wasn't sure she could get them straight. Then she saw the cord. Double damn. It had been slashed. Of course they wouldn't have left any phones intact.

Time to get up...time to conduct reconnaissance. Do it slowly, cautiously, carefully. She smiled. Like when she was a girl and pretended she was Nancy Drew, super sleuth, sneaking up on her adversary. No not like when she was a girl. She had to get to the cockpit to assess her situation and decide on an appropriate course of action.

Study the various scenarios and develop strategic alternatives...she stopped for a moment...where did that kind of straight, cold, professional language come from? The thought popped to the front as her eyes narrowed. She wasn't Nancy Drew super sleuth. Right now she wasn't even Captain Skye Madison, pilot. At this moment she was Special Agent Skyler Madison and she had a job to do.

Slowly and soundlessly she got up. She shook her head to clear it but only succeeded in making herself dizzy. Taking another cleansing breath to brace herself, she started toward the cockpit. Look out hijackers, she thought. Did you ever snatch the wrong airplane. Special Agent Skyler Nancy Madison Drew was awake and on the prowl.

Skye warily peeked in the back to see if there was any movement. There wasn't. Moving past the lavatories she longingly looked at the doors. Both unoccupied. Later. First things first. Cautiously taking another step, she suddenly noticed she was limping. That stopped her for a moment. Had they hit her? Looking down she nearly laughed out loud. She was missing a shoe. She paused, her mission momentarily forgotten. She was utterly fascinated with the shoeless foot. Hey Cinderella, she thought. Stay too late at the ball? Then a flash of Prince Charming came through. Tall, handsome, beautiful blue eyes. Her Prince Charming. She shook herself. Skye, if you don't get down to business, you will never, ever see him again. That sobered her up completely and she took another few tentative steps.

The door to the cockpit was closed, but when she put her ear to it, she could hear voices. Several male voices. They sounded like they knew what they were doing. Sounded like pilot talk. She turned the doorknob slightly to test it. It was unlocked. Okay, she could get in if she had to. She had to trust for now the hijackers didn't have a death wish. Her passengers and crew were all still alive back here for a reason and that reason would bring them in safely. She hoped.

Her immediate need was to send out information and ascertain what the outside world knew about what was happening. She would go back and see what she could do about rewiring the phone and making a call. Looking out the window, she still saw ocean. The sun was on her right, so they were southbound. At this moment due south. No way to tell anyone exactly where she was, but she could provide direction. She looked at her watch and was surprised to see she'd been out for a couple of hours. And time. They would be able to plot a search grid.

The plane would have to land within the next four or five hours. That was all the fuel they had left. On her way back to her designated seat, she stopped off at the lavatory and took care of that little bit of business.

When she got back to the seat, she felt more refreshed, certainly less desperate, and ready to fight the menace. Her head was clearing fast now and the special agent was firmly in control. She had a black belt in Tae Kwon Do, a bright and now functioning brain, a love for close hand-to-hand, and experience in weaponry. She could fly anything with wings. Seasoned, well-trained, and pissed as hell. These assholes were toast.

CHAPTER 3

The air traffic controller and her supervisor were in the auxiliary room off the main control tower. Also present were key personnel from International Airlines and representatives from the FAA and the National Transportation and Safety Board, the department responsible for investigating aviation accidents. They introduced themselves, with Jim being appropriately cryptic about the reason for his and Alex's presence. Amanda kept a lower profile by staying behind in a nearby conference room.

Rhoda McBride from the NTSB appeared to be the woman in charge. She was coordinating the collection and dissemination of information. She had already provided a preliminary report stating that Flight 127 from London with 107 passengers and ten crewmembers was overdue. At 14:05, the plane had disappeared from radar. The Navy and Air Force had been scrambled to launch a search and rescue mission to determine if there were visible debris fields or survivors.

Alex was getting impatient with the speculation and conjecture flying around the room. The discussion assigned probabilities to several possible scenarios. Each scenario pierced Alex's heart since all of them put Skye in harm's way. A crash seemed the most likely. Hijacking was also considered a high possibility.

"Okay. What do you know?" asked Jim with authority. The people in the Tower had received calls from the Attorney General of the United States, the Secretary of Transportation, and the head of the Air Traffic Controllers union, so they knew he was a man who was connected. The first to speak was the air traffic controller. She wasted no words.

"At 1240 hours, Flight 127 transferred from International Air Route Traffic control to the Dulles Control Tower. This is routine. We had it on radar and all reports were on schedule and positive. Here is the transmission received from Captain Skyler Madison at the time of the transfer."

Alex held his breath in anticipation of the sound of Skye's voice on tape. As he expected it was strong and authoritative. She was completely in control. Because he knew her so well, he also noticed a touch of humor in her tone, as if she was sharing a joke with her copilot just prior to turning on the radio for transmission.

"As you heard, it's very routine, very standard. Captain Madison is precise and a stickler for procedures and details." When the people from International Airlines nodded, the air traffic controller smiled. "And I've been informed that despite her relatively young age, she's a seasoned pilot and their brightest tactician. If there's trouble, she's the best person to be in the cockpit." Only Jim looked at Alex. No one else in the room realized what a beating he was taking with every word being expressed.

"Please refer to the forward screen and I'll show you what came next."

They all looked at the screen in the front of the room. An air traffic control screen appeared with hundreds of tiny blips, each one labeled with the number of the flight.

"We'll run this frame by frame for the time period 13:57 to 14:07." They watched as Skye's plane traveled in a steady, unmistakable line toward the airport.

"There," said the controller. "Right there. At 14:05." They all clearly saw the little blip with IA127 below it disappear. "That means the transponder was either turned off or destroyed…or the plane was. In this case we know it wasn't the plane because of what came after, but this was our first indication there was trouble. Switch to the international radar screen."

There was a slight fade, then another screen appeared. "You see here?" She indicated a blip with no corresponding number. "The plane is still in the air, even though it's not sending out any signals. It's descending rapidly…not falling or tumbling or raining down in pieces as it would if there were a midair explosion." She cleared her throat.

"That's a very rapid descent, indicating either a mechanical problem, and uncontrolled dive, or a purposeful drop to go under the radar." Just as she said the words, the plane went below the 500-foot mark and disappeared. The room went completely silent.

The controller cleared her throat again and went on. "We're asking for the cooperation of ground and water sources as spotters, but if we assume the pilot pulled up and is still flying over water and under the radar, there will be little chance of a visual sighting.

"The maximum number of hours the plane can be in the air with the amount of fuel it carried is another five to six hours. It will certainly have enough fuel to reach any landmass, but it makes our search grid huge. If we can't narrow it down, it will be virtually impossible for us to locate the aircraft.

"Now the final and most important clue as to what happened. We received this communiqué from the captain just prior to the transponder failure. Approximately three minutes before."

She played it. It sounded like Skye, but her voice was breathy and soft. Alex's throat closed and he swallowed hard. Like it sounded when she was whispering to him while they were making love.

"What did she say?" asked nearly everyone as the room erupted in conjecture.

"Sterohydroxophene," said Alex. "She said sterohydroxophene. It's a non-toxic gas. Extremely effective in closed areas. Once it got into the ventilation system of the aircraft, it would take only seconds before everyone on the plane is out."

"Gassed?" The room erupted again and Alex looked at Jim. He didn't know if this was good news or bad. It could mean that everyone was unconscious when they flew straight into the ocean and a deep, cold, watery grave, or it could mean that someone wanted the passengers and crew alive and was going to ransom them, make public demands, create a media frenzy for a political forum, or some combination. Alex could only accept the later. It was a chilling alternative, but not a disaster.

Everyone in the room turned to Alex now. He seemed to know something about what was happening the others did not.

"How long would they be unconscious if we assume they're still alive and still in the air?" asked Ms. McBride.

"Six to eight hours, I'd say. It depends on the dose, the size of the person, and the length of exposure," answered Alex.

Everyone did the math…six hours of fuel maximum, six hours unconscious minimum. "So, if both Captain Madison and Co-Captain Modesto breathed this stuff, there's probably no one to land the plane…it was obviously taken off autopilot," said Ms. McBride.

"Captain Madison wouldn't have been awake three minutes after that transmission," Alex said his mind working the time line. "She was already going under when she transmitted…even that was an incredible effort. The gas is extremely fast acting. Someone else turned off the transponder and put the plane into a dive." When he saw the gathered experts nodding, he continued. "If this is a hijacking, then it is a well-planned and executed operation. I would assume there was oxygen on board for the person or persons piloting the plane. Check the manifest and see if you had a passenger request a permit for bottled oxygen."

"What about the gas?" asked the controller.

"The amount of sterohydroxophene needed to render a plane full of people unconscious could be contained in a small canister. It could be hidden in a can of hair spray," responded Alex. "No help there."

"If it's a hijacking, and we sincerely hope at this point that this is the case, then there should be some contact soon," said Ms. McBride.

"Were there any other transmissions?" asked Jim.

"No. Everything went dead after the captain managed to send us the name of the gas."

A fax came through and a woman brought it over to Alex. He read it and nodded grimly. "This may be good news. A Mr. Stratton requested permission to bring two tanks of oxygen for his trip across the ocean. First Class, seat 2B. Where would they have been stored?"

"Probably in the first class closet," responded the representative from International Airlines. He turned to Ms. McBride. "Should we put this out in the media?"

"Not yet. Let's keep this information close for the time being. Hopefully we'll hear from the hijackers. Let's trust they have a skilled pilot in the cockpit and they're better served with the passengers alive. We'll prepare a negotiation team to stand on call. That's all we have for now." The room jumped with activity, everyone knowing their respective duties.

Jim looked at Alex. "Sounds like they have some good people in here and everything is under control. Let's go back to the conference room and start building a strategy of our own."

Alex nodded. Things were bad, but not hopeless. This was terror. It was meant to be frightening, even debilitating. But they were not without information and resources of their own. The hijackers were flying with a highly skilled and well-trained agent on board and Skye had managed to get some information through that was already proving helpful in the investigation.

Amanda was waiting for them, pacing the room, talking on her cell phone and running through her mental list of people she could contact to help with the investigation. She realized she didn't have nearly enough data to begin a tactical plan. When Jim and Alex came in they gave her all the information they had.

"She did an excellent job. Well done. It isn't much, but we can build on it," said Amanda. "It's helpful to know there was no mechanical or pilot error and that the plane didn't explode. Non-lethal gas is good news. Whether they contact us or not, because of the captain's intelligence, we know the passengers are most likely alive and that there are people on board who are probably awake and at the controls. Because of the information on the oxygen tanks, there's a higher probability of hijacking rather than sabotage." That took a great weight off her shoulders and she felt she could think more clearly now.

"Agreed," said Jim. "Mr. Stratton is a good place to start. We'll get going on the security video from the gate, double check the no-fly list and pull together everything we can on this Stratton," said Jim.

"Do you have a list of passengers?" she asked.

"We have."

"How many hijackers do you think there are?" asked Amanda.

"There would need to be at least four or five...a pilot, copilot for backup, and at least two or three guards." Alex responded. "The passengers are out, but they would still want someone for security. If I'm getting the picture in my head correctly, Stratton would be the gas person. He would breathe the oxygen while releasing the gas into the cabin. He's most likely the pilot. They wouldn't want to risk an error and would give him the most efficient breathing device. The other hijackers would use IBA's, individual breathing apparatus. They would be good for 5-10 minutes. That's all they would need to gas the plane, then vent the air. The IBA's could have been disguised as anything."

Alex placed himself in the role of hijacker as he saw various scenarios. Some of it sounded like a James Bond movie, but the technology was well advanced and known to both Amanda and Jim. Alex had reason to know that the tiny IBA's worked quite well. "I wish we knew if they're armed. If they got guns on board, we can pursue that angle, investigating how that happened. If not, it would be a red herring and a waste of time and resources."

Amanda looked at Alex. "You're going with the hijacking theory exclusively?"

"Yes. It not only makes the most sense and fits the evidence the best, but if it isn't the case, then the plane is in the ocean and I don't give a damn." Alex's blue eyes turned to ice cold fury. Amanda now saw the agent, dangerous, intense, and on the edge. There wasn't much left of the suave businessperson she first met. She knew that if the plane was in the ocean, his only mission would be vengeance. Their eyes met in complete understanding and implicit partnership. If the plane was in the ocean, the people responsible would have nowhere to hide.

Jim cleared his throat. "It's a hijacking. Let's proceed."

Amanda looked thoughtful. "Are there any VIPs on the flight?"

"A few. We're checking that now. Do you think it might be more of a kidnapping?" asked Jim.

"It's pretty elaborate, but it's possible. Most terrorists would have brought the plane down right away, or used a lethal gas...in other words maximum shock. There's amazing coordination here, but little actual terror yet. It could be someone on board was their target, for either a financial or political agenda…perhaps both. Do you have a team?"

"Yes," said Jim. "We're calling in some people Skye has worked with in the past. Also some experts on terrorism from the FBI and from Langley to keep up with the terrorist angle. Although I agree with both of you that it doesn't feel like the traditional terrorist act, we can't afford to abandon that possibility."

"I recommend McKenzie Allen at the CIA. She's the best over there. And Dylan Brown at the FBI. Would you like me to call Andy?" asked Amanda.

"No. I've been assured we'll get full cooperation. I'm sure they'll assign them to this if we make the request. If you'd call McKenzie directly and fill her in I'd appreciate it. Her first priority should be to identify Mr. Stratton and determine if there were any weapons on board. She can be very helpful in tracing the source and uncovering the breach in security."

Amanda nodded in agreement and got on her cell phone.

"Who's Andy?" Alex asked Jim as they watched Amanda punch in codes and talk in commanding tones.

"The President, son."

"Whoa…she trained him, too?"

"No, she didn't. The President was never in the intelligence community. Her son was in his class in undergraduate school. He used to bunk in with them when he went to Georgetown to complete his PhD…he was in and out of her house for nearly four years. That's a lot of time to misbehave so I imagine she has quite a dossier on him," said Jim. "Anyway, I know they think the world of each other. She was instrumental in drumming up support in his early campaigns. You could say she was the woman behind the man. And since she's an excellent judge of character and the President is a good man, I would say she did the country a favor."

"And I would say we have a President on our side," said Alex thoughtfully.

"Indeed."

CHAPTER 4

Skye's head was clear now, steady and focused. She needed to communicate their predicament to Jim and Alex, to let them know they were alive and apparently hijacked. Perhaps the men in the cockpit or their co-conspirators had already contacted people in power, but they would still benefit from inside intelligence. She would be the eyes and ears on the inside and she would start now. With a few deft moves, Skye reconnected the severed wires and was ready to test the telephone line.

She put the phone to her ear to make the call. Damn, nothing. No dial tone, no pre-recorded instructions, no annoying little voice telling her what button to push. She re-inspected the wires. Maybe she had them attached in the wrong order. She was a pilot, not a goddamn phone repairperson. Impatiently pulling the wires apart, she started over again.

Suddenly her finely tuned instincts detected a change in the sound of the engines and the attitude of the fuselage. The plane was slowing and banking and she knew instantly they were preparing for a landing. At least she hoped it was a landing rather than a plunge into the ocean but she couldn't think of that now…she had to hustle her bustle. Jim and Alex had to be informed that the plane was still over the ocean but preparing to land. That would narrow down the search grid. She had to get this call through and it felt like time was almost up.

She continued to work swiftly and calmly, her fingers quick and skilled. Her mind was centered on the task rather than on her personal safety or what would come next. One thing at a time. Focus. She barely registered the sound of the cockpit door clicking and the elevated voices. This could be her only chance to reach the outside. Her hands were perfectly steady as she re-spliced the last wire.

She put the phone to her ear. Buzzing! Yes! Success! God, she was superwoman! It pumped more adrenalin into her system. Skye was an adrenalin junkie. It made her fearless and focused.

The door was opening as she tapped in the number. Her heart begged her to call Alex, but she knew that Jim's secure line would be automatically recorded. If she could get some information through, they could listen to it over and over again. She had to put aside the woman in her. Duty. Responsibility. She was now a special agent relaying vital information to assist in the search and rescue of the passengers and crew aboard her aircraft. Hers!

Skye was ready to rip someone apart for taking her plane, especially on her last flight, but she held her considerable temper in check. She dutifully tapped in her credit card number when prompted by the mechanical voice on the phone. This was working, she thought. She only needed a few more seconds. Come on. Come on. God, this phone was more complicated than her cockpit. Now she had to dial the seventeen-digit code for Jim's secure cell phone. She sure hoped the gas was all out of her system. It wouldn't be amusing if the jokester still lurking on the edges decided it would be great fun to order a pizza.

Hearing several voices as the cockpit door opened, she realized she was trapped. She couldn't play possum. If she stopped now, she may not get her message through. The landing gear was lowering and the plane was gliding into a landing pattern. She had to allow herself to be discovered and then improvise to relay any information she could. Hearing the glorious sound of Jim's voice she knew she had made the connection. Hot damn, she was good!

She could feel the hijackers coming through the door, sense their presence. Protect the phone and its location, her brain screamed. Get the information out! Put the phone down. Now! Quickly she stuffed it in the side of the seat, the earpiece between the cushions to drown out anything Jim might say and leaving the mouthpiece up and in a position to carry any messages she could send. Then she rose slowly, deliberately, prepared to divert the hijacker's attention away from the repairs she made.

Three men came out of the cockpit door laughing. They were all armed but relaxed, obviously not expecting to see anyone up and moving about. Skye caught a quick glimpse of two additional men in the cockpit and an island with a long concrete strip just coming in to view through the forward window. The plane was coming in for a landing and the crew looked competent. That was enough to reassure her and eliminate the need to try and take the cockpit.

Her attention returned to the situation inside the cabin, her sharp eyes taking in everything. The assessment was instantaneous and chilling.

Damn, she thought. How did they get those guns on board? It drastically reduced her options. There were three of them and the narrow fuselage didn't give her the space to stand and fight. Obviously there was no escape route until the plane was on the ground. In addition, the men were fully armed and there would be civilian casualties if they started shooting, not to mention damage to the fuselage and to her. All of her hand-to-hand training was useless here. Until she could use it she had to remain, in the eyes of her captors, helpless, soft and unprepared for this kind of event. She needed to bring down their guard and distract them. So, she improvised. One of her specialties.

Pretending to be groggy and disoriented, she blinked her eyes and swayed. She wanted them to concentrate on her and divert their attention away from the repaired phone.

"What's going on?" she asked the startled men, putting a confused look on her face and fear in her eyes. "Why is someone else landing my plane?" she asked, slurring her words. "Where are we?"

Shocked at seeing her conscious, they raised their weapons and looked around to see if anyone else was moving. The man who appeared to be the leader came over and roughly grabbed her.

"Why are you awake?" he demanded as he dug his fingers painfully into her arm and shoved a gun under her chin. Standing at nearly six feet, they were about the same height so she could look into his eyes as he was fighting for control. She took his measure. Mean but not strong, she thought. Damn, she wished she were on the ground. He would have been begging for mercy in three seconds flat. Maybe later. For now, she had a part to play.

Cringing, she stood passively as though in shock. It galled her. He was holding the gun too loosely and he stood in a vulnerable position. Her mind raced with the few swift efficient moves she could make on him, then on the two idiots standing behind him. Out of the corner of her eye, she saw the copilot stand, drawing a weapon. Ruthlessly suppressing her instincts, she kept her itchy feet planted and her lethal hands at her side. She had other people to think of. Making her eyes appear terrified, she opened them wide and forced herself to shudder with terror.

"Please...please I...I don't know," she pleaded, the fear in her voice sounding strange to her, but it seemed to work on the hijacker. He became emboldened and obviously saw her as absolutely no threat.

Lowering his gun, he looked around. His confusion turned to anger at the unexpected difficulty and he took it out on her. His hand shot out and he brutally slapped her across the face. The force of the blow whirled her around. Obviously the asshole knew how to slap a woman, she thought. Reading his eyes and anticipating it, she had moved with the slap, lessening its impact. Working to make it look more serious than it was, she fell to her knees. The rabid gleam in his eye gave her more information on the man. Animal. He was enjoying the physical punishment.

Shaking her head, she cranked up her best whining voice knowing it would feed his cruelty.

"Please...please don't hurt me."

Noticing the other two men were watching with anticipation she felt confidence surge through her. It reinforced her game plan. She could play them. It was going to hurt, but it was going to work. She was going to get information to Jim. This was her training. This was what she had to do. They wouldn't see the phone if they were enjoying the show. All right you cowardly bastards. Act two.

"I have little ones at home. There are five of them." This time the whine was grating even to her ears but they would be less likely to hear her words if she coated them in a voice that was detestable to them.

She had to get the messages home. She knew things, saw things that would provide them with clues and she had no doubt that a team was already assembled. Shaking off the stinging pain in her cheek, she concentrated on her task.

"Sonny was right," she cried and sniffed, enunciating her words clearly so Jim would be sure to get it. She wanted the hijackers to hold her in contempt. To underestimate her. She would take this punishment, because she knew her time would come. She was well trained. She was the best.

"Shut up you stupid woman!" Another slap on the other side. When men thought you were weak, they slapped with an open hand. It stung like hell, but didn't really do much damage.

"They love to play with guns," she said distinctly, but in a voice dripping with fear. "All of them."

"Stupid woman, what are you babbling about? I said shut up!" He pulled her up off the floor then slapped her again. This one made her ears ring and it caused her to bite the inside of her cheek. Good. That would generate some blood. Men like these enjoyed seeing tangible evidence of their cruelty. Taking a deep breath, she spit out the blood that was pooling in her mouth.

"We are landing? You have a pilot?"

God, she thought, seeing him ball his fist. He was going for the gut. Reflexively she tightened her stomach muscles. She brutally censored her natural inbred need to defend as the man drove his fist into her stomach. She went down again fighting to get her breath back. Any other place, any other time and she would have had no trouble putting this man down into a whole hellish universe of hurt before pounding him into a fleshy puddle.

Going out of her body, she fought him in her mind. It was a technique she employed when situations required that she remain passive. Every move was clear. She earned a sixth degree black belt when she was a teenager. On the ground she could have taken out all three of these men in less than a minute. Instead, she drew in a slow wheezing breath and got back up on her feet. Her vision was beginning to blur and she had to fight the nausea, but she needed to project her voice toward the phone.

"It's...it's so warm in here...tropical. Land has small green eyes, the little deadhead." Skye coughed out some more blood. Now the man was incensed. Fisting his hand, he delivered another cruel body blow.

Whoa, that hurt. Skye bent over struggling to breathe through the pain. She needed to communicate more, but there wasn't much left in her. Letting out a breath and sucking in another one, she started speaking in Italian. She hoped it sounded like she was saying a prayer. Appropriate under the circumstances, she thought.

"Stop that praying," he shouted, but she kept up the steady stream of Italian.

He was winding up for another blow to her stomach and she knew it was going to be harder to shake off. Her ribs were just healing from a fight she had a few months before and she twisted to protect her right side. Might as well have matching bruises. Come on, asshole, put one on the left side. And he did. She flew up against the bulkhead and slid to the floor. This one made the darkness descend.

One last thing. She knew she was losing consciousness and she had to get out one more message. One for the families and friends. One for the airlines. She got back up on her knees, then to her feet. Looking back at the people who were in her care, swaying and barely conscious, she leaned against the bulkhead.

"All the passengers are alive and sleeping, why are you doing this?"

This time, the man put all his fury into the punch. He hit her in the face and it was his fist this time. Whirling from the force of the blow she went down. And stayed down.

Still frustrated, he kicked her viciously in the side one last time. There was a satisfying crunch of cracking bone. The pain got through her unconscious state and she moaned in agony. Winding up for another blow he stopped when he spotted the phone. Surprised, he snatched it up and listened. There was no sound. No dial tone.

"Foolish woman thought she could reconnect it," he smiled maliciously to the two men standing with him. Snorting with derision, he pulled it out again. "Leave her there and buckle in. She is nothing."

CHAPTER 5

Jim heard his secure phone chirp. Taking it out his pocket, he opened it up, punched a seven-digit number and was instantly connected.

"Jim Stryker," he said frowning. "Hello? Hello?"

No answer. His heart lifted when he heard Skye's voice but his relief quickly dissolved as he listened.

He heard the scene as it played out and paced out his anger and anxiety. It didn't take long, and every sound ripped through him. His face registered amazement, then relief, then shock, then white-hot anger, then pain. The hand that was gripping the phone shook a little and the knuckles went white with tension. He looked at Alex's face. Then Amanda's. They knew something was up, but they also knew he would tell them when he could. Unconsciously, they braced for bad news.

Finally, Jim held up his hand communicating to them to hold their questions while he punched another set of buttons on his phone.

"Barclay? This is Jim. At your desk? Good. I've placed a call on my secure line on hold. The line may still be open. I want you to trace it." He listened for a moment. "Call me with the information. It may take you awhile. I'm fairly sure it's a cabin phone from a Boeing 767. That's right." He smiled grimly at Alex and Amanda. "Skye's plane."

Alex's heart leapt with relief. The plane was still intact. This was excellent news. But he also saw the pain and anger on Jim's face and it twisted his gut. There was going to be something bad in his report.

Jim quickly punched another number. "You got some recording equipment? Good, bring it up, will you? And a phone-to-disk hookup. Fine."

Jim's phone chirped again. "Barclay? Damn it. Goddamn it. I was afraid of that. Okay. Thanks for the attempt. Call Linda in and stand by. We'll be finished here shortly and we'll want to start working on finding her. I'll brief you both soon."

41

A woman from the communications van stationed outside the building came running in with the equipment Jim had requested. Alex could hear his pulse throb in his ears and was nearly bursting with the need to hear what Jim knew. He admired Amanda's restraint. She appeared calm, poised, anticipatory.

"Jim," he demanded, slowly coming to his feet as the woman left the room. He simply couldn't sit there and wait for a report. This wasn't just another assigned case. This wasn't about a random hijacking. This was about Skye. This was about his life. He wanted answers.

"Now!" he growled.

Jim glanced up while he hooked up his phone and efficiently began pushing buttons. "That was Skye on the phone, Alex. It was in real time. She's alive."

"Christ, thank God." Alex hadn't realized he'd been holding his breath. He let it out in a rush and closed his eyes. Relief flooded though him like a wave of warm water. It was Skye on the phone. She was alive. His heart had known it, but it had been doing battle with his head and his terror since that first minute the International Airlines officials had come into the gate. Now all that fear and anxiety settled into steely determination. She was alive and he was going to get her back.

Amanda came up beside him and took his arm. "Alex, this is really good news." She, too, was nearly at her limit, but if Skye was alive then chances were great that the plane was still in the air and her grandson was okay.

Jim was still working with the equipment. "From what I can gather, she must have shaken off the effect of the drug. We expected them to be under for hours yet, but she has incredibly quick reflexes. I guess she took action the moment she sensed danger and held her breath. They're still in the air, Alex, but coming in for a landing. She dropped several clues and we'll need to go back to confirm my memory." He looked at Alex. "I know she probably wanted to call you first, but she had to report to me. She knew there would be a recording if she was on my phone and from what I heard, she only had one chance…"

"That's okay. Doesn't matter." Although for a second it did. His heart took a hit when he realized she'd used her time to call Jim first. But it made sense. Their agent was alive and working. On the inside. She was doing her job. His fiancée was in there too, but she would come to him when her plane was home and her passengers were safe. Watching Jim closely, he couldn't get past the look on the man's face. It was far too grim for good news.

"I've replayed the call and placed it into the recording disk in this machine."

"Let's hear it," demanded Alex. He was anxious to hear her voice. Just to hear her voice.

Jim knew that too, but he had to prepare both the agent and the man for what he was going to hear.

"Sit down, Alex."

Alex felt cold sweat forming on his skin and sat down without question…without argument.

"This is bad?"

"Yes, son." There was compassion in his eyes and a horrible look of foreboding on his face. Alex preferred the anger. It didn't scare him as much.

"What is it?" asked Amanda as she moved nearer to Alex, prepared to stand beside him.

"Here is what I know." Jim forced himself into the role of director. "Skye called me from a cabin phone. Alive, awake, and aware. Alex, she wasn't talking directly to me. That was her on the phone, but she was…" Jim hesitated. He didn't know how Alex was going to take it. Besides Skye, Alex was the best agent he had. But he was also Skye's future husband. Jim had consented to put them together in the field in the future and he figured this would be the first test as to whether that had been a good decision.

"Go on," said Alex, his voice cold, but steady. There was ice flowing through his veins now. He resisted the urge to shiver.

"It was obvious she was trying to divert them from the position of the phone." Jim had to clear his voice. He looked at Amanda. "I'm speculating, but I think she assessed the situation and realized she couldn't fight her way out of it. The quarters were too tight, they were armed, and they were still in the air. She couldn't risk revealing herself or her special skills. It would uncover her training and the time and place weren't optimal."

"So she went down," whispered Amanda. Knowing what that meant. Feeling the pain. Her hand clutched Alex's shoulder and communicated her sympathy and support.

"Yes," replied Jim, never taking his steady gaze off Alex. Alex saw both pride and pain in Jim's eyes. He knew what Jim meant, too. You go down, take the beating. Don't show them your strength. Be a Clark Kent. Disguise your true nature. Hold back. Bide your time.

"Are you saying she took a few blows?" he asked between clenched teeth.

Jim nodded. "Not before she was able to get some information to us through the phone line. Maybe enough vital information for us to narrow down the search." Jim hesitated, then continued. "But it sounded like she did it in true Skyler fashion."

"Are you saying she took it to the limit?" asked Alex through the tension in his jaw…although he already knew the answer and pain tore through him.

"I would say from what I heard, she punched right through the limit. Alex, this is going to be very difficult. I would suggest you leave while Amanda and I get what we can from the disk."

"Do you have reason to believe that she is still alive?"

"I do. Yes."

Jim stared at Alex. He wouldn't order him out, but his eyes begged him to go. Alex shook his head slowly. As much as it wounded him, Jim nodded. His decision had been the correct one. Now for the real test. "Okay. But Alex…listen to me. This recording is…is going to be brutal."

Alex jerked as he felt Amanda's hand move from his shoulder to his arm. He shook it off and glared at Jim.

"Just play the fucking thing and let me deal with it," he snarled.

Jim stared at him for a moment, saw the agent inside the man and pressed play. Alex's muscles tensed to concrete as he recognized the voice of his future wife. He had to remind himself that she was also Special Agent Madison, his colleague. Soon to be his partner. Brave, resourceful, well-trained, and fearless.

Even though Alex steeled himself the reality of the recording left his heart and soul in shreds. Every time he heard a blow to the body of the woman he loved he took it himself. The woman who should have been in his arms tonight. The woman who laughed with him, fought with him, worked with him. She was performing her job with skill and proficiency. And she was killing him by doing it.

They obtained a great deal from her words and decided to listen again. Alex got up and started pacing. He looked at a chair in the corner and for some reason, it offended him. Delivering a driving sidekick, he shattered it into a score of small pieces and splinters went flying. Staring for a moment at the pile of busted wood, he turned and leaned against the wall. He needed to shake the haze of red-hot fury from his brain.

Alex's head had to remain clear and focused but his soul was shattered. Just like that unfortunate chair. He kept hearing the echo of punches and knowing she was playing the part perfectly didn't help. Alex tried to tune out the sound of flesh on flesh that was replaying a continuous loop in his mind. It was the last groan that did him in...bringing him to the brink of losing it completely.

"Alex." Alex heard Amanda through the haze. She was standing next to him. Jim had wisely accepted her unspoken offer to take on this challenge. "She played this exactly right. You can hear their contempt for her and her apparent weakness. All along she was playing them. They didn't hear what she was saying because of how she was saying it. She was brilliant. And so brave. It wasn't easy to just take a beating, but she was doing it to save her life and the lives of her passengers. She will endure, Alex. And she'll win in the end because her incredible performance today will help us find her."

"Fuck that Amanda. I don't give a damn about her brilliance or her courage. She couldn't just go down? Why couldn't she just stay in the fucking seat in the first place and let this play out?" He covered his face, then ran his fingers through his hair. In his mind, he heard another vicious slap and her cry of pain and it ripped right through him. He was losing control and the chair didn't do it for him.

He closed his eyes, but he could see her falling so he opened them again and stared. Skye, his voice whispered in his head, the price I'm paying to love you is getting higher and higher. Then he heard her voice again. *Come for me. I love you.* Applying his tremendous self-discipline he fought back the murderous feelings threatening to break him. When he looked at Amanda, his eyes had the glint of blue steel. "Those hijackers are dead men."

"Yes," she said evenly. "I believe they are. Now come. We mustn't allow her courageous sacrifice to be wasted. We must get every last clue we can out of that disk."

"I don't know if I can stand listening to it again," he whispered through a constricted throat.

"Special Agent Springfield," said Amanda sharply, hoping to get through to him. She knew he was in a mild form of shock. "If that resourceful agent can take the blows of a cruel and vicious man, then you can sit down and help us work the clues she so boldly sent us. Everything she said has potential. You're the one who insisted on listening. I admire that. Now don't disappoint me. Don't disappoint Skye."

That got through. Alex looked down at the alert, intelligent green eyes and knew she understood completely. So he did listen again, even though his mind screamed, *stay down, Skye. Dear Jesus, just stay down!*

Finally, Jim called a halt to the listening and asked for analysis. Alex was numb and relieved, but his brain was focused and sharp.

"Skye must have held her breath for quite a while. She was out for only about, what, two hours? It should have kept her under for at least six to eight," commented Jim.

"Yes, that would be right," nodded Alex.

"Damn, she reacts fast," said Amanda.

"She does, yes," agreed Jim.

"She said there was someone landing her plane, so at 4:37 Eastern time, the plane was descending and should be down by now. Excellent. That will help us develop a perimeter," said Amanda. She had some ideas on how to conduct the search now that they could narrow it down. "This is a critical bit of information."

The men nodded.

"So there are five children. This woman's been busy. It tells us two things," said Amanda, ticking off the clues.

"There are five of them on the plane," said Alex, stating the most obvious.

"Yes, and her captors are stupid. They weren't catching the most basic of ploys. They are inexperienced so chalk one up for our side."

"Agreed," breathed Alex. "When Skye comes to, they won't know what hit them. I hope she saves a few for us." He stared into Amanda's cool green glare.

That made Jim's mouth turn up at the edges as he nodded in agreement. "Five people. That isn't many considering the size of the operation."

"The gas was supposed to make everyone on the plane immobile. That should explain the lower number of hijackers. If this is a major op there will be more when they land, I'm sure," speculated Alex. He was feeling better. They were moving. They would find her. And he would be able to pay back her tormentors. That fact was driving him now. That and his love for Skye. They had a date at the altar. He touched the box, still in his pocket. That was where it was going to stay until he could put it on her finger.

"'Sunny was right'. That was a good one. She doesn't only act fast, Alex, she thinks fast," said Amanda. "Sun on the right, they're headed south."

Alex's lips quirked. "When she gets back here for the debriefing, I hope you will give her proper applause for that one. She doesn't mind a few curtain calls among colleagues and associates."

"I'm very much looking forward to meeting her. I'm assuming she's also Level Three?" Jim nodded. She smiled. "That incredible young woman and I will do more than get acquainted. We'll share stories, show each other our scars, and generally bash the bad guys all over again."

"They're armed," said Jim, back to business.

"Indeed. We'll get McKenzie on that right away. The hijackers were able to get guns on board an international flight. She'll be able to trace the source and the method they used to smuggle them on the plane."

Alex and Jim looked at Amanda quizzically. She looked back at them and shrugged. "I trained her."

"Figures. The area is tropical. And then the small green eyes, deadhead. I'm assuming that's a small green island, dead ahead," said Alex and got confirming nods.

"Yes. So we're looking for a tropical island and we can eliminate all the mainland airstrips or anything north of our location," said Amanda.

"That's huge. If we would have included the mainland in our search of the perimeter, there would be thousands of airports, private airstrips, and general aviation terminals," said Jim.

"They're probably going to land on an established airstrip. Maybe abandoned. They aren't going to be landing at an international terminal, unless they intend to make a huge media splash," said Alex. He looked at his watch. It had been almost a half-hour since Jim's phone rang. "We would know by now or at least real soon if the hijacking is to be open and public. The plane has landed. If there's no media coverage or attempt to reach people in power in another few hours, we'll know that the hijacking was meant to be secretive and guarded."

"We have to have a complete media blackout on all this data...we can't let the hijackers suspect we have someone on the inside," said Jim. "Chances are they're monitoring all the coverage. We can do our part to lull them into thinking everything is going according to their plan."

"Not just the media, Jim," said Amanda grimly. "Everyone. I feel badly for the friends and families, but we can't let what we just heard go beyond our team."

"The people who took the plane don't know what we know. The airlines and the governmental agencies know about the gas but they have agreed to keep that very close for now. Everyone is under strict orders to keep the lid on. No leaks," said Jim.

"Agreed. We know about the gas, that the plane is still intact, has already landed on an island, and was taken by armed hijackers. This information is priceless," said Amanda.

"Oh, it had a price," said Alex softly, fury accenting his tone. He knew he wouldn't sleep until Skye was back in his arms.

Jim nodded in agreement and ran a hand that was not too steady through his silver hair.

"Yes, and that incredible woman took that last horrible blow just to tell us our families are safe." Amanda sniffed. It was getting to her, too. She thought she was almost immune to the pain that could be part of covert operations. She'd been forced to do just what Skye had done on a few occasions. "That was completely unnecessary, but so very brave and compassionate."

"Not for the captain inside her. That part will always put the protection and security of her passengers before any personal safety or comfort," said Alex and was a little amazed at the pride that got through the worry and anger. A calm settled over him. There was still that radiating fury but he was sure he would be able to channel it into action. "Until she leaves the terminal on her last flight, she will be the captain of Flight 127."

"Then I do believe my grandson will be coming home to me." This time a tear slipped by Amanda's defenses. "Now…let's analyze that foreign language, shall we?"

They listened again to the string of Italian, delivered in a soft, singsong voice. Jim wasn't quick enough to turn it off before they heard the vicious blow that followed.

"Sorry Alex," said Jim when he saw his agent's face flinch once again. "We have to get a translation for that part. She was speaking too fast for me to catch any of it."

"That was Italian, wasn't it?" asked Amanda.

Alex nodded. "Skye speaks several languages. Comes from being the daughter of a European diplomat. When she's wired and angry, her Italian blood boils and she cusses like an enraged Mafioso. It may have been a way to vent some of her frustration. Although she didn't deliver it with her usual panache."

"Bless her, but we need to be sure there was no deeper message. My guess is that she didn't waste her breath," said Amanda.

"I agree. You don't speak Italian?" asked Alex. He had heard it often enough from Skye, but didn't pay much attention since she usually reserved that language for when she was angry.

"No. My languages were Russian and Chinese…back in the cold war, that was pretty much all us spooks needed. We have to get someone to come in and translate. The sooner, the better. Who do you have?"

"Sloane could translate. She's at the townhouse," suggested Jim.

"No, there's no way we could put her through that. Skye would have our skins for even thinking of it," said Alex firmly. He was still shaking inside and didn't want Sloane to have to go through listening to her sister being brutalized.

"Who's Sloane?" asked Amanda.

"I am."

Alex, Jim, and Amanda whirled around. A beautiful, petite young woman was standing in the room as pale as death. "Skye's alive. And I'm not leaving so you better put me to work before I call the National Inquirer and tell them you two mate with space aliens and you," she nodded at Amanda, "are their love child."

"Sloane." Alex went over to her and wrapped Skye's young sister in his arms. "You shouldn't be here."

"How did you get here?" asked Jim suspiciously.

"Duncan brought me."

"No, I mean how did you get in *here*? This is a secure location."

"The door was ajar."

Jim looked at her for a few heartbeats. "You're going to have to lie better than that if you're ever going to be a special agent."

"Damn."

He held out his hand and she reached in her pocket and pulled out what looked like an ordinary charge card.

"What's this?"

"Something I've been working on."

"And…"

"And, it works!" She smiled brashly into the face of the Director of the Intelligence Division of the Justice Department. She knew who he was and what he was and it didn't intimidate her a bit.

Jim sighed and shook his head, but looked at the device with interest, then handed it to Alex who turned it around in his hand.

"We'll have to find you something to do for our team. I sure would hate to have you go over to the dark side," said Alex, looking into Sloane's golden eyes and seeing the dread and pain under the bravado. He knew she would see the same haunted look in his own eyes.

"Who is this child and why does she seem to be privy to Level Three information?" Amanda's tone was sharp and Alex had a glimpse of what she must have been like in the training room. She looked like a woman you wouldn't want to cross.

"This is Skye's sister, Sloane Madison. She knows about Skye and Alex because she, ah, hacked into our secure records last summer seeking information about the cause of a serious injury to Skye. I didn't prosecute her because she was so distraught over her sister and because I have sentenced her to a more productive endeavor. She's currently interning with me to build in more safeguards so no one else will be able to do what she did." Jim took the device from Alex and put it in his pocket, determined to get the schematics from Sloane later.

"But she's just a child," said Amanda, still horrified with the breach of both security and protocol.

"And you're an old lady," spat out Sloane as they stared each other down. "What's your point?"

"This 'child' has been tested with an IQ of 235. She has degrees in physics and history and she's a dissertation away from a graduate degree in mechanical engineering. She should have a PhD in Computer Information Systems by the end of the year," said Jim.

"Then you can call me Doctor, Granny," said Sloane with a sneer.

"Unless you fall off your bike on the way to school."

"At least I'm still on the upside of my learning curve."

"We have a hijacked plane, child!"

"And my sister is its captain, old lady."

They continued to stare. Sloane was not going to back down. Amanda used the few seconds to assess and evaluate. The two men wisely stayed clear of the minefield.

Amanda's lips twitched first. Then Sloane's.

"Okay," sighed Sloane. "Look, I realize that chronologically I'm a kid and most of the time I'm perfectly content to be a kid. I don't want to be an adult. I like hanging at the mall and testing the limits of my sister's subjectively established parental rules." Her eyes filled with tears. "But now…now I want to put this pain of a brain to work. I need to." Her voice hitched and Alex reached out and pulled her against his chest as she cried out some of her fear.

"My God, there are two of them," said Amanda with both compassion and admiration.

"Indeed," said Jim. He looked at Amanda and at her nod, he smiled. "Lord help me…my team. The Granny, the Kid, and the Fiancé."

"And the agent on the inside," said Alex as he held his future sister-in-law. "As terrible as it is for us, sweetheart, having Skye on that plane increases the chances of those people coming out of this alive and well."

"Yeah, one bad assed, totally wicked, super she-bitch on the inside," said Sloane as she blinked back the last of her tears. It made Alex smile and feel a whole lot better…and it worked to reduce some of the tension.

"In the meantime, we could use you. We have her on disk. She managed to get a message out. But I want to warn you, it's going to be very, very difficult," said Alex.

"It proves she's alive, doesn't it?"

Simple, direct, and right to the heart of the matter. That was Sloane. He nodded. As horrific as the disk was to listen to, Skye was alive and that was an enormous relief. It was all relative. A few hours ago they thought she might be dead. The fact that she was alive in any condition lifted a huge burden from their hearts.

Sloane listened to the disk without comment. Alex could see she felt every blow, taking it stoically, concentrating on the words. It obviously took all of her willpower and self-control. She was naturally less disciplined than her older sister. More outgoing and impulsive. Seeing the toll it was taking, he almost stopped the tape twice. Sloane gently put her trembling hand on his and shook her head.

"If you can take it, so can I," she whispered. Feeling him shudder she squeezed his hand. Hard.

"Would you like to write it down?" asked Amanda softly. Alex glanced over and saw that now that she was convinced Sloane could do the job, she was in her corner all the way.

"No, I have it all in my head now." Sloane could remember everything she heard or saw. "I take it you have chased all the clues from her chatter?"

"We have. We figure there are five hijackers. They're armed. They're still over water going in a southerly direction and are about to land on a tropical island. And…" He looked at Amanda. "All the passengers are safe and sleeping."

"I've never heard her beg. That was pretty good begging." Sloane took a deep breath and brushed at the fresh tears on her pale cheeks. "Of course," she continued, looking Alex up and down. "I'm not completely sure what goes on in the bedroom. Could be a lot of begging and pleading there too, I suppose."

"Sloane," warned Jim.

"Okay. I'm digressing. Trying to lighten the mood." She looked at Amanda, whose admiration was evident on her face. She wasn't fooled for a minute. Nothing had lightened in the poor girl's eyes. "I tend to do that. Digress. It comes from having this brain like a sponge. Anyway. To the Italian." She took a deep breath and braced herself.

"I won't translate most of it...don't need to. It was Skye's way of venting some of her true feelings. She was cussing really, really bad. Um...I'll write it down if you want, but neither grannies nor kids should be privy to this kind of language. And as her godfather, you should have a talk with her when she gets back. And I do mean *when*," said Sloane with confidence. "She's going to bide her time, then kick the hijackers' collective ass, take over the plane, turn it around, and bring them all safely home."

"No doubt," said Jim. "Go on."

"Yeah. Okay," Sloane continued. "She weaved more into it. A man...actually she called more of a...well...something to do with his male part...anyway, he has a snake tattoo. Right forearm. Brown eyes and hair. Her height. Scar on the right cheek. Two more in the cabin. Same description, no scars. The plane is being flown by a competent pilot. A man in the copilot's seat. They are not in immediate peril. All the hijackers have guns. Semi-automatic. Swiss made. SG 552 Commando."

"Good girl!" exclaimed Amanda, not even trying to hide her awe of the instant and perfect translation. "Excellent intelligence! We'll start searching for the men based on descriptions. And we should be able to trace the guns. They're a compact assault rifle and far less popular than the Russian AKS-74U."

"You got all that?" asked Alex, still staring at Sloane.

"It was all very fast and very cleverly woven into the cussing, but yes. And she made it all sound like a prayer. And we know something for sure," said Sloane.

"That would be?"

"The hijackers don't speak Italian. She said some uncomplimentary things about the man's...ah...man thing."

She stopped and took a deep breath. "Plus there was something else. When, when that man...." Her voice shook and she had to start over again. "When that man who sounded like he...Oh God, Alex." Her eyes filled with tears.

Alex's voice was steady, professional, even as his stomach continued to ache miserably. He looked at Sloane, knowing what she had to report was important. Leaning forward, he kissed her forehead. "Sloane, just give us the data."

It helped. It helped remind her of her purpose. Sloane swallowed the huge lump in her throat and whispered. "When it sounded like he kicked her, he said, 'Stupid woman. Why do they allow women to drive the plane' Or something to that effect. When I see Skye, I'm going to tell her he said that, then back away. She'll take him apart molecule by molecule. He's standing in a pile of shit and he doesn't even know it."

They all looked at each other, confused.

"Sloane, we didn't hear anything like that," said Jim with gentle compassion. "There are some parts of the tape that are unclear, but we would have heard some of those words or phrases, I'm sure of it."

When Jim reached to replay the disk Sloane put her hand on the top of his. "Um. Please. I don't think I can."

Jim pulled back and nodded sympathetically. "It isn't that important anyway. We all know they hold her in contempt. It was part of Skye's plan."

"I think it is important Uncle Jim." Her voice was intense now…commanding attention. She sounded so much like Skye at that moment that Alex felt a tremor go through his gut. Definite, determined, and certain of her facts. "You missed it probably because it sounded like an unintelligible oath of some kind. That wasn't it. It was very fast and very angry, but it was Shakanwa."

They all looked at her confused.

"I'm kind of a natural with languages. I can't speak them like Skye. I don't really want to. Too utterly bogus for someone like me. I might swing into one of them like Skye does and scare the coolies out of some of my friends. I'm already kind of a freakazoid. I don't want to call attention to my whiz kid status. But I can remember and translate them just fine."

"And?" prompted Jim gently.

"Yeah. Well, I took a course at George Washington a few years ago for fun. It was called the obscure languages of Central and South America. Shakanwa was one of them. It doesn't translate directly into English all that well. It's a combination of several languages, including Spanish, Portuguese, and native peoples. It's an old language. These guys, or at least one of them, speaks it. Since they're conversing in English all the other times, I think he only spoke it when he was so royally pissed, it just came out. The guy didn't use it until he…he. Until Skye was…was…"

Suddenly it was all too much. Sloane shot up and ran to the bathroom where she got violently sick. When he heard the water running Alex went in. She was washing out her mouth and crying and cursing in Italian. So she did know how to speak the language. Alex's heart both filled and cracked. She was a piece of Skye and she was so dear to him. Brave and smart, but still just a kid.

"You okay?"

"*Idioti! Non sapranno ciò che ha colpito loro!* Yeah. I'm platinum. Must have been something I ate. Carter and Bill had all sorts of great grub at the party and Al and Jason and I filled our faces fast before Aunt Hazel could put her unique twist to the food. She was talking about putting green jelly beans on the avocado dip...you know, kind of a green theme." She took a deep shuddering breath.

"Oh Alex!" Turning, she flew into his waiting arms. "Skye wasn't all that well yet. Those ribs were still sore, I know they were. The broken ribs were still doing their dance. She tried to cover it up, you know? She was healing okay, but that guy was punching her hard. What if he kicked her there? How can she stand it? How can we stand it?" She was sobbing out all of his fears, all of his thoughts and his arms held her tighter. The constriction in his throat was unbearable. "She just took it, because she knew she had to be alive to save them. To come back to us. Will she, Alex? Will she come back to us?"

"Yes," he managed to get out. "There's no way you're going to get out of getting all dressed up and standing beside her at our wedding. She's coming back. If she doesn't get here on her own, I'm going in after her."

Sloane sniffed and looked up at him. She saw that he meant it and she knew he could do it. "Okay, okay," she sighed and let go of her death grip on his waist. Alex looked into her lovely hazel eyes. Skye favored her father...tall, lean, and fair-haired. Sloane inherited her mother's dark Italian beauty. But she was going to be a stunner, just like her sister.

"I think I got it all out. For now, that is. Can I see it? Will you show it to me again? I didn't tell anyone...I wanted to, but I didn't."

He took the ring out of his pocket and handed it to her.

She opened the box. "This is our talisman," she whispered. "You'll carry it until it goes on her finger...until you put it there personally," she sighed. "I know that was too adorably and grossly quixotic, but it's how I feel...in here." She tapped her chest. "When it's on her finger, she'll be safe. You'll put it there, won't you Alex?"

She looked up at him with all the trust and faith of a child. "I will under one condition, sweetheart," said Alex, kissing the top of her head.

"Sure. Name it."

"You tell me what the hell quixotic means."

"Oh yeah, I forgot. Skye loves you for your body, not your mind. Quixotic...ah, romantic, dreamy, wistful...need more?"

"I think I get the picture, professor."

"Ah...Alex?"

"Yeah?"

"I saw a chair in the corner that looked like a stack of firewood. You do that?"

"Yeah. I felt better, too."

"At least you didn't barf buckets."

"But I felt like it."

"Okay."

"Okay."

"You're just the Grand Canyon of men." Sloane gave him one last hug and stepped back. "Now let's get out of this truly gross bathroom and I'll tell you where Shakanwa is spoken."

Jim and Amanda stared at the door of the bathroom. "You helped raise these two girls after Perry died?" Amanda asked.

Jim nodded. "I did. I've known them their whole lives. Skye is my godchild. Perry and Angela were killed before they chose godparents for Sloane, so I've pretty much taken on the role for her as well."

"Perry Madison and Jim Stryker," said Amanda. "I remember you both from field operations. The cowboy and the strategist. Whom does Skye favor?"

"She's a fine combination of both. Brilliant and an incredible leader. She's been Special Agent in Charge of several important operations. On the other hand, she prefers hands on work. Fearless and physical as hell. Scares the shit out of me on a regular basis."

"Like her father."

"Exactly like her father. I originally tried to talk her out of joining the department, but she was determined. Besides Alex and her family, she has two passions in her life. Flying and justice. When she couldn't be persuaded to concentrate only on flying, I tried to talk her into administrative work. That didn't appeal to her at all, so I gave in and put her through the most rigorous training available. She took to it like a natural. She's Perry's girl, through and through."

"Given her father was a legendary field agent known for his solo work and incorrigible daring, she probably has it in her genes."

"Since joining the Department, Skye's created her own legends. And now she's right in the middle of another incident, with Sloane right behind her. I put Sloane to work after she uncovered all of Skye's secrets…and Alex's too. Damn, she hacked into Skye's files before she was ten. She has an incredible mind and is already making a difference. There will be another Madison crafting legends before she's through."

"She's just a child."

"Yes, but her brain is ancient."

"You did a fine job."

"I had a lot to work with."

"Well then give that child a Level Seven clearance right now, James. And groom her. She clearly has infinite potential and we need that kind of brain on our side," Amanda said with feeling as she heard them come back into the room.

"Sorry," said Sloane a bit sheepishly. "I thought I would be able to hold that in."

"No doubt Hazel got through Cynthia into the kitchen," smiled Jim, hugging her and kissing the top of the head. He remembered doing that for Skye. Until she got as tall as him and he couldn't reach the top of her head any longer. Skye. Who was now in peril...in pain. He put it away. He had work to do.

"Yeah." She smiled weakly at Amanda. "Hazel is my great aunt and the swankiest woman I know, but her food is always a mystery. If you can guess what it is by the end of the meal, you don't have clean up duties afterward. It was a game Skye and I played to keep us from running from the dining room screaming some nights." She looked at Amanda, who was smiling at her. "I think you two would really hit it off. You know, the spook and the spooky."

Amanda looked sharply at Alex and frowned.

"Didn't say a word," said Alex.

"Adults. They think they can fool a kid. Skye thought for years I was clueless. I just let her think so. Two plus two still equals four, Granny." She winked, smiled, and then went back to work. "Anyway, Uncle Jim, I have a bit more. While I was blowing chunks in there, I was reviewing the possible countries where these assholes...may I say assholes?" When Alex nodded she continued. "Where these assholes come from. There are only two or three. It isn't all that common, especially since he wasn't just using words or random phrases as we would when interjecting a language into our own. Like when my friend Frankie says 'numero uno' when referring to his own conceited, but hunky self. This asshole spoke it naturally and in a complete sentence. Like it was his native and preferred tongue."

Sloane continued. "We can get on the Internet and find out for sure where else he may be from, but I'll write down the areas and the countries that come to mind. Frankly, I wasn't paying a lot of attention in class. The professor looked too much like Orlando Blume. Hey. Maybe we can bring him in as a consultant?"

Alex smiled. Some of the kid was coming back. He was relieved, but he shook his head.

"Ah, well. Anyway, here's the list." She scribbled names of countries, including the regions within the countries where the language was spoken.

"Linda and Barclay are in the process of setting up a headquarters now," said Jim. "Let's go."

"Is there any reason someone should stay here?" asked Alex.

"None. The airline officials will be issuing a statement soon. The official line will be that the flight is still missing and that a search and rescue team has been sent out to the last known location. If the hijackers are monitoring the media they may not be so careful with security."

"Exactly," agreed Alex. "If it is a hijacking they should be trying to contact someone. Amanda, do you have contacts in the state department?"

"I do."

"My contacts are with the business community. So I suggest we play the grieving grandma and panicked fiancé roles and start tapping our sources to see if they know anything."

"Fine."

"Can I play the enraged, but heroically stoic sister?" asked Sloane grinning.

Alex actually laughed. "And who would stop you?"

"Um. One last thing." Sloane looked right at Alex. "I was kind of saving this. I thought you might want to be alone."

He looked at her, confused.

"You wouldn't have perceived it. It got kind of lost in all that Italian." She went over to the disk player. Her photographic memory knew just where the tiny section was in the playback. "You have a copy of this disk?" she asked Jim.

"Several."

Her clever fingers worked over the keys of the equipment until she spliced the portion she was looking for and transferred it to a file. Then she slipped a disk inside and pressed save.

"Just push play when you want to hear. We'll wait for you downstairs."

Now he was confused. When they had left, he pushed the play button. It was Skye's voice, caressing him, soothing him. *Alex, J'taime, mon chere. J'taime.* Brief, no more than a whisper. No more than a few seconds. Yet, it healed the open wound in his soul.

"I love you too, my darling," he whispered to his heart. "And I'm coming for you."

Alex played it again as he leaned over the machine and braced himself on the table. She was with him in that moment. Almost a physical presence. He blinked back the tears. She knew he would be right there. She knew he would be on duty for her.

Bless Sloane. They had a plan, they had information, they had someone on the inside, they were ready to roll. Action was the antidote for dread. And he was determined to keep the fear at bay. Skye was counting on that. She was counting on him. He slipped the disk out of the player and went to join his team. The granny, the godfather, and the kid.

CHAPTER 6

Loris Terrin looked up at the huge mechanical bird. Impressive. And massive in this hangar. It barely fit, but it was necessary. They weren't in any shipping lanes and certainly no craft ever flew over the deserted island, but he didn't want to take any chances. Details were important. If everything went as planned, Flight 127 would disappear and forever be a mystery of aviation…like Amelia Earhart.

Terrin's wicked smile revealed straight white teeth and a shadow of the charm he used when moving through high-level political and commercial circles. He was a beautifully handsome man with caramel colored skin and thick, wavy black hair. Only in unguarded moments like this did his eyes reveal his true depraved nature. Right now they flashed with satisfaction and self-importance. He did it. He was not only powerful, attractive, and wealthy, he was brilliant. He was a God! Life and death was in the palm of his hand.

And soon all the world would know his name. But not as the mastermind behind the hijacking of Flight127. He was about to emerge as a leader of a tiny but rich nation and the world was going to be his stage. The entire incident would be a springboard to his success but would soon become only a footnote in the history of his country.

None of the men he recruited to this mission…the hijackers, the men who smuggled in the guns, even the pilot…would be allowed to survive to tell the tale. Only his elite guard, the ones he had handpicked and personally trained, would be privy to the true fate of this flight. And even their life expectancy would be strangely short. He smiled. He enjoyed the rush of power it gave him. Evil always triumphed over good. Evil was stronger.

There was no movement from the plane. Most of the passengers were still under. He had thought of killing them all…of unleashing his men with automatics and plenty of ammunition, or putting poison in their food or drink. But there was still a remote possibility he would need them. He was sure the radar wouldn't have picked them up, but he knew the frailties of man and hundreds of things could go wrong if fate was having a bad day. His pilot may not have been as good as he thought he was. Those pig Americans may have some new technology they haven't yet shared with the world. Someone might have talked before he sequestered them on the island. Hundreds of things. He would know in 24 hours if anyone had his location. If it came to that, the negotiators for the soft, weak United States would fold and buckle to save even one useless soul.

Yes, he needed them for a little while yet. But when he left the island, he would leave them behind…along with the rag tag team of men he had recruited from the streets and hills of his island country. They would be cleanly destroyed together in one huge, magnificent conflagration. There was enough C-4 explosives around this hangar to incinerate everything. No evidence. No bodies. No witnesses. No mess.

So far, everything went exactly as he planned. Perfectly executed. He smiled again and checked his watch. The pilot was even now being thrown into the ocean for the sharks…perfectly executed. He snorted. The fool thought he would be set up for life and live like a king. He was an excellent pilot, but he was too weak to trust. The man had just the right skills and was wonderfully corruptible, but there was a significant flaw that made his continued existence dangerous and unacceptable. He drank too much. Which was why he had been fired from British West Indies Airlines and was available for this flight in the first place. Terrin hated flaws.

His childhood friend Nadir, an idiot but unbelievably loyal, told him there was a woman…one of the crew…who had regained consciousness just before the landing. Not a flaw exactly. More like a puzzle, but then life was full of them. Nadir said she was easily subdued. He beat her and that was good. Terrin spat. Women. They were put on this earth for only one thing. Fucking. That was it. A woman in uniform. Disgraceful. And men of her country allowed it. Even more disgraceful. They were weak…both the women and the men who allowed them to work along side them. Terrin hated weakness almost as much as he hated flaws.

Turning, he strode back to the command station in a room at the far end of the hangar. The generator hummed steadily, keeping it cool and dry. He wouldn't need it much longer. The curtain was coming up on the final act and he was ready to finish it.

Skye's mind came slowly into consciousness. Her body hurt all over. No, she thought perhaps that was a slight exaggeration. She shifted. Nope. No exaggeration. Her body definitely had no part that wasn't screaming at her. Every nerve let her know they wanted a vote next time she decided to take a fall for the cause of ultimate freedom. Checking in with her brain, she found that she remembered everything, every detail. Good. Nothing was wrong with the cognitive skills.

She wiggled her toes and moved her fingers. Extremities working. No spinal injury. She wasn't ready yet to open her eyes to see if it was night or day. That part of her assessment could wait. She was still dealing with the body inventory. God, she could use a painkiller. A shot of morphine would be just the ticket right about now. Why couldn't the body just stay unconscious until everything healed up?

She was in a lying position on a hard surface. Someone had covered her. She could feel a blanket or something over her. Maybe she should just lie still and wait for rescue. Her body was coming on strong, getting behind that idea with enthusiasm. She moved her right arm and there was no pain. She was a superb fighter in close contact hand-to-hand and her right hand was lethal. Okay, so she had a weapon. Left arm, you in for the good fight? Left arm came through. A bit sore from an old injury, but game. So now she was armed. She nearly snorted. Must still be some of that gas in her, but she was feeling better knowing she could move. They hadn't restrained her. Hell, after her performance she was sure they thought all they would have to do is say "boo" and she would cower in the corner and shake herself into a catatonic state. That would change, she thought with determination.

"Captain?" She recognized the voice. It was Amy. Skye last remembered seeing her on the floor of the plane and was relieved that her voice sounded strong. Concerned, but strong. "Skye? Can you hear me?"

Time to go to work. Captain Skyler Madison was being summoned. She slowly opened her eyes. Actually it was just one eye. The other one had a bit of a problem. Christ, she was going to have a shiner. It was the last punch that did it.

She blinked a couple of times and Amy's face gradually came into focus. Good. Nothing wrong with the vision. For a pilot that was critical. Had to be 20/20. The look on her pretty flight attendant's face matched her voice. There was deep concern. Not for herself or their predicament, but for Skye.

I must look a mess, Skye thought. Amy had a glass of water in her hand

and for the first time, Skye realized how parched she was. When she tried to sit up the real serious pain kicked in. Her ribs were in an uproar. She took a moment to force the darkness that was threatening to overcome her back into the corner where it belonged. She was not going to pass out in front of her stalwart flight attendants and cockpit crew. But she couldn't keep a groan from escaping her cracked lip as Amy helped her into a sitting position.

"Amy," her voice came out as a croak, so she took the water and swallowed some gratefully. The finest wine of Italy didn't taste as sweet and wonderful as that stale lukewarm water. She tried again. "Amy, give me a report."

"Oh, Captain. What did they do to you?" Skye noticed Amy went from calling her Skye back to addressing her as captain. Good. It meant the captain was back and in charge. "We woke up and they forced us to carry you in here."

"I hope you didn't hurt yourself." Amy was all of 5'2".

Amy giggled and Skye smiled at her. Good to keep the crew morale up. Hijacking 101.

"You were semi-conscious and talking in Italian."

"I further hope none of you are fluent in Italian." She looked behind Amy and saw all of her crew was gathering around her. "I...ah...get a little racy. I learned a lot of my Italian from our gardener in Rome. By the time my mother found out what I was saying it was too late. I was attached to the words and phrases."

"I speak a little," said Brian, a seasoned international flight attendant who flew with Skye regularly. "You sure were mad at someone."

"See this face? I'm way beyond mad. I wasn't planning on wearing a veil at my wedding." They all laughed. Mission accomplished. Laughter would keep the fear from grabbing them and clouding their judgment. Or worse yet...keep them from taking action. "And if you think I'm mad, Carter and Bill are going to be really pissed that we missed the party and you have seen nothing until you have seen them on a tear."

"It was supposed to be a surprise," said Beth, another flight attendant and sat down next to her.

"Like those boys could ever keep anything a secret."

"No, but they can throw one hell of a party."

"What time is it?"

"0700," said her copilot, Stuart Modesto. He looked none the worse for wear. He'd taken off his jacket and Skye noticed that was what she'd been laying on.

"Damn. I've been out for fourteen hours?"

"More or less, Captain. Um…we were all quite worried."

"Let's start by filling each other in. I need information. Where are we? Where are the passengers? Is everyone okay? Where is the plane?" She looked around. "What is this place? Have you seen any landmarks?" And where is my flight bag, she thought. She carried a weapon in a secret compartment in the bag and would very much like to have it right now.

Since Stuart was officially second in command, he reported for all of them. Amy made herself useful, along with three other attendants by helping Skye get into a more comfortable position. There were no chairs or furniture in the room. As a matter of fact, it looked like there was nothing in the room. Off to one side was a bathroom. Thank God for small favors. She really wanted to wash up. She felt dried blood on her face and could see some on her hands.

"I'm not sure how much I can tell you. I don't know when we landed and I'm not sure what happened before we landed," said Stuart, a confused look on his youthful face.

"We were all gassed. Sterohydroxophene. It makes you happy, gives you a buzz, then puts you out," said Skye. None of her crew asked her how she knew. Skye always seemed to be incredibly well informed. "When did you regain consciousness?"

"We were all out until about 20-2100. Some of the passengers experienced nausea, so we were quite busy making everyone comfortable. The hijackers have said little. We're inside a hangar and there's a small window."

"Vegetation? Landmarks? Buildings?"

"Palms and some undergrowth. No visible town. We couldn't see much out the little window in the hangar and as you can see, in here we're blind."

"They're armed with large guns," said Beth.

"I saw them," said Skye. "SG 552's…those are very large guns, indeed. I wonder how they got them through the metal detectors."

"They were armed on the plane?" asked an incredulous Brian.

Skye nodded, then moved them right along. "How many hijackers?"

"There were at least five on the plane and more than a dozen on the ground. With guns like that, we pretty much did what they wanted."

"Very smart, and you will continue to do so. Did all of our passengers arrive safely?"

"That was our first duty. One man appeared to have a slight heart attack. We asked for medical assistance and were denied," said Katherine.

Skye looked at the small bruise on her face. "You the one who made the request?"

"Yes, Captain," answered Katherine. Skye's eyes grew dark with fury. It was one thing for her to be battered and bruised, but it was quite another for one of her crew to be abused.

"One more thing we owe them for. You're very brave." Skye smiled at the beaming Katherine. "What about the passenger?" Skye didn't intend to lose one.

"Oh, he was okay by the time we left. His wife gave him a nitro tablet and he seemed to be fine."

"Good. Proceed."

"They separated us. They brought the crew in here. Stuart and Brian helped you here and the rest of us came along. We all grabbed what we could from the first aid kits," said Amy.

Skye touched her tender face. She could feel the cream they must have put on her wounds.

"Good thinking. Anyone bring an aspirin?"

"Oh, we all knew you'd be hurting, so..." Every crewmember reached in his or her pocket and produced small packets of aspirin, Tylenol, and Advil. They presented them to her like a tribute to their empress.

She took them gratefully. "May I say, that no gift I've received in my entire life has ever reached the level of magnificence as these little bags of pure gold." She ripped open four of them, threw them in her mouth and washed them down with more water from Amy.

Now they all beamed. Admiration, loyalty, affection. It filled the space around her and threw a warm wave of optimism over her crew.

"Do you know the location and the condition of the passengers?"

"We asked to stay with them, but were refused. We haven't seen them since we were separated almost eight hours ago. We haven't heard any...um...."

"Gunfire?" prompted Skye.

"Yes. And the plane is in the hangar right outside that door."

"Good. That's good. They're close. Did you see any fuel tanks?"

They stared at her.

"You know, in case we want to retake the plane, refuel, and fly back home."

They continued to stare. She took pity on them. She shrugged. Big mistake. Pain shot through her. "Just a thought," she said, gasping.

"Actually there are fuel tanks right outside the door," Brian offered.

"But I don't think I would trust them. They're pretty rusty. There's a small outbuilding and an office in the corner of this one. Looks like some kind of living quarters on the second floor. And there's a beat up old Piper Cub at the end of the runway."

"Since last night, we haven't seen any of the hijackers. There are three deadbolts on the door, external locks that can only be opened with a key," added Brian.

"Very good. I'm proud of all of you. Well done. This is a very difficult experience. A nightmare, really. We've been trained for this eventuality and you have all comported yourselves professionally and with dignity. I couldn't be more pleased."

"What about you, Captain? Tell us what happened. I just about fainted when I saw what they did to you," said Amy.

Skye gave her a flying ace smile. "Let's just say I woke up early and asked them to please give me my plane back," she said with such nonchalance, that her entire crew gaped. "They said no." Then she moved right along. She didn't want them to get too curious. "Could someone help me up? My ribs are mush."

They all made the move, but Stuart and Amy pulled rank. They gently got her to her feet where she swayed a bit until Stuart's steady arm went around her. She blew out a breath and worked out some of the kinks in her back and legs.

"Not too bad," she said gratefully. She was able to go with most of the punches and slaps to keep the damage to a minimum. It was that last hit, and something else. She vaguely remembered a kick.

"Do you think you should be standing?" asked Amy, noticing some of the color draining from Skye's face.

"Yeah. I want to go wash up." She looked down into Amy's worried face. "But if I go down, don't try to catch me. I don't want any member of my crew to come home fractured." When Amy smiled, she was satisfied.

"I was missing a shoe." She could remember something about Cinderella. She must have been really buzzed.

"Here, Captain," said Kristie. "I found them both and brought them. We all know how you are about shoes. Even regulation black pumps."

"I would smile again, but I'm afraid my lips would fall off," replied Skye, but gratefully took them.

She limped over to the bathroom on Stuart's arm. "Thanks. I'll take it from here." She walked into the bathroom under her own steam. When she got in, she shut the door, and nearly collapsed on the floor. Reaching for the sink, she braced herself while she caught her breath. All that bravado and straight-backed authority was a sham. She was hurting and hurting bad. Something was broken in there, she thought. Removing her jacket, slowly, gingerly she lifted her blouse and saw she was a mass of bruises. One at the lower right rib cage was a particularly ugly specimen. Snake Tattoo must have kicked her when she was unconscious. Cowardly bastard. She was going to kick him back at the first opportunity. That was a promise.

Then she turned and looked at herself in the mirror. A string of Italian came pouring out as she stared at the discoloration and swelling. Let Brian translate...she felt better with every word and she vented her entire vocabulary as she began the task of transforming into something other than the bride of Frankenstein.

When she came back out, even though her face was heavily bruised and her eye was still very tender looking, she had managed to wash off most of the blood. She had restyled her hair and it was back in place. Her uniform slacks were a little wrinkled, but they were made to sit in for long periods of time, so she was able to brush out most of the creases. Pantyhose were regulation but they were a complete waste. She figured that under the circumstances, she could waive the dress code. Captain's privilege.

Most importantly, the medication took the edge off the pain. It made her feel human again. Now the dominant feeling was anger...she was mad as hell and ready for a fight.

Her crew turned and immediately stood a little straighter when they saw the transformation. Skye could still see concern in their eyes, but no fear. She smiled and they smiled back. This was to be a moment legends were made of and if they ever got out of there, they could say they were there when Captain Skyler Madison rose above the pain and came out in glorious victory. Skye, on the other hand, was just glad she could walk.

They were sitting in a circle and planning their escape strategy when they heard keys in the lock. Stuart jumped up and gave Skye his hand. Gratefully accepting it, she stood up and took her position in front of her crew.

With her shoes on, she was a good two inches taller than Stuart and was in fact the tallest person in the room. She stood out and she stood forward. Her posture was rigid. If the crew didn't know it was because her ribs were hurting her so badly, then that was okay with Skye. Putting her head up, she waited for the door to open. No fear, no weakness.

Five men came in with food. It smelled wonderful and they were all tempted to dive into it. But they stood their ground, waiting for Skye's lead.

Snake Tattoo wasn't among the five.

"Good morning," said one of the hijackers. "We have here some food for you and would invite you to eat."

"We eat nothing provided by you," said Skye. There was only a slight chance that there were drugs in the food but she didn't want to risk it. "I would like to talk with whomever is in charge."

"Well," grinned the man. "This is very unfortunate. For he would like to talk with the captain of the craft, not a woman." The man turned to Stuart. "Please come with me."

"I'm the captain of Flight 127," said Skye stepping closer to the man and smiling down at him. Little chauvinistic putz. "And I would be glad to come with you."

The guard looked up at her and stared, his skepticism obvious and insulting. She turned to her crew. "I know this is asking a great deal of you. But the food could be drugged. They've put us under before. Please refrain from consuming anything that's opened or cooked by their hand." She examined the soft drink cans carefully. No holes or tell tale scratches. "These look okay," she smiled. "But stay away from the coffee."

Amy sniffed. "I wanted to lose a few pounds anyway." She recognized the soft drinks from their own supply. "And since they stole these from our galley, we're fortunate to have our captain's favorite." She opened the can of Diet Pepsi. "Would you like a drink before you go?"

Skye smiled. It reopened the cut on her lip but what the hell. Taking the can, she drank deeply, making the guards wait. To the delight of her crew and the confusion of her captors, she smacked her lips and said. "Thanks I needed that." Actually the little rush of caffeine did feel pretty good. "All of you stay here. If I don't return, Stuart, you're in charge. We'll go by strict chain of command until we touch down in the United States and are out of the terminal."

Stuart nodded, although she could see he was reluctant to have her go where they couldn't keep an eye on her. He would hold though. It was his job...and they just took on a 24/7 shift.

"Shall we go? *Pistola! Testa di cazzo,*" she suggested to the little man, who couldn't help himself. He gaped at her as she walked out the door as if she was in command.

"What was that?" Stuart asked Brian when all of the locks had been shoved back into place.

"Some equivalent to male chauvinist pig."

"Oooh yes," laughed Stuart. He just couldn't help himself. The look on the hijacker's face was something he wouldn't soon forget. "Now they have made her really mad. Messing up her face and stealing her plane is one thing. Not thinking that a woman can be a captain...well. Now they've done it. And it's only seventeen to one."

That was exactly what Skye was thinking as her eyes traveled over everything. Her plane was sitting in the middle of a large hangar. Seeing anxious faces at the windows, she waved her assurance. Moving quickly, she lengthened her stride until the little flyspeck holding the gun had to trot alongside.

Observing everything without appearing to do so, she mentally assessed what she already knew about the hijackers. Amateurs. Poorly trained. Cannon fodder for her if she was 100 percent, a challenge now that she wasn't. Snake Tattoo would be easy to take down. She already knew his weaknesses. Then there was Pilot and Copilot. They may or may not have other combat training. They may not even still be here. They seemed to have done a skillful job of landing her plane and she was grateful to them, but she figured she could take them too.

The five people with her now were the cooks and the servers. All but one of them...the one on the far right, didn't even know how to carry a Commando, much less how to shoot one.

Then her heart sank as she was escorted into the small office. Oh shit, she thought, here they are. The professionals. The mercenaries. The real danger to her crew and her passengers. There were seven of them. None of them were holding weapons, but they all had a sidearm. They looked lean, mean, and tough. Their posture was disciplined and their eyes were alert. This was not good.

She barely moved her eyes, but she took in everything. Great communications system. Phones, faxes, computers. It was air-conditioned and clean. The men were coordinated. When one moved, the others reacted. They had a perimeter they were maintaining and right now it was around a man. A very handsome, well groomed man. He looked like he should be sitting behind a desk at a professional law office, not in this old hangar on an island. He was dressed casually but stylishly right down to his diamond ring and Movado watch. There was a designer look about him.

"I said I wanted to talk with the captain. Who is this?" asked the man with a low cultured voice. He spoke English with slight British undertones.

Skye saw the man look her up and down and there was appreciation in his eyes despite the bruises on her face.

"I said who is this?" he repeated to the guard as he slowly stood up. Skye saw that he too was a bit shorter than her. She always liked that...it gave her an edge. To accent the advantage, she never broke eye contact. When the guard began to speak, she interrupted and answered the question herself. Petty power plays, but what the hell.

"Captain Skyler Madison. First officer of Flight 127. You sent for the captain. You got the captain."

Terrin frowned.

"They did not tell me there was a woman in the cockpit."

"Did you ask?"

"No, I simply assumed the captain would be a man." He stopped when he realized what she was doing. She was interrogating him. His eyes narrowed.

Skye saw the rush of surprise and anger. Then he leered at her and blatantly looked down at her captain's wings, running his eyes over the swell of her generous breasts at the same time and in a transparently insulting voice said. "I guess my assumptions were not correct for you are definitely female."

"I guess that makes you a chauvinistic asshole," Skye said in a casual tone, soft and honey coated.

A man behind her audibly gasped. Terrin's eyes snapped back to her face letting the insult wash through him...then he laughed. So he was going to let it go for now, she thought. Good. That meant he wasn't all that quick. Also overconfident.

"My name is Loris Terrin. You are my guest here on this island," he said in an icy tone...civil on the surface, deadly underneath. "I see you have been marked. What did you do to make Nadir so angry?"

Ignoring his question, she had one of her own. "When do you plan to release my passengers and crew?"

"How badly do you want them to be released?" His gaze went from her face back to her chest. He was looking like a man who needed to find the upper hand.

"It's top on my list of priorities," she said, still looking at him straight and steady.

Terrin slowly came around the desk and moved into her personal space, lightly touching her hair. Still she didn't move. She knew he wanted her to cringe. He was close enough so she could feel the annoyance bubbling up inside him. She didn't respond except to put on a slight smile…like she knew something he didn't. Like his zipper was down and she thought it was all a big joke.

Angry now, he grabbed her hair and turned her head toward him. She impaled him with her steady brown eyes. No pain, no fear.

"Would you stay here with me, perhaps? Give your body to me?" He said it in a sneering tone. His men snickered and Terrin began playing to them. His hand ran down her unbruised cheek then wrapped around her neck.

"If that's what it takes. When I see the entire plane of passengers and crew, no one injured, no one dead, flying off the island under the command of Co-Captain Stuart Modesto, then I would indeed give you this body."

Never varying her voice, she called his bluff…and won the hand.

He yanked on her hair. "You forget, bitch, who has the guns." His tone picked up a dangerous edge.

"Oh. I won't forget who needs the guns. It's easy to have your way when you're armed. Little men need big guns." Her eyes traveled around the room. "Twelve guns."

He stared for a minute more, then retreated just a step and Skye had an accurate read of the man she was up against. And she was satisfied.

"Back to business. I'll need you to take care of some correspondence. We'll be sending out demands to five governments within the next few days."

"That I'll be glad to do. And what will this correspondence entail? Political demands or monetary ransom?"

"Both actually. Your government is now in its seventeenth hour of a search and rescue mission. We'll wait until 24 hours have elapsed. Then we'll make the first contact."

"Why not right now? Why put the families of my passengers through any more agony?" As a special agent, she wanted to get messages out as quickly as possible. She could get more information to Jim and Alex. As she swept the room with her peripheral vision she itched to send along what she saw.

"Perhaps we wish to put the families through agony," he snarled. She could see he was trying to find steadier ground.

She'd cooperate, of course, but her gut was telling her there was more under the surface. And she was afraid it wasn't going to be in the best interest of her passengers, plane, and crew. Nothing to do until she could get something more concrete, so she threw him a bone. She had stretched her luck far enough.

"All right, you're in charge," she said, lowering her gaze. "I would however, like to assess the condition of our passengers. I would like to go aboard my craft. I would also like to bring my flight bag into my cell."

"You would like a great deal."

"If you want me to correspond, I need to know if everyone is all right. I'm responsible for my airplane and I wasn't conscious when they shut it down. I wish to look it over to be sure there is no danger of any spontaneous combustion." That was bullshit, but it sounded serious and she was banking on the fact that Terrin wasn't a pilot. "And I would like my flight bag...well, for personal, feminine reasons."

She saw Terrin register mild disgust. Men always cringed when a woman mentioned anything female. She bet she got her flight bag though, and that was all she cared about.

Nodding his assent, he told his minions to take her aboard. He made it sound like it was his idea and that was fine with her.

Terrin watched the tall woman in uniform as she walked between his men toward the plane. A female captain. What were the men of her country thinking allowing such a thing? Any nation that allowed this kind of foolishness wasn't worthy of another thought. This captain was going to wish she had stayed home and made a man happy. The bitch would cooperate. He could see that. Terrin knew his plan and it had nothing to do with political demands or ransom. He wanted her to have hope before he stripped it from her. He liked playing the game.

He remembered the eyes...direct and fearless. That would change. He would see to it. It would be a battle with only one outcome...not really a battle at all. More of a massacre. He'd been bored on this island. This was going to make a very pleasant diversion. She was proud, arrogant, confident. He would strip away her pride. It would make his victory sweet indeed. He would break her. Then he would kill her, but not *too* quickly. He liked maneuvering events, controlling people, and implementing tactical operations...but he particularly liked one-on-one contact...dominance, degradation, and brutality. His early years were filled with pleasant hours of cutting, raping, and torturing. He missed it. Command and high authority separated him too much from the blood of death and sweat of fear. It really was lonely at the top.

Too bad Nadir used his fists on her...pig. He had little regard for women, but he appreciated beauty. It was unfortunate that he needed to bring these ignorant peasants like Nadir with him on this mission. On the other hand, they were all expendable and would be sacrificed in the end...so in the final analysis, the pig would pay for his lack of restraint.

Terrin grew up poor on the small but prosperous island of Soteras. He and his gang of thugs formed a cohesive unit realizing early in life that a band of determined young men could rule through intimidation and fear much more effectively than through laws and legitimate power. Crime was his game and he was the best player in the history of his island country. Once he had the power, he wielded it with cruelty and enthusiasm so that the people who didn't join him disappeared, died, or were seriously disabled.

Soon his control over the island underworld was nearly absolute. His gang became a syndicate and as their leader, he reached out to other crime lords in the region, joining their larger more sinister brotherhood. They called themselves the *Catalla antabra Fra*...the Serpent and the Spear. He absentmindedly rubbed his forearm where a ceremonial tattoo was prominent.

First he was one of many, then one of three. Soon he would be the dominant lord. Once he achieved that, the next step in his life plan was legitimacy. He would be President of his island someday and the rest of the world would know what the people knew...he was a man of destiny. He wanted to be invited to the White House, the Kremlin, and Parliament. The only barrier he saw to fulfilling his ultimate plan was to be eliminated here on the soil of a remote and deserted island.

Once he became President, he could really begin the rape of his country. His island, the source of his wealth, was about to make him a whole lot richer. A few years before he'd hired a private firm of geologists to uncover what had initially begun as a rumor in a small village on the relatively unpopulated northern part of Soteras. Oil. Lots of it. Buried under the ocean floor near the coastline. The scientists who wrote the original documentation were all buried near the place where they delivered their findings...their enthusiasm and confidential assurances of huge deposits sealing their fate.

Mentally, Terrin went over the timetable for this part of the operation. The two other lords of the cartel, Lomar and Faneta, would be arriving on the island in the morning. They were his partners in this venture and were coming soon to supervise the loading of the cargo...payoff for their part in the hijacking. Then they were to leave the island together destroying all the evidence. On the other hand...he secretly planned a contingency.

Terrin hated sharing the power and wealth almost as much as he hated sharing the spotlight. He needed Lomar and Faneta's assistance and contacts to execute this complex operation but it was nearly finished. They didn't know about the oil and he wasn't sure he wanted to share.

With the oil as his ticket, legitimate representatives from all over the world would come to him. He, Lomar, and Faneta were a triumvirate...but perhaps now was the time to make it a sole dictatorship. Terrin's smile became malevolent and guarded as he pushed up his sleeve and stared at his tattoo. Yes. Perhaps now was the time.

As she approached the plane with her entourage of guards, Skye took inventory of the outside of the fuselage. It looked good. Nothing dented, damaged, or destroyed. They stopped at the bottom of the stairs and her escorts told the men guarding the door that she was to enter. She recognized the two men and bet they would just let her pass and go in alone. They were the ones who witnessed her stunning show of pathetic weakness and wouldn't consider her a threat.

Her ribs ached terribly and negotiating stairs was particularly painful, so what they saw etched on her face was genuine. They just thought it was fear instead of pain. Maybe there was a doctor on board she could talk to. That would have to wait, however. She wanted to be sure that everyone on board was doing well; to see if the radios were operative, if the plane could be easily fired up again, read the fuel gauge, and assess the general condition of the cockpit. She intended to cooperate and work for a peaceful outcome, but instinct told her to prepare to flee.

As she expected, the guards completely ignored her and let her pass through the doorway alone. They sniggered and raised their guns to frighten her. She made appropriate scared noises. They laughed. She scoffed at them when they turned their backs. She got what she wanted. They got another charge of superiority. Everyone was happy. The only thing was the men had no idea there was a time bomb ticking in Skye's fisted hands and that at the first opportunity, they would be just so much debris on the hangar floor.

A few of the passengers were softly conversing in small groups throughout the plane. When she walked into the cabin and looked around, all conversation ceased. Most of the passengers were sleeping. There was no weeping or hysteria. Those who were awake were apprehensive and there was curiosity on their faces, but as far as she could see everything was subdued. She frowned. Too subdued. Maybe the food *was* drugged. Since the passengers who were sleeping appeared to be breathing normally, perhaps it wasn't a bad thing. Let them sleep through most of it.

A small, elderly man in an old fashioned suit was going from seat to seat taking people's pulses and generally acting doctor-like. Good, she would talk to him before she left. She smiled as the passengers turned to her.

"Good morning, ladies and gentlemen. It appears we have taken a detour. I would welcome you to this island, but I have no idea yet what island we're on." Keep it light. Keep it confident. Be as informative as you can. "As you know, the plane has been hijacked. I'm sure you have seen the little men with the big guns. We were gassed with sterohydroxophene. It's neither lethal, nor particularly dangerous…unless you're operating heavy equipment or flying a plane." She smiled reassuringly and took off her hat.

"They do that to you, Captain?" asked a large man leaning against a seat in the aisle. A sleeping woman and two children were in the seats next to him. It was obvious that he had placed himself in a position to defend.

"Indeed." She put her hand to her face. "It looks worse than it is. And I can assure you that when the time comes," she said smiling with as much bravado as she could muster with a swollen face and a cracked lip. "That when the time comes, I'm physically ready and able to fly us home."

The man smiled grimly, then looked down at his family. "We're counting on that, Captain." He looked around. "It seems there might have been additional drugs in the food. We've been talking." He indicated the handful of people still awake. "Most of us ate very little and didn't drink the coffee or juice." He looked at his sleeping family. "My children aren't normally this quiet. If this drug has no side effects, I guess I'm grateful."

The man coming down the aisle toward them turned out to be a doctor, as Skye had originally thought. He introduced himself as Dr. Livingston Lacy, retired.

"Everyone is sleeping. It's a mild sedative, I would imagine. It appears as though it was administered through the drink, as we all ate the food. Those who helped themselves to more than their share of the coffee and juice," he pointed to a large man in first class, "seem to be out deeper than the others."

"That's not all bad," said the large man, who introduced himself as Cliff Mawer of the D.C. fire department. "He wasn't easy to subdue. He's some CEO of a major electronics firm in Atlanta. He was making all sorts of demands. Ranting about a meeting he was missing. Generally making an ass of himself."

Dr. Lacy smiled at Cliff. "Cliff here pretty much convinced Mr. CEO to take his seat and shut up. Of course I'm paraphrasing."

"Yeah," said a girl coming out of the lavatory. "It was really cool. My brother rented an R-rated movie once and whoa. The same words." She looked at Cliff with what could only be described as hero worship. "He was just like the guy in the movie."

"Trying circumstances test people's character. Some are cowards." She looked at the snoring CEO. "And some are heroes." She looked at Cliff, the doctor, and the other people standing around. They all stood a little straighter. And Skye had just recruited her team. She would need them to keep order and reduce the trauma for the other passengers and she told them so.

"What else can you tell us?" asked a woman in a very wrinkled linen suit.

Skye told them everything she knew, which wasn't much. She didn't tell them about her contact with Jim. While it might give them hope, it was far too sensitive. He and Alex should be able to build on some of the things she was able to get through. She could picture Alex, Jim and their operations team working the clues. Scanning the maps. Poking through the Internet. She knew she would have backup and that was a great advantage…an advantage the hijackers had no way of knowing.

"Do you have a plan?"

"We have protocol for situations like this," said Skye. "My primary responsibility is to the passengers and crew. I'm to cooperate and work hard to keep things from getting unstable. Other than that, I have a great deal of discretion. Unless I see imminent danger to all the people here, I'll cooperate fully with the demands of the hijackers. In the event that things begin to deteriorate, the fools they have guarding us would be relatively easy to subdue."

"Shit, define relatively," said Cliff, smiling in spite of their dire situation. Skye drew back from her assessment a little. She was talking to civilians, after all.

"I was just in with the leader. Around him are seven extremely well-trained and well-armed men. They are the ones that concern me the most. There are fifteen others scattered around the perimeter."

"We haven't seen the leader or the other men you're talking about," said Cliff.

"Do any of you have a communication device? Cell phones are useless here, but a satellite phone or any other piece of equipment?"

They all shook their heads. "We were searched pretty thoroughly while we slept. They took phones, cameras, valuables, cash, our carry-on luggage."

"My Game Boy," said the girl, aggrieved. "Creeps!"

Skye smiled. "Now that's nasty!" She liked the girl's nerve.

Another passenger then voiced a concern. "Captain. I think we're missing someone. I mean other than the five hijackers who were on our flight."

Skye became immediately alert. "Tell me."

She nodded. "I was sitting next to this very pleasant man. Very friendly, although we didn't talk much. I was so jet lagged from my D.C. to London flight a few days ago, I zonked right out. Anyway, when we woke up from that drug they put into the system, he was gone."

"Did he leave anything behind? Maybe he was one of the hijackers."

"I thought about that. But the ones we have seen so far aren't him. Besides, he was so nice. Kind of noble, I guess. Like he had a mission. Anyway, I'm getting too fanciful. He was very tall, handsome, dressed in a dark blue business suit. Not designer. Black hair. Dark eyes."

"Could he have switched seats?"

"Thought of that, too, but I went up and down the aisles earlier. He isn't here."

"I'll ask about him when I see this Terrin again. Thank you for your information."

Skye's mind was absorbing the information and already analyzing the implications. Could he have been another ringleader? One she had not yet seen? Or could he have been the target? Was this a kidnapping?

"Let us keep order here," said Cliff and the others nodded. "Then you concentrate on the negotiations and taking care of whatever you need to do to get us out of here."

Skye nodded. "We're in pretty good shape, actually. The plane looks unharmed. I'm going up to the cockpit to assess the damage there. The fact that someone flew us in here means the plane is air worthy, but I don't know what they did since we landed. I want to see if I can fly us back out, if necessary. We're parked inside a hangar, so it will be cooler in here, although it's likely to get increasingly more uncomfortable. The water supply is limited, but you should only drink that or liquid in unopened cans or bottles. I would suggest playing a nice game of possum. You don't want to draw attention to yourselves. Unless there's a compelling reason to do so, stay in your seats."

They all nodded in agreement.

"Doctor. I would appreciate it if you could accompany me to the cockpit. I would like you to examine a little problem I might have with my ribs."

"I would like to take a look at that eye, as well." He went to his seat to get his bag. It had been searched, but nothing had been taken. He thought a heavy dose of painkiller would be in order for their courageous captain. You couldn't fool a doctor. She put on a good performance but he saw agony in her eyes. There was a good deal more wrong with her than a bruised face and a swollen eye.

To the others, Skye smiled grimly. "We're alive and that's not only a favorable outcome it is incredibly significant. They apparently want us passive, but not dead. That we can accommodate. I'll do everything necessary to get us all back home."

They nodded and smiled back. The small band of passengers felt both confident and determined. They had a leader. She had a plan. They had hope.

Skye walked down the familiar aisle to the cockpit. It was all surreal. Like a dream. Her eyes swept the sleeping faces. Revise that. More like a nightmare. She was walking through her plane, the passengers asleep. This she had done many times. But the familiar feel of the pulsating engines was absent. She was on the ground, had no idea where they were, and there were armed men surrounding the plane. Well, she thought. Could be worse. They could have been parked out in the hot sun. She could have had a broken leg. Damn. Then she thought of the ocean. It could have been much, much worse.

Walking into the cockpit, her palms itched to start the engines and get the hell out of there. She looked out the front of the plane from the vantage point of the captain's seat. Like most hangars, there were doors at the front and back. One need only open the doors in the front and she could get this bird off the ground. She read the fuel gage. She had a quarter in each wing. That was good. They could refuel here, but she wasn't sure they should risk using the jet fuel from the tanks even if there was some left in them. Depending on where they were, she could get the plane to a safe airport on what they had. Maybe even the southeastern coast of the United States.

The radios were completely fried. Some of the navigational equipment was also gone. Idiots. *Gli idioti.* They probably thought her directional gyro was a radio. Probably was Snake Tattoo. She hadn't seen him yet. Maybe it wasn't his shift. She would be unable to communicate. Otherwise it gave her heart a lift to see everything else looking good. She closed her eyes. Everything else felt good. If she could overpower seventeen armed boobs, seven highly skilled mercenaries, an evil leader, get the front door of the hangar open, turn on the engines, and get to the runway, she could get everyone out of here. Six steps to freedom. She snorted. Well at least she had a plan.

Reaching into the pocket of her captain's seat, she took out an old battered compass. It belonged to her dad. He was the one who infected her with a love of flying back when she couldn't even reach the foot controls. She carried this compass on every flight she took. Rubbing its surface, she felt her father's presence. She remembered hearing his voice when she came out of the gas-induced fog. Now she had another man in her life. Another man who *was* her life. She remembered her mind calling to him when she was going under. She looked out the window and into the hangar. What was he doing right now?

The doctor walked into the small space. "Captain?"

She put the compass back into her seat pocket. If she were going to fly this plane out, she would want it close to her.

"Will you show me now what is causing you such agony?" he asked sternly.

She looked at the doctor strangely.

"You're good, my dear. But I'm a trained physician. You're barely able to walk and you haven't moved your torso since you entered the plane."

She nodded. Then he helped her shrug out of her jacket and she removed her blouse. The doctor muttered a curse. "Bastards." He also recognized old knife and surgery scars and looked up at her with compassion.

Skye smiled wanly. "It's a long story."

"I would be interested in hearing it some day. But right now it appears as though you have a very serious problem."

"Shit. Shit. I knew it." She leaned against the arm of her seat as the doctor gently probed her rib cage. She couldn't control her sharp intake of breath and the flash of tears as he touched the spot on her right side.

"Tell me about your ribs, please."

"A few months ago I cracked several of them."

The doctor raised his eyebrows. "You seem to be quite accident prone."

She let out a short breath. "You could say that, yes."

"Well it appears that they have been nicely re-broken."

"I suspected that. Can you do anything to give me some relief?" asked Skye.

"I certainly can," said Dr. Lacy. "The hijackers had no idea what I have in here or they probably wouldn't have left it. It's a nice strong painkiller. I would suggest that I administer it immediately and that you stay off your feet until we are rescued and I can get you to a hospital."

"I'll gladly take a shot, but I want it to assist me to stay *on* my feet."

"The amount of the drug I need to give you to make this pain tolerable will knock you out. You'll have to rely on other members of your crew." The doctor was not going to allow his patient to abuse her body. She needed to be down.

"This isn't negotiable. I'll take nothing if it means either my judgment is impaired or my movement is restricted."

They stared each other down for a moment, then the doctor nodded. He knew absolute willfulness when he saw it.

"I understand the parameters. Now let me help you."

"I would really, really appreciate it," she said and surrendered a bit of her control to this healer.

"Okay. First of all, please protect this side at all costs. You can't sustain another hard blow to these ribs without puncturing your lung and that would be life threatening. This is not an ordinary contusion. The discoloration would indicate that you might have already nicked the outside of your lung. It could collapse." He looked at her solemnly. "I think you will be okay for another two or three days. After that, you may have some difficulty getting a deep breath. This would be serious enough if I had access to a medical facility, but since I don't, you will have to be very, very careful. Just in case you need any extra incentive to get us off this island, you have until the end of the week before I start to really worry."

"I understand." Tell her something she didn't know, she thought. She knew this was more than a popped rib and Mr. Snake Tattoo was going to pay.

"I'll wrap it. It doesn't help the healing process, but it will make you more comfortable." She nodded, very grateful. "Then I'll administer a shot of morphine." When he saw her stiffen, he smiled. "Not enough to impair you in any way, just enough to take the sharp edge off the pain." He looked at her scars. "I'm sure you're familiar with the various levels of pain management, from complete absence of feeling to just a bit of relief."

"You and I are going to be best friends," she said sincerely.

"Give me your arm and we'll consummate our relationship."

She gave the elderly doctor her most dazzling smile.

79

"I'm yours."

"Please, my dear. Don't diddle with a heart as old as parchment."

Skye wasn't quite sure what diddle meant, but she enjoyed the narcotic as soon as it hit her system and could see why people got hooked on the stuff. She almost got on her knees and worshiped the good doctor as a God. Closing her eyes for a moment, she let the relief wash over her.

"Thanks. I really needed that," she sighed. There was still a throbbing ache but she could easily live with what was left.

"I'm going to wrap up the painkiller in tablet form for you. I want you to take two of these every four hours."

"I'll take one every six hours."

The doctor sighed. "Thought maybe I could get one past you."

She tapped her chest as she reached for her blouse. "I'm experienced, remember?"

"Ah yes." He helped her into her blouse and jacket and slipped the pills in the pocket. She gathered up her flight bag and filled it with some of the bags of peanuts and pretzels. It was a cliché to provide these for her crew, but they would be better than nothing. She left all the bottled water and soda for the passengers.

"I appreciate you helping out with the passengers. Tell me. In your professional opinion, will they all be okay?"

"I'm not sure of the long-term effects of the initial drug we were subjected to, but everyone is in good shape." Skye knew about the effects of sterohydroxophene, but didn't want to reveal her superior knowledge of various forms of gas to the doctor. They all had to take whiffs of the non-lethal varieties during training. This one was everyone's favorite. They used to schedule the parties to coincide with the whiffing sessions. There were some nasty ones, too. Remembering one that induced vomiting and diarrhea, she decided she definitely didn't want to go there. Instead, she added the fact that the hijackers didn't use that particular gas to her list of things to be thankful for.

Skye heard a commotion in the back of the plane. "I think I'd better get back out there. I've stayed in here long enough." Grabbing her flight bag, she put her hat back on and started down the aisle. It was Snake Tattoo and he was staring at her from the doorway.

"So it's the bitch who couldn't shut up. You learned your lesson, whore?"

It was all she could do to keep from breaking his nose and turning him into a vegetable with one punch. But he had two of his men behind him and she knew just how many more there were.

Out of the corner of her eye she saw Cliff making a move to stand up. Shaking her head slightly, she waved him off. Catching her nonverbal message, he sat quietly.

Snake Tattoo came forward and held the muzzle of his gun to her chest. He was confused because she didn't cower this time. Must be putting on a show to impress the passengers, he thought.

Skye didn't say a word. Didn't make a move. Damn. The safety was on and there was no bullet in the chamber of his gun. She could take it away from him and be armed in two seconds. Discipline Skye, she thought. Discipline. She still would only have one weapon against all the others. Even with the element of surprise, she wouldn't be able to pull it off. She'd wait. Bide her time. And comfort herself with the certainty that this asshole was hers.

Suddenly a boy came out of one of the seats and walked right to her. He was tall and very nice looking. His eyes were right on Skye's, a silent message in them. Not knowing who he was, she had no idea what the message could be. But it did serve to distract Snake Tattoo and his friends.

"Sit down," said Skye firmly, but not unkindly.

"Oh please!" cried the boy in a very loud, whining voice that seemed incongruous with the confident way he was carrying himself. "Please sir. Let me go with my aunt. I need to be with my aunt." He grabbed Skye's hand and gently squeezed it. Play along, it said. "I want to go home. You said this was going to be a fun trip." His voice cracked and he started to hyperventilate. He was actually getting himself all worked up, although the hand she held was steady and dry.

"Jason." She could only think of Alex's nephew's name. "Now get back to your seat. You're going to make yourself sick."

"Pleeeeeese. Take me with you!" He really was making a scene now. Skye would have hated to see this boy in his terrible two's. "I'm soooooo scared." Skye realized he was playing this perfectly...showing fear. That would appeal to the hijacker's need for dominance. And the bonus was that he was taking all the attention away from her. A very good thing, considering she was about a heartbeat away from either another slap or some equally painful confrontation. The teenager obviously wanted to go with her for some reason. Normally she would have insisted he stay on the plane, but there was something about the boy. Something about the firm pressure of his hand.

As the hijackers watched, revolted, the kid began to make awful, whining, sucking noises. She was quite sure it would annoy the hell out of their captors and maybe they would just give in rather than fight it. They obviously wanted the passengers quiet and submissive. This boy was anything but. Now he was launching into a full-fledged tantrum. Wow. She almost applauded.

The boy must have assessed his chances of being shot and realized that for some reason, no passenger had been injured. He calculated the risk and took his chances. He started screaming, kicking the seat, and getting red in the face. The three armed men could probably have faced a platoon of invaders easier than one screaming, obnoxious child. They looked at each other, consternation on their faces.

"Jason, honey." She turned imploring, submissive eyes to Snake Tattoo who was finding the situation deteriorating as the passengers who were awake started murmuring and a few were moving to get up. "Could I just take him with me. I need to calm him down." Appeal to his need to control. Kiss his ass.

She looked the boy right in the eye. He had beautifully expressive green eyes. His phony tears didn't hide their intensity. "Jason. If this man allows me to take you with me, will you settle down?"

"I'm so scared. This guy is really scaring me!" And he dissolved in tears on Skye's chest, adding a few shakes and shudders. God this kid was good. She put an arm around him. His arms went around her waist and she noticed that even though it appeared to be a death grip, it was very, very gentle. He knew she was hurting. Suddenly, she wanted to take this kid back to the room. For some reason he wanted to go with her and it wasn't just a whim, she was sure of it.

She looked at Snake Tattoo beseechingly. "Please?" This was just about killing her to be so passive, but she had passengers to think about. "Oh please." She was begging now. She could see it was working. Nodding importantly, Snake Tattoo poked the boy with the muzzle of his gun. Skye stiffened but she felt the boy softly tap the back of her waist. It was okay. Still, he whimpered in fright. That sealed it. Snake Tattoo accompanied them off the plane and enjoyed prodding him all the way back to the room with the crew. The boy played Snake like a violin, whimpering and letting out little frightened squeals every time he got a poke.

Skye walked back to the room that was her prison working hard to suppress a smile…she had assessed the dangers, obtained valuable intelligence, evaluated the shape of her plane, checked on the passenger situation, received some good painkillers, and had acquired her flight bag and a kid. A good morning's work.

Cliff, the doctor and a few of the passengers looked out the window. "The two of them played that perfectly," said Cliff with a grin. They all nodded.

"If our hijackers are that stupid, we have a chance," agreed one of the women.

"From what the captain said, these men aren't the problem. There's a formidable adversary on the premises." He watched the captain as she and the boy disappeared behind the door near the front of the hangar. "But perhaps he has met his match."

The doctor nodded, but a shadow of concern passed over his expressive face. She better make her play quickly or he was afraid the match would go to the terrorists by default.

Stuart and the others heard the locks disengage and watched as Skye, with a boy wrapped around her, was shoved roughly into the room. Skye almost lost her balance, but the kid held tightly to her waist and kept her from stumbling. He wailed some more and Snake Tattoo snorted in derision as he slammed the door and locked it.

Instantly the kid transformed. He stood up straight and looked at Skye. "Figured he'd be a door slammer. When you can't get it up, you slap women, torment kids, and slam doors." He shook off the last of the award-winning performance and wiped his face with his hands.

Skye just stared at him. "Who the hell are you?"

"Why I'm your nephew, Jason," he said sticking out his hand. "Otherwise known as Fisher Mitchell. My friends call me Fish. My enemies call me Shark." His grin was absolutely infectious and his green eyes were intelligent, alert, and way on the other side of cocky.

She grinned back. "You sure were convincing."

"Sorry I had to trip all over you like that, but I really needed to get here."

"Do you always get what you want?"

"With my talent for tantrums? Need you ask?"

Then as the crew gathered around her, she filled them in on all that had happened. "Okay, Fish," said Skye. "You got in here, now do you mind telling us why it was so important?"

"Jeesh, you really remind me of my grandma. Tight. Anyway." With a flourish and a swaggering grin he pulled a small thin device out of one of his many pockets and presented it to her. "No one ever pulled a rabbit out of a hat without putting one in there in the first place, as my dear grandma is fond of saying."

Recognizing it immediately, Skye felt a surge of excitement sweep through her. "How come they didn't take this from you?"

Fisher looked at the multitude of pockets in his cargo pants. "Well, the only thing I can figure out is that they got tired of rummaging around all the really cool stuff I carry in here." He shook his pants...and it was obvious there were more treasures in his pockets than in his luggage. "I don't travel light. Anyway, they did take my cell phone and Game Boy. Buttheads. That little honey was stuck down there in my lower left leg pocket with all the Bubbliscious wrappers. I never litter, so that pocket becomes my wrapper carrier. I don't think they search a kid real close, anyway. Never expected something that sweet on a child."

"What is it?" asked Brian.

"It's a PDA with a satellite communication system." She looked at Fisher for confirmation and he nodded. "We have email capability."

They all started talking at once, but Skye saw from Fisher's face that there was more and it wasn't good.

She nodded at him to continue his report.

"Yeah. Before you get all stoked, the reason it was in the wrapper pocket is that the battery was way low."

"You have the cord?"

"No. It was in my backpack and that was taken. There's a reason I wanted this to get to you." He was serious now. An amazing transformation. This boy had many faces, many facets. Skye was fascinated, but she put it aside for now. "I estimate we have maybe three to five minutes of power left in the string. You'll need to isolate someone other than my own mailbox dudes to get a hot point to. I thought of my grandma, she was waiting for me at the gate, but that would have been selfish. I figure if you compose your dope, we quick turn it on, tune it in and flash it over...we can get maybe one or two flats out, smoking."

"Did he say we could get a message out?" Amy asked Brian. She figured if he knew Italian, he might know kid speak.

"That's what I heard," said Skye. She understood perfectly. She lived with a fourteen-year-old. And she knew exactly whom she was going to get the hot point out to.

"Here is what I know. Let's tick these things off. Fisher, you add anything you've seen or heard." He nodded. He liked how she didn't just dismiss him now that he gave her his tool. He was part of her lunch bunch. Cool.

"There are at least seventeen armed men. Idiots, but with SIG Commandos, each with 20-30 rounds." Her crew looked at her with amazement. "Pilots are trained to recognize various models.

"One vicious, self-absorbed leader named Loris Terrin," Skye continued. "Seven close body guards, skilled and well trained, side arms only. Terrin has state-of-the-art equipment. Isencompt computers were turned on and I saw a manual for the international Internet connection EarthCom5. I'm hoping the person I'll be sending this to will be able to hack into his system. Our plane is in excellent shape, except for the radios and transponders. All passengers are well, although drugged, and their situation doesn't appear to be dire."

"Um...," interrupted Fisher. She nodded.

"I'm not sure if this means anything." She noticed he was focused and solemn. He knew instinctively that what he saw did mean something. He'd even lost his kid speak. "But the really dangerous guys, as you called them, were stringing wire around the perimeter of the building early this morning while most people were sleeping and I don't think it was fiber optics for the modems. They were working with what looked like clay." Skye jerked. He nodded. "Plastic explosives."

Skye raised her eyebrows and Fisher waggled his. "I like action movies. I know the lingo."

Skye nodded. She knew exactly what plastic looked like and he described it perfectly. It was effective and very dangerous. It meant they were surrounded by explosives. Things just got a lot hotter.

"Damn. I think we have to amend the not dire scenario. That may be a defensive move in case they're attacked, but we can't count on it. If they're laying it to use it, we may not be able to just wait for rescue or release," said Skye, all business now. "Okay, let's inventory our assets. First of all, a healthy, hungry, clear-headed crew."

Her healthy and hungry, but clear-headed crew responded.

"Great weather," said Amy.

"A hangar that we can get out of in a hurry. We don't have to move the plane first since there are two doors," said Brian.

"Plenty of fuel."

"Some pretty big passengers," said Fisher thinking of Cliff and some of the others. "They will fight to save their families."

"Peanuts and pretzels," said Beth who was put in charge of dolling them out. "Water and a clean bathroom."

"And from the flight bag, soap, toothpaste, and shampoo."

"And, if we have to get out of here on our own, two pilots." Skye looked around at everyone in the room, getting serious. "As self serving as this sounds, you will all protect the pilots. If we have to make our own escape plans, we need the skill."

She looked at Stuart. "You will stand down, Co-Captain Modesto and stay back. You will never confront any of the hijackers or run to the aid of any of the passengers or us…ever. You will stand behind me and the rest of the crew. That's an order. When and if we get in the cockpit, I'll be your backup only. As much as I want to fly this baby back home, according to the doctor, I may be unable to by the end of the week."

She heard the gasps and saw the horror on their faces. She smiled weakly. "I'm sorry to have to tell you. I was hoping to keep that little bit of dicey information to myself, but you all have to know everything."

"I knew you were hurting more than you were letting on," said Amy with alarm. "How bad is it?" Skye told them.

"Right now, I'm feeling relatively good. The doctor got me fixed up. But that will be the last shot I'll be taking until I have Stuart in the cockpit. I want eight hours between the shot and any possibility of having to fly. I don't see things happening that fast. Stuart. You're field promoted to captain. If we have to get off the island, you will be in the left seat."

Stuart swallowed hard. Every pilot's dream and all he wanted to do was shout 'no way.' He would do his job though and he simply nodded.

Skye didn't mention the gun she had in her flight bag, or her special training. They were assets that she held in reserve.

"Let's get a message out first, then we can talk strategy and tactics."

Soon, they all gathered around Fisher and Skye who sat with their backs resting against the wall. Katherine was listening at the door. No sound from the other side.

When they had gone over the message several times, refining it and prioritizing the information, Skye nodded at Fisher and handed him back his PDA. His green eyes blazed with pride and purpose. She was letting him do it, trusting him to do it right. Opening it up, he prayed he hadn't screwed up and left it on or something. He breathed a sigh of relief when he heard the familiar, sweet whir of the little mechanism. Turning off the volume, he waited for everything to boot up. Then he used quick, efficient, highly skilled movements to load all the appropriate software and get on-line. Shit. The little battery signal was flashing in the corner. Teasing, Urgent.

He quickly typed in the address Skye had given him and then the words as Skye dictated them…he didn't worry about spelling or syntax. Except for wanting to get the names exactly right, the receiver would get the message.

The blinking battery was flashing faster. Mocking him. Trying to make him nervous, but his hands were steady and his fingers were swift. "Hurry," he breathed. "Hurry. I have to push send now, Captain. I have to."

"Send it," she breathed. She would have liked to get in more descriptions, more observations, but the most important stuff was loaded. Fisher pushed send just as the screen went blank. Frustration overwhelmed the boy. He wasn't sure it got out. Making a fist around the device, he hurled it across the room where it smashed into several pieces.

"Hell! Hell!" he said as he covered his face with his hands. Tears, real this time, were in his eyes. "I'm not sure it got out, Captain. I'm sorry. I underestimated the time we had."

Smiling confidently Skye put an appreciative arm around Fisher's shuddering shoulders. She trusted the boy's quick hands and remarkable reflexes. "It got out," she said. "And the person catching it will know just what to do with it."

CHAPTER 7

A team of exhausted but dedicated people were working around the clock in a conference room in the Justice building in Washington D.C. There was a sense of urgency, but no panic or wasted movement. Linda Hauser, Barclay Kimkoski and Sloane were working on the computers. Linda had been with Skye since they met at training camp in Colorado. They'd been good friends and colleagues ever since. Barclay had worked with Skye on several important ops and was a genius on computers. Not quite at Sloane's level, but one of the best in the department.

Sloane and Barclay were working on finding connections between the passenger list and any known terrorist groups. Linda was communicating with British authorities on what they had gathered from Heathrow Airport in London and searching for the man with the tattoo and scar.

Jim had been in contact with the airlines, the State Department, the United Nations, and the media. No one had heard from the hijackers. Neither Amanda nor Alex learned anything from all of their global contacts. As far as the world was concerned, the plane was in the ocean. The only people who knew it was still intact and on some kind of island were in this room or had top-secret clearance.

Alex and Jim were still pouring over maps where Alex had circled several possible islands in the boundaries they had set. Amanda was currently working on convincing Langley to divert some of their satellite assets to move over the area of possible landing sites.

"I don't give a flying fuck if you have to wake up the goddamn director, the President, the general secretary of the United Nations and good God almighty!" She continued to swear at the person she was talking to.

"My, my," he said to Jim. "Very un-old ladylike. Wow. Where did she learn that one?"

Finally, Amanda slammed down the phone. "Done! We'll have pictures by this afternoon. If there's an International Airlines plane parked up the ass of the mayor in an obscure town in the fucking foothills of the mountains of Outer Nowhere, we're going to know about it."

Looking up with bloodshot eyes, Sloane poked Barclay, giving a little victory squeal. "You owe me a pizza and a full body massage at Serenity Spa. Huh! Eat your heart out and your liver, too," she grinned at Barclay. "Amateur." And since Barclay worshiped anyone who could hack into the computers at the Kremlin for a little hide and seek, he grinned right back.

"I have the target." Sloane declared as she went to the printer, and picked up a printout. She shot it across the table toward Alex, Amanda, and Jim.

Amanda just stared. She had to remind herself this was a child.

"Sloane Madison, girl genius. Roll over and torpedo your fan, 'cause this fantasmo Zelda can rock." She popped another huge bubble.

Ah yes, there was the fourteen year old. They all stared at the picture of a nice looking man of about 40 waving and smiling to the camera. There was more there too…charisma. A commanding presence.

"Emilio Moreno. He's the Soterian ambassador to England," said Sloane. "He was returning home for good because he's running for President. His platform is reform…a very dangerous stand. There's lots of organized crime in the area and vicious cartel leaders have terrorized his country for years. He is determined to get the criminals and seedy element off his island…an island where the native tongue is Shakanwa. Mostly English educated middle and upper class. The hill people still speak the native tongue. Poor, uneducated. The reason the slime ball pig who whaled on Skye spoke English was to impress. To be more imposing. It was a sign of movement to an upper class. Leadership perhaps. It was only after she pushed him over and…and was out that he babbled in his native tongue."

"An elaborate kidnapping?" speculated Alex.

"Perhaps," responded Jim.

Amanda nodded and said. "Or an assassination…but why such a complicated take down?"

Linda came over with her own contribution. "I used your suspicion Alex, and it connects exactly with Sloane's data. The tattoo is one used by a crime syndicate throughout the West Indies, Venezuela, and other parts of South America. It's used as a badge. Here's a picture of it now."

The printer whirred and they looked at the tattoo Skye had described. "I'm still looking for the guy with the cheek scar, but if he's known to the authorities down there, we should have his picture soon."

"That one belongs to me," said Alex. "I want to see his face."

He looked very dangerous and very determined. He hadn't shaved or slept and the combination gave him a sinister look. The man with the scar on his cheek was marked and they had no doubt Alex was going to get him.

"If it's a kidnapping I think we would have heard from them by now," said Jim.

"Maybe Amanda's right and it's a cover for an assassination," said Alex, rubbing his tired eyes. He'd tried to nap in the chair a few hours earlier but whenever he closed his eyes, he'd see a scar-faced man hitting Skye and hear that last horrendous kick. His eyes would fly open and he'd break out in a cold sweat. Better to stay awake. Alex continued, "Maybe they'll shoot him as one of the passengers and have the world think he was a victim of terrorists."

"In that case we may not be talking about negotiation or ransom," said Jim, thinking out loud. He was operating on no sleep as well. "It's a simple murder cloaked in a complicated deception to cover the cartel's duplicity. Seems terribly elaborate, however. Why not kill the man in his sleep?"

Amanda frowned. "We need more information and more data before we can decide if we should go in after them or risk waiting for contact and negotiations. If it's an assassination, they may just want the whole plane to disappear. Then we need to go in. If it's a kidnapping, demands should be coming soon. We would want to play it very cool. Standing back. If he's their only target, and I know this sounds cold, but if it's true, then the rest of the passengers might be safe. He may be their only casualty. Or one of very few."

"Let's work all scenarios," said Jim. "It will be more difficult, but I don't see any alternative."

Sloane went back to her computer. She was using her own laptop because she had modified some of the software and a few of the things were not just quite altogether...well...legal. Or at least no real international laws had been established that covered everything she could do.

She heard all the beeps, indicating she had received new email, but she'd been ignoring it all night. She slept fitfully on the coach for a few hours, but mostly she'd been working on digging into the files of the passengers. Her email would have to wait. Now she wanted to find out more about Emilio Moreno.

Her new mail indicator beeped again and she looked down automatically to see whom it was from. The little box in the corner said Shark. She didn't know anyone named Shark. Sighing, she poised her finger over the delete key. Not much got through her multiple levels of anti-spam software, but sometimes an unwanted email from some imbecilic company promising paradise popped up. Apparently the underworld of commerce had no respect for her need to stay focused on the current crisis. Her finger moved to zap the email out of her computer but it hesitated. Whether it was intuition or a couple of cells in her remarkable brain had registered the name and made instant connections, she would never know. She stopped. Her finger hovered for a moment, then slowly made its way to the email. When she opened it, she didn't care.

"Oh my God," she said in an unsteady voice. Everyone in the room stopped and looked at her. Sloane had been unshakable throughout the night but now she was sitting in her chair trembling and running her fingers through her dark brown curls. "Oh my God!" she said again. Her entire vocabulary in dozens of different languages completely let her down. She had no words in her. Her fingers flew over the keys to uncover the true name of the sender. "Oh my God!" she said again.

"What is it?" demanded Alex, putting down the map he'd been working on. Sloane looked at him...looked through him. Her eyes were shiny with tears. "Before I answer that, Alex," she pulled her gaze away from him to Amanda. The intensity of Sloane's face gave Amanda a little jolt. She hadn't expected Sloane to look right at her next. "Tell me again the name of your grandson, Amanda. His full name, please."

"Fisher Taylor Stanaslov Mitchell." Amanda didn't hesitate, didn't ask for explanations. Sloane was, on a certain level, her colleague and as such deserved instant cooperation. When Sloane raised her eyebrows, Amanda explained. "He had four godfathers. One was a former Russian KGB agent."

"Ah." Then Sloane grinned...just like a sunrise. "Well, everyone." She looked right at Alex. "Fisher Taylor Stanaslov Mitchell, otherwise known as Shark, has just sent us a message from Skye."

The room erupted with noise, excitement, and energy.

"Are you sure?" asked Jim, not wanting to have any distractions. It was his job to assess the validity of all correspondence and he'd uncovered several bogus messages already.

Sloane turned her steady gaze on Jim, anticipating that exact question. "I'm sure. Skye starts the message with her social security number and," her shiny eyes went to tears and they started sliding down her cheeks in two tiny silver rivers. Alex went over and she put her arms around his waist. Thus protected, she could finish. "And the name of my teddy bear."

"You have a teddy bear?" asked Barclay, stunned. They all looked at him. Sometimes the poor man was completely clueless. This was one of those times. He shrugged and fiddled with his pocket protector. "Never seemed the type," he mumbled. "I never had a teddy bear. It wouldn't be that difficult to figure out the name of a teddy bear. It's Teddy for God's sake." His voice trailed off and he went back to the protection of his keyboard. His fingers tapped the keys and he projected the message from Sloane's computer to the large screen on the wall.

They all stared at the information. Concise, clearly written and filled with valuable information. Sloane took a deep breath, let go of Alex and went back to work.

"Skye dictated it, it's her style," said Jim.

"But she didn't type it in," griped Sloane. "Too many typos."

They all slid a look at Amanda who'd been busy working with a handkerchief and something in her eye. They all smiled. Hard crust, soft middle. Just like a loaf of the best French bread.

"Must be Shark's work. Boneheaded flakeboy, can't even spell semi-automatic. Good thing I can translate just about any bit of gibberish," mumbled Sloane as she swiftly cleaned up the spelling and enlarged the font. I bugged her just a little that there was someone right there with Skye. Someone who could touch her and talk to her and be with her. Shark, huh. Didn't he have a stupid spell check?

"We have a lot to work with here." Alex read the message then threw his arm around Amanda and squeezed. Squeezed so hard a few more tears came out of her eyes. "They're together Amanda. As remarkable as that seems, they're working together." They looked at each other. For some reason, it was a great comfort. To both of them.

"Can we get a message back to her on Fisher's unit?" asked Alex.

Sloane shook her head. "I'm afraid not. Look, see this little imperfection?" Alex didn't really see much, but he nodded anyway. "It's a battery mark. Your idiot grandson must have been emailing across the Atlantic and ran down the batteries. Most models with this capability will have two, three hours of battery power. They were six hours over the Atlantic when they were taken. He may have had only a few minutes of power left. I've been trying since we got the message to hack through to him, but he's gone."

Her gaze went to Amanda. They all realized there was the possibility that they had been discovered and stopped, maybe even injured or killed.

"Then let's concentrate on what we have. Isencompt computers," said Jim, looking at the message on the screen. "I've never heard of them." Barclay and Sloane looked at each other and rolled their eyes. Sloane gave Barclay a little nod.

"They're a South American manufacturer. Stole all the patents from Micron." Sometimes it just paid to be a nerd. He may not be the stud of the century, but he knew things. And some people thought that was sexy. Enough people to make Barclay happy, anyway.

"They have some unique features, but they're really very simple machines. It's the Internet connection that's the most important place for us to start, though," Barclay continued.

"EarthCom5," said Sloane, reading from the message.

"Yes. This is very good news. Their security is incredibly lax. We have the guy's name...good going, Skye...so we should be able to gain access relatively fast," said Sloane.

"Define relative," said Alex.

Barclay and Sloane looked at each other.

"Ready?"

They looked at the clock. "Mark the time," said Sloane, then placed her fingers on the keys of her computer.

"Raspberry cheesecake," said Barclay, then wished he hadn't said it out loud. Sounded so soft.

"A trip to Jamaica," said Sloane. Barclay stared at her, his fingers poised over his keys. "Okay. Just thought I would try to slip one by you."

"Do I look that stupid?"

Sloane tactfully refused to answer. Instead she said, "Saunders hot fudge."

They nodded and for the next twenty minutes the only sound was the dueling keyboards. Barclay was sweating. Sloane was blowing bubbles and snapping them back in her mouth. She had a thing for Bubbliscious gum. Helped her think, kept her alert. And annoyed the hell out of Barclay.

"Yes!" Sloane said jumping up in victory. "Mark the time!"

"21 minutes and 17 seconds," said Linda.

"Damn," said Barclay, but he was grinning. "I wasn't even close. I kept jigging right instead of left. I couldn't get the door open on the 23rd level."

"Hey!" said the grinning Sloane generously. "You were right behind me. You had only about eight left."

She sat back down and punched a few more keys. Her screen was projected on the large unit on the wall. "In a minute I can upload all this guy's email."

Amanda and Alex had been at the maps again. Jim was on the phones coordinating a possible rescue team. They would be mobilized as soon as they pinpointed the island. They all looked up at Sloane and marveled at her future in intelligence work. Sloane grinned at Amanda and winked.

"Where you had to sneak around men's bedrooms and dig through private papers, I can pop into anyone's computer and get away clean without having to leave my room. Good thing, too, since I'm constantly being grounded by unenlightened adults." She looked over at Jim, who gave her a mock frown.

She turned to Alex. "There's a problem, though."

"What?"

"He may have a detector unit. If he does, he'll know he's been raided. I'm not sure how he'll react. If his units are on, and from Skye's observations it seems as though they are, the warning may be audio. In other words it's like a security system. The alarm will go off as soon as I press this key. Then he may have an automatic dump. He could have put everything on disk and the email file is just a convenience. If everything is dumped, it will be a real race. My program against his. It will be like chasing a cat's tail that's going 100 miles an hour."

"On foot," said Barclay, his admiration for Sloane and her work evident in his face.

Alex smiled. His confidence showing. "So tell me what's the problem?"

Nodding, Sloane gave him a particularly Skye-like smile that tugged at his heart, took a deep breath, spit the bubble gum out of her mouth and put it on top of her printer to keep the three wads already there company. She flexed her fingers, strong, long and capable, just like her sister's. She looked at Barclay who nodded. He didn't have her capabilities, would never have them, but his confidence was important to her. And his own self-respect would stay in tact only if he felt part of the experience. With that one look, she included him in the race, and he would feel a part of the victory. Alex felt another tug. She knew how to lead, just like her sister.

Then Sloane, girl genius, the fantasmo Zelda, punched the key and got started. Information spilled on the screen and then started to melt away…liquefying like an ice cube on a hot stove.

"He has a detector!" shouted Barclay, in spite of himself. "Shit. Go Sloane go!" Barclay had never watched a sporting event in his life, but he knew what a cheerleader was for. Quiet, nerdy, clueless Barclay was jumping, shouting, and rooting for the home team.

"She's got it…she's got it." He would say every time she beat the incredible erasing mechanism and captured some or all of the dissolving material. Sloane's fingers were a blur. They were cramping and still she didn't reduce their speed, didn't flag for a minute, didn't even take the time to blink. Alex could see the strain on her face, could see the muscles in her wrists and arms jumping with fatigue and still she didn't stop. Everyone surrounded her joining in the chant. Jim had his arm around Amanda, whose eyes started leaking again.

Alex was watching Sloane, the pain evident on her face. She was beginning to tense up. His compassion for the girl conflicting with his need for the information. Alex almost called a halt to it when Sloane's eyes started to tear. She hadn't even blinked, couldn't afford the distraction. Finally, as abruptly as it began, the screen went blank and Sloane stopped. She was breathing heavily and was completely zoned. Her fingers had stopped, but her hands were shaking from fatigue. Finally she allowed herself to blink, then almost collapsed over her computer. Alex knelt beside her and gathered her in his arms as she wept out her pain and frustration.

"Alex. Alex. I think I got a lot of it. Oh. Alex. It has to help." And she just let herself be held for a while.

Amanda watched. "James, the price these two young women, these sisters, no less, have paid is almost too much to bear. I thought I was out of the game. Out of the agony, out of the need to watch the sacrifice and the toll on people's emotions." Then she pulled something out of her pocket and went over to Sloane, who was wiping her face and swallowing her anxiety.

"Got to get back to work," Sloane said with a big watery sigh as she tried to work the cramps out of her talented hands. She looked up at Amanda as she came over. The truce was solid, but still in its infancy. She waited.

"In that case," Amanda said with a compassionate smile, handing Sloane a package of Bubbliscious gum. "I imagine you will need this."

"Watermelon. Chilled ice! My absolute favorite. You chew?"

"No." Amanda laughed in spite of herself. This was like talking to her grandson. "It's Fisher's favorite too."

"So he's connected. A boss player with at least a little knobby groove."

"Ah, yes. I guess. Anyway, I would love for you to meet when we get them all back home," said Amanda, putting her arm around the pretty, but troubled child.

"Yeah. Okay." Sloane had a picture of a short skinny, geeky, pimply kid with freckles, braces, and a booger fetish. But she liked Amanda and would shake the kid's hand...especially since he got the message through. And of course there was the Bubbliscious connection. But she was sure going to remind him he had a spell check, moron. She popped three pieces in her mouth and managed to chew them into submission before she turned to start work on what she had captured.

Barclay was the expert in the area of reconstructing broken lines of text. Before long he and Sloane were engaged in a new round of contests and Barclay actually won a few. As soon as they had a bit of useful data, they would turn it over to Linda, Alex, Amanda and Jim. It was up to them to make sense of it and decide how to use it.

Over the next few hours the team was energized with renewed vigor and focus. They all had their tasks, the most important being the location of the island, the biographies of the players, and any other relevant information that could be hacked out of the seemingly random strands of data.

In his office a few thousand miles away, Terrin was swearing and screaming at his computer screen. He was frantically pulling plugs and flipping switches.

"What is it?" asked one of his elite guard. There was a buzzing sound coming from the computer system. They all had their guns drawn and were moving to defend, alerted by a blaring that seemed more like a security breach than a computer malfunction. But it soon became obvious that the enemy was unseen and electronic, so they stood down.

"Someone just tried to hack into my system," said Terrin, smiling confidently as he flipped the last power switch. "But what he doesn't know is that no one can get in without my knowledge. This is a state-of-the-art detection system. The very best on the market. As soon as anyone even knocks on the door, it begins erasing and burning all the files. Everything is gone. No one can retrieve anything. It would have been damn inconvenient a few weeks ago, but since this unit and the entire hangar is going to be blown to hell in two days, it doesn't really matter. I have everything I need already transferred to my laptop or placed on disk."

His bodyguards smiled. Their leader was a genius and they were proud to serve him. "Who do you think it was?"

Terrin's smile faded. "I have a pretty good idea...and I think he has just made up my mind on how to proceed in the next few days. Whoever it was has betrayed my trust and can no longer be part of the future."

A few of the men nodded. They were paid militia, assassins and soldiers. The inactivity on the island was making them restless. Their hunger for blood needed to be fed and it sounded like their leader was singing their song.

"Now where were we before we were so rudely interrupted? Is everything ready?"

"Yes. We expect Lomar and his people tomorrow. He will have Faneta from Venezuela with him. They will be meeting in the Trinidad airport and fly over by helicopter."

"Lomar and I have been communicating with Faneta for the past year. This is the perfect place for us all to meet. I met Lomar personally two years ago and then again last month when we were putting the last steps of this plan together. Faneta provided us with the gas, the guns and the London connection. He's never come out of his lair before. He trusts no one. This will be our first meeting so I want intense security."

He looked at his dead computers thoughtfully. "I wonder. I wonder which one tried to get in. I suspect Faneta. He's more of a mystery. I ran with his brother who was a courageous and useful soldier for the Serpent and the Spear, but I only know this man by his deeds. He is ruthless. Without mercy. Even his brother, who feared nothing, was afraid of Faneta."

"He was responsible for the bombing of the high court on the south island?"

"Yes, he was. The entire court. He has stayed alive because of his cunning and his caution. And tomorrow we will meet. The three of us will open the crates and enjoy a celebration. Then we will leave here, destroy all the evidence, and return to our country to begin our reign. By this time next month, we will be planning our Presidential campaign. Within the year, I will be dining in the President's private residence. The country is ours. Its oil is ours. The people will be ours."

He turned and looked out the window at the runway and the pile of boxes and crates stacked near the hangar. A year in the planning, a week in the execution. Victory was near. No one knew where they were. The media was still reporting the plane as missing and presumed down. The U.S. military was racing around looking for debris. Fools. Tomorrow night, after Faneta and Lomar left with the cargo, he would allow himself to celebrate. He would drink, take that arrogant captain to his bed, play with her like a cat plays with a mouse, then leave her broken and dead. Then the day after that he would leave with his guard and pull the plug on Flight 127. No one would ever know what happened. The plane and the entire island would be blasted into oblivion. He smiled. Yes, victory was near and nothing or no one could stop him.

"We have the location!" shouted Amanda, slamming down the phone for the hundredth time in three hours. "Alex, grab the map. Right here." She pointed to a tiny speck. Even on this enhanced map, it was hardly noticeable.

"According to our satellites, there are over a hundred bodies on the island."

She saw Sloane's head jerk up and turn to her. "Alive, honey. To put it bluntly, if they weren't alive, they wouldn't be putting out this much heat. The bodies are concentrated in a pattern consistent with an airliner. They will be sending the pictures over in a few minutes. Linda, prepare to receive them and put them on screen."

"Who are 'they'?" whispered Barclay to Sloane.

"Don't ask," she said. Sloane knew that 'they' were the Central Intelligence Agency. She'd already hacked into the CIA files and read the deep cover, complete file on one Amanda Lakeside Lambert Mitchell. It was under several layers of intense security and a real challenge to access. And while she was there, she snagged the file for one Cameron Mitchell as well. She skimmed part of it while waiting for a website to load earlier that afternoon. It was information she was definitely keeping to herself. She took pride in keeping secrets. She figured she was knee deep in trouble again…well, since it was CIA, maybe up to her neck. She didn't care. Let them arrest her, put her in irons, give her bread and water for the rest of her life. She needed to know whom she was working with. And, as it turned out, it was the best. She was able to relax her jittery nerves and calm her devastating fears. And that made her better. Besides. She'd proven she could keep a secret. She'd known about Skye for years. Cranked her dossier when she was only nine…and a half. Never told a soul until she confessed a few months ago.

"The island is northwest of Trinidad. A very small island. The visual pictures show a hangar and airstrip. They never would have been able to locate it if Skye hadn't sent the original message and given them the parameters to work with," said Amanda. "She did fine work."

As it turned out, Sloane had mined for pure gold as well. She and Barclay were getting entire paragraphs from Terrin's email. Much of it was useless, but they were trying to secure every line they could.

When Sloane went off for a bathroom break, Barclay sat back in his chair and stared after her. "You know Alex, I don't think there's an instrument or a test yet devised that can begin to measure that girl's intelligence. She humors people and takes the standard exams, but nothing has come close to finding the bottom of that well."

"All that and she's well adjusted," added Amanda.

"Chalk one up for Skye," said Linda simply. She was nibbling on a piece of Barclay's raspberry cheesecake.

Even though he lost, Sloane had ordered it from a local bakery for him. They didn't know she had charged it to Alex's open account. Alex was so easy, Sloane thought. He just didn't care much about his money. It was there and that was that. The fact that Sloane knew the extent of his wealth better than he wouldn't have shocked him. He had a real knack for making it. Then he would lose interest and delegate the operations to someone he trusted and go make more. It was the chase that excited him. And since he joined the Justice Department, even that became less important. He much preferred to chase bad guys now.

Alex was studying the dossiers of Lomar, Terrin, and Faneta. Barclay and Sloane had uncovered their names from the email correspondence and Amanda had secured their files from the CIA. He was frowning over the details of this man Terrin's life and it wasn't as alarming as it could have been. The man got where he was and survived through intimidation and an army of mercenaries. No real finesse or intelligence. Skye would be able to handle him. Of course he was also the type who would be threatened by her if she cranked up her need to control a situation. She didn't like backing down, but he knew she would if she felt she had to. Her natural charisma and personal power could dominate a room. It was to her credit that she could turn it down and play a submissive role when the situation dictated the need. She was a real chameleon and it was one of the reasons she was Jim Stryker's best. One of two, he thought, letting his own ego take a bow. The terrible pain in his chest was easing with every bit of information they were gathering. Her situation was dangerous, but not dire. The terror was beginning to dissipate.

According to the emails they were reading, Lomar was bringing in a helicopter to Trinidad and meeting Faneta at the airport. Faneta seemed like the real wild card. Someone who was deeply hidden from direct contact but did all the dirty work. Very, very dangerous, but never seen by the other two. This was to be their initial meeting. To merge the factions.

Alex knew they could plan and execute a raid within 48 hours but held it as a last resort. There were just too many passengers and an incursion would be bloody. He read the emails again and a plan was beginning to formulate in his mind. He would need a great deal more information. He looked at Sloane, blowing bubbles and conferring with Barclay. And he knew right where to get it.

Sloane and Barclay both straightened at the same time. "Oh God," said Sloane with alarm. Barclay looked over at Alex. "Get everyone in here. We have some very important, very alarming news."

When everyone was assembled, Barclay reported. "They don't intend to, nor have they ever intended to have anyone leave the island alive. The explosives Skye mentioned in her message are not for containment. They're for complete destruction. They mention cargo and getting it off the island. Then they talk about the execution of Emilio Moreno. Sloane was right. He was the target all along." Barclay took a deep breath and told them what they didn't yet know. "When Terrin leaves the island, they intend to blow up the plane and all of the passengers."

"When," demanded Alex.

"Their meeting is tomorrow. Terrin plans on leaving the next day. I suspect it will be soon after."

"48 hours."

"We have to go in after them," said Jim.

"It's going to be really tight," responded Amanda, knowing how long it took logistically to get an incursion team together.

"We have to get to Skye," said Alex. "She mentions the plane looks airworthy and it's in good shape. Sloane, how much fuel would they still have in the tanks?" Sloane's fingers flew.

"A good four to five hours."

"And how far is this island from the U.S....say, somewhere in Florida?" asked Alex.

"Three hours max."

"Great. She has to get prepared to fly out if we can't get to her in time and she needs to know about Terrin's plans."

"We have to get a message to them," said Alex. "Jim is working on a rescue force?" He looked at Amanda. She nodded. Alex said to the rest of the team. "Carry on. Amanda and I will be conferring for the next hour or so."

CHAPTER 8

Skye and her crew were dozing and chatting, playing word games, and generally trying to pass the time. They discussed the missing passenger at length. Megan, one of the flight attendants working the business class remembered him vaguely. "Tall, handsome. Very distinguished. I think he was a VIP of some sort. An ambassador or something. I just can't remember. We were serving the dinner and we were busy. He was very polite and had a great smile. I think he was reading most of the time."

"I thought that man Terrin was going to have you assist him in formulating letters to the various governments." said Katherine.

"I thought so too. He said he wanted the families to suffer. It's been 20 hours since we talked." She looked at her watch. "I don't know if that's good news or bad news, but I do know I'm getting impatient."

Skye wasn't used to inactivity, but pulled back hard on her temptation to start something. She and her crew were in pretty good shape, all things considered. They'd been drinking water from the tap, not trusting the canned soda anymore. They dined on the little bags of pretzels and peanuts. It was actually a pretty good source of protein and carbohydrates. She took the pills the doctor had given her and remained very still so she was beginning to feel alive again. Stiff, but ready for battle.

In the 24th hour, Skye sat against the wall with her arm draped around Fisher's shoulders. He was, after all, just a teenager. As brave and resourceful as he'd been, he was in a very terrifying situation. He rested his head against her and sighed.

"There's someone I would like you to meet when we return home," she said to the top of his head. "A real cyber phenomenon."

"Sounds radical. Just don't disturb me now. I'm living every fifteen year old boy's dream." She looked down. He had one arm around the back of her waist and his head resting on her shoulder. It gave him a nice view of cleavage.

She slapped him playfully along the side of his head. "Why you little animal!"

"Hey!" He straightened and grinned. "I'm just a cub. Treat me like a mamma."

"Help me up cub. The party's over."

Standing, he gave her a hand. He was going to be a tall one. The boy shark still had some growing to do and he was almost at her level already. She looked at him with a fresh eye. He really was a nice looking kid. All arms and legs now, but with great potential. Still, it wasn't his looks that one noticed right away. It was his attitude. He had a real chilled 'tude, as Sloane would say. Yes, she was anxious to get the two together some day. She was sure they would hit it off.

Suddenly, they heard the rattle of the locks. Skye straightened and walked over to the door, ready to face her captors...preferring the possibility of combat to the hours of boredom and inactivity. She needed an opportunity to take action and that was not going to happen in this small, cramped room. They figured Fisher got some information out to Sloane, but she wasn't sure how her team and those involved would apply what she sent. She didn't know what help was coming from the outside and it put her at a distinct disadvantage. Should she sit and wait, or should she plot to make a break? She decided to let her instincts guide her.

The door opened and the usual brigade of men strode in, guns pointed at her and her crew. Half-wits. The way they held them, she was sure they'd never competently fired them, and if they had, they never hit what they were shooting at. The pain in her side had subsided and the temptation to take them was so great she could feel the muscles in her legs preparing for a brawl.

Then the atmosphere changed as a very tall man came in behind them. He was unshaven, and his hair was the color of coal. He was dressed all in black from his turtleneck down to his boots. A cap, pulled down over his forehead, hooded his eyes. There was unmistakable menace in his clear, penetrating gaze. Dark, sinister, and authoritative. His sharp eyes took everything in. Here was someone who was not a minion or a lackey. He was heavily armed with a pair of Beretta 15 round pistols in a holster around his waist. Definitely comfortable with the heavy pieces, he appeared to be no stranger to violence. The muscles in Skye's legs tightened even more. If she was to get through this, the stakes just got higher.

The man was powerfully built and gave the impression of being ruthless. He looked around the room slowly until his eyes fixed on Skye. Her crew instinctively moved closer. Fisher swallowed hard. He hadn't been really afraid up to now, but when he saw the cold look of rage flash in this man's eyes when he spotted the captain, Fisher was terrified. Still he came closer to Skye. He wouldn't be able to do much, but he wasn't going to hide either. They'd heard a helicopter a few hours before and figured correctly that's how he'd arrived.

"Go back to your fucking posts, I wish to interrogate the crew myself," the stranger demanded sharply. Fury seemed to radiate from him, out of proportion to the situation. He spoke in heavily accented English, his inflections not clearly identifiable. Perhaps a mix of Spanish and Portuguese. His manner and posture sent signals to the crew that he could be brutal...would be brutal if crossed. He kept staring into the face of the captain and she was defiantly staring back. This must have angered him for the heat that simmered just below the surface was scorching.

The armed men looked at him and then at each other. Faneta was someone whose cruelty and viciousness were obvious and legendary and they wanted his anger firmly concentrated on the prisoners, not them. He'd already sent one of their numbers to the infirmary when the poor man spilled coffee on his hand. Just lashed out with his booted foot and nearly broke the man's neck. They would do as he commanded. As much as they wanted to stick around to see him abuse the prisoners, they valued their own safety more.

The leader of the small group of guards was still more afraid of Terrin than this fuming newcomer. "I need to get authority," he said, a tremor in his voice betraying the fixed scowl and stubborn look on his face.

The tall man dragged his penetrating brown eyes from the captain, who'd been staring into them, and turned the full force of his naked anger on the man. He violently pushed up his sleeve and growled. "This is all the fucking authority I need."

The guard looked down at the stranger's forearm and paled. He stared at the tattoo of a snake wrapped around a spear. Skye and the crew had seen the snake tattoo on all of the arms of their captors, but this one was different. It must have been a far more dangerous version of the mark because the five men who escorted him all straightened and backed away.

"Tatanawa!" the man shouted, pushing his sleeve back over his wrist. This got the guards moving and they almost fell over their feet getting themselves clear of the threatening notice of this man.

When the last of them left and shut the door, the stranger stared at it in contempt. Then he gradually turned his attention back to the captain. The members of the crew came closer to her as his searing eyes looked into hers. When the locks were reengaged, he walked slowly over to her, never taking his eyes off her face. His boots made clicking sounds on the hardwood floor. It was the only sound in the room.

Fury was pouring out of him. Brian and Amy moved in front of Stuart and closer to Skye. She was tall, but he was taller and she had to look up at him. He raised his hands and took her face in them. As he stared into her deep bottomless brown eyes, she stared back. The rest of her crew stepped to her side, ready to defend and protect her. The man had his hands on their captain.

Skye stopped all comment and attempts to intervene by putting up her hand. "It's okay." Her voice was just above a whisper, but there was steel in the tone. "Back away."

The crew was used to obeying the captain's orders without question and did as she commanded. They slowly backed away. Skye kept her head up and her eyes fixed. She seemed mesmerized by him. She looked at the dark, enraged man without fear as he bent down and gently, almost tenderly kissed her lips, her bruised cheek, her swollen eye. The fury was still in his eyes, but there was also compassion and concern.

"You will tell me which of those vermin did this to you?" he asked softly in the same menacing tone, but this time there was also what seemed to be warmth behind the tough voice. He saw in her eyes the stubborn spark of command, but he also saw the dullness of intense pain. She could fool her crew, perhaps, but she couldn't fool him. He recognized the look. The tall boy behind her whom he figured was Fisher stood with his hands in fists by his side, a combative look on his face.

The captain actually smiled into the blazing dark brown eyes. "The little putz who did this will be easy to recognize. He'll be the one hanging from his tiny black and blue balls."

Skye and the stranger continued to stare at each other a minute. Her crew could feel the heat; sense the powerful emotions passing between them. Stuart cleared his throat and was the first to break the silence. "Ah...you know each other?"

Skye shook herself and grasped Alex's wrists. She slowly lowered his hands, feeling the tension in him and knowing he was trying hard to suppress his rage. Keeping her hand firmly in his, she turned to her crew. "I do." She smiled at Fisher. "I can safely say that our message got through."

Alex looked down at her as the crew all rushed over to shake his hand. She didn't introduce him, doubting they would recognize him when they returned to the states. If they did, she would have to rely on their discretion.

Skye never let go of his hand. It soothed some of the waves of simmering temper that were pulsating through him. He'd heard her take the beating, but when he was confronted with the reality of it, he nearly lost control completely. When he saw her battered face, he almost pulled his guns and started shooting. He restrained himself, however by both his iron will and the unspoken message that passed from Skye to him in that moment their eyes locked. Not yet, she told him through her steady look. Wait. Our time will come.

Alex was a master of changing his look. It wasn't so much the outward appearance; although the black hair, dark contact lenses and stubble were good, it was the attitude, the voice, how he walked, and the manner of speech.

Skye watched him. When he first came into the room, even she was fooled. She'd never seen him in deep covert before. It was only a few seconds, but enough to make her stomach knot up. Impressive, she thought.

Alex took his cue from Skye. Looking down at her he actually smiled...because of his role, it was more of a sneer. He took a deep breath. He really was so glad to see her. Bruised, but standing. In obvious pain, but alive and relatively unharmed.

"Actually, Bill and Carter sent me. When you and all these fine people didn't show up for your party, they were really upset," he said in a rough voice, keeping the accent. He was playing the commando...and he was doing a spectacular job at it. He needed to keep his identity from her crew as well as from the rest of the world.

"I told the crew they'd be ticked."

"To put it mildly. Just what do you do with acres of cake and tons of fresh shrimp?"

"Oh stop. The sound you hear is our stomachs growling," said Skye. "We've avoided all food and drink from our captors."

"Good thing. From what I've seen of the passengers, they have not," said Alex.

"Yes, but since the drugs don't seem life threatening, that may not be a bad thing. It keeps them calm and saves them from living the horror of the situation."

"And is this Fisher Tyler Stanaslov Mitchell." Alex turned to the youth, who was still scowling at him. Alex looked every bit like Fisher's idea of a dangerous villain. And he wasn't quite sure if he liked the kissing part, either. Seemed kind of uncalled for under the circumstances. But he took Alex's hand and gave it a firm shake.

"I take it you got the entire message," he said stiffly, impressed, in spite of himself, with the man and the grip.

"Enough of it. I'm here to coordinate all communication. Including this from your grandma." He pulled a small pin of one of the seven dwarfs out of his pocket and handed it to Fisher. "Save Disney buttons, huh kid?" Again the sneer.

"Oh, cripes. Not since I was 6."

Alex stared at him.

"Okay. Not since I gave them up last year. Grandma must have found Dopey...sort of makes my collection complete." He gave Alex a cockeyed smile. "Kind of bitchin', though. But it's a red face moment."

"It was either that, or a hug and kiss. Take your punches like a man, kid."

The guy wasn't so bad after all, Fisher thought. He had a great set of guns and he was, well, super radical.

"May I talk with you in private, Captain?"

She gave a short laugh. "Certainly, please step into my office. Carry on crew."

When they went into the bathroom and shut the door, Alex sniffed the air. He'd expected a repulsive foul smelling little room and instead, it seemed fresh and filled with the scent of Skye's shampoo and lotions. He thought his mind must have been projecting his wishful thinking, but Skye chuckled.

"Beth has spent her entire time here cleaning the bathroom. And I was able to secure my flight bag. We've made use of all the bare essentials. Shampoo, hairspray, toothpaste, makeup...you know...the armor against misery and despair."

When he turned to her, he saw her strong, straight back collapse a bit. He gently took her arm and leaned her against the low counter next to the sink. "How bad?" he demanded.

She considered lying to him, but it wouldn't work. He could see right through her into her soul and she didn't have the strength to put up a veil against his powers of observation.

"I think the asshole might have kicked me after I went down. I was able to protect my right side while I was conscious, but the cowardly bastard must have taken another shot." Her body shifted with the memory, a movement she couldn't control. "I've been finding it difficult to take a deep breath."

"Let me see."

"Um. I think we have more important things to do than assess my bruises."

"Let me see," he said sharply, some of the fury returning.

"Okay, okay." She pulled her blouse out of her waistband and pulled it up. She had removed the wrap just a few hours before; it was making it hard for her to breathe. Damn. She wished now there was another layer between the bruise and Alex's sharp eyes.

Alex did see how even this movement made her flinch and had to suppress the urge to put his fist through the wall. What he saw almost snapped what little control he had left.

"That son-of-a-bitch is a dead man," he said through clenched teeth. He gently touched the bruise and realized it was more than a simple surface contusion.

"Is there a doctor on board?"

"Yes."

"And?" It was like pulling on the leash of a stubborn dog. A very large and very stubborn dog.

"He feels that one or two of the ribs have definitely rebroken and one of them may be causing a slow leak in the lungs."

"How long before this becomes a real problem?"

"Well, nothing definite. He doesn't have X-ray eyes, for God's sake. Let's discuss issues we can do something about."

"Skye?"

"Okay. Maybe another 48 hours. Then I'm pretty much out of commission. I was getting a bit concerned about how it was all going to play out. See how timely the arrival of my personal commando is?"

She tried to keep her voice light and soothing, but she could see from the tense set of his jaw it wasn't working. So she decided on some direct action of her own. Taking his rough face in her hands she kissed him thoroughly. Feeling him respond, there was the sweetest, most wonderful feeling of release. She felt anything was possible now. They were together. They were an unbeatable team. He felt it too, and let go of some of the incredible stress from the last few days. He deepened the kiss and tried to absorb some of the pain.

She reluctantly pulled away. "Is that unshaven, black haired, brown eyed desperado look going to be a new thing for you? If so, I recommend a pieced ear. You look like a pirate."

He ran a hand over his beard, then through the dyed hair. "I thought it would add just the right dash of menace. And also helps disguise the polished and debonair financier that lurks underneath. These contacts are a bitch, though. I'm not used to them, but the blue eyes had to go. There wasn't a blue-eyed person in any of the files we were able to locate."

He reached for her but she put her hand up reluctantly. "Darling, I would like to melt in your arms right now, but if I do that, I won't be able to get my backbone set again."

"Can I hold you?" asked Alex.

She shook her head. "Not now. After we're out of here, I won't want to leave your arms for a week. For now, I have to keep bodily contact to a minimum. These ribs are really beginning to annoy me."

He nodded, his eyes snapping, his fists clenched.

"Alex, please. Put that away. Fill me in on what's happening on the outside. How did you get here? Then I'll tell you what has been happening here. Let's do this fast and efficiently."

Alex nodded. If they were ever going to be a proficient husband and wife team, they would have to get right to business when it was necessary. It took less than ten minutes for Alex to tell her everything. About the election and the society of the Serpent and the Spear. Alex touched her face again. It was awful what the sight of that face did to his gut. "Your clues were valuable, darling, even though the price was dear."

She turned her head and kissed his palm. "Everything will heal. Not such a big price."

He nodded and kissed her bruised lips gently. He understood.

"Where was Sloane when she got the email?"

"Well…ah…" stammered Alex.

"Alex." Skye suspected from his reaction she wasn't going to like the answer and Alex knew for a fact she wasn't going to like it.

"She was right in the OCC," he admitted.

"The Operational Command Center? Are you crazy? What if she would have heard the recording of the…" She saw the look in his eyes and knew. Anger. Horror. Heartache. "Oh God," she whispered. "You had her translate. You insensitive, thoughtless, unfeeling…"

Alex actually laughed and Skye was so shocked, she ran out of words.

"Skye. Sloane broke into a highly secured section of the airport. Threatened Jim, Fisher's grandmother and me, and insisted she be a part of the op. And, if I could be so boastful, since she's going to be my sister-in-law, she was invaluable…absolutely irreplaceable. I'm here because of what she uncovered. Barclay is good, but Sloane is light years ahead of him. She hacked into Terrin's computer with barely a bump and Barclay told me he couldn't have done it in a month. Seems she's developed some special equipment…some modifications of software that isn't even on the market yet."

"I don't think I want to hear this. Sometimes, I'm afraid for that girl. Is she really okay?" asked Skye with concern.

"Yes, she is." He told her about how she translated some obscure language.

"She's one unbelievable teen," said Skye, shaking her head.

"Seems like you had your own teenager to deal with," said Alex.

"Yes, he's a remarkable young man." She filled him in quickly and Alex gave her a run down on his grandmother.

"That explains a lot. He was such a natural. Must be in the genes." Skye shifted and winced. Alex noticed she couldn't stand in one position for very long and hoped he would get a chance to pay her captors back soon.

Skye went on quickly, trying to distract him. He needed a clear head and she wanted him farther back from the edge. "So Sloane received the message. All of it?"

"Enough, anyway. We were able to narrow down the search area from your original message. Amanda had some of the CIA satellites diverted to take a few pictures. Even though the hangar is well concealed, the satellite tracks according to temperature. A hundred plus bodies generate a lot of heat."

She smiled at him. "Well one thing for sure." She looked him in the eye and he got the message loud and clear. "The heat you were pushing out a moment ago would have fried their circuits. Let's hope they're on the other side of the globe right now."

He stared at her for a few seconds. "If you'd like to get naked, I could get a lot hotter."

She just shook her head and smiled. Their situation was dire, but her body was still reacting to his voice, his suggestion with its own heat. Funny how the pain in her side had backed off a bit, too. "I liked the tattoo, by the way. Kind of goes with the whole mood."

"Linda got all the information on this little band of criminals. Thank goodness she did or I would have been toast in the first three seconds. Terrin, and Lomar pushed up their sleeve as soon as we got off the helicopter, like some goddamn fraternity ritual. I had a pretty tattoo of my own to show them. It matched, I passed.

"Amanda arranged to have the real Faneta taken as he was getting off a plane in Trinidad. He was coming in from Venezuela. We got all of this from Sloane's journey into Terrin's email. He saves everything according to Sloane. It took a while for us to find relevant stuff…the creep likes child porn. But that's not important now. Seems these three amigos formed a criminal cartel to take over the little island of Soteras. Terrin found out about a rich oil reserve and wants to suck it all out. He's been working with geologists and oil consultants. We get the impression that the other two think it's a simple crime syndicate. At some point we suspect he will arrange for their demise. Apparently he needed them to make all the arrangements for the hijacking."

"But why the hijacking?"

"Ambassador Moreno is running for President and from all accounts he is determined, honest, and very popular. He not only has broad-based support, but has been on the international scene for quite a few years and has developed invaluable worldwide contacts. Linda's assessment indicates he is almost assured a victory."

She told him about the suspected missing passenger and they compared descriptions.

"He must be the ambassador. They could be taking him with them tomorrow, blowing him up with the rest of you, or maybe he's already dead."

"I don't know. This Terrin guy likes an audience. If there's a mirror in the room, I'm sure he would spend his time in front of it. I think he would keep the ambassador alive just to flaunt his success, then kill him in front of his two partners…a show."

Alex nodded. "Good assessment. I agree."

"But Alex, why not just assassinate him? This seems like an awfully elaborate way to rid themselves of a Presidential candidate."

"A couple of reasons. First, he is heavily guarded. He's escorted to and from planes by a small army of loyal followers. About the only time he's alone is when he's physically on a plane. They count on airport security to keep him safe from port to port. In addition, to prevent a groundswell of anti-cartel sentiment, they decided to have him fall with a plane full of men, women, and children in a random tragedy or terrorist attack. That way he isn't a martyr and he isn't alive. They needed both. He's extremely popular and they needed him out of the way without making it look like they were responsible."

"Why didn't they just put a bomb in the plane?"

Alex shuddered and frowned at her direct question.

"Sorry, darling, but it's a relevant question."

"How about close to a billion, that's with a 'b', in gold, currency, and precious gems?"

Skye's eyes widened.

"Amanda dug this one up from her sources in Eastern Europe and some assets she was aware of in Panama. It appears as though the ambassador successfully impounded, then took possession of the combined bank vaults of about a dozen current and past Serpent and Spear kingpins. This is what initially got them so pissed off. He will be going back after more when he wins the election. He was planning to make a major announcement upon his return and he wanted the actual physical merchandise to show to the world. He and his staff were scheduled to take possession of it at the airport, then carry it in triumph to their federal bank in Soteras."

"That must be what they've been hauling out of the cargo hold since we arrived. Probably the reason the plane is still intact."

"That's our assessment."

"What now?"

"There's an invasion force on its way. We'll have an air incursion team on the ground in Trinidad in less than 24 hours. The sea force is taking longer to get here. Maybe a day and a half out. All of this is a last resort. And we think it will all be moot anyway." Alex told her about Terrin's plan to blast the hangar and all the occupants.

"So either we bring the air incursion team in here tomorrow, or we try to fly the plane out." Her preference was the latter. She would like to bring the plane home intact, with all the passengers on board. Invasion by Special Forces might mean casualties amongst her passengers. "There have been no demands…no messages to outside sources?" asked Skye thoughtfully.

"None."

"Then they simply intended for the plane, passengers, and crew to disappear."

"That's right. We think time is of the essence."

Skye smiled, a surge of confidence filling her with energy. "Then we better look for our opportunities and act. The main body of guards are not adept. You probably saw that for yourself. Our major problem is going to be the elite guard around Terrin and the men you brought in with you."

"Agreed," he said. "I'm going to try to stir things up and get some distrust going. I would like them to start fighting among themselves so we can make our move during the confusion."

"I'm armed." She looked him over. "And you certainly are. We don't need a whole lot of time to get the plane up and running. We'll need to close and lock the cargo doors and open the hangar door at the front."

"If things get too hot, the air incursion team will move in at my signal."

"You wired?"

"No. Too risky. But I do have a secure satellite phone direct to Jim."

"Excellent."

"They should be a sufficient diversion if we need one. We'll place ourselves with the passengers and crew."

"I'll want to locate the ambassador and bring him back on board."

"I can do that. Tonight, I'll look around…ask a few questions. I'll find out what happened to him and if he's still alive."

"I don't want to lose one, Alex," she said with troubled eyes.

"I know, darling. You won't. We have a plan…if other opportunities present themselves, we'll move spontaneously."

She nodded. They were both used to quick, decisive action.

He put his hand on her bruised cheek, then kissed it. "Just remember, the man who hit you is mine."

She nodded. She would have liked to take Snake Tattoo down herself, but as she stared into his brown eyes she saw the lingering shadows of fury and fear. It was so strange not to see the color of the sky in them. There were residual ghosts haunting him and she would stand back and allow him to do what he needed to do.

"Just one more bit of business," said Alex shaking off the commando for a minute and resurrecting the fiancé. "Sloane and I went shopping."

"Uh oh."

"Indeed. Anyway, we purchased a talisman," said Alex.

"A what?"

"Well, it wasn't a talisman when we bought it, but right after we listened to the tape of your…your…" He couldn't find the words. She understood and gave him an assist.

"My brilliant and dazzling effort to communicate clues," she prompted, smiling easily and giving her head a little tilt.

"Sometimes my darling," said Alex as he touched her swollen lip. "I wish you'd have just been satisfied with flying planes."

"And if I would have done that, we never would have met. And besides, even though my little adventure hurt a bit, the fact that you're here and we have a strategy means it all worked out as I planned." She raised her eyebrows in triumph. Case made, argument won.

"Anyway," said Alex, conceding the point and wanting to get on with the talisman presentation ceremony, as Sloane called it. He reached into his pocket.

She looked down, a slight frown on her face. "You brought me a weapon?"

"Yes, a weapon against all the dark powers of the universe, against solitude and against sorrow. It will protect you and your heart from ever having to beat alone again. There will always be a steady heart beating beside you."

Now there was confusion on her face, but her heart did a dance as it picked up the beat of his beautiful words. Looking up at him she saw love, passion, and a poignancy flash in his eyes.

She lowered her gaze and he opened his fist. In the palm of his hand was her future, her life. She saw the brilliant diamond set in the exquisite gold band. In this tiny bathroom behind a locked door where both danger and possible death lurked, time stood still.

She stared at the ring in his hand for so long that Alex's stomach started to pitch. Was she going to refuse it? Had he made a monumental mistake? Stupid, he thought. Why did he think that this time, this place, was appropriate to present the woman who was his life a token of his love and devotion?

Skye looked up at him. For just that moment there was no pain. Literally, all of her misery was gone, momentarily dispelled by the flood of love and pleasure that was pouring through her.

He saw the pain leave her eyes, a hint of color return to her cheeks. He saw the glistening of tears forming in her wonderful deep brown eyes.

They were transported to another place for that instant and she knew that regardless of what happened in the next few hours, the next few days, she would face it knowing she had lived a lifetime in these few seconds. Their souls touched, danced, and merged. She could feel it all unfold and it opened her heart.

Alex saw it all happening, too. She took him with her on her journey. Out of their bodies, out of this room, out of this place in time. It was just the two of them. The room faded from their vision. He thought he had seen all of her smiles, but here was one she hadn't yet revealed. Her lips moved and she smiled the most touching and enchanted smile he'd ever seen. Artists have tried over the centuries to capture a look like that and he would forever carry it in his heart.

She opened her left hand and presented it to him, palm down. Her long fingers waiting with great anticipation for the adornment that would rest there for a lifetime. Smiling back, his expression mirroring hers, he slipped it on. It was a perfect fit…both the size and the sentiment.

No words were necessary. No words could convey the feeling or express the joy. No words could possibly capture the perfect matching of two souls. When she looked down, she knew she had totally opened her heart once more and that it would never be completely hers again.

Leaning over, he softly kissed her. His eyes were open and he could see into the depths of hers. Not just love and devotion, but something that was much, much harder for Skye to give…trust. Even when she accepted his proposal a few weeks before, she had held something of herself back, protecting a heart that had been broken too often. Now she held nothing back. She gave him her heart to keep safe. And he would. The ring was his promise.

Suddenly, there was a knock. "Um, sorry Captain, but there's some shouting outside. Perhaps it would be better if they didn't catch the two of you alone in the bathroom."

Skye didn't move. She was staring down at her talisman.

"Captain?" said Alex.

"Hmm?" She looked up. For a moment, her eyes sparkled as brilliantly as the diamond on her finger. The timing was horrible, the circumstances dire, but this was one of the happiest moments of her life.

"Maybe I had better tuck your blouse back in or your perceptive crew will think we spent our time in here getting naked and fooling around."

"That would have been nice."

He started tucking in the blouse and around the back he felt a familiar shape. "How did you get that?"

"It was in the bottom of my flight bag."

"Just the right accessory for an event like this."

"I like this one better," she said as she held the ring up to the light for one more look. She let Alex tuck her shirt in and help her into her jacket. "But I'm afraid I'm going to have to move the sparkle to the inside. I can't afford to have it exposed." She looked up at him and gently removed the ring, kissed it and placed it in her inside jacket pocket. "My talisman and my guardian. I'm now invincible." She smiled that wonderful smile again and they sealed the engagement with a beautiful, gentle kiss. Then she squared her shoulders, opened the door, and went to fill in her crew.

Skye and Alex told them what they thought was relevant, leaving out anything that would reveal their sources or the identity of their team. Morale was very high by the time they finished, even though there was deep concern over the news that the explosives were intended to actually explode.

They all turned when they heard the key in the locks. Alex and Skye moved apart, ready to assume their respective roles. The crew took the look of hope off their faces. Fisher was the only one in the room still staring at Alex, assessing, thinking, appraising. He may be a soldier, Fisher thought, but he was a damn sight more than that. Then he looked at Skye. She too was more than your everyday garden-variety airline pilot. Two of a kind. He looked down at the stupid pin from his grandma. Make that three of a kind.

Terrin strode in followed by the seven bodyguards. His other men remained outside the door, standing at some kind of attention. God, what a pompous ass, Alex thought as he assessed in a glance the armaments and the men holding them. He stood with his arms folded, relaxed but ready. He had a gun in the small of his back, one in his boot and two in the holster around his waist. He knew that if there was shooting, he could take at least five or six. Skye had a gun and could maybe take out three more. It still didn't add up. No. Now was not the time or place.

Alex casually took out a cigarette and slid it between his sneering lips. Skye almost gaped in shock, but she caught herself and remained stoic. He lit it with a lighter they had taken off Faneta, one that Terrin recognized. He had one just like it with a snake engraved on its face. Alex actually looked like he knew what he was doing. It was a good move, Skye decided. It added to the role and the casual exposure of something only Faneta would possess was a detail that would sooth any suspicion. In addition, if Faneta was a heavy smoker, the lack of cigarettes would have sent signals to someone as paranoid as Terrin.

"You have talked with these people?" Asked Terrin, determined to take center stage.

"I have." Alex blew out smoke and sneered. "They know nothing and are totally unprepared for this situation. They will not present a problem. We can proceed. I would suggest you move some of your guards from this door to the task of getting the cargo prepared for transport. Let us go to your office and complete our planning. These people are not players. All they are is an audience to what is happening."

Terrin liked an audience and wanted to impress this man. "You are right." He looked at Skye and then grabbed her arm. "And after tomorrow, they will not even be that."

"You will be sending us home tomorrow?" asked Skye in an optimistic voice, never flinching, but giving an impression of submission.

Well done, Skye, thought Alex. He knew what it cost her to hold back her anger and her natural tendency to fight.

She knew what it was costing him to see this animal's hand on his fiancée.

"Have you heard from our company? Our country?" Skye went on quickly, keeping her tone hopeful. She managed to put a little tremor in her arm for good measure.

Alex looked at her with disdain and then over to Terrin, bonding with the man in a shared irony. "You will be off the island by this time tomorrow, Captain," he said in a sarcastic, disrespectful tone.

Terrin nodded his approval. He shoved Skye and Stuart was right there to keep her from falling. It took all of Alex's will power not to move and assist her. She was beneath contempt, after all, not the love of his life. Stuart had a steady hand; he would have to content himself with that…for now.

"I came here to find you and to ask you if you have any information on who hacked into my computers." Terrin showed his disregard for the crew by discussing sensitive matters in front of them. Both Alex and Skye knew that meant he planned for them to be dead and didn't need to worry about what they knew. "It seems there is a traitor in the Serpent and the Spear."

"I have no knowledge of what you are talking about. I met Lomar in Trinidad. He brought with him a heavily armed guard. We are to merge and combine forces. As far as I know Lomar is a loyal follower of the Catalla and the Fra. We will take care of our business here. We will try Moreno and execute him on this island." Alex thought now might be a good time to drop a bomb." Then we'll return to Soteras to mourn with the rest of the country. The three of us will divide the country and its rich oil reserves."

Terrin's eyes narrowed. No one knew about the oil…unless they got the information from some of his emails with the geologists.

"And how do you know about the oil?"

"We know everything. Lomar has informed me of your geological findings." Divide and conquer. Cause trouble among the thieves.

"Someone has been monitoring my communications and has gone into my files." He spun around and barked at his men. "Where is Lomar?"

"He is checking on the perimeter. He wants to be sure everything is ready for the final show," said one of his men.

"You will join us?" asked Terrin, looking at Alex. He didn't want to insist, but he wanted to keep an eye on Faneta. This cartel was rapidly deteriorating and he wanted to act fast and decisively.

Alex nodded. He was improvising and the fish took the bait. Terrin now knew that either he or Lomar hacked into his computer.

Skye knew exactly what Alex was doing. It was very risky. She approved of his tactics, even though she feared for his safety. If there was going to be warfare among the players, Alex would be right in the middle of it. There was already bad blood caused by too many strong-willed men and an absolute lack of both conscience and trust.

"Bring her." Terrin nodded at Skye, looking at her with condescension.

"Why continue with this charade?" snapped Alex, stepping slightly closer to Skye. He wanted her here, behind the locked door, until he could determine if there was going to be a bloody feud. He needed about twelve more hours before he could call in the Special Forces. Even with the explosives around the hangar, he figured as long as Terrin was in residence, everyone was safe. He wanted to be free to continue to stir the pot. With Skye in here, there wouldn't be that distraction.

"Why not tell these people their fate?" He sneered and Skye thought it was a marvelous sneer. But she didn't show any pride. She didn't show anything.

"I want to have this woman assist me with my communications. Now bring her." Both Skye and Alex knew exactly what he meant...he wanted to have the woman, all right, but not to assist him. Skye made the slightest of motions with her hand. I can handle it she told Alex with the gesture. Trust me to do my job. You go do yours. We're now special agents, not lovers. Alex took a deep breath and did nothing.

When the man nearest Skye grabbed her arm, he had to ratchet up the willpower another notch, but Alex stayed in his role. When Fisher started forward, Alex flicked his cigarette at him. Fisher dodged beautifully and swore admirably. Stuart took his arm and pulled him back from danger.

Skye shook off the guard's hand, straightened her jacket, and walked out the door with a commanding attitude. Alex didn't like this development, but there was little he could do without breaking his cover.

"I will join you. I am finished here," he said and they all left together. The crew let out a collective breath. Fisher stared after them, then went and picked up the captain's hat. He intended to hold it for her and give it to her when they were safely on their way home.

When they were out the door Terrin turned on Alex. "Find Lomar and wait for me by the cargo. We will begin the process of assessing what will go with you and what we will want to transport tomorrow. We have a great deal to talk about and plan for. When the cargo is properly divided, we can talk about our future." Alex's eyes went for a brief moment to Skye. She would be all right her eyes told him. She touched her jacket in the place where her ring rested. Go do your job. I am protected.

Nodding curtly to the man, Alex went swiftly in the direction of the runway. Skye caught a subtle look pass between Terrin and a guard to his left. This man veered off as they approached the office. It gave Skye a prickly feeling in her spine but she had to trust that Alex's plan would work...and that he could take care of himself.

Skye walked unassisted into the office, taking her place in front of the desk. From where she stood, she could see the helicopter and most of the airstrip. She was hoping to catch a glimpse of Alex, but he wasn't in her range of vision. Terrin looked at the men in the room and something passed between them too. It was a conspiratorial look. She didn't like it. She felt a heaviness in the air, like the island was holding its breath, waiting for something to happen.

"You had a nice chat with Faneta." Terrin had little regard for this woman, but he wanted to know if Faneta had revealed anything to her.

"We barely talked."

"He was in there for a long time."

"He questioned each of us individually. He was concerned about what had been said since we arrived and what we had seen." She looked at Terrin. Might as well stir the pot some more. "Most particularly if I had seen anything related to the unloading of the cargo. The cargo seemed to particularly interest him. Number of boxes, shape, size. I told him with few exceptions, we had been locked in a windowless room and had no knowledge of it. Of course as captain, I'm privy to certain, shall we say...more sensitive issues related to cargo."

"What are you saying?"

"I'm saying that there's a valuable consignment aboard and it's less of a secret than you think." She was making things up. Anything to throw him off balance. She could see the mounting fury and at that moment she knew she needed to get her passengers out of there. An invasion would result in civilian casualties and at this point she had the strong feeling that the main forces wouldn't arrive in time anyway. Maybe if she could get him preoccupied with irrelevant information and misdirection, he would be too distracted to notice a few missing men. A few missing guns. Alex played on his paranoia and she would too. There would be the added bonus of diverting his attention away from her.

"When we take that much precious metal and other assets on board, I know about it. Be sure you count it carefully...some of it didn't arrive," she improvised smoothly and with sincerity. She was completely believable. "I believe it was diverted at the last minute because it was on the original manifest."

"I will take care of things," said Terrin, his mind quickly jumping from one possibility to another, sidetracked for a moment from his original intent. Then he stopped and stared at her...he wanted to get her into his personal rooms in the back of the hangar where he would come to her later and show her the ways of a real man.

He would take care of business, but from that first encounter, she had teased his mind, been on the edge of his thoughts. He was near the dawn of a new phase of his life and career and he wanted to celebrate. She would be such sweet entertainment. Screaming, crying, on her knees with his gun to her head. She would have him in her mouth and he would threaten to shoot if she didn't comply. He saw her with fear in her eyes and tears sliding down her face. His whole body was tensing up with anticipation. A thin film of sweat covered his face but he was a disciplined man and he had work to do before he could indulge himself.

Just a sample, he thought, before he completed his business. He walked over to her. Touching the side of her neck, he ran his long thin fingers down the front of her chest and just under the v of her blouse. Her skin was soft and warm. Already hungry for more, he went back up and then suddenly grabbed her neck and squeezed. Skye never moved, but kept her eyes straight forward. Impassive. Unresponsive.

"You do not react, whore. But you will. You will." Skye knew just the move to take him down and completely immobilize him. She was sure of her abilities and of his lack of them. But she marshaled all of her willpower and remained motionless.

Disgusted with her lack of reaction, he let go of her and told one of the men to take her to his quarters. There would be time later. Time to move her from this frigid bearing.

When she was led out of the room Terrin stood for a long time. He stared at the computers and frowned. Then he made a decision. He moved to his contingency plan...one that he had originally preferred anyway. As profitable as a third of the island reserves of oil would be, one hundred percent was better. He had his two rivals right here on the island. Lomar had only six bodyguards, Faneta always traveled alone. Terrin had seven of his elite troop, seventeen of the dimwits he recruited from the street with promises of wealth and women, and two of his own that came in with the helicopter. Plus he had some unrevealed reserves just in case and it seemed like this was the perfect time to play his "just in case" card.

There would be bloodshed, but he had superior forces and surprise on his side. If he pulled this off, the entire cargo, what was left of it, would be his as well. A very good bonus. He could leave in the morning, then blow up the island...after executing that misguided reform candidate with it. No way the ambassador was going to be able to change anything from the burning grave. He would tell Lomar and Faneta's followers that they got caught in an explosion caused by an outside incursion. He barely escaped with his life. He would be heartbroken. He saw no flaws in the plan. Success was assured.

CHAPTER 9

As soon as they walked out of the office, Skye let out the breath she'd been holding. That man was going down. She felt his fingers on her and fought the shudder of revulsion. In addition, her blood was boiling with frustration and suppressed rage. Never in her life had she just had to take that kind of insult, the fondling and the scorn. She always fought back, no matter what. But then, she told herself firmly, never before had over 100 people depended on her to stay cool. Cool, she thought. Ice. Colder than ice. Outer space, far side of the moon cold. She could do it. She had to do it.

She took in everything as the guard led her up a flight of stairs to a suite of rooms. She was elated when she saw a man sitting on a cot in a storeroom she passed. He wasn't locked in, but she noticed he was shackled and cuffed to a pipe in the room. Her quick assessment of the pipe was hopeful. It looked like it could be cracked with a few good kicks. It made her ribs ache to think about it, but she had to plan. It was the face of the man who had been described to her. She was sure he was the future President of Soteras…more importantly to her right now, he was one of her passengers and he was going back on the plane. He had a ticket to the United States on Flight 127 and he was going to get there, by God. Their eyes met for the briefest of moments. He caught the look of reassurance she sent him. Help was on the way. His smile signaled he would be ready.

The guard opened the door to Terrin's private quarters with the same kind of master key the guards used to open the door to the crew. Hello. She saw the one she wanted on his key ring. It was silver and a bit longer than the rest. She would need that to get back to her crew. Pretending to stumble, she had it off his ring in less than a second. She palmed it and when the guard closed the door, she hid it in the inside pocket of her jacket, right next to her talisman. It was working already. She smirked. It didn't pay to underestimate her.

The room was surprisingly spacious and richly furnished. Terrin obviously liked luxury, even when away from home. Good. It would make putting him away in a little gray cell even more satisfying. Skye collapsed on the bed for just a little rest. A bed. A real live mattress. She laid back on it. Just five minutes, she told herself. It felt so good under her tired and sore ribs. Her body screamed for a nap. Her ruthless mind said no. Twenty glorious minutes later she had to force herself to get up and check out the room before her body launched a full-fledged campaign to stretch out and take a little siesta.

She walked over to the window. What an idiot. A window that could easily be broken and used as a path to escape. It was on the second floor and it had a security system around it, but she could take care of that with no problem. This man either was so egotistical that he thought she would be panting for more of his ever-so-talented fingers, or he thought there was nowhere else for her to go on the island.

Then she remembered her original ploy. She smiled. She had a reputation on this island and she should remember that. With Terrin she was unresponsive and cold, but he still thought of her as a weak, whimpering female. Smiling cagily, she rubbed her hands together. It was so unlike her that she forgot how well she got into the role and how convincing she'd been. Terrin was underestimating her. He put her in this room because he thought she was cowed, intimidated, and afraid. He already expressed his disdain for woman in general. Well, let him think what he wanted. If it helped her get everyone home safe, she didn't really care.

Skye acknowledged the window as a possible out, but she would rather go through the door. Down the hall was one of her passengers and she wanted him. She inspected the lock. Unfortunately, it was a good one. She had her gun in the small of her back, but she wouldn't want to risk using that to blow the door. She would have to play this out and see what happened.

She heard shouting outside and hurried over to take a look. There was the love of her life, pacing, arms crossed over his chest. God, he looked dangerous. And oh so good. She watched him flex his muscles, stop pacing, and light up again. He leaned against a crate and chatted with another heavily armed man. Must be the other kingpin. Lomar. She looked again at Alex. Was there any of Alex Springfield in that stance? Any hint of subterfuge? No. It was perfect. He was perfect. Lomar was alert, but at ease. No suspicion.

Taking out her ring, she stared into the diamond. When they got home, she and Alex had a new life to plan and implement. They were merging both their personal and professional lives. Alex had designed a perfect strategy so they could execute the primary function of their shadow existence while simultaneously pursuing their chosen careers. She smiled and shook her head. Christ, listen to her. Her friend and copilot, Bill McGee, used to tease her about her rather perfunctory, cold way of referring to her relationships with men. Planning, implementing, and designing perfect strategies sounded like an op and she was Special Agent in Charge, or something. Well she was sort of in charge. A bride usually was. And when she got home, she was going to add bride to her multiple roles. She would start planning Operation Matrimony.

Skye continued to stare into the diamond, mesmerized by its beauty. She knew their situation was dire, but she wanted just a few seconds to feel the wash of love and anticipation. So she took it. She was so in love with Alex. Their new life was going to be lived with excitement, passion, and devotion. No matter what, she would always have him to come home to and that was like living a dream. So, Bill, no planning and implementing...how about dreaming, drifting, and following your heart? Alex was her heart. He was her life. She needed no other plan than that.

Before she'd met Alex, her heart had been tucked neatly away inside an iron box. She placed the box behind a steel door and surrounded it all with a protective shield of ice. Staring into the brilliant gem, she floated back. This wasn't her first diamond ring. She'd been engaged to a wonderful man...a man who had made her take out her heart after she buried it once before. When she was 15, she'd witnessed the car bombing of her parents...feeling her heart shatter as she watched them burn to death. She would have been in the car herself except she'd begged them to stop for bakery. They never found the people who killed her beautiful, intelligent mother and fun-loving father. It was one of the things that drove her to seek justice...drove her to become a Special Agent. And she kept her heart safe by not allowing anyone to have any part of it.

She'd known Jeff Lewin practically her whole life. He'd loved her and she had tolerated him until he wore her down with his wit and his easygoing manner. He was a police officer in Washington D.C. when she discovered that the life long acquaintance had blossomed into love. Opening the path to her heart, she gave it freely to him and discovered the warm, wonderful feeling of passion and desire. They became engaged and together they planned a spring wedding. She had her dress, attended the showers, and made meticulous plans for a perfect reception. Two weeks before the wedding her heart was completely shattered once again when his captain and the chaplain paid her a visit. He had been killed in the line of duty. One week before the wedding, she eulogized him near the altar where they would have taken their vows.

She took a different vow that day. She swore she would never, ever allow herself to be that vulnerable to heartache again. She wouldn't date, much less fall in love with...anyone remotely associated with law enforcement. No man with a gun, a badge, or a job with danger. She lost her parents and sealed her heart. Jeff wore down the seal and she risked giving it to him. When her heart broke again, she put the pieces away and vowed she would only take it out if she found a nice, safe man in a nice, safe occupation.

She looked out the window at her fiancé. And here she was completely in love with and officially engaged to a man carrying two Berettas in his belt. Damn.

When she first met Alex and fell in love with him, she didn't know he was a fellow agent. When she finally found out, she resisted him. Pulled away and fought like hell. Her own needs and her latent heart's desire betrayed her and jumped in firmly on the side of Alex. And still she refused to give in. She tried to defy destiny until she didn't have the strength to resist any longer. Alex shattered the ice, melted the steel and opened the box that contained her heart. And now it was out and beating red again.

Being this vulnerable scared her witless, but she knew she couldn't live without him now. Couldn't live without his love, his laughter, his touch.

Standing up straighter, she tucked the ring securely back in her pocket, and stared at the scene below. Back to work...back into the here and now. She needed to watch her future husband's back.

A few minutes later, Terrin strode out of the building. Where was his elite guard? He was alone. She didn't like the way things felt. Terrin walked over to Alex and the other man started talking. They began shouting and soon it escalated to angry accusations. She couldn't exactly tell what they were saying, but Alex, Terrin, and the other man were shouting at each other...and the argument was getting more heated. Alex stirred the pot all right and there was some real ugly soup going on.

Down below, Alex was pacing by the crates and boxes. Lomar was there with his selected guard. Alex wondered why Faneta didn't have any men surrounding him. Maybe he was a real tough guy. Good enough. He could be tough. Or maybe he just didn't trust anyone, which was more likely. He seemed paranoid. Alex decided he could do a real fine paranoid as well.

As a matter of fact, things were feeling very tense and distrustful right now between all the factions and he didn't think it was paranoia talking. The suspicious grumbling and guarded looks were getting very heavy.

The air was thick with bad feeling and Alex felt a familiar prickle. Danger. Watch your back. In a conscious tactical move, he relocated so that his back was to a crate and he had a better view of the entire area.

Skye watched her lover work. He was placing himself in a more defensible position. Was he expecting trouble? If so, why not get the hell out of harm's way? He was a splendid sight standing there at the ready, his hands just inches from his guns, but he was only one man. Would Lomar fall in with him? If so there were several very well armed men standing with the two of them. She wished they had their guns up and ready. If there was trouble, Alex could tear off into the jungle. It was only a few yards from where he stood and there were crates and a bunker between him and most of the other men. Alex positioned himself beautifully for either fight or flight. She sincerely hoped he would opt for the latter.

Skye realized she was holding her breath. It made her very dizzy and she leaned against the windowsill for support. Her lungs were beginning to act up and things around her started to lose focus. She shook her head to clear it. Damn. She really needed to get off this island. Modify that. She needed to kick Snake Tattoo's balls up to his earlobes, then get off the island.

Looking over to the end of the runway, she saw Terrin's missing elite and about eight of the hijackers coming around the other side behind Lomar. She shouted at the precise moment Terrin's men opened fire with Kalashnikov AK 47's and the blood bath started. Lomar went down first. The back of his head exploded and his body fell. She could see it all unfold. It was like the action was running in slow motion, a lifetime in just a few minutes. The end of her life in the blink of an eye.

Alex had no idea he was being observed from a second story window. He was feeling the danger, but he was also very concerned for Skye. He knew she was a fellow agent and worthy of his trust. He'd seen her in action several times and she could take care of herself. But he also knew she was not in the best shape right now. He had to shake the sight of her

125

bruised face and bashed in ribs from his mind or he would start shooting right now. He had to get her off this island. And soon.

When Terrin came out of the hangar, Alex's eyes narrowed. There was a hot, predatory gleam in the man's eye. And he had been in there with Skye for more than fifteen minutes. Where was she? Alex hadn't seen her come out. His palms itched. He wanted to draw his guns and blow off the man's face. Contain the anger, Alex, he told himself. This isn't about you and Skye. This is about the passengers and crew of Flight 127. This is about the future President of Soteras.

Terrin turned to Lomar. "Yesterday morning, my computers were raided. I want to know if you had anything to do with that."

Lomar looked at Terrin. He always thought Terrin was caught up in his own self-importance and so his body did not communicate respect. Terrin noticed and bristled.

"I don't know what you're talking about. What is this nonsense? Let's get on with the inspection of this cargo, then we'll talk about the execution of Moreno and our return to the island. Faneta has been in exile long enough. It's time we move things along."

"You know about the oil. How did you know?" barked Terrin.

"I don't know what the hell you're talking about!" shouted Lomar.

"You got into my computers and found the reports," Terrin persisted, anger flashing in his eyes.

"What reports you fucking imbecile? Make sense," Lomar retorted with a snort.

"I'll bring them out and show you. Wait here. Then we'll open these crates and start loading the contents into the helicopters." Lomar had sealed his fate the second he had called Terrin an imbecile. Terrin could handle anger and deceit. He worked with it every day...expected it. At some level admired it. But he would never stand for insults. He demanded respect. The fact that the only way he ever got it was through intimidation made it even more important to his ego.

"We'll open them now," said Lomar to his men. "I don't want to see any goddamn reports. I'm not a politician. I'm a dealer." He nodded at the closest of his bodyguards and indicated one of the crates.

Turning, Terrin went back toward the hangar. Lomar was watching the man opening the crates. Alex already had both his guns drawn. He saw the movement and felt the threat.

"Behind you," he shouted to Lomar, but too late. The man's head exploded and pieces of his brain flew into the faces of his guards. They lifted their guns as Terrin's guard and several hijackers came out of the bushes and around the open door of the hangar. Four of Lomar's men were killed instantly, the other two got off several bursts. They took three of the hijackers and one of the guards with them before they went down. Alex dove as a volley slammed into the place where he had just been standing.

Alex did not take random shots, but focused on the well-trained elite guards. He took head shots, assuming, correctly, that they were vested. Raising both guns, he used his superior marksmanship to pick off two of them as he sailed through the air and dove behind a crate closer to the dense trees to his left. Seeing three more men by the door to the hangar, he turned, and exposed himself for a split second while he took all three of them in a deliberate and precise volley of well-placed bullets. Being left handed, he found that gun emptied first. Getting safely back behind the crates, he dropped the empty magazine and shoved another one into the empty gun in one smooth practiced move.

Okay. He wiped the sweat out of his eyes. He could either dip his toe into the water or he could dive right in. Dive, he thought. Taking a deep breath, he left the shelter of the crate and ran to another critical vantage point, shooting and covering his own ass as he went. The hijackers ducked for cover, but not before Alex wounded two and killed another one.

A few reluctant hijackers decided it was their day to be a hero and rushed him from the right. He employed both of his pistols and took the two of them out with chest shots, already knowing from his earlier assessment that they weren't wearing vests. Throwing the empty guns aside, he drew his pistol from the small of his back, flipped the safety and took stock of his situation. Fifteen rounds. He counted his targets. There were at least three fully operational elite guard and six hijackers. Two others were wounded and possibly still in the game. And the two that came in today with the helicopter. If the pilots and Terrin wanted in, that was three more.

Skye's information was proving vital again. He blew out a breath. He needed more bullets. Reaching down he got the gun from his boot. He was clear headed and focused. His hands were steady and he was confident of his ability to hit the targets both stationary and moving. So much adrenalin was pumping through his body, he thought he could fly over this island. He took another deep breath and blew it out. Thirty rounds before he had to reload. This reminded him of some of his favorite video games, except no live rounds flew at him from those. He took several more deep breaths to send oxygen to his brain. His destination was the dense trees on the other side of the runway. To get there, he needed to take out a few more of the targets.

The impatient guards wanted to flush him out, but they weren't going to take him on directly. They held back, respecting his proficiency. The evidence of it was lying all over the ground. Three of the best-trained commandos Terrin could buy were lying dead just inside the hangar. Most of the men standing were not brave and not good with a gun. The site of the fallen chosen ones was frightening so they just emptied their guns in the general direction of the crates. Alex actually smiled. He was pumped and he was confident. He might get splintered to death back here, but no bullets were getting through. He'd better move, though. It would only be a matter of time before someone got a lucky shot.

From the sound and placing of the volleys, Alex pinpointed the locations of the shooters in his mind. When the gunmen stopped to reload, Alex jumped up from behind the crate and took two more hijackers and one guard before he dove behind some concrete pilings. He was in pretty good shape. Not a scratch and plenty of ammunition. He figured he would take a few more shots, then head for the heavy cover of the jungle and from there call in the Special Forces. There may not be an entire team deployed yet, but they could send in a forward unit and provide the distraction he needed to go back, find Skye, and get the passengers to safety. He could do some sniping from the trees while he waited for them to arrive. His lips formed into a diabolical, menacing smile. He was particularly proficient in sniping. Maybe the man with the scar would come into his sights. He would take a head shot only after he took out the guy's kneecaps. He savored the thought for a few seconds, then risked a quick peek around the corner of the piling. The shooters were reloading again. Damn, what amateurs. They were all reloading at once, giving him opportunity and a wide-open corridor.

Alex was planning his next move when suddenly the door of a shed opened behind him and five men he hadn't seen before poured out. This was Terrin's ace in the hole...his backup in case he decided to put an end to the partnership. Oh shit, was all that Alex processed. He was primed and ready and managed to take out four before they even brought up their weapons.

The fifth man remained standing and released a full volley of bullets, catching Alex in the chest, propelling him across the short lawn, and slamming him up against the hangar. Blood splashed on the gray wall and Alex fell hard behind a bank of tall bushes where he lay motionless and forgotten.

Some of Lomar's men were still in the game and the firefight continued. Terrin's men located all the remaining resistance and took them out with superior firepower. There was pandemonium as the mercenaries shouted to each other and several less efficient guards unloaded their weapons at any hostile target. The wounded moaned for help. Those unscathed carried the bodies of their fallen friends to a makeshift infirmary in the hangar. Armed guards subdued the few passengers who were awake with threats and shouts. Soon there was calm and smoke from the gunfire began to dissipate.

Terrin surveyed the scene from a broken out window on the second floor. The cost of his treachery was dear. There were dead and dying lying all over the field. Faneta fought like a madman. Very entertaining. He was true to his legend, but in the end, he was outnumbered and outgunned. He would leave his body where it lay, to be blown to bits with the rest of the island.

Terrin was satisfied. He could easily replace the lowborn gunmen. His close personal guard would be more difficult to restore to full strength, but with one hundred percent of the country and its wealth, he was sure he could surround himself once again with highly trained commandos. He let the thrill of the victory wash over him, then turned to deal with the blonde bitch.

Twenty minutes before, Terrin had decided to watch the attack from the window of his bedroom...completely out of the fight, out of the danger. He was not a man who liked putting himself in harm's way. He'd come in just as the stupid woman was going to pitch a chair out the window. One of the two guards he chose to accompany him ran in and hit her in the back with the muzzle of his AK-47.

Skye went down in a cloud of pain. She couldn't get her breath. The guard put the end of the muzzle to her temple. Terrin had no idea she was more in agony over what was happening outside the hangar than anything they could do to her in this room. Holding her side, she tried to get up. When she heard another volley of bullets, she didn't care any more. She suppressed the pain, slapped the muzzle back, stood up, shot a foot out, and caught one of the guards in the kneecap. She heard a satisfying crunch and grabbed his gun as it dropped from his hand.

If Skye would have trained the weapon on the men in the room, she would have been killed instantly, but instead blew out the window with another vicious kick. She looked down just in time to see the five men burst out of the small shed right behind Alex. Bringing the weapon to her shoulder, she took aim. She saw Alex turn, raise his pistols and though he thought he took out four of the five men, it was actually Skye who got two of them plus one wounded hijacker who popped up at Alex's back.

The two greatest flashes of agony Skye ever experienced in her life happened simultaneously. She was hit in the ribs again by Terrin's man as he pulled the gun from her grasp and she saw Alex go down in a hail of bullets. She gasped, grabbed her side and passed out from the excruciating physical pain. But the agony of her screaming side was nothing compared to the image of Alex just before she fell to her knees and lost consciousness. She saw him fly through the air, propelled by a volley of life-ending bullets. His blood on the side of the hangar. His body lying still. Skye moaned. Her soul was ripped to shreds and that was the worst pain of all.

CHAPTER 10

Skye slowly, reluctantly came to consciousness. There was no disorientation. No moment of blessed confusion. She knew exactly where she was and she knew she wanted to die. She willed her heart to stop beating, but it wouldn't obey. She willed her mind to let her slip back into unconsciousness. It wouldn't comply. She couldn't even cry. There was absolutely nothing inside. She was hollow. Hollow and completely void of feeling. She knew she was in shock. She recognized the symptoms because she had been down this road before. Twice.

Damn him. Damn him. She thought of the ring in her pocket and if she would have had the energy she would have taken it and thrown it out the window. She never wanted to see it again. Damn him to hell. He persisted until she could no longer resist. He kept it up, insisting it would be a better life with him than without him. What life? What life now? She had no life because she had no soul. It was shattered and lying in pieces like his body out there in the night.

She heard night sounds. Low talking, some pounding. The sound of machinery. She was alone, lying on the monster's bed. She moved her arms and legs. He still hadn't tied her down. Even when he saw her grab a gun and shoot three people, he didn't think of her as a threat. That should have made her angry, but it didn't. She was feeling nothing. She was completely without sensation. She wondered for a moment if she was paralyzed, then realized she didn't care much if she was. She just didn't care.

Hearing a key in the lock, she automatically closed her eyes. She knew who it was. She smelled that horrible cologne he wore. He was saying something to a guard outside the door and she could see through her eyelids that he had turned on the light by the bedside.

"So, Captain," said Terrin in a low voice. "There's a bite, not just a bark, as they say in your country." She wasn't sure if he was talking to himself, or if he thought she was awake. She didn't care.

"I just want you to know that by this time tomorrow all of the passengers and crew of Flight 127 will be blown to paradise. We have just tried Moreno and have decided to execute him at dawn. The rest of you will perish as soon as I leave the island and fly to safety. I may be persuaded to take you with me. Show a little appreciation and I will think about it."

Skye just lay there, completely still. Completely lifeless. She felt cold, inside and out. And it was what saved her that night from rape, injury, and death. Had she been feeling anything, she would have played the encounter differently and Terrin wouldn't have left her alive. The irony was, her imminent death was averted only by her basic, fundamental wish to die. Her complete lack of response infuriated Terrin. He didn't hit her again, however. He knew that would make her go unconscious once more and he wanted to torture her and break her spirit more than he wanted to bring her physical pain. He wanted her arrogance and her pride to be stripped from her.

He brought his hands up and stroked her cheek. "All your passengers. All those children blown up. Never to grow up." He ran his hands over her breasts, unbuttoning her jacket, then slowly unbuttoning her blouse.

"Your responsibility, Captain. They were your responsibility. You failed." He watched her face, but there was nothing. He knew she was awake, he could sense it. Opening her blouse and seeing the luscious curve of her breasts, he could feel the satisfying heat move through him, making him hard and ready. It wasn't just her physical beauty turning him on. It was his ability to control. To dominate. He ran his fingers under her bra, then flicked open the hook and exposed her flesh. He bent down and ran his tongue down her neck as his hands roughly stroked her breasts. Nothing, he was getting absolutely no reaction. His hands started to shake with frustration. Anger seethed through him along with the lust. He moved his hand to her leg.

"We will see if you can lie still when I am inside you, bitch." He growled, running his hand up her thigh. Still nothing. No fear, no begging. No cringing. There was no recoil under his hands. She didn't even flinch. This was no act, he thought. She really was frigid. His own physical reaction began to cool as well. He needed the terrified struggle...the horror...the panic...the pitiful resistance. He enjoyed rape. It was practically the only way he could get true satisfaction, but this was like touching a stiff dead body. Her chest was moving...she was still warm, but the thought of sticking himself into her was becoming less pleasing. He could feel his desire slip away.

Suddenly, he heard a shout coming from outside. Reluctantly he removed his hand from her thigh and throat and went over to the broken window. It came from the crew he directed to load the crates. They were frantically motioning him down. He looked over at the woman. She still hadn't moved. Not a muscle. It was a good excuse to end this torture and seduction before his own manhood suffered. He went back to Skye, lying on his bed in the same exact position he left her.

"Whore, slut," he said and gave her a vicious punch in the stomach. "Lie here and think about dying. I'm not going to make it quick. Think about the explosion ripping through your body. Think about the screams of the children. I'll be back, bitch. Think of me."

His fist went back and he punched her again. He missed her broken ribs by less than an inch, missed killing her by a fraction. When she sensed the second punch coming, she stiffened her stomach muscles and shifted her body to the left. She saved her own life. She still had a job to do. Because she gave a low, long groan, and was left gasping for breath, Terrin was satisfied. He strode out of the room ordering the guard to stand watch at the door.

When he left, Skye opened her watering eyes, trying to get a breath. The wind had been completely knocked out of her and the pain was mind numbing, but she had protected her life. There was something inside that wanted to survive. No. That needed to survive. She had to bring her passengers home. No babies screaming on her watch. Terrin was right. They were her responsibility. She tried to move but couldn't. Now that she let one feeling in, others poured in with it. None of them were good.

Outside she heard Terrin screaming about stolen gold and currency. From what she could gather, he had discovered nothing but stone and gravel in the crates. Well. Pave your driveway moron, because that's all you're going to get, Skye thought. He had been deceived and the thought was satisfying. Score one for the good guys. It gave her a tiny boost.

She tried moving again. Just one leg over the edge of the bed, then sit up. The very thought of it made her sweat. Shifting again, she found she could move...but not without excruciating pain. Her chest was on fire and she felt unconsciousness flowing into the corners of her vision. She forced the darkness back. Gasping for air, she knew she needed to recapture some control of her breathing...get oxygen into her system. She stopped struggling to get up. Maybe a little rest to get her breath back, then she would act. Her eyes remained open. She had one thing to do before she could rest, however. Even though every move was agonizing, she hooked her bra, buttoned all the buttons on her blouse and tucked it into the front of her waistband.

Then she relaxed her muscles and channeled whatever energy she had left to her ribs. She would move before dawn. A few moments before, she wanted to die, wouldn't have cared how. But it wasn't her time...not yet. She still had a mission. She would put Emilio Moreno back on the plane, secure Stuart in the left seat, strap everyone in, get the hangar doors open, then let Flight 127 take off while she covered its escape.

Skye intended to stay on this island and die in the explosion. Stay on the island with Alex. She would find his body and wait with him for death to relieve her of the indescribable suffering in her soul.

Now she needed to concentrate. Surround the ache, then get it the hell off her back. She breathed in energy, breathed out pain. It was working on the ribs, but didn't make a dent in the cold, hard pain around the hole in her chest where her heart used to be. That was okay. Before the next sunset, the explosion would send her body where her soul had gone. She would be dead.

Skye lay in the lamplight. Pale as death. Dawn was breaking, but she was in a healing sleep. A hand came over her mouth and her eyes flew open. "Shhh." She heard it in her ear. "Wake up, but keep your voice low."

She nodded. "Okay," she agreed and closed her eyes again. She heard a familiar chuckle.

"Don't go back to sleep, my darling." His breath on her ear was warming her. She frowned.

"Am I dead?" she whispered. She thought she must be. It was the voice of...of her guardian angel. He was here to greet her. How nice. "If I'm dead," she asked in confusion. "Why do I hurt?"

Another chuckle. "Darling. You're not dead."

"Oh." Then her eyes opened and she turned her head. It was Alex. He was smiling. He was dirty and there was blood on him. It looked like he wasn't doing real well, either, but he was alive. Or was she dreaming? She blinked.

"Can you move?" asked Alex.

"What part?" replied Skye.

"Any part."

She moved her foot.

"Good. That's good."

"Thanks," she said and closed her eyes again. This was a cruel dream. Alex was dead.

"Darling. We have to get out of here. I heard them talking. Terrin is flying out this morning. They found out the cargo was bogus so they're leaving early. We have to rescue the crew and then get the plane off the ground. There isn't time to bring anyone in to assist. You and I are it."

"Boy. Are they in trouble. A ghost and a ghost walking."

"Sweetheart. You're not making sense. Let me help you sit up."

"Why not? I don't have other plans." She was still completely groggy and thought she was talking to a dead man.

When Alex placed his arm under her shoulders and pivoted her gently into a sitting position, her ribs woke her up with a ferocity that knocked the breath right out of her lungs. She must have passed out for a second, because Alex's cursing faded in and out.

When she came back around, she had an arm around his neck. Shaking her head, she tried to focus on his face, then moved to his mouth. She looked at his lips, Alex's lips. They were set in a grim line, but they looked warm and alive. She dove into them.

"Alex? Alex?" She kissed him until she had to pull back for air. She shook her head again to clear it. "What are you doing here?"

"Searching the premises."

"I mean…" Then she looked down at the bullet holes in his shirt and the bloody sleeve coming off his right shoulder.

"Superman?" she asked, still not processing it. Not wanting the hope to invade her heart until she was sure she was awake and alive. And that he was alive…that what she was seeing was not a hallucination. The hollow part of her was begging to be filled, but she was ruthlessly keeping the door closed until she was sure. Alex could see the war going on and thought it was one of her usual waking up and getting started rituals.

"Kevlar," he grinned rapping on his chest. "One did get through but it was at such short range it went in one side and out the other. We can have the doctor on board take a look. Bled like a bitch and hurts like hell, but I'll live."

"You will live," she said softly. Touching the bullet holes she looked into his still brown eyes. They were smudged with pain and fatigue, but they were full of life. She swayed with both pain and relief.

"Can you walk, or shall I carry you?" asked Alex, holding her against him, frowning and instantly serious. She had absolutely no color and her eyes were still radiating terrible waves of pain.

"Carry me, hell." She put her feet on the floor. "Get my shoes, will you? I can't bend over." She was still groggy and unable to fully fathom Alex's miraculous return from the dead, but no one was going to carry her. Alex helped her sit up, and nearly did pick her up when she bent over and groaned.

"Did you take another hit?" She seemed far worse to him physically than the day before. He could hear her labored breathing and feel the shudder of pain rip through her.

She looked into Alex's angry eyes. "No worse than yours. Just give me a minute."

Skye shook off the throbbing ache in her side. Taking Alex's arm...his warm, living arm...she opened the door and welcomed life back in...enjoying the rush and channeling the energy. A few seconds passed and then the special agent returned to command as she outlined her plan to escape the island. "First, we have to get Moreno back on the plane. I saw him last night. He's alive and looks unharmed, but they're planning on executing him before they leave the island."

"Where is he?"

"Two doors down on the left," responded Skye.

"Okay. Wait here."

"Oh no." She reached behind her, a move that sent new shards of pain through her chest. Gasping, but game, she drew her gun. "The pompous prick didn't even search me. Deadheaded, pea brained schmuck. I'm at your back."

"Doesn't pay to underestimate the best."

He grinned. She grinned. They were battered, bleeding, bruised, sore and just this side of standing, but they were together. They were a team. Skye shook off the last of her cold, hard, night. She couldn't think of it now. Later. She would think about it later.

"When we get him aboard, we'll need to go free the crew."

"Ah," said Skye. She reached in her pocket. "Voila. The key."

"Darling." Alex beamed at his resourceful fiancée...rather his ingenious and quick-fingered colleague. "Do you have breakfast in there, too?"

She shook her head, smiling. "Sorry."

They had to move, but first things first. He took her gently in his arms and kissed her. They both winced. "Kevlar." He heard her whisper.

"Should we do something with that?" she asked pointing at his bloody shoulder. "Shouldn't I be ripping up petticoats or something?"

He looked down at her trim slacks. No petticoats there. "Shucks, ma'am. It was only a flesh wound." Standing, he extended his hand. She looked up into his beautiful, marvelous, wonderful, alive brown eyes and slapped her hand in his.

"Okay, pardner. Let's get the hell out of Dodge." He gently helped her to her feet. She swayed but held her ground.

"Are you sure you're all right?" There was more concern than anger in his voice. He made a move to hold her, but she put up her hand to stop him.

"Just hungry. I haven't eaten since…well, I can't remember. Promise you'll take me to the Mariners for a steak when we get back home. Now let's move before I stiffen up."

Okay, if she wanted to play it tough, he would let her. He would just keep her very, very close. "I'll buy you a whole fucking cow." He swept his good arm toward the door. "After you."

Alex had snatched a SIG-552 and extra magazines from a dead guard before he came up. When he had seen Skye lying there, he thought she was dead. Her skin was so pale; she was lying so still. Then he had seen her chest move and knew she was just asleep or unconscious. She moved with horrible stiffness and he saw the agony in her face, but that they would deal with when they got off the island. For now he had to set aside his concern and concentrate on getting her home.

They moved slowly, silently. When they got to the room holding Moreno, Alex whispered, "Go in and identify yourself. He'll recognize and trust you. I'll cover your back."

Skye made her way into the dark room, her weapon drawn.

"Mr. Moreno?" she whispered. "Ambassador?"

"Who are you?" She nearly jumped when she heard his voice, clear and awake. He kept it low, however. Smart man.

"Captain Skyler Madison. Please stay very still. I want you back onboard the aircraft. I'm with a friend. We're going to try to take down this pipe to correspond with the pounding outside." Alex came in behind her and handed her the rifle.

"I understand, Captain." No panic. Calm compliance. He recognized the voice of a friend and he would do his part.

With each pound from outside, Alex hit the pipe with a punishing sidekick. His shoulder protested violently, but he ignored it. It took only three tries and the pipe snapped. He deftly caught it before it clamored to the ground.

Skye and Moreno pulled the restraints through the pipe and he was free to move. "We'll worry about getting those off you later," she whispered.

"A minor inconvenience, Captain."

"You know what they're planning?" asked Skye.

"Terrin has taken great pleasure in telling me everything."

"We're going to take the plane home."

"The other passengers?"

"All safe and well on the plane," said Skye.

"Thank God." It had weighed heavily on his heart that over 100 people were going to die because these animals from his country wanted him dead.

"We're going to get you on the plane, then go for our crew. They're locked in the room on the other side of the hangar."

"I heard shots."

"That was our man making the odds a bit more favorable." She indicated Alex, who was moving quickly back to the door to be sure they hadn't been heard.

"I would like to meet this hero," said Moreno.

"You will, sir," said Skye.

"His name?"

"No sir." He grinned at her. She could see the flash of teeth in the light of the dawning day. She grinned back. He thought he had never seen anything so lovely as this woman. He remembered her confident look the night before when their eyes had briefly met. She had obviously taken some punishment, but it didn't diminish the stunning quality of her timeless beauty. He found himself hoping he would be able to repay her in a very personal way when they got off the island. For he had no doubt that these two people would complete the rescue. "Maybe when you're President and you get special clearance."

"I understand," he said again, simply.

"Ready to move out?"

"I am."

The three of them left the room with Alex in the lead. They moved quickly and silently down the hallway toward the plane. If they were lucky, all the remaining guards and hijackers would be preparing to leave and there would be only minor resistance. She could see Alex out in front of them, checking each corridor. No one. They were catching some luck.

When they got to the door of the hangar, Alex took a quick look and saw only two guards at the bottom of the stairs. He guessed no guards were on the plane. Things had been very quiet when he had passed there earlier looking for Skye.

His shoulder was hindering him more than he was letting on. When he went flying into the side of the building, he had been stunned for a moment. He thought he might have passed out. Vest or no vest, there was a powerful force behind those bullets. He saw death coming at him and he felt it breathe down his neck. He knew he had to stay down and play possum until the sun went down. He must have passed out again, because he didn't wake up until about an hour ago. Then his only thought was to find Skye. Shifting, preparing for battle, he took a deep breath of air into his lungs. He was a little lightheaded from blood loss, but nothing too serious. Finding her and having her here beside him was all the medicine he needed right now.

Skye and Moreno came up behind him. He looked at her and put up two fingers, then brought one up to his lips. She caught the message. Two guards. Make it silent, deadly, and quick. She indicated right. He nodded. She put up her palm to Moreno's chest. He hesitated, then nodded. They all had their tasks. Action.

It was indeed silent, deadly, and quick. They were well trained and determined. Skye crouched, silently moved across the hangar and positioned herself behind the guard on the right; then grabbed him, twisted his neck, chopped at his skull. Alex was beside her to catch him. He had taken his man out already. He dragged the bodies into the shadows as Skye motioned to Moreno, then walked slowly, quietly up the stairs and into the dark interior of the plane. Just as Alex had suspected, they hadn't wasted any manpower here. The passengers were mostly sleeping. She smiled when she saw Cliff and waved him over. He whispered something to the other passenger standing guard and came over.

"You here to rescue us?" he asked glibly. Then saw that it was exactly what she was doing. Straightening, he helped her into the cabin. Moreno was right behind her. Cliff nodded at him "The missing passenger. Well done, Captain." Then he stiffened when he saw Alex.

"Good guy," she whispered and Cliff nodded, eyeing the dirty, bloody commando suspiciously. "Cliff, could you help Senor Moreno out of his restraints?"

"Sure. I'm so hungry right now maybe I can gnaw them off."

"Not necessary, I hope." Opening her fist, she let a set of keys dangle from her fingers. "I lifted these off the guard. See if any of them fit Senor Moreno's restraints." She did it with such a flourish, Alex chuckled before he went back to scanning every corner of the hangar. Damn, he loved this woman.

"We're going after the crew. Keep everyone calm and spread the word. We're going to have to fly out of here."

Cliff's eyes sparkled with excitement, but his face registered concern. "Need help?" he asked. "You two look like the walking wounded."

"You'll help me a great deal if you stay here," she squeezed his arm. Cliff nodded as he went through the ring of keys and in a few moments Moreno was out of the cuffs and rubbing his wrists. Alex gave Cliff one of the guns he took off the guard at the bottom of the stairs.

"You look like you can handle this." Cliff nodded grimly. He'd never had a gun in his hand in his life, but that was his family back there and he was a fast learner.

Alex handed the other gun to Moreno. "I read your dossier. I know you know which end of this is dangerous." Moreno grinned. He had been a sergeant in the national guard of his country before he went into politics…that explained his ability to move quickly and follow orders.

"Speaking of the walking wounded," she said looking down the aisle. "I was going to fetch the doctor to have him take a look at your shoulder, but here he comes." The doctor had risen and was coming fast. He saw the blood on the stranger and thought he might be needed.

Skye looked at Alex who was leaning against the bulkhead, favoring his shoulder. "You'll have the doctor look at that wound before we go on the next leg of our adventure."

He nodded. He knew when to be macho and when to be smart. Right now he was going to be smart.

"Let's go to the crew section in back."

Cliff and Moreno stayed at their station at the door, while Skye, Alex and the doctor went to the relative privacy of the rear section.

Alex sat down gratefully. The doctor's eyes nearly popped out when he saw the line of bullet holes in Alex's sweater and the flattened slugs that showed through them. He was a general practitioner and while he had worked with some bullet wounds, he most certainly had never seen anything like this.

"Can you get that vest off?" he asked, helping Alex pull the bulky turtleneck over his head. Pain shot through his shoulder and sweat started to roll down his spine.

"Maybe later, doctor. I'm kind of fond of it right now."

"I understand. I'll work around it, but as soon as we get off the ground and over the ocean toward home I want the two of you to allow me to properly care for you." The doctor used some of the towels from the galley and some sterile water from his bag to wash the wound. He also washed some of the blood from Alex's neck, shoulder and arm. Alex had him leave the dirt. He wanted to look as little like himself as possible. There may be some who would recognize him later, but they would never be quite sure. "Good grief, boy. You had to go rolling around in the dirt? I see bits of branch in the exit wound." Alex gritted his teeth as the doctor started to probe and clean the wound. "And the captain. Well, she shouldn't even be walking around. That leak is too dangerous. Her lung could collapse and if pneumothorax occurs, I have no way to surgically help her. A tube thoracostomy would be impossible. This isn't a fully functioning medical center you know. I could give her oxygen to increase the nitrogen gradient from the lung to the pleura, but if that doesn't increase the rate of absorption, I need..." The little doctor continued to grumble unmindful that he had lost his audience.

Skye and Alex looked at each other and she made a wide-eyed, good grief face. He smiled, then winced hugely as the doctor hit a nerve. He had to use all of his willpower not to scream ouch and pop the guy down the aisle.

"It looks okay," said the doctor as he applied antibiotic cream and closed the wound with bandages. "I'll want to do a bit of sewing when you return, but the bullet went right through. It hit no bones or major arteries. You have a good steady pulse in your right arm. No nerve damage. You're a very lucky young man."

"If you say so," rasped Alex. When he saw Skye's eyes start to tear, he smiled a weak little smile, gave the love of his life a wink, and leaned against the wall of the galley.

"I already know the captain's feelings on painkillers." The doctor looked into Alex's eyes. "Tell me yours. Will you allow me to give you a shot for the pain?"

"You have a shot you could have given her?" frowned Alex.

"I do."

"Then why is she still in so much pain?" demanded Alex.

"She wouldn't take my advice."

"Let's not get into this now," she said. "Take the shot."

The doctor stared at them. He had the shot ready and was waiting for the go ahead.

"I will if you will," said Alex, looking steadily into her stubborn face.

"I can't. I can't have anything narcotic based. I may have to fly."

Alex stared into her eyes, pulsating with pain. But he also recognized the stubborn look and willful set of her mouth, so he gave up and nodded. There was no way to budge that mountain. "Then eat your heart out, darling." He presented his well-muscled arm to the doctor. "I'm not as brave as the captain," Alex said with a wicked grin.

"Or as stupid," mumbled the doctor. "Killing herself. Won't listen to simple advice. Could probably fly this plane in her sleep."

"As soon as I bring the copilot on board and we're off the ground, I expect you will have one of those for the captain?" asked Alex in a voice that suggested he would hold her down if he needed to.

"I've had one ready for two days. Don't know what is keeping her on her feet. Foolish woman."

Skye would have shrugged, but she was too sore.

Alex gingerly put the shirt back on and as he pulled it over his head, he caught a very haunted look on Skye's face as the bullet holes passed his eyes. By the time his head popped though the neck, the look was gone. Something to think about later. He rotated his shoulder. He was already feeling much better.

Picking up his weapon with his left hand, he started back down the aisle toward the door. The passengers were coming awake, sensing something happening and stared at him with anxiety. He looked more dangerous than the men who had been guarding them the last few days. When they saw their captain behind him, they were comforted with the confidence she was doing something to get them home.

Alex looked out the door. All was quiet. Dark and still. The plane was cast in shadows, but he could discern soft shades of light licking up the dark wall of night on the eastern horizon. Time to move. Fast.

Alex turned to Skye. "Cliff, Moreno, I'm going to need some help here." Cliff nodded at the stranger…not sure who he was, but knowing authority when he heard it. Moreno already trusted him.

"Captain," said Alex as he turned to her and took her arm. She was ready to move out and frowned at the hand on her arm. "Captain." He deliberately used the more formal address. He wanted her to think like the captain of this aircraft. She looked up into his eyes. Not her lover's eyes. The eyes of Special Agent Alexander Springfield.

"You have to stay here." Both Cliff and Moreno moved closer.

"The hell I will," whispered Skye though clenched teeth. She jerked her arm out of his grasp and glowered at him. "I'll be going after my crew." And watching his back, she thought.

"Captain." He wanted to say darling, he really wanted to say darling, but he knew that would change the feel of the moment. Looking at her steadily, he had to appeal to the captain in her. "First of all, you can hardly walk. You have to get off your feet. You have to conserve what energy you have left."

The doctor saw her color and nodded. "I agree."

"I can still walk," insisted Skye, getting angry now. Why was he wasting time? "Don't worry about me. Now move out. I'll be right behind you."

Shaking his head, he went on as if she hadn't spoken. "And more importantly," he said in a commanding whisper, looking at her as Cliff put his hand gently on her shoulder. "You're the only one on board who can fly this plane out of here."

He saw that one hit its mark. Cliff and Moreno looked at each other. They got it too.

"Stuart."

"Stuart is in a room across the hangar from here. If things go bad, you're going to have to get this plane off the ground. You need to stay here. We can't have both pilots out there."

"Please," she said. She knew what he was saying. They might not make it back. Alex, her crew, Fisher. They might not be able to get back to the plane.

"I'll bring them, Captain. I'll bring them here, but we have to have a back-up plan."

To his relief, she nodded. He was presenting the best tactical plan to Special Agent Madison. She couldn't let her personal feelings, her preferences, her love, get in the way of saving all these people. Looking around the cabin to strengthen her resolve, she saw the heads of the souls who were in her care. It gave her the discipline to let him go alone.

"I'll bring them back," he repeated.

"See that you do." Suddenly, she didn't care what Cliff, or the doctor or the future President of Soteras thought at that moment. She was going to send him off with her love on his lips. Taking his rough face in her hands, she gave him a farewell kiss that would have blasted a lesser man into orbit. When she started to pull away, Alex decided to take some reserves with him and returned the favor. Cliff and Moreno discretely checked out the hangar, the passengers, and the time on their respective watches. The doctor just gaped.

"See you soon, Captain," said Alex, throwing the rifle over his good shoulder and pulling out two pistols.

She nodded, not knowing what she was feeling. There he went again into the dusky hangar. The eastern sky was getting lighter, casting long shadows. She may never see him again. Remembering the cold feeling from the night before, her inner self started to construct a wall around her heart. Not ice this time. Not steel. But an impenetrable combination of both. She swallowed hard. The wall helped clear her head.

CHAPTER 11

Amy, Stuart, Fisher and the rest of the crew were waiting, pacing, and talking among themselves. They heard the gunfire the day before and no one had come since so they were formulating a plan for escape. They assumed Skye wouldn't be back, and it weighed heavily on their hearts. Stuart took over leadership now as second in command. When the door opened again, they were going to go through it, even if it cost some of them their lives.

It was almost daybreak when there was a scratch at the lock. As one they faced the door, prepared to overpower the guards and get to the passengers.

Alex opened the door and looked in. They stared at the bloody commando with an assault rifle at the ready.

"Anyone want to go home?" he asked in a low voice.

No one moved right away. Suspicion clearly written on their faces.

"Where's Skye?" asked Stuart in a commanding tone. "Where is the captain? We don't leave without her."

"She's waiting for you on the plane and would like your help."

That was all it took. Grabbing their jackets they started toward the door moving quickly and efficiently. Amy snatched up Skye's flight bag. Her captain would want to freshen up sometime during the flight. She always liked to look really good when they landed. Fisher brought her hat. If the captain was on the plane, they knew they were going home.

They went out silently, in single file, walking past two prone figures in the hall. The hijackers looked dead, but the crew didn't want to know. Didn't care.

Skye watched anxiously from the top of the stairs. There was too much light coming into the hangar. She knew Terrin was planning on executing Moreno at dawn. It was now officially dawn, she thought. She'd taken Cliff's gun from him so he and his crew of brave passengers could quietly prepare everyone for the flight. She would have to send some of them out to open the hangar door if Alex didn't return in the next few seconds.

Nothing was happening and Skye was getting tensed up to act when two things occurred simultaneously. There was a shout from the hallway where Skye and Moreno had been held and Alex came around the corner on the opposite side of the hangar with the crew. She had to trust Alex to get the crew to where they needed to be. Her only concern right now was to stop the group of men in the hallway...coming on the run after discovering the empty rooms. They were pouring into the hangar, shouting an alarm.

Damn. A few more minutes and we would have been clear, she thought. Tough shit. Didn't happen. In a heartbeat, all hell broke loose.

Her reactions were automatic, quick, and deadly. Adrenalin, a great natural painkiller, flowed through Skye's system. She ran down the steps laying a covering blast of gunfire and drawing the attention to her so Alex could get the crew across the hangar floor over to the stairs. Three of the guards flew back into the hallway and stayed down. The rest scattered and slowly started to return fire. Most of the inexperienced hijackers fumbled with their weapons. Skye took cover behind a stack of huge boxes, drawing what fire there was away from the entrance of the plane. She continued to exchange shots with the men, aware that she had been right about their pitiful training. Bullets whizzed by, but none close enough to concern her.

Seeing Skye's more vulnerable position and watching the concentrated gunfire aimed in her direction, Alex laid cover fire from the other end of the hangar. The crew ran quickly across the floor and safely up the stairs as the hijackers and guards kept their heads and weapons down.

Moreno had his rifle ready and watched for a signal from Alex. Skye saw Alex nod and while Moreno began giving him protective cover from the doorway of the plane, he moved closer to Skye's position. Standing, Skye emptied her pistol to keep the men in the hallway down. She was operating according to standard procedure and she was magnificent.

Alex had to suppress his natural terror at seeing her so exposed and remind himself that she was a fellow agent now, not the woman he loved. What the hell, he thought. Either way he wanted to protect her. Coming around to get a better angle on the hallway, he began to pick off the hijackers one at a time as he swiftly made his way to Skye's side.

"Draw the fire away from the passengers and the fuselage," shouted Skye.

Suddenly, she felt Alex beside her and there was no stopping their natural instincts and intense training. Alex handed her an automatic rifle and they formed a two-person team running together toward the danger. Shooting, finding protection, providing cover for each other. It was a spectacular sight. Like a well-choreographed movie, only this was reality. The bullets that whizzed by them were very real, their peril was not a script. Skye's original assessment of the men's abilities with firearms was correct...and it gave her heart. They were no match for Alex's deadly aim. Skye wasn't nearly as proficient, but she was good enough.

When they saw the crew was safely on board, they started to move back, sweeping the hangar with their rifles. Skye could feel her magazine was almost empty. Alex didn't have much left either and they both emptied their weapons on a threat from the left. The volley brought down three more hijackers foolish enough to try and stop them and scattered the survivors, now in complete retreat.

"Get the hangar door open!" shouted Skye. "I'll cover you." She threw her empty weapon down, brought her arm up to Moreno, who was still standing in the doorway, waved her fingers at him and in perfect synchronization, he threw the weapon to her, she caught it, turned and shot a lone hijacker who was coming up from the right.

"Go back and get in your seat," she shouted up to him. Now that Stuart was on board, the plane had a pilot. She was going to stay down here and cover her partner.

Alex ran to the front of the hangar and worked the wheel to open the big door. He was hampered by his bad shoulder and it was only going up by inches. Skye felt someone run past her and grinned. Cliff. Together, he and Alex got the door up and secured. Skye kept her eyes sweeping the perimeter. There was no movement anywhere from inside or outside the hangar.

There didn't appear to be any more guards but according to Skye's count there were more...plus Terrin. Then they heard the helicopter. They knew what that meant. Terrin and his remaining men were deserting the island. As soon as they cleared the land, he could detonate the explosives around the plane.

"Hurry!" shouted Skye. "Terrin's leaving."

Cliff took the stairs two at a time and Alex grabbed the automatic from Skye. "Get on board, Captain," he shouted. "Now!" Alex ran forward to make sure no one was coming into the hangar from the front. "If he left any behind, they will be desperate to get on board our plane."

Skye didn't argue. Turning, she started toward the stairs when a man who had been cowering behind some crates jumped her from behind. Alex twisted around and raised his gun, but he couldn't get a clear shot. Didn't matter. Skye's movements were swift and automatic. She grabbed the man's arm and drew him around her body, then initiated an effective sidekick into his chest, snapping his sternum and putting him out of commission.

Another man ran from where he'd been hiding and grabbed her around the throat. Putting a knife next to her jugular, he pointed her toward Alex. Skye saw his face. The scar. It was Snake Tattoo. Perfect. He was smiling. He thought he had her. The asshole was still underestimating her. And this time it cost him his life. She brought her arm up and over, ignoring completely the intense shot of pain in her side. Over her shoulder he went, and in the same deft move, she grabbed the wrist with the knife and broke the bone. He screamed in agony as the knife went flying. Then she planted a vicious kick into this gut, propelling him in Alex's direction.

Snake Tattoo, strengthened by fury and pain grabbed a rifle from one of his fallen comrades. "Bitch, you die!" he screamed pulling the gun up for firing.

"He's all yours!" shouted Skye, turning her back on the armed man and walking quickly to the plane.

Fisher was watching with appreciation, as were most of the passengers. "Whoa. That was pretty!" he exclaimed. Then had to swallow hard as Alex put one shot through the man's head...right between the eyes.

Alex knew exactly who the man was. He had studied his picture. Skye had just handed him an opportunity for retribution...allowed him to settle the score. His eyes narrowed as he lowered his rifle and the passengers all backed up from the windows. If that man was coming onto the plane, they wanted to be in their seats and cooperating fully.

Starting up the stairs Skye stopped as the whole plane started to lose focus. Her legs weren't responding to her brain's desperate plea to move. She wasn't sure she could make it. Then suddenly Alex was beside her, taking her around the waist as gently as he could. He helped her up the stairs, his gun still sweeping the hangar, his eyes still alert for danger.

Skye had to stop at the top of the stairs to pound the pain in her side back into submission. Getting her wind back, she nodded to Alex who went back down to guard the perimeter. Taking a deep breath she stood as straight as she could. Show time.

"Crew to your stations," she called when she came through the doorway. "Prepare for a very fast preflight check. Brian, Beth, Katherine, check the inner skin carefully to be sure there are no bullet holes in the fuselage. If there are, note their locations and report. Fisher, take your seat." He'd been standing in the aisle gaping at her.

"Stuart!" she said to her copilot, who had just completed his sweep of the instruments. "I have to ask you to go back out and do a quick visual inspection. If any bullets hit the wing, check to be sure they missed all the hydraulics. I can't do it and we have to be sure everything is operational. There should be no danger. The rats have deserted the ship and you will have protection. I'll start the cockpit checklist and close the cargo door."

They were trying to get back into rhythm. Each one knew their duties. "We're going to try to do this as close to the book as possible." They knew that they would have to compress their usual careful preflight procedure but the safety of all the people on the plane depended on them. She noticed with satisfaction and pride that her crew was quietly and competently going about their usual preflight routines.

"Ladies and gentlemen," Skye said in a clear confident tone as she hurried toward the cockpit. "Please get to your seats and buckle in." The passengers promptly started to do as she bid. Skye had to stop midway down the aisle and catch her breath. The pain in her side was horrible.

Cliff came up behind her. "Give you a hand, Captain?" he asked discreetly. She nodded, gratefully. Over her head, he caught the doctor's eye. Dr. Lacy and his bag were already on the way forward and fell in behind them. For the sake of the passengers' peace of mind, nothing was said. They just got Skye to where she needed to be. Cliff eased her into the familiar captain's seat. She would switch over to the right seat when Stuart was back inside and in place.

"Thanks," she said and squeezed Cliff's hand. "Now go back to your family."

"I will," he said and smiled. "We're in good hands."

Alex guarded Stuart's back, scanning the trees, the buildings, the air. He knew there still might be people alive on the island. He just wasn't sure how committed they were to the cause now that their leader wasn't there to direct their efforts. Stuart checked the tires, fuselage, cargo door, engines, gear housings, brakes, and the skin of the airplane. Everything looked airworthy.

Then Alex saw some movement near one of the outbuildings on the far side of the grounds. Grabbing Stuart, he propelled him toward the stairs. "Get on board. Now!" shouted Alex. "Skye needs you in the cockpit." Alex knew that Skye was just about at the end of her endurance and was counting on Stuart to take the controls and get the plane up.

When he saw Stuart go through the door, Alex ran up the stairs himself. A man jumped out from behind a barrel near the far end of the hangar and shot one last volley at him. Alex heard the bullets clatter on the stairs below him, whirled and fired at the same time. He caught the foolish man across the chest and effectively ended the threat. Cliff was right there to assist as he dove through the opening. He grabbed Alex's wrist and together they kicked away the staircase.

"Inform Skye that everyone is on board and ready to go," he shouted to Brian. "We'll secure the door when we start to taxi. I want it open so I can discourage anyone from getting brave and attacking the plane."

"Thanks for the hand, Cliff." Alex grinned at the firefighter from D.C. "Take your seat, we're going home." Cliff grinned back. He wouldn't have wished this on his family, but that wasn't his choice to make. Now that he was in the middle of it and was confident they were going home safely, he was loving the adventure. It was an adrenalin rush and he would have stories for the firehouse gang for a year. His kids seemed to be oblivious to the actual danger anyway. They reacted to the gunfire like it was some sophisticated video game. They knew mommy and daddy were there and that meant nothing bad could happen to them. Cliff took the seat next to his wife and they held hands as they waited for the plane to taxi out.

The passengers were filled with hope and anticipation as they looked out the window and at each other. They had been given no food or water since the night before so most of them were awake and alert. It was really happening. The flight that began four days before in London was going to finish its journey. There were smiles and cheerful banter, sprinkled with some apprehension and natural anxiety. They had confidence in their captain and that made a big difference in their attitude.

Amy was right behind Stuart, who was walking purposefully toward the cockpit. He was just about through the first class cabin when he heard an angry shout. Frank Sills, CEO of Astron Corporation and carrier of the International Airlines Platinum Card was furious. He was used to being in charge. He had Amy by the arm and was asking her in an enraged voice if they had enough fuel to make it back to the states.

"How do you know if there's enough!" Sills demanded. "I think the best course of action is to stay here and wait for rescue."

"Look, sir," said Amy patiently but firmly trying to pry his fingers off her arm. "You must get back to your seat now. We have to take off." Sills didn't budge. He glared at Amy with flashing eyes and a malicious look on his face. He didn't like people defying him. Grabbing Amy's other arm, he started to shake her.

"Answer my question, little lady. How do we know we'll have enough fuel to take us back to the United States? I'm an important person...I'm sure there are several senators arranging for special forces as we speak. Why try a foolhardy escape?"

Stuart impatiently grabbed the man's arm. "Get back into your seat right now sir. You're in violation of international law. Assaulting a flight attendant is an extremely serious charge. We'll have you arrested when we reach our destination if you don't get into your seat and strap in immediately."

The other passengers were beginning to shout at him to shut up and sit down. That seemed to incense the man even more. He was now not only losing control of himself; he was losing control of the situation.

Alex, who looked up from his station by the door assessed the trouble and started to move forward.

"You just try and have me arrested and I'll add that to my lawsuit against this half-assed airline!" What happened next was sudden and totally unexpected. The man shoved Stuart and slapped Amy with the back of his hand. Alex was on him in a flash, but not before Stuart went down hard. Alex picked Sills up off the floor of the plane by his lapels.

"You will take your fucking seat, now, asshole. And when we return to the states, you'll be answering to the charge of assault. Add to that the fact that it was an in-air emergency and you'll be looking at doing time."

"Who are you? Who let you on this plane? How do we know you aren't one of them?"

Alex shoved him back into his first class seat. He grabbed the seat belt and secured it around the struggling form. Sills was a large man, but no match for the hard muscle and solid grip of Alex.

"You move from this spot and I will come back...and I swear to you that when I'm finished, you'll no longer be able to fuck your mistress." Mr. Sills saw the furious look in Alex's eyes and fear brought him to bay. He sat growling, but subdued.

"You will be mentioned in the lawsuit!" he said as a parting shot.

"And you will be mentioned in the indictment," said an equally angry Alex.

When he turned to assess Amy's situation, he found her kneeing over an unconscious Stuart. There was a gash in his head where it had hit the corner of the bulkhead. Alex's blood ran cold.

"Goddamn it! How bad is it?" he asked as he hurried over to kneel next to Amy.

"He's breathing okay," she said. "But I can't revive him."

"I'll get the doctor," said Brian and hurried toward the cockpit.

Dr. Lacy was standing behind Skye with a hypodermic in his hand. He was waiting for her signal to administer the strong painkiller. He knew she couldn't suppress the agony much longer. The pain was keeping her from taking deep breaths, and that was a dangerous problem. Her lungs could fill and she could get pneumonia as a result. He looked at her flushed cheeks. Her temperature was slightly elevated already. Had she not such a strong immune system and powerful constitution, she would have been down the day before.

"Please, Dr. Lacy. Could you come with me?" asked Brian.

"Go ahead," said Skye. "I have another few minutes here, anyway." Skye was still concentrating hard on her checklist and turning on switches so she didn't see the look on Brian's face.

"Of course," said the doctor and quickly followed Brain, because he did see the look on his face.

Alex knew before the doctor could confirm it that while the head wound was not life threatening and would require a few stitches, Stuart was not going to regain consciousness any time soon.

"He won't be able to fly this plane, will he?" asked Alex.

The doctor shook his head with a look of deep concern.

"And Skye?"

"She will do what she has to do. I would have said that she wouldn't have been able to move after the beating she took, but she's proven to have resources beyond the norm. Then I saw her take out five of our captors with even a deeper well of willpower and internal strength. I'll not again underestimate that young woman's fortitude. If she is the only hope for us getting this plane off the ground and home, then I expect to be seeing the coastline of the United States before lunchtime." All the while he talked he was gently cleaning and bandaging Stuart's wound.

Alex nodded, his heart slamming against his chest. How much more did his fearless warrior have to endure?

"Brian, you and Amy are going to have to take the door. Let's just close it now. Stay clear of the opening. We don't want to add to the casualties."

"She'll do what she has to do," repeated Amy, looking into Alex's troubled eyes and squeezing his arm. "I'll get the others to help put

Stuart in a first class seat. Brian and I'll take the door. You scared everyone out there so much, no one is going to stop us now. You two get back to the cockpit and help the captain."

"You go ahead," said the doctor, not looking up. "I want to finish with the bandage."

"Where's Stuart?" asked Skye, looking up briefly from her preflight checklist. She was trying to do this take off by the book, but the words were beginning to blur. She saw it on his face before he uttered the words.

"Shit, Alex. What happened? Did something happen to Stu?" There was alarm in her voice and concern on her face. Not for her own predicament, but for Stuart's safety.

"I'm so sorry, Skye," he knelt beside her seat and looked at her pale and pain racked face. "He intervened with a hysterical passenger and was shoved. He hit his head on the corner of the bulkhead. He's out cold and I don't think he'll be able to help you in here."

"Is the doctor with him?"

"He is."

"Okay. Unfortunately I can't take an extra minute to make sure he's all right. We'll have to trust him to the doctor. Here." She handed him the checklist. "Read this off to me while I start the engines. Did Stuart finish the visual?"

"He did and found everything okay." Alex smiled at his chosen one. No hysterics. No panic. No displeasure. Just take the blow and get back to business without even missing a step.

"Excellent." Her hands were swift and confident as she started the two huge GE engines. They were screaming within seconds. Skye's exhaustion faded in the face of the adrenalin pouring in to her system. As Alex read off the list, she checked her instruments. Simultaneously, she lined up the plane and applied power to bring it to the end of the runway.

It was a splendid sight. The huge metal bird so graceful in the air lumbering slowly out of the hangar that had kept it prisoner. A slight, victorious smile passed over Skye's face as she passed from shadows into the light.

Alex watched her hands. It was just as he imagined they would be…competent, confident, and controlled. Her fingers were spread wide over the throttle as she pushed it forward. Her experience was obvious. She moved through instinct. Effortlessly, without any hesitation, she automatically moved the throttle precisely where it needed to be. Her eyes took in everything the instruments communicated to her. It was routine, even if the circumstances weren't.

She got on the intercom and raised Amy. "Have you completed the internal inspection for holes?"

"We saw none, Captain."

"When we get above 8000 feet, you know what to look for as I pressurize the cabin."

"Yes, Captain." If they had to, they could fly home at 8,000-10,000 feet, where there was breathable air. But she preferred to climb much higher and that required the fuselage to be intact.

"Flight crew, buckle in and prepare for take off."

"Yes, Captain."

She looked over at Alex and smiled. "You ready?" He nodded realizing he was never more in love than he was right at that moment.

"Ready, Captain."

Skye grabbed the intercom. This was one announcement she wanted to make herself. "Ladies and gentlemen. This is your captain speaking. Please fasten yourself in and prepare to leave this island in our wake. Let's go home."

Passengers were looking out the windows as the hangar disappeared and the heavily wooded landscape came into view. Some had tears in their eyes, some cheered, some were still in a mild form of shock. They all heard the word home, however, and unexpectedly the incident seemed less like a deadly situation and more like a once-in-a-lifetime adventure. It restored the group's energy and optimism.

Skye glanced over to Alex one more time and gave him a 'let's give them hell' smile then pushed the throttles to full. Her eyes went forward as the engines spooled up and didn't leave her instruments until she felt the plane defy the pull of gravity, the wings giving her the lift necessary to leave the land behind and soar to the freedom of the sky.

Never in her life had the feeling of take off felt so sweet. So satisfying. Skye banked slightly to the left until she had the bearing she desired to get her to her destination. She continued to climb, the exhilaration of being in the air, of flying free momentarily countering the pain.

The doctor came into the cockpit soon after they reached altitude.

Skye glanced back. "How's Stuart?"

"He'll be fine, but I'm afraid he's still unconscious. His left pupil is still unresponsive. I'm so sorry, Captain. I think you're going to have to fly us home."

She nodded, the mere act of doing so causing her great distress.

Ignoring it, she began pressurizing the cabin, watching her instruments carefully. They caught some luck. No structural damage. They would be able to climb to a safer altitude. It would also assure her enough fuel to get them back to the United States.

Alex kept a close eye on her, but knew he was nearly useless in the cockpit. She was the only one on board capable of this task. He was frustrated and very disturbed, but forced himself to suppress both feelings. If he couldn't help her in this primary task, he could offer his support in any other way.

"Darling, you will have to tell us what we can do for you. To help you." Her eyes slid to his for a second. She couldn't move her body without inviting excruciating pain, so she only moved her head slightly.

"In a moment I'll be putting us on autopilot. I'm having trouble focusing on the instruments, so you'll have to keep a running dialog with me. Go from left to right and read what the instruments have to say."

Without warning, there was a terrific concussion in the air currents and the plane bucked in the turbulence. Skye checked all of her instruments. What the hell?

Alex looked out and back at the island. The hangar and half the runway were completely engulfed in smoke and fire. He reported what he saw to Skye, then wiped the sweat off his face.

Skye quickly got on the intercom to reassure her passengers. Her voice was pleasant and soothing.

"Ladies and gentlemen, it appears as though our hosts never planned on negotiating our release. The turbulence you felt was the shock wave caused by multiple explosions on the island. As some of you can see, the hangar and runway are now gone. I want you to know you're perfectly safe. All that little blast did was give us a nice shove home. I'm looking at all of the instruments right now and they tell me everything is registering excellent conditions. The weather is perfect and the plane has plenty of fuel. I apologize that there will be no beverage service, but I'm sure when we arrive in the United States, there will be plenty of pampering for all of you."

Reaching over, she tried to put the intercom microphone back into its cradle. She missed and couldn't seem to get it where she wanted it. Alex gently took it from her hand and placed it in its designated spot.

"Please, Captain. Let me give you something for the pain," the doctor begged. "You can't keep on like this. There's a limit to how much a body can stand before it has to shut down. I can give you a shot that will make you more comfortable. Those Tylenol simply aren't enough."

"No," said Skye, gritting her teeth against the waves of pain coming from her injured ribs. She was finding it difficult to take a deep breath. "I will not fly under the influence of drugs. I can't. Alex, could you please reach there to the right and hand me the oxygen mask? I'll get some pure oxygen into me to clear my head and keep me alert. I'm breathing too shallowly. Then could you please ask Amy to bring me a really strong cup of coffee if there's anything left in the galley?"

"Strong coffee and oxygen will only work for awhile. You shouldn't even be standing!" cried Dr. Lacy.

"I'm not standing, Doctor. I'm sitting." It was her own unique brand of Skye logic. "I'll take any antibiotics you think will be necessary, but nothing narcotic-based. I've got to retain my balance and keep my head as clear as possible. I'm a seasoned pilot and could probably bring this plane in with my eyes closed, but regulations are uncompromising on this issue. I'm responsible for over 100 souls and insist on being completely aware."

"You have an incredible ability to channel your pain and compartmentalize it, but there are limits to even your remarkable body. Your will cannot change your anatomy."

"Doctor, thank you for your concern. I'll take the shot as soon as we've landed and I've shut down the engines. Please, look after Stuart. If he regains complete consciousness, let me know immediately. I'll want him up here with me if it's at all possible." She looked over at Alex. He only saw pain and steely determination in the eyes of his lover. "No offense."

"None taken. I wouldn't mind seeing Stuart up and about myself. Anything to get you to take care of yourself."

"First I need to get my passengers and crew safely on the ground, then I can worry about a few broken ribs." She shifted in her seat again, desperate for some relief, but there was no position that afforded any less agony. She checked her instruments and the amount of time she had left in the air. "Three more hours." Just three hours and she would be able to rest. She could do it. She had no choice.

Amy brought her and Alex strong coffee. The crew managed to dig up some coffee grounds in a cupboard in the galley. There was no other food or drink but Skye couldn't have tolerated anything, anyway. An hour into their flight, when everything was going smoothly and the plane was on autopilot, Amy helped Skye into the lavatory and stayed with her to freshen up. Amy was a wise woman. When Skye came out, all polished and pampered, her make-up on, her hair neatly styled, she felt alive again. It was better than a shot. Her spirit was refreshed and her fortitude was refueled. Alex appreciated the look and whistled, but he wasn't fooled by the shine on the outside. He saw into her soul and knew she was fading.

Alex's satellite phone survived the night and he was on it with Jim almost constantly. While it wasn't completely secure, it was far too dangerous for them to be flying toward the continental United States with absolutely no communication. Jim passed on all the coded and cryptic messages to Amanda and the rest of the team. International Airlines representatives were already preparing the families and friends to be transported to an alternate location.

Alex asked that Jim check out Dr. Lacy for possible clearance so he could continue to work with Skye. They had developed a rapport and Alex wanted seamless care for her. A half-hour later, a delighted Jim reported that Dr. Lacy's background check was exemplary. He was a fine and distinguished general practitioner, recently retired. No family. A bachelor his entire life. Completely trustworthy.

The doctor in question fussed over Alex some more. Checking his wounded shoulder and giving him another shot to counteract the soreness that had been throbbing through his chest.

"Some healer," Alex griped when the doctor went back to check on Stuart again. "Every time he touches me, he finds a new way to administer pain." Alex had removed the Kevlar vest, giving him tremendous relief. He kept his cap on low over his forehead and borrowed Stuart's sunglasses. He wanted the contacts out before they melted into his burning eyes, so the sunglasses stayed on until they were home and out of the airport. The posture and manner of the commando were still perfectly played. He didn't break cover. But he looked exhausted and Skye's superior peripheral vision caught him periodically rubbing his chest.

"When is the last time you slept?" asked Skye, as Alex had to blink a few times to read the altimeter.

"Does being unconscious count?"

"You wish." She gave a little laugh that ended in a cough. It was agonizing. Alex reached over and lightly covered her hand with his.

"We'll be home soon," he said gently. "We'll sleep then."

She glanced at him. The tender tone of his voice was so incongruous with his menacing appearance. She'd seen him shoot down men just two hours ago. Hell, what was she saying? *She* shot down men. Now that the heat of battle was wearing off, she wondered what she thought about that. She searched her emotions. She was okay. The people they killed were trying to injure and murder innocent men, women, and children trusted in her care. They beat her and shot Alex. They were without moral fiber. They would have murdered everyone on this plane to assassinate a future President. From what Alex had told her, he was a good man. She searched again for regret, remorse, or guilt. There was none. She wondered if that made her flawed somehow.

A few months ago, she would have had no one to talk to about this except paid professional counselors. There were her fellow agents, of course, but no one who would have the experience so freshly in their mind. They were alone in the cockpit 30,000 feet above the surface of the earth. There wasn't much to occupy her since the autopilot was on and set for home. The sky was a beautiful, endless blue. A perfect setting for confidences and questions.

"Alex?" she asked softly.

He shifted, alarmed by her quiet, breathy tone. "You okay?" he asked. He'd been drifting a bit. The blood loss had been significant and he was feeling the effects.

"I don't know. I want to ask you something."

"Anything."

Skye looked over at him. She hadn't had to move in awhile and the periodic doses of pure oxygen had helped. More alert now, she was beginning to see the strain on Alex's face. He looked utterly exhausted, but the eyes behind the sunglasses were watchful and attentive. She swallowed. How to put this without sounding melodramatic. Directly, that was how. He was beginning to frown. Better get this out now, or he was going to start worrying on a whole new level.

"Have you ever had to kill anyone before?"

"Yes," he said simply, relief running through him. It wasn't a worsening of her physical symptoms. It was the posttraumatic self-analysis. Just as painful, but not debilitating if a context was established right away.

"Do you remember their faces?"

"No. I don't." He shifted again. "Darling. We're soldiers. We usually use tools that aren't as deadly as those we used on the island. When we do have to back up our convictions with force, it tests both our physical training and conditioning and our mental and emotional commitment to what we're doing." He didn't know exactly how to explain it, but he knew exactly what was going through her mind right now. "This is a tough time. There's a fine line between overemphasizing the importance of taking a life that's malevolent and devaluing life in general. We've seen desensitized agents and they're nearly as bad as the people we're fighting."

She sat very still. She heard and, more importantly, she felt every word.

He stared out at the blue sky.

"I want you to replay the scenes in your mind. Just once. If there's to be moral justification and ethical validation in what we do, then I ask you. Would you trade what we have here now, all those people back there for the lives we sacrificed last night and this morning? For that's what surely would have happened. If we would have waited. If we would have done nothing. If we would have stood back and not taken direct action they would be dead. Amy. Stuart. Fisher. Cliff. His family. The sleeping baby in seat 14D. The doctor. A future President…all the lives each of those people will touch and have an impact on. There is evil. We're its enemy. We're on the right side. We'll always value life, but sometimes we have to use our judgment as to which lives are more important. It's in the balance, my love. And we're the keepers of the scale. We took an oath. We made a promise. We are justice."

She got it. He really was a good person to talk to…to share this with. She did value life. These last few days, she didn't just stand on the sidelines while corruption or immorality or evil pursued its course. Looking out over the ocean, she processed what he said. She did replay her direct actions. Once. Then she conjured up in her mind the faces of the innocent. The scales were balanced. She could rest. Alex remained quiet, knowing this was a journey one took alone. Finally, she looked at him and nodded.

"It's gone, Alex," she said softly, but with finality and assurance. His hand was still on hers. She wrapped her fingers through his and was content to just feel his strength. These hands were not the hands of a killer. They were the hands of a defender.

He nodded back, knowing precisely what she meant. The ghosts of guilt and remorse were gone. He had banished his only a few moments before she brought it up. Putting his fingers through hers, he held on. It was important to remember what was essential and at the core of their purpose. They sat in a comfortable, companionable silence, enjoying the stillness, sensing the vibration of the engines, feeling validated by the hum of voices from the cabin. They were doing important work. And they were doing it together.

"Darling, before the doctor comes back, before we land," Alex looked down at her left hand. "I would really like to see the ring on your finger."

Smiling, she took it out of her pocket. "My talisman. It got us off the ground. We're in the sky. We're on the way home."

Taking it from her, he put it on her finger. It flashed in the sunlight. He saw her stare at it. There was none of the joy he saw on her face when he gave it to her the first time. He felt a pang of unease. Must be the pain, he thought. But she was in pain before, too. The ring seemed to take it away earlier, now it seemed to add to it. He looked down at her other hand poised gently over the throttle. Hell, she was in the cockpit of an airplane full of passengers, her copilot incapacitated. She had more than marriage on her mind.

Leaning over, he gave her a soft kiss. "Just to seal the deal." He looked at her and frowned. He saw none of her earlier enchantment.

"I love you, Captain." He waited for her to say something, but she just continued to stare at the bright lights inside the diamond.

Skye hadn't even heard him. She was flashing to some very unpleasant thoughts, feelings, and memories. She decided very deliberately to put them away for now. She had to get this plane safely on the ground. No time to think about other things. When Amy came in a few minutes later, Skye twirled the diamond to the inside of her hand, and Alex pulled back into his seat. He shook off the edgy feeling. The ring was on her finger. That made it official. Leaning his head back against the comfortable seat, he flexed his injured shoulder. He was shot, exhausted, hungry, and sore as hell. He looked over at his future bride…safe and on the way home. He'd never been happier in his life.

An hour later, Skye saw the first F16 fighter jet dispatched from Miami. She would have an escort until they landed. She would keep her plane and passengers safe by flying exactly the path Alex indicated to Jim, who had communicated it to the military. She smiled. Alex had told her that Fisher's grandma called the President Andy. That was comfort enough for her, but those fighters looked all business. She thought the passengers might need some reassurance, so she took the intercom and opened up the connection to the cabin.

"Ladies and gentlemen. You know who this is. I want you to take a look outside the windows. We have an escort. We're coming in without radios or other transponder signals. I don't need them to land, but we'll be unable to go into Dulles. Our escort is here for our safety and protection and to assure everyone we're coming home under our own steam. Perhaps if you wave and flash a few peace signs, they will understand we come in peace."

She could hear much laughter and movement. That should keep them occupied and their minds off the scary sight of fully armed F16's.

Skye shifted again, trying to find any kind of relief. She was sweating now and feeling more than a little nauseous. Alex had moved from concern to a burning anger. She was killing herself. He knew there were few alternatives, but she could have put the plane down an hour ago or more. They could have landed in Aruba, the Caymans, even the Bahamas, but Skye was as stubborn as she was valiant. She was going to take her plane home to the U.S. She knew her limits and would never endanger the passengers, so he had to trust her judgment.

He had been in contact with Jim and the team all through the flight and they had been busy. They decided to land the plane on a small airfield on Amelia Island off the northeast coast of Florida. It was long enough to land the jet and was not in a major news hub. There would be no cameras or videos allowed on the airfield. The family and friends were so excited about the news of the plane being in the air, they were willing to comply with any request.

Jim knew he wouldn't be able to keep a low profile on this event. It was already major news, but he wanted to do his best to protect his two agents. They would begin shuttling family and friends down to Fernandina Beach Municipal Airport within the hour. In addition, Alex owned a beachfront home on the island. It was secluded and private and had a state-of-the-art security system. A perfect place for Skye to rest, recover and hide out for a few weeks.

He made calls to Sloane and Hazel as well as his family. They all agreed to meet at the property rather than go to the airport. Sloane was the only one who knew he was calling from the cockpit. He told the others he'd received a report from the officials at the airlines and was taking a shuttle to the small airport to pick her up. He warned them in low tones what to expect when they saw Skye.

Alex talked openly to Dr. Lacy when Jim gave him clearance. The good doctor was delighted to make a prolonged house call, as he referred to it, and stay with Skye during her transportation to the estate. He also agreed, since he was retired and felt he owed Skye his life, to stay on throughout her recuperation. Using Alex's phone, he made all the arrangements for the transportation of medical supplies to Alex's estate and the use of the emergency room in a small medical facility on the island for both Skye and Stuart. Stuart remained unconscious and unresponsive.

"I want two ambulances at the airport," he said looking at Alex seriously, the phone in his hand. "One for Stuart and one for our intrepid pilot here. Two stretchers."

"Absolutely not. I forbid it," said Skye, frowning at him and interrupting his call. She wiped sweat from her forehead. She was beyond feeling, beyond exhausted. She was running on pure guts and grit. "I will not be taken out of my plane on a stretcher. You give me a shot for pain, then I'll walk out under my own power. This is my last flight and I'm not going to be carried out of it."

The doctor opened his mouth to argue, but shut it again when Alex shook his head. Shrugging, he requested only one ambulance and went to stand behind her like a sentinel. "At least let me take your pulse and temperature and give yourself some more of that oxygen."

Nodding, Skye held up her wrist. The doctor's frown deepened when he counted the heartbeats and read the thermometer. Looking over at Alex, he shook his head. He was about to make his opinion known again but Skye beat him to it.

"I still have fuel in my reserve tank, doctor. Trust me. I wouldn't jeopardize the passengers and crew out of stubbornness or misplaced bravado. I'll get us home. When we're on the ground, you can take over, but until then, this is my cockpit and I'm the law."

Alex shrugged at the doctor, turned and grinned at her. She had on a roguish, daring look she reserved for moments like this. He called it her daredevil, barnstormer look. Although he had observed her do it better, he was glad to see the attempt. She was in charge all right. She treated herself to more pure oxygen. It cleared her head, but also intensified the pain screaming through her body. Just when she thought she might actually scream herself from the agonizing throb in her side, she visually spotted what her instruments had been telling her was just over the horizon. A fresh wave of energy surged through her as she took the plane out of automatic pilot.

"There it is...Florida! We made it!" She grinned and looked at Alex. There was a gleam in her eye that was not from fever, not from pain. She was the adventurer, the victorious audacious pilot. As she did many times before, she reminded him of the daring aviatrix from the early years of aviation. She loved flying, not just being in the air, but driving the plane and feeling it respond to her direction. Through the agony, through the fear, through the anger, the pure thrill of having the craft under her and reacting to her touch was enough to get her to her destination and safely on the ground. Even though her body was wracked with aches and pains, her hands on the yoke were strong and steady.

Skye picked up the microphone for the intercom. "Ladies and gentlemen and crew of Flight 127, this is your captain. Florida is just ahead. I'll be beginning my descent, so if you will kindly take your seats and buckle in, we'll be on the ground soon." She had to take another breath to clear the emotion out of her voice. She needed to sound steady and in command.

"I want to thank you again for your collective courage and positive attitude through this difficult time. This kind of incident tests both bravery and resilience. If you ever wondered what you were made of, what you would do if your character and heroism were tested, you no longer have to speculate. You have a story to tell to your children and grandchildren. You will be able to tell them you were threatened, subjected to grave peril, and stood tough. You didn't lose your heads, you didn't lose your hope, you didn't lose your faith. The criminals who took our plane didn't know what they were getting themselves into when they hijacked us."

The passengers in the cabin looked at each other, many of them bringing tissues to their eyes.

"So now ladies and gentlemen and crew of Flight 127, please prepare for landing. We'll be touching down on Amelia Island in Florida in about ten minutes. We apologize for the delay and for the diversion into an alternative airport. Your friends and family will be there to greet you, as will representatives of International Airlines. They will work with you to get you to where you need or want to be. And kids...we're only about three hours from Disney World. Now might be a good time to make your move. I'll be working to get this plane down, so the next time we talk, it will be on U.S. soil."

Handing the microphone to Alex she settled into her landing posture as best she could. "Will you go get Fisher? I think he's earned a seat in the cockpit," she asked, focused on the instruments and satisfied with what they told her. She looked to the ground to confirm her rate of descent and location of the runway.

Alex nodded and returned in less than a minute with the beaming boy.

"Holy schnikies, Captain. This is mega, mega chilled. Wait 'til I tell my home team. They will flip. I wish the creepazoids hadn't taken my camera. To snap this would have been in the Milky Way. And look. The escorts are so close. I just decided what I want to be. Always thought I would be a teacher like my mom or an architect, like my dad. But not now. I've had an epiphany. I want to be a fighter pilot. Look at those guys flying those tanks. Rippin! Completely out of sight. I hope my grandma is down there when we land. I really want her to meet you."

Skye's mouth turned up and she even felt a bit better. "Look, Fisher. There's someone I want you to meet too. I think you would hit it off just perfectly."

"Not a girl, I hope." He snorted, his brilliant green eyes reflecting the contempt he had for anything female.

"I'm a girl," said Skye mildly, still smiling.

Alex looked back at him and smiled. "You may want to quit while you're only slightly in the hole on that one, kid. She may just lock you in the lavatories with the other chauvinists."

"You aren't a girl," insisted Fisher, his still-changing voice cracking under the weight of his enthusiasm. "You're a pilot. You wear a uniform. And you can kick the crap out of armed guards. Take the air and put it in the wind, Captain. You're only, like, a part-time girl. It's not your full-time job."

Alex actually laughed out loud and Skye chuckled then immediately regretted it as it ended in a wheezing spasm. The smile evaporated from Alex's lips as he watched her try to recapture her breath, holding her right side, each cough accompanied by a feeling of a knife to the side. It was so intense there were tears in her eyes. The doctor stood up but she waved him back.

"Strap in," she gasped. "I'm...I'm all right."

"I think maybe you should stop talking for a minute and allow Skye to catch her breath," said the doctor to Fisher.

"Consider my lips buttoned and sealed," he said cheerfully, unaware of the dire condition of his idol. He was blissfully oblivious to her situation. He knew she had been beaten and secretly thought it was the most radical thing he could imagine on the cool and courageous meter, but he didn't understand the amount of pain or dangerous consequences of her beating. So he excitedly looked around at all the outstanding instruments and the landmass getting larger in the windscreen.

It was all surreal to Skye. No copilot. Alex in the cockpit. She wasn't communicating with the tower to get her usual instructions. She was just flying in using her own discretion and her own instincts. She knew they had opened the airspace for her exclusive use and could see the runway in clear relief against the green of the surrounding countryside. She saw cars stopped on the road to look up at the spectacular sight of the hijacked plane returning home under its own power. Lining up the plane, she headed in. Her fighter escorts waggled their wings and pealed off.

"Whoa. Awesome!" Apparently the button had popped on Fisher's lips. "Sorry," he said, grinning. "That just slipped out."

Alex watched as Skye's hands moved confidently and automatically over the instruments. There was no hesitation to her swift, competent movements. She pulled back on the throttle and the plane smoothly responded. Magnificent, he thought, swallowing hard against the intense emotion that seemed to collect in his throat and move down his chest.

Skye put the plane down right in the middle of the runway, concentrating on the feel of the wheels touching the ground. There was barely a bump. She grinned broadly...she hadn't lost her touch. It was a sweet and gentle landing and she could hear the cheering from the back of the plane.

As she moved down the runway toward the terminal, she glanced over at Alex. Their eyes met in an intense connection. Glad to be alive. Glad to be together. Her eyes were watering from the emotion, the relief, and the ever-present pain, but the joy in them came through.

As pilot in command, she taxied the plane skillfully to just the proper angle in front of the terminal and cut the engines. For a moment, all was completely silent. Then the cabin erupted with sound. Talking, laughing, weeping, applauding, children scrambling. Parents directing. Seat belts clicking. It was all so normal.

Amy popped in to report that everything was running smoothly. Everyone was feeling charitable, helpful, and generous. Morale was high and the mood was festive. Excited to be home. Grateful to be alive. Thankful to the captain for their survival and liberation. There were tears, laughter, and general high spirits. Amy and her team of flight attendants prepared the doors and welcomed the crew rolling the stairway to the plane. The passengers were going to be walking in the sunshine across the runway to the terminal where they would greet their families and loved ones.

Back in the cockpit, Skye reached up and turned off all the controls and instruments. It was more habit than necessity since personnel from International Airlines would be taking possession of the aircraft as soon as the passengers were dispatched. She ran her hand over the beloved controls of her Boeing 767.

"My last flight for International. It was a hell of a trip." She sighed and looked at Alex with both elation and sadness etched between the lines of fatigue on her face. Turning, she gave him and his heart a wonderful gift. "It was nice we could make this last leg together."

He leaned over and touched her lips in a gentle, loving kiss and in a voice only she could hear. "A hell of a trip, my darling," he agreed.

"We'll celebrate later. Now you take care of yourself." He kissed her again.

They smiled at each other when they heard Fisher's snort of disgust.

"Absolutely bogus to the nth degree. Get a room and lock the door." He hadn't heard the words but that celebratory lip lock was a little too hot for the confined space inside the cockpit. Unlocking his seat belt, he stood up to stretch and yawn. Skye envied his ease of movement.

"Come here, Fisher," rasped Skye. When he came over, she unpinned her captain's wings and put them in his hand. His eyes nearly bugged out of his head.

"Until you get your own, you can have these."

For once, Fisher was speechless. But only for a heartbeat. "Wow! I know we'll be friends forever, Captain, but does this mean we're going steady or something?" His eyes flashed with mischief and gratitude as he looked at Skye, then slid his gaze over to Alex. He wasn't the least bit intimidated by the tall, commanding man with the bad attitude. He wiggled his eyebrows and said, "I don't see any wings pinned on you."

"Should look real good next to Dumbo," said Alex in a low menacing voice.

"That's Dopey," grinned Fisher, his eyes steady, wishing he could see behind the man's shades.

"I thought so too," responded Alex, glad the boy couldn't see the amused twinkle behind the sunglasses.

"See you soon, Fisher," said Skye, smiling, but unable to work up enough energy to laugh. Fisher disappeared through the doorway into the cabin to prepare to depart and meet his grandma.

Taking her left hand, he turned the ring around so that the diamond showed. "That, my boy, is going steady," he said softly, chuckling, now that it was just the two of them and the good doctor in the cockpit.

"My goodness, did you find that on the island?" asked the doctor.

Alex looked up at him. "Special delivery. We'll fill you in when you get official clearance."

Dr. Lacy just nodded. He was more interested in taking care of his patient than what she was wearing.

Skye removed her hand from Alex, not roughly jerking it away, but forcefully in a way that pulled more than her hand back...he felt her pulling herself back. He frowned, but he was just too tired and worried to think about it.

"We're safely on the ground, Captain, so now I'm in charge. Please take off your jacket and roll up your sleeve," said the doctor in a surprisingly commanding tone.

Skye looked at him, completely done in. She didn't think she would be able to comply with this simple request. Looking over at Alex she telegraphed her distress and he stood up to stand over her. "I can't," she whispered. "I can't move."

Alex gently pushed her sleeve up her arm, exposing enough flesh for the Doctor to insert the hypodermic needle. He administered the maximum amount of the painkiller right into her vein.

"There," he said, rubbing the spot with alcohol. "You should feel better within minutes. I'm going to see to the stretcher for Stuart." Skye's eyes closed as she sat still, listening to the sounds of departing passengers. It was a wonderful and familiar humming. A fantastic feeling.

"We didn't lose one, Alex. Not one," she said as she let her head rest on the back of the seat. Alex captured the single tear that slid down her battered cheek with his fingertips.

"No," he responded, never taking his eyes from her ravaged face, his heart full, his throat tight. "You did it, my darling. Now rest. Take care of yourself."

Skye took her first really deep breath in hours, already feeling the welcome relief of the painkiller. "Better," she said simply knowing she could at least move now. She'd be unable to get out of her seat without assistance but she knew Alex was there for her. Alex. He came for her...he was with her...they were home. She allowed herself to float on the cloud of blessed relief.

After the last passenger left, she opened her eyes. "Alex?"

"Yes, darling."

"Help me up, will you?"

Placing his arm gently around her waist, he slowly got her to her feet. She looked into his face and managed a smile. He still had on dark glasses, a hat, and an attitude...and a fine layer of island grime. Hopefully it would continue to keep people from making a connection between him and the polished Alex Springfield.

"When I get to the doorway, please let me make my own way. I want to walk off the plane under my own power," said Skye.

Even though he would have preferred to carry his wounded warrior from the scene, he knew she needed this. He respected her wishes, but was going to stay close. Very close. She knew that and it helped.

"I understand," he said.

Skye stood up straight, nearly moaned, but caught it in her throat. Swallowing hard she stood still for a moment while the cockpit righted itself. Then she smoothed the creases out of her uniform and patted her hair into submission. The ribs were protesting in a chorus of screeching pain, but Skye ignored them as best she could. Reaching into the pocket behind her seat, she took out her lipstick and a small hand-held mirror. Applying a coat of Luscious Rose, she was starting to feel human again. Then she put on her aviator sunglasses to cover the swollen and bruised eye and grabbed the captain's hat that Fisher had brought in earlier. This she placed on her head and positioned at the precise regulation point and angle. Alex thought she was just about the most glorious thing he'd ever seen and his pride was being crowded out by a full dose of lust. Beaten, battered, and bruised, she still managed to maintain both her dignity and her beauty.

She reached into the pocket again and brought out her dad's compass. He'd given her the love of flying, taught her all its valuable lessons, then after his death had been by her side every time she took to the air. With his compass near her, she could always feel him, sense his presence, hear his words. In her heart and mind she believed it always kept her safe, brought her home. One more time, it did its magic, she thought. Putting it in her pocket, she ran her hands over her seat, checked all the familiar instruments, turned, and was ready to leave her last flight as captain for International Airlines.

Alex kept his arm around her as she slowly made her way out of the cockpit and down the aisle. He could feel her body tremble and knew she was using the last bit of her willpower to stay erect. When they got to the doorway, he stood back. Her shadow, her guardian, standing behind her. Gingerly, she reached for the rail and stepped into the sun.

The passengers looked up as one. They'd been waiting for her, forming two lines on either side of the walkway from the bottom of the stairs to the doors of the terminal. They stared at the magnificent captain, valiant and heroic, noble in her straight, proud stance, and for a moment there was complete silence. Then the crowd erupted in loud cheers and applause. Skye's eyes filled with tears and she would have stumbled, but Alex discreetly placed his hand under her elbow.

"Steady, my love. Let them say thank you."

She nodded and smiled. Slowly, deliberately, she walked down the stairs. When she reached the bottom of the stairway, she shook hands and talked with each passenger and every member of the crew. She looked like a queen greeting her subjects. Never hurrying, always listening to the person who had her hand. No one was rushing to leave. They wanted to extend the moment...as if her touch was magic and her presence was enchanted. It was a flash of history and they would always be a part of it. Alex remained at her side, silent, impatient, feeling the tremors run through her body, but knowing he couldn't rush her. When it came time to say goodbye to her crew, the tremble became more pronounced.

"The party is still on," promised Skye. "But just like this flight, delayed a bit."

"Take care of yourself, Captain," said Amy, tears running down her cheeks unchecked. "I've never been so proud to be a part of a crew."

"Good bye, Amy. You're truly a credit to your profession. We'll stay in touch. Please don't expect to hear from me right away. I think I'm going to have to be down for awhile."

"We'll be expecting an invitation to a wedding soon."

Skye just smiled and nodded, hardly acknowledging the idea that there was to be a wedding soon. Alex noticed with a pang of uneasiness that she was backing away from the commitment she so clearly made when he had presented the talisman, her ring. The ring that was now turned back around, the diamond hidden in her palm. She was leaning on him, which was pleasant, but it was as if he really was a commando, a rescuer, not her lover and future husband. He reminded himself that for this audience, that was exactly what he was. It gave him some comfort. But there still seemed like a part of her that was very, very distant. The part that held her heart and soul, and it was moving at a rapid pace away from him. Then he admonished himself again. She was barely able to walk, why should she be thinking of marriage, her engagement, a wedding?

"Where's Fisher?" Skye asked, when the last person had been touched and talked to. They were walking alone through the terminal toward the exit, where the doctor would be waiting to transport Skye to the medical center in Alex's limo.

"I suspect he is halfway to Washington by now," Alex said in a confidential tone. "His grandma had one of the Joint Chiefs send a jet down to get him. She couldn't leave. She's coordinating the search for Terrin and getting the London connection cleaned up. Her contacts in South America have been invaluable, but most of them will only deal with her."

"Could we make that recuperation time start now?" asked the doctor testily as he came over to her. "Your car and driver are outside waiting. We'll be taking you to an emergency room, where I can treat you. We should have left an hour ago."

Skye's eyes started to glaze over as she looked at Alex. "Will you take me to your home on the beach after they look at me there?"

She went back to *your* home, not *our* home or just home, he thought with some frustration. It wasn't his imagination. She was pulling away from him again. He couldn't say anything however, when he saw the heightened color on her cheeks.

"Please. I don't want to be in a hospital again." There was something about the contrast between her tough looking sunglasses and uniform and the pleading tone in her voice that drained his frustration and fueled his concern.

"Of course, baby. Everything has been arranged." He removed her hat and kissed her forehead. He was alarmed at how hot it was. Removing her sunglasses, he saw the lack of focus in her brown eyes.

"Thank you." Her voice was raspy, hollow to her ears. A tear escaped and ran down her cheek. "I'm feeling a bit...a bit..." Then she couldn't even talk anymore. It was too much effort.

Alex had her out the door and could see his limo waiting by the curb. The media had been kept out of this portion of the parking lot completely. The story was a big one, but if Skye remained in seclusion for the next couple of weeks, their incredible account would be replaced by the next sensational story.

Duncan, Alex's young driver, held open the door. Not wanting to speculate why Alex looked like some movie villain, he recognized his boss's voice and that was enough. He'd never asked about any of his boss's activities, strange as they seemed sometimes. It was one of the reasons Alex trusted and relied on him. He also never asked about the lady's penchant for getting into serious...ah...difficulties. He knew about the hijacking, of course. And he knew his boss had disappeared for a few days. They were back and Duncan was glad to see them, but he was concerned about their general condition. Even though their actions were none of his business, the two of them were. He frowned at the state she was in, and his boss didn't look all that much better.

Just a few more steps, Skye thought, just a few more steps. One foot in front of the other. She could see the open door, the leather seats. She could see the end of her journey, the end of her obligation, the end of her ordeal. Looking up, she gave Duncan a weak smile. Why did he look so concerned? There was usually a wide grin for her on his beautiful black face. Must be the traffic or something. Why was he fading? Where was he going? And suddenly, she couldn't force herself to go on. Not another step, not another inch. She was empty. The reserves were completely used up.

"Alex," she whispered and he turned to her, alarmed at her fading and breathy voice. "Alex," she repeated and slowly started to collapse. Catching her and painfully holding her against his own battered chest, he carried her unconscious over to the car. Her head rested on his shoulder, her eyes were closed. He looked down to see her breathing had become very labored.

"Doctor!" he shouted and found that the man was right behind him. He could feel the wound on his shoulder tear open and the hot blood run down his side, but he didn't feel the pain. He was too intent on Skye to feel anything but alarm.

"To the hospital. Now!" said the doctor in an authoritative voice Alex hadn't heard before. The medical center was less than fifteen minutes away, but Duncan was there in five. Alex held Skye all the way and when they arrived at the emergency room door, he refused to place her on a gurney. Carrying her himself, he ignored his aching and bleeding shoulder...taking her directly into the room that had been prepared for her and laying her gently on the examining table.

Jim was there clearing the way, keeping the media uninformed. They hadn't found her yet. Admissions forms and requests were ignored. There would be no official records of her whereabouts or her condition. Alex stood back, but remained close, never taking his eyes from her, never moving. His job wasn't finished, his mission wasn't complete. He was sent to bring her home and keep her safe. Shaking off Jim's concern when he saw the wounded shoulder, he crossed his arms and ignored his own pain and exhaustion.

Skye was unconscious throughout the examination and knew nothing of this. She had a high fever, a punctured lung, multiple contusions, broken ribs and suffered from general exhaustion. Alex swallowed hard against the rage when he saw how her side had deteriorated.

"She took another hit after I saw her," said the doctor, appalled. "How did she stand the pain? A little more to the right and it would have collapsed her lung and there would have been nothing I could have done for her. She would have drowned in her own blood."

The words slammed into Alex. He thought of her lying on the bed, so still and pale. A little more to the right and he would have found her dead. She wouldn't have been lying here and he knew he wouldn't have been here either. He would have gone after Terrin, instead of the plane. As selfish as that sounded now, he was sure he wouldn't have been able to control his emotions and need for retribution. It made him sweat and he felt a wave of light-headedness. Bracing himself and gritting his teeth, he fought back the darkness. He would stay on his feet until she was out of danger. It was his job, his duty, his role. She was the hunter, he was the guardian.

A team of specialists worked on her for over an hour before they felt she was stable enough to move. Alex resisted Doctor Lacy's pleas to have her admitted and placed in a room. He'd promised her there would be no more hospitals. Jim concurred knowing that Skye would be more secure at Alex's compound. The doctor finally gave in to their combined resolve and went off to arrange for all the supplies he would need...where his patient went, he was going to follow. That was one argument he didn't intend to lose. When she was breathing better, he would take her to this man's home...whoever the heck he turned out to be. Diamond rings, Kevlar vests, machine guns, explosives. And the scary guy seemed to have lost his accent, too. Well, he didn't care much for any of that. His attention was focused on one thing...the patient. And she was a very, very sick young woman.

The doctor initially tried to fuss over Alex too, and to get the emergency room team involved in his care, but Alex shook his head. "We'll wait until we're home. I don't want anyone here to get a closer look."

Dr. Lacy nodded and gave up. He was very big on discretion. Alex already knew that Jim had checked out Livingston Lacy and would be administering an oath before the end of the day. Alex felt confident that the doctor would be able to treat him solo and was glad the field recruitment was going to allow the man to become part of their team. As soon as Dr. Lacy obtained clearance, they would be able to be more open around him.

Jim was reluctant to leave his two top agents and even more reluctant to leave his godchild, but he was needed to continue the coordination of all the details of the debriefing of passengers and crew. When Dr. Lacy told him Skye was not in any immediate danger, he decided he could get back to the plane. The doctor suspected her infection would deteriorate into pneumonia, but he was giving her intravenous antibiotics and to keep her stable.

Standing over his sleeping agent, Jim studied her face and touched her unbruised cheek. Leaning over, he softly smoothed the wet curls around her temple, then, as he did with every case she wrapped up for him, he whispered his pride and gratitude. She was her father's daughter all right...the daring Perry Madison's little girl had grown up and was now his. The pride he felt helped contain the anxiety.

"You did well, Special Agent Madison. Your father would have been proud." He thought she might have heard him on some level, because the small frown between her eyes relaxed and disappeared. Then he switched roles and kissed the fevered forehead of his beloved godchild. "You scared the shit out of me again, sweetheart. Another few years of my life just blew away like lawn furniture in a hurricane. You owe me now, honey. No more fooling around. Get well. You asked me to walk you down the aisle and I consider that a date."

Looking up at a smiling Alex, he recognized the signs of fatigue and pain around the eyes. He knew his other top agent was near collapse as well. "And as for you, Special Agent Springfield, I knew when you went in it was going to be perilous for you. From the preliminary reports it seems you will be getting another citation to add to your collection." He looked down at Skye, unconscious and bruised, but alive and back in their care. "But I think you got all the reward you need right here."

Alex nodded. It was all he had the energy for.

"And you got the men who did this?"

Alex nodded again. "Most of them…Terrin got away."

"Take care of yourself and heal up. We'll debrief when you're ready. Then we'll go after the one that got away." Jim put his hand on Alex's good shoulder and squeezed. His agent was fading away and the concerned fiancé was taking its place. Jim understood that, respected that. "Thanks for bringing her back, son. It feels inadequate to say well done, but I'm going to say it anyway. Well done, Special Agent. I think now I'll be able to breathe again."

Alex looked into the warm, compassionate eyes of his boss, less the Director of Intelligence now and more the surrogate father. His praise was far from inadequate, it warmed him. He both liked and respected this man. They maintained eye contact for a few more seconds, allowing all the thoughts to be communicated without being said. So was the way of two strong, commanding men.

Then Jim took one final look at the face of his special Special Agent and went to do his job. He wanted to reinforce the passengers' impressions while the experience was still fresh in their minds. He needed to get people to describe the man who aided in the rescue fairly consistently and he needed them to describe a man completely unlike Alexander Springfield. Little details would be planted in their minds. Jim was a master at integrating false impressions and memories into the real ones. Through subtle suggestion he could get people to admit to seeing pretty much what he wanted them to, within certain parameters.

Brown eyes, black hair, and the impression of a body much heavier, somewhat shorter were already there. He would have them remember the pronounced accent, perhaps Latino. Jim was extremely gratified that Alex had taken care of his own identity misdirection and disguise.

People's perceptions generally were both filtered and faulty. And their recollections were worse. Jim used this fact and did so very successfully. He wanted to add age to their collective memory of this man…someone in his low-to mid-forties would be good. Alex was a decade younger. And if Jim could get someone to remember a scar, say on his left cheek, a chipped tooth and a tattoo of an eagle on his wrist, all the better.

When Skye began breathing easier, Alex found a small pocket of reserve strength and carried her out to the car to a pacing Duncan. The doctor was close at his heels, tut tutting over Alex's lack of regard for his own injuries. How was the shoulder going to heal when he was straining it all the time? And it was bleeding again. He hadn't rested since he got off the plane…wouldn't even sit down. Foolish boy. All the medical supplies he needed were being delivered to his home and now the good doctor just wanted to get both his patients into a bed. For at least a week.

Duncan drove them quickly to Alex's estate. Skye was still unconscious, but the doctor assured Alex and the anxious Duncan that this was a good thing. He had her lying across the back under a soft blanket. Alex never took his eyes from her, but grabbed the opportunity to rub away some of the dirt and grime on his face and hands with the wet towels the doctor brought with him. He drank a gallon of bottled water and tried to work out some of the soreness in his back and legs. Duncan drove fast, knowing that they would be covered if anyone in law enforcement took exception with his driving.

Leaning over, Alex gently brushed back some stray curls from her face. It was like a miracle. When he came to in the bushes in the early hours before dawn, he wasn't even sure he would find her alive. Now they were in the back of his air-conditioned limo on their way home to sleep in the same bed. Together in a nice soft bed, with clean sheets and the smell of the ocean filtering through the windows.

Smiling, he looked at her bruised face. It would heal. His eyes felt like sandpaper and his shoulder was pounding with pain, but he couldn't relax…couldn't shake the image of her standing, gun in hand, taking shots at the hijackers. Bullets kicking up dust all around her. Damn she was a bold one, his intrepid pilot. He was grateful there were no holes in her.

Never taking his eyes from her face, he jerked in surprise when Duncan threw open the back door. Home already? He looked out at the luxurious ocean front mansion. Yes, that was his, all right. He hadn't noticed Duncan driving through the gated entrance. Of course that was probably because Duncan hadn't slowed down...he never did. He liked to play his brand of chicken with the gates. He would push the button on the dashboard, then punch the gas to see how close he could come to beating the pace of the ornate metal gates swinging open. Once in a while he caught a nick or a scrape on the side of the car, but since he was the guy who took care of all repairs, Alex let him enjoy his little pleasures.

Duncan held out his hand and Alex gratefully took it. Getting out, he straightened, and swayed just a bit. He shook his head to clear it, as Duncan laid his hand on the small of his back. He was just about at the end of his rope and his knees were becoming unsteady.

Duncan had been watching some of the early reports from several of the passengers on the small TV in the back of the limo when the Bossman and the Captain had been in the hospital. Apparently, there was a fierce and experienced commando who helped rescue them and they thought he'd been injured. Duncan saw the bulge of the bandages on Alex's shoulder and didn't need a calculator to add it all up. Duncan was proud that the boss trusted him to keep his secrets. He always had. He always would.

"Easy now, Bossman," Duncan said in a low voice. Alex tried to turn to reach in for his precious package, but Duncan gently pushed him aside.

"Please. Let me." Duncan, all 6'6" of him, nearly filled the back seat as he reached in and gently picked up Skye. The doctor was a little unsure of the giant, but it seemed as though Alex was okay with it so he didn't protest. He really didn't want Alex to carry anything right now anyway.

Duncan walked up the front stairs as Cynthia threw open the door with exclamations of both joy and concern. Alex had called her from the hospital so she was prepared, but the reality of seeing Skye bruised, deathly pale, and unconscious was shocking. Duncan quickly carried Skye up the sweeping staircase to the huge master suite on the second floor. Dr. Lacy followed him trying not to gawk at the fabulous foyer and luxurious house.

Cynthia pulled down the cover and fluffed the pillows. Duncan gently laid Skye on the bed and her eyes fluttered open as she sensed the end of her long journey.

"Alex?" His name came out in a breathy whisper and then she was out again. Alex's heart rolled in his chest as he, too, felt the end of the

174

nightmare. She was home. The woman who defined his happiness, his future was back in their bed. It gave him a few more moments of backbone as he felt the relief wash away some of the numbing fatigue. Somewhere deep inside there was a celebration going on and he felt the smile even though he was sure his mouth didn't move. She had called his name…and he was a happy man.

Cynthia shooed the men out of the room, even though one was Skye's lover and her boss and another was apparently a doctor. She picked a pretty cotton nightgown, knowing it would keep her cool during her fight with a high fever and helped a groggy and compliant Skye into it. Then she took down Skye's hair and brushed it out.

She smiled at the small, but sincere "thank you" that Skye mumbled as she sighed and laid back down. As soon as Skye's head hit the pillow, she was out again. Completely under. Cynthia looked down at the young woman who had captured the heart of her employer and tenderly kissed her hot cheek. She hadn't known Skye long, but she loved her.

"You enjoy your sleep. When you're feeling up to it, I'll make you pancakes," she whispered. Skye loved pancakes for breakfast and she most particularly liked Cynthia's pancakes. Cynthia unconsciously patted her heart. She hadn't taken a happy breath since the moment Alex had called her from the airport a few short days before. Now her dear Skye was home, sleeping between clean sheets. Lying there, she looked like a princess in a fairy tale. Beautiful, sleeping, and very vulnerable.

When the doctor and Alex came back into the room, Duncan followed Cynthia down to the kitchen to beg some snacks and to share the relief. She kept bushels of Romaine lettuce, baskets of broccoli, and tons of baby carrots just for him. He was a strict vegetation and never abused his body with unwholesome treats. His weakness for peanut butter cookies was their little secret and she had baked a few dozen just that morning. They talked about the doctor, the hijacking, the captain's heroic heart…and never brought up the fact that the boss looked like he was going for a brand new look. They both believed in discretion and wouldn't discuss the obvious.

Duncan had been Alex's driver and mechanic for years. He'd been a dropout street punk when Alex had befriended him…actually, when he caught Duncan in his garage hotwiring his antique MG, claiming he only wanted to take the old car for a joy ride. Alex was so impressed with Duncan's ability to get around his security system; he threw him the keys and told him that if he brought the car back, he would give him a job. If he didn't, he would consider it a learning experience and write the car off as a loss on his next tax return. Duncan brought the car back. It was over a week later, but the car was purring like a kitten. Since then, Duncan was a permanent, if unconventional, fixture on the grounds.

Duncan was huge, very dark-skinned, over 250 pounds, with long dreadlocks and a beautiful gold tooth that would flash every time he smiled. And he smiled a lot. To add to his arsenal, he liked tattoos, body piercing, and leather. On the other hand, he didn't drink, smoke, or do drugs of any kind. He considered his body a temple…well, more like a cathedral…a very large, Notre Dame type cathedral. He was a magician with anything mechanical and Alex relied on him heavily to keep everything running smoothly. He'd never been disappointed.

When Dr. Lacy assured himself that Skye was breathing well and the fever wasn't too severe, he turned on Alex.

"Okay, young man. I know you outweigh me, are 40 years younger, and have some kind of special training or whatever. But if you don't sit down right now and let me see to you, I'm going to take you down. Don't think I can't."

Alex looked down at the little man, then assessed how lousy he really did feel. He must look even worse. He thought all he needed was a shower, a shave to get this stubble off, and a bottle of strong shampoo to get the black out of his hair. But the adrenalin was gone, he hadn't eaten since, well, he couldn't remember when and he couldn't remember what. He was a little fuzzy on details right now and fading fast…actually everything was getting a little blurred, including the doctor. His shoulder was really beginning to pound and it seemed his head wanted to join the chorus. Looking at the doctor again he decided the little guy probably could take him down right now. So he sat.

"Take off your shirt." Alex thought it was a good suggestion, but his arms didn't. He just leaned his head against the back of his chair and was sound asleep when the doctor reached over and gently cut it off his patient. He took off the blood soaked bandages and inspected the wounds. The blood was running, but it was red and clear. He was proud of the work he did on the island, but he cleaned the wound again and did some stitching. Alex never stirred even when the doctor probed the larger exit wound in his back. The pain didn't make it through the healing fog of deep sleep.

"Damn fool. Doesn't even know when to drop. They're just alike. Good thing I'm here or they would both be out dancing." He administered another powerful painkiller into the thick, solid muscle of

Alex's upper arm, then went downstairs to supervise the unpacking of the supplies he ordered.

When Cynthia came in an hour later, Alex still hadn't moved. She put the sandwiches down on the table next to the chair, and covered him with a quilt. Touching his bandage, she noticed the other bruising on his chest. Shaking her head slowly, she looked over at the sleeping woman in the bed.

"You two are going to take years off my life with all these shenanigans," she said to her sleeping employer and his beautiful bride to be. She always called Alex's adventures shenanigans and now it seemed he was going to marry someone in the same line of work. Shenanigans. Unknown to her, she had been checked out by Jim many years before. She'd never taken an oath, she wasn't privy to all the secrets, but she was smart. And she was perceptive. Hard not to be when Alex's appearance changed like this. But she loved these two, so even though they were carving away at her natural life span, she would never leave them and would always make sure they had a warm, comfortable home to come back to.

Alex woke up a few hours later. The edge had been taken off his exhaustion and the painkillers had reduced the soreness in his shoulder. He looked down at himself and then over at the sandwiches. As hungry as he was, he wasn't going to touch food until after he scrubbed off the island. He stood up slowly and groaned, then went over to check on Skye. She hadn't moved. The doctor smiled reassuringly up at him.

"She's sleeping, Alex. It's the best thing for her right now." The doctor used his name. Jim must have gotten him all buttoned up. That was good.

"Jim's been here, huh?" asked Alex trying to stretch out some of the kinks and deciding he wasn't up for that level of torture.

"Yes," said the doctor. "He came in and made some comment about you sleeping on the job, then filled me in. I'm officially on your team. I must say, I'm thrilled. My retirement was a bit disappointing."

Alex just nodded. He hadn't taken his eyes off of Skye.

"And all those old scars? Are you going to tell me about those?" asked the doctor, looking at Skye's sleeping face.

Alex shook his head. That was another case, another time.

The doctor sighed. "Okay. I'm just glad I don't have to go golfing."

The house was a stately ten-bedroom mansion right on the ocean. There was a high fence surrounding the property and state-of-the-art security system. Few people knew about it since it was listed under a name Alex had picked at random. It was his safe house. A place where he could go to get away from everything. A secure place, out of harm's way. He brought his future wife here to recover, recuperate, and heal. He had a very strong feeling that it was not just her body that needed the secluded location and time away. There was something about her that was remote, changed. He would let her body mend, then confront the internal wounds when he thought she was ready. And he would import some reinforcements. He looked at his watch. They should be here any time. He needed to change his look before they did.

Alex took a bath when he was warned by the doctor to protect the healing wound in his shoulder. The hot water soothed his muscles and using a special shampoo, he washed the black rinse out of his hair. He soaped the tattoo on his arm and watched as it faded. Home…they were home. Looking out the window at the ocean, he replayed some of the last few days. Then he shook his head. Plenty of time to debrief later. He just wanted to enjoy the little pleasures. Soap. Hot water. The soothing bubbles of the Jacuzzi. Closing his eyes, he fell asleep again.

CHAPTER 12

Sloane and Hazel arrived a short time later. Anxious to see Skye, they tiptoed into the huge master suite to touch her fevered forehead and kiss her hot cheeks. Alex had dragged himself out of the tub and was there to meet them. He felt like and looked like Alexander Springfield again. Casually dressed, his loose shirt covering the bandages on his shoulder. Sloane was the first to notice the ring. She now had clearance, but Hazel did not so the elderly woman assumed he put the ring on her finger when the plane landed.

"Hot damn," said Sloane. "You gave it to her, Alex! I knew you would! Did she like it? Of course she did. She has it on, doesn't she?"

"Yeah," Alex said remembering her reaction, wishing he could express in words how it felt to have her look at him with such love. Such trust. Of opening herself up completely and handing him the source of her existence.

Aunt Hazel looked down at the ring. She didn't want Sloane and Alex to see the tears so she threw on her sunglasses. "Cri-yi Diddly. There's a blinder. Why didn't you just go out and brand her, son. Couldn't you find anything bigger? It'll make her look like a lighthouse. Tall as one. Now she has a beacon. Don't let her stand on the beach with that, boy, or we'll have ships going aground."

Hazel was particularly stunning in an array of beads, bangles, and stars. She admitted to being 80 and was all of five feet. She was wacky and loving and hadn't known anything about how to raise children when she came to live with Sloane and Skye 14 years before. Sloane always said she raised Hazel, not the other way around, but that was an old debate. Hazel loved her girls with a ferocious passion and was one of the reasons they were both accomplished and unorthodox. Today, she was wearing something tilted on her head and Alex couldn't determine if it was supposed to be a bird or a plate of Fettuccini. She had on a green multi layered blouse and matching full skirt. Brown cowboy boots completed the ensemble.

"We call it her Christmas tree look," Sloane said in a low tone. "All she needs is lights and people would start throwing presents under her skirt."

As if sensing her sister and aunt, Skye's eyes slowly came open. She was so sick and so tired; she could hardly keep them that way. Sighing, she wanted to just sleep for a week. Turning her pain-glazed eyes to the two faces of her childhood, she tried to get them to focus.

"Hi," she smiled weakly. It was so good to see them.

"You're late," said Hazel, suspiciously wiping her eyes. "Ruined a perfectly good party."

Skye shifted. She felt so weak. Damn, she hated that. "I see you're still dressed for it," she said softly, her eyes glowing with love. "I like the hat."

"It's not a hat, love. Some bird landed on it and just decided to stay for the summer. It was hot and wanted to enjoy some h'air conditioning."

Skye smiled. Her eyes were tacking, but not focusing. Her breathing was labored and there was a soft rattling sound coming from deep in her chest.

"Somewhere on this globe, every ten seconds, there's a woman giving birth to a child," said Hazel.

"She must be found and stopped," replied Skye softly, beginning to drift back into sleep.

"Have you heard of the upcoming Schizophrenics' Convention?" asked Hazel.

"Anybody who's everybody will be there," mumbled Skye with her eyes closed.

"You don't have to agree with me." One more test, thought Hazel.

"But it's quicker," said Skye as she went back under. Hazel leaned over and kissed her treasured niece's hot forehead.

Straightening, she looked at Sloane and Alex and grinned broadly. "It's called Aunt Hazel's test of brain function. She'll live. And now, young man," said Hazel as she turned to Alex. "What about you? You look like shit. I know you were worried, but did you have to let yourself go like that?" She saw the circles under his eyes and something else. Pain? Well he was in love with her niece and very empathetic, so it probably was a lot of pain.

"I feel great, Hazel." His eyes slid to Skye, as they did nearly every minute he was in the room with her. "Your eye sight is failing."

"I know bags when I see them. I look at them every morning when I stare in the mirror and those under your eyes are doing more than giving you that sexy sleepy look."

"Why don't we let them rest?" laughed Sloane. She was dying to hear everything, but she knew she had to wait.

"Sure. Dandy idea. Hey Alex, why are lawyers like nuclear weapons?"

"If one side has one, the other side has to get one," he responded easily. He was always getting emails from his dad, who was also an attorney, with one lawyer joke or another.

"Why does California have the most attorneys, and New Jersey have the most toxic waste dumps?"

"New Jersey got first pick."

"What do you have when a lawyer is buried up to his neck in wet cement?"

"Not enough cement."

"If you drop a snake and an attorney off the Empire State Building, which one hits first?" Hazel thought one more should do it.

"Who cares?" whispered Skye in her sleep. Alex, Hazel, and Sloane looked down at her, then burst out laughing. It felt so good.

Just then Dr. Lacy came into the room. He frowned at them. Laughing in a sick room, indeed. Hazel took one look at him and straightened her hat. "Helllooo handsome," she said under her breath. "Who is that hunk?"

Alex looked over at Dr. Lacy who just nodded absentmindedly and walked over to the bedside table to check on all the medications. Alex was quite sure no one had ever called him a hunk before.

"The name's Dr. Lacy. He is a bachelor." Alex thought a dose of Hazel might be just what the doctor needed. Hazel, a gunshot wound, and a hijacking in the same week. The man might need a pacemaker to get through the cumulative shock of it.

Hazel said to Sloane. "Unpack my bags, girl. I'm staying for a week. You know I like them young and sexy." She walked over and touched the doctor's arm. He raised his head, then looked absolutely terrified. Something to build on, thought Alex and smiled as the doctor seemed to forget every word he ever learned as Hazel began her assault.

That night was their first in this bedroom, in this house. He thought about giving her privacy, maybe staying in one of the other bedrooms, but he wanted to be near her and have her know he was there. Besides, the bed was huge. She could have plenty of healing space. There was also something inside him that wanted to establish the habit of being in her bed at night. The doctor discreetly excused himself after administering the evening's medication obviously assuming they were going to sleep together.

They were alone. For the first time since their return. The house was quiet. The sound of the surf outside was a comforting backdrop to the rising moon and lengthening shadows in the room.

Alex struggled with the pillows, trying to get into a comfortable position. He was freshly stitched and it gave him the itches as well as the aches. The chest bruises were deep and uncomfortable, but that was minor. Reminded him he was still alive. The doctor would check on him when he made his regular visits to Skye, but he felt he would be back in excellent form in a week.

Alex, Sloane, Connie, Duncan, and Hazel had been watching CNN since early evening. The accounts of the hijacking and subsequent escape from the island were dramatic and fairly vague. The passengers didn't know much...didn't see much. Alex filled in what he could as both he and Sloane reinvented the truth.

Stuart called and was doing very well. He would be in the hospital overnight and wanted to stop by and see Skye before he flew back to Washington D.C. for debriefing. He was itching for a fight with one Frank Sills, CEO of Astron, Corporation. Mr. CEO had been arrested in mid tirade right in front of the cameras of CNN. Alex was planning to add his considerable influence to the fight, as well. Stuart would be over the next day for a visit and a strategy session.

Alex shifted restlessly and thought of the week ahead. After an operation of this magnitude, there would be reports, debriefings, and lots of paperwork. He and Skye would have to give detailed statements to various agencies in the intelligence community. Terrin was still out there and that was a concern. A lot of loose ends. Looking over at Skye, outlined in the moonlight, he didn't care about any of them. All that could wait.

Now that it was over and they were sleeping in their bed by the ocean, with cool breezes coming through the French doors, the darkness surrounding them, he allowed himself to fully feel the impact of his emotions. Another near miss. He almost lost her again. His hands shook a bit as his heart raced with relief. He'd held all his fears in check while there was work to be done. He could ignore the dread when direct action was possible. But now...God. So close. So deadly.

When he looked back that morning at the explosion that rocked the hangar, he realized how close he'd come to losing her, despite their hard work back here. What if they'd decided on a different course of action?

He'd pushed hard to go in, against the advice of the strategists and the wishes of the State Department. Only Jim and Amanda had pushed with him. They were the ones who ultimately got him to the island...and just in time. If they would have hesitated, taken a safer, more conservative course of action, he would be alone tonight. Really, completely, forever alone. Breaking out in a cold sweat, he had to work hard to control his breathing.

Getting up, despite his fatigue and discomfort, he paced the floor. He had to get this pent up fury, frustration, and anxiety out of his system. He remembered sitting in the airport four days ago with a ring in his pocket and flowers in his hand, waiting for Skye to arrive. Filled with anticipation and excitement. Happy. Exhilarated. She was supposed to step off the plane and into his arms. It seemed like a lifetime ago.

Walking over to her, he stared at her sleeping face. Reaching out, he gently touched it. It was bruised, her eye was swollen, and her breathing was shallow and labored. It moved him as much as it distressed him to see her so wounded. The bruises and injuries were the result of her bravery and courage. Would he have her be less bold? Would he have her be less daring? He couldn't answer that. It was so much a part of what she was. Of who she was. He listened to the surf crashing on the sand. Could he stop the tide? No.

His troubled mind fired snapshots of the last 36 hours. He saw her standing defiantly with her crew, unafraid; her eyes shining with love when he gave her the ring; lying as quiet and pale as death on the bed in the room with the broken window; running toward armed men with an assault rifle as bullets were whizzing by her; tossing him the man with the snake tattoo and then turning, trusting him to do his job and watch her back; then flying home, shifting in her seat trying to get comfortable, not giving in to a debilitating pain; picking up her father's compass, walking through the passengers, giving each of them a piece of herself; fainting into his arms when she could go no further. He hoped he would always be there to catch her.

The passengers aboard Flight 127 were alive for one reason and she was sleeping in his bed. If there had been any other pilot on that flight, the friends and family who stood to greet the passengers this morning may never have found out what happened. He loved her, but more than that he was in awe of her. He looked at her with both love and admiration. Sometimes he couldn't believe she was his. That she gave herself to him. He wanted to hold her and touch her and make love to her so badly. But he would wait and in the meantime he would keep watch.

His body started to shake from exhaustion so he finally gave it up and got back into bed. He took one last look at her face, pounded a few pillows into submission, laid back, and was almost instantly asleep. On a very basic level, however, he was still listening, ever alert to any changes in Skye's breathing.

Alex's eyes came open and for a moment he had to lie still to determine why he had come so suddenly awake. He looked over at Skye. God it was so good to be able to just turn his head and see her. The night-lights cast a glow and he could see her frowning and shifting. She was restless, which was surprising, considering how many drugs she had in her system. He looked down at her left hand. The ring sparkled, even in the low light of the room.

Suddenly her eyes opened. She moved her head. Even that bit of motion hurt and she softly moaned.

"Alex?" she whispered. Her hands moved and she seemed agitated. "Are you awake?"

He moved closer and kissed her forehead. It was too warm, but he was relieved somehow that she had assumed he would be in her bed. She looked at him for a long time. Her face was expressionless. Something inside Alex shifted. He didn't like the blank stare, the lack of animation.

"Are you okay?" she asked.

"Yes, darling."

"Is Stuart okay?"

"He's nearly fully recovered."

"Am I okay?" He smiled down at her. So direct, yet third in line.

"You will be. Do you want me to hold you?" asked Alex, anticipating her move into his arms. She'd made a habit of coming to him when she needed comfort. She called it her safe place.

Looking up at him, she hesitated. That small pause hurt worse than the bullet in the shoulder. Before she could answer, she sighed, her eyes went closed, and she was back under again.

What was that all about, he thought. He lay in the dark for a long, long time. This was the time to be rid of his anxiety. To celebrate. Why did he feel apprehensive? He looked down at Skye. Something pulled at him. He would figure it out. Later. He rearranged the pillows again and tried to sleep.

The doctor entered the room in the night and checked on both his patients. Alex came immediately awake and the doctor answered the question he could see was foremost on his mind. Her temperature was up, but not dangerously so. While he wouldn't declare Skye out of the woods, he whispered to Alex it would only be a matter of days before he could.

Just before daybreak, Skye moaned and opened her eyes. There were tears on her cheeks. She raised a shaking hand and brushed them away. Must be the drugs, she thought. The edges of something monstrous were lurking just beyond her consciousness.

She felt Alex stir.

"Skye. You okay?" He had felt her jerk awake and assumed it was pain. "Shall I call Dr. Lacy?"

"No," she whispered. Talking in the dark always seemed to inspire whispers. "What time is it?" She felt him shift.

"A little after 4:00 a.m."

"Are you sleeping?"

"Not at the moment."

"Would you do something for me?" asked Skye.

"Anything."

"Does this swanky room come with a terrace?"

His Skye was peeking through. He smiled.

"It does."

"Does it have one of those really posh lounge chairs like we had in London?" They'd spent one of their first nights together in a lounge chair on a terrace...at least part of a night.

"I ordered them special."

"That's the ocean I hear, isn't it?"

"I ordered that special too."

"I want to watch the sun come up."

"You do? Okay...who are you and what have you done with Skyler Madison?" Skye had seen many sunrises in the cockpit, but she rarely saw one by choice on the ground. Morning was not her favorite time of day. She always said she was living in the wrong time zone.

"I kicked her out of the bed a few hours ago. I wanted her spot," she said, her voice getting a little stronger.

"Ah."

She smiled. "And did you order the white Gardenias?" They were her favorite flowers. Alex had ordered a room full so she could wake up to their lovely fragrance and feel at home. Since she had consented to marry him, he sent them to her every day, wherever she was.

"That would be me," admitted Alex.

He got up painfully on his side of the bed. He had on only a pair of old sweatpants. Skye could clearly see the outline of the bandage on his tanned chest and immediately regretted her request. He'd been through a great deal on the island too and needed his rest.

Coming over to her side of the bed, he stretched gingerly, testing the range of motion on his injured shoulder.

She tried to get up on her own, but wasn't too successful.

"Wait, darling," he said. "Don't try to do that without me."

"But your shoulder," she said. "I shouldn't have bothered you."

"Is there someone else in this room?" he asked.

"No."

"Is there someone else you'd rather help you?"

"Besides Ewan McGregor?"

"He's in the guest room."

"Don't wake him."

"Then I'm it, my love," said Alex. He threw the covers back and reached over to pick her up.

"No, Alex. Just help me. Don't pick me up."

"Darling, when you're in my arms, I feel no pain." When he did pick her up, that wasn't entirely true.

She gave a sharp intake of breath as she got a pretty substantial shot of pain herself. He did the same thing as his stitches reminded him of their existence.

She rested her head against his good shoulder and chuckled. "So much for the pain-free argument."

"At least we can share the experience."

"There's that."

Skye watched the sun come up from the cradle of Alex's arm. She couldn't turn into him like she used to. She couldn't turn at all…she was far too stiff and sore. So he just snaked his good arm around her shoulders and she rested her head against him.

He'd fallen back to sleep. She looked up at him. No wonder. He had no sleep for days, and then he got shot and lost a lot of blood. In the light of predawn, she saw the large purple bruises on his chest for the first time. The Kevlar saved his life, but the bullets still had quite a punch.

One was right over his heart. God. What if he hadn't protected himself? The outcome would have been exactly how she thought it had played out originally. It froze her. She remembered the nightmare now. What had woken her up. The monsters. Come on sun, she thought. She was always able to function when the sun scared the monsters away. She started to shiver. It hurt her ribs so badly she had to bite her lip to keep from whimpering. Tears started sliding down her cheeks. Finally, she couldn't hold it back anymore, she moaned.

Alex's eyes flew open. He looked over at Skye curled up at his side, shivering violently. "Shit, Skye," he said and gently pulled his arm out from around her. Hurrying into the bedroom he pulled blankets off the bed. He hadn't thought it was that cold, but then he didn't have a fever. When he came back out Skye was gasping for air, which absolutely terrified him. She couldn't cough without waves of excruciating pain and she couldn't clear her lungs without coughing. It caused such tension in her chest that she passed out. At least that stopped the brutal trembling.

Wrapping her in blankets, he carried her back into the bedroom and called Dr. Lacy. Then he held her, talking to her in a gentle soothing voice, telling her she was going to be all right. He could feel her labored breathing through the layers of blankets and he found it hard to breathe himself. Her color was bad and she didn't respond when he whispered her name. He was scared witless by the time the doctor came hurrying in.

Dr. Lacy got her stabilized with an injection to help her breathe. He was alarmed by the spike in her temperature and told Alex that if it didn't come down within the next few hours, he was taking her to a hospital. He started giving her intravenous antibiotics again, diagnosing a case of aggressive bacterial pneumonia. Alex refused to leave but the doctor insisted Hazel and Sloane keep their visits short. He stayed with Skye until the late afternoon when she finally came around. She was still feverish and achy, but she wasn't in crisis anymore. Alex was sitting in a chair near the bed and watching her when her eyes came slowly open. She looked right at Alex, then at the sun pouring in from one of the windows.

"I think I missed another sunrise," she said, annoyed at the raspy quality of her voice.

Dr. Lacy took her temperature. "Much better," he said. "Are you feeling more comfortable?" he asked solicitously.

"Yes. I think so."

"That's good, my dear." Then he let loose and scolded for a full twenty minutes. She shouldn't be out of bed. Relapse possible. She had pneumonia. A real possibility of hospitalization. Pneumothorax still a real threat. Remarkable recuperative powers, but still human. What were they thinking? Could have re-injured herself. Should have used her head. She was not out of danger. He was appalled.

It made Skye wish she hadn't opened her eyes. She looked over at Alex and gave her eyes a little roll.

187

"And how did she get out there?" asked the doctor.

"I carried her," said Alex bravely, because he knew he was next.

"You did what? I know this lady is skin and bones, but skin and bones weigh something you know. Could have pulled out your stitches. You were shot, young man, not hit with a stick...and those chest bruises aren't just for show. They go deep. I told you that you weren't supposed to lift anything heavier than a loaf of bread and boy," he pointed at Skye. "That's no loaf of bread." He went on for another ten minutes. Alex considered himself lucky.

"Am I going to have to climb into that gigantic bed with the two of you and make sure you behave?"

That did it. They both solemnly promised to exercise better judgment.

"Now you." He pointed a finger at Alex. "You get back into that bed and don't move for at least four hours. Order up some food. Lots of it. And be sure to stay on your side of the bed."

Then he left to call in more prescriptions.

"I guess he told us," her lips quivered.

"You don't look too contrite, now that he's out of the room."

"I just had a flash of him lying right there...between us. I wonder if he wears pajamas?" asked Skye.

"I think he sleeps in a chair, in his clothes. He sure got here fast."

"I would laugh, but it's too painful. A loaf of bread?"

"Any way you slice it," quipped Alex.

They looked at each other.

"Just loafing around." They said in unison and smiled together. It was pretty lame, but then they both were less than 100%.

Within minutes, Cynthia flew in with a tray filled with pancakes and the daily newspapers. Skye and the story of her heroic return were all over the headlines. Alex was described in a variety of interesting ways. One passenger was sure he was one of the hijackers so smitten with the captain that he turned on his former colleagues and helped Skye fly to safety. The eagle tattoo and scar were noted and confirmed by several different passengers. The man was deadly and greatly feared. He was also admired and called a hero. The two heroes sat in bed, surrounded by their daring story and faced another angry tirade.

Cynthia put her hand on her hips and gave them a piece of her mind as well. They were to stay in bed for the rest of the day and the next. And they were to eat all the pancakes, every crumb. Poor Skye missed her breakfast but she wouldn't miss her favorite breakfast food. She watched over them as they gamely ate. Skye could do little more than pick at the food, but she made yum yum sounds often enough to satisfy Cynthia. Alex liked the pancakes pretty much, but liked the show even better.

When Cynthia left, Skye looked at Alex from her side of the bed. She was drinking hot tea and honey. Alex looked at her from his side of the bed. He was drinking hot coffee.

"Goodness. All this bed time and I'm afraid there's little I can do besides drink tea." Her voice was so raspy, it was nearly gone. And her energy was beginning to flag as well.

"We'll have plenty of time for quality bedtime later."

"Is that what you call a bedtime story?"

"Absolutely," said Alex.

Skye coughed and her eyes watered from the pain. Her cup rattled and she wheezed in another breath.

"Darling, I'm sorry. I shouldn't have carried you out there. The doctor did say you weren't to be moved."

"I just wanted to see the sun, Alex. I wanted to see it come up. It's like I needed the light. It was so dark in here." Out of the blue her mood changed. Tears were running down her cheeks. That alarmed Alex more than her elevated temperature. He put down his coffee and scooted over. He took her cup away from her so she wouldn't spill hot liquid all over her hands.

"I'm sorry." Skye wiped at the tears. "It must be the drugs. I want off of them as soon as possible." She took a deep breath and immediately regretted it. "Damn. I can't even take a deep breath."

Alex smiled and kissed her cheeks, then her lips. "I love you." She didn't move. Alex waited, then frowned. No response.

"Darling, what is it?" He felt there was more to her unreceptive behavior than her injuries, as serious as they might be.

"I just hate being sick," she griped.

Alex kissed the tip of her nose. "I'll fix it."

"The sick part?"

"No, the seeing the sunrise part."

And he did. Later that evening when Dr. Lacy went downstairs for a rest, Alex called Duncan to come to the room.

"You're looking more like yourself, Bossman," said Duncan, smiling broadly. He was sure his employer had a hand in bringing the plane back, but he would never mention it. "Where's the captain?" he asked with concern.

"Bath stuff," said Alex.

"Ah. The real medicine for the ladies. That will perk her right up. The doctor was up here a long time this morning and Ms. Cookie was in a tizzy. Ms. High Pockets and Ms. Brainchild were pacing a hole in the stone terrace. You doing something stupid in here?"

"Do you ever forget you work for me?"

"Every day but payday, Bossman."

"When is the next one?"

"Why that would be Friday," answered Duncan.

"Are you sure?"

"You terminating my employment, Bossman?"

"I can't now. The captain has taken a shine to you for some reason."

"Must be my natural charm."

"No doubt. Would you do her a favor?"

"She need a kidney?"

"No." Alex had to laugh. "Something heavier." He looked at the huge bed. "You may wish it was only a kidney."

With Alex assisting as best he could with one arm, Duncan shoved the bed so that it faced the French doors. When Alex opened them, there was a perfect view of the ocean.

"That will help heal her," said Duncan. He had seen her condition the day before and was worried.

Alex smiled. "I think so, too."

Duncan stuck around for a few more minutes, re-arranging the furniture and moving some other pieces around. When Skye emerged from the bathroom on Sloane's arm, she looked fresh and beautiful. Her hair was piled high and she used cosmetics to cover the bruises. There wasn't much she could do about the swollen eye. They'd iced it, but it was going to have to come down on its own. She put on a pair of light yellow rimless sunglasses to hide the eye while allowing maximum light. She was dressed in a long purple terry cloth robe and because it was from Hazel, there were very large, jumping, gray porpoises all over it. Alex was partial to the porpoise jumping into her cleavage.

"Lucky fish," said Duncan in his low rumbling voice as he carried a huge vase of Gardenias to a side table.

"Don't make me have to hurt you, Duncan."

"I'm real scared, Bossman."

Skye looked at the bed, then at the open doors, then at the ocean beyond. Alex figured Duncan had stuck around for just this moment. There was such a look of genuine delight and gratitude on her face; both men were humbled by it. It was a simple gift, but she looked like she'd just been presented the crown jewels.

"The best medicine," she said, looking at the two men. "I'll heal twice as fast now." And she meant it.

Then she crooked her finger at them. They dutifully lined up while she gave them each a kiss on the cheek.

Duncan beamed, then presented Skye with a white gardenia he'd hidden behind his back. She gave him a brilliant smile, a kiss on the other cheek, and went to add the bloom to one of the several vases around the room.

"Pure sugar," Duncan said rubbing his cheek.

Alex looked at him and said in a low tone, "yeah, well just remember, the sugar bowl is all mine."

"Don't make me have to hurt you, Bossman," said Duncan.

"I'm real scared," said Alex.

"I got a real pretty smile for that little flower," Duncan said, a chuckle rumbling in his chest.

"I gave her the whole bouquet," said Alex, looking at him, raising an eyebrow and letting the implication hang in the air.

Sloane and Skye thought they were both daffy.

When Hazel came in later for a visit, she stopped and looked at the location of the bed. Skye was sound asleep again. Alex was lounging in a chair next to the bed, working on a laptop computer. He still had a day job and he needed to get some contracts drafted. He looked up and smiled. Hazel had decided to go for the Florida look today. Florescent pink flamingo earrings accented her bright blue caftan.

Setting his laptop aside, Alex went to sit down on the bed next to Skye. He liked to touch her; to reassure himself that she was breathing okay and it had been almost ten minutes since the last time he took her hand. Hazel smiled fondly at him.

"You move this bed or were you two shagging so hot and heavy that it hopped on over here?"

"She woke up early this morning and wanted to see the sun come up over the ocean," explained Alex.

"Our Skye? Are you sure there wasn't a switch on that island...you know like one of those cloning experimental things?" Hazel loved conspiracy theories. She truly believed that Elvis was alive and living in seclusion in the Canadian Rockies.

Alex smiled. "My reaction exactly. But it was her and it seemed important. With the bed this way, she'll be able to see the sunrise by just opening her eyes." He smiled and leaned over to kiss her cheek. He couldn't help himself. The cheek was just lying there, exposed and soft and…he found himself swallowing a powerful hit of desire.

Hazel usually caught things like that and had something to say, but her brow was furrowed with thought…and memory.

"Was she like almost obsessed with it? Like it was a needful thing?"

Alex dragged his eyes away from Skye's face. "That almost perfectly describes it…why?" Her expression of anxiety, so uncharacteristic of her, caused him to be more than a little uneasy.

"It's happened before Alex…twice."

"Oh hell," said Alex, sickened by the thought of Skye in misery. Twice. He understood immediately. Two horrific traumas in her life, both shattering her heart. "Do you think what happened on the island reopened something?"

"More like closed it up, Alex, although I don't know why it would. It wasn't like you were in any danger or anything."

"Tell me about before," he said, absentmindedly rubbing the bruises on his chest. That was all there was on the island…danger.

"She's not afraid of the dark. Skye has never been afraid of anything according to my recollection. It's what happens to her at night, when she sleeps. The nightmares were horrible, Alex. You can't imagine. She would scream in the night and wake up sobbing. Came to a point where she wouldn't sleep hardly at all. In the mornings she would be absolutely fine. The sun seemed to represent more than light…it was kind of a reprieve. She needed to see the sun come up. I would find her sometimes on the porch roof outside her window. It faced the east. She would have her blanket and sleep out there so she could feel the sun's first light." Hazel went over and touched Skye's cheek.

"We all heal in different ways, dear. Skye finds things that work for her. She is wise and brave and smart. Daylight has always been her refuge. She was always more controlled after her parents died, but in the daylight she would laugh and smile and be…well happy, I guess. She was too plucky and spirited to let the nightmares have her days. But the nights, Alex. She suffered so." Hazel shook her head and sighed.

"I'll tell you, though, she will not open up. Not to you, not to anyone. We sent her to therapists after she saw her parents burning alive right in front of her. She babbled platitudes to them and they thought they were helping her cope. They had no idea she was taking on the demons by herself. Then after Jeff, she didn't even pretend to talk with anyone, she just closed up. She is someone who fights alone. Everything I'm saying to you I figured out on my own. I put it all together. I didn't destroy all of my brain cells in the 60s, you know. The price she pays for not allowing her nights and her anguish to take her over...well, you know her iron will. You'll need to stick to her like glue. Don't let her push you away, because a part of her will want to push hard. She will try to fight it herself, but even this dear girl has her limits." Hazel shook herself and looked around. "And I think the bed is real nice here."

Just then, Sloane came sweeping in to check on Skye. Alex looked into Hazel's eyes and she saw what she needed to see. He would be patient. He wasn't going anywhere. Alex looked down at his future wife. And neither was she.

CHAPTER 13

Skye hardly stirred for the next few nights and days. Her body shut down for repairs and the doctor was satisfied with her continuous improvement. When she was awake, she begged to talk with friends and family and managed to touch base with nearly everyone who had placed a call, or sent a card, flowers, or email.

Alex kept a close eye on her, not wanting her to exhaust herself. But she would defy him and push the limit, sometimes drifting away in the middle of a conversation. Alex's mother called his cell phone one afternoon, alarmed because Skye hadn't responded to a question. When he checked on her, he found her fast asleep with the phone near her ear. He picked up the receiver, nibbled the ear, got a snarl from her, backed off, and told his mom that it must have been a boring conversation. She begged to differ. They had been chatting about guns. They had been talking about the SIG-552 Commandoes and the more traditional AK-47's used on the island and were comparing their relative efficiency. Alex just shook his head.

His mom was a Chicago cop and his future wife was a special agent. He almost asked her why they didn't talk about normal things like shopping, clothes, and the state of her face, but caught himself just in time. When the women in your life were armed, you didn't say foolish, chauvinistic things.

On the morning of the fifth day, Skye found herself alone in the bedroom propped up on a dozen pillows. She felt better now and she was bored. Alex was out, Sloane was on a conference call with her dissertation committee, and Hazel was out gathering shells. Skye could only imagine what Hazel was going to make with them. She and Sloane better get prepared for seashell accessories for their birthday and holiday gifts this year. She could imagine the seashell purses, perfectly matched with the seashell earrings and necklaces.

It wasn't bad if Hazel could stop at a few items, but when she got on a theme, it usually got to be Guinness Book Of World Records weird. Skye could see seashell napkin holders, centerpieces, tissue dispensers, picture frames, vases, key rings. And, worse yet, Hazel might think it would be a great activity to keep Skye occupied. She was fully prepared to go into immediate cardiac arrest if Hazel brought in shells and Elmer's glue. Both she and Sloane could smell Elmer's glue at 100 paces and knew when to run for the hills. She couldn't run yet, but she could play dead. She refused to make things. Particularly things out of shells.

God, Skye thought, she had to find something to do. She sighed. It hurt. So she sighed again. She was up for feeling some pain. Kept her alert. If she was going to be awake more than a few minutes at a time, she was going to need a diversion. She picked up a paperback Sloane had brought. The *Calculus of Consent* by James Buchanan. Shit. A little light reading, Sloane? She probably had to buy it for one of her classes and decided to recycle it through the sick room. Had a pretty cover, though. Skye threw it back on the bedside table. She'd rather make seashell jewelry.

Suddenly, she heard familiar voices outside the bedroom. Hallelujah! Salvation! If she would have been able, she would have done a little happy dance. She heard Alex's deep chuckle, as he came around the corner with two familiar, beaming faces.

"Linda, Barclay!" Skye smiled broadly at her friends and colleagues. Then she immediately put on a show when her excitement activated a spasm of coughing. It made her side ache so badly her eyes teared up. Barclay nearly passed out in panic, but Linda was right behind Alex as he came over, knelt beside the bed, and took her hand.

Skye could only nod and grin in response to the unasked question in his eyes. When her chest settled, she could finally get some words out.

"Okay," she gasped, looking up at Linda her eyes were dancing the happy dance instead of her feet. "I'm...okay. Just...let me...get my...breath back." She opened her arms and Linda gave her a gentle hug. Standing up, Alex ruffled her hair in a casual gesture that Linda thought was just as adorable as could be.

Barclay was still trying to decide if he should call 911.

It was great to see them, two people with whom she could share everything. She didn't have to be cryptic or secretive. Alex told her a great deal when they were laying together in bed, but she always liked the telling and retelling of a really great op with colleagues who were a part of the experience. The only group who came close to the same love of storytelling was pilots. And Skye was both. Linda sat on the edge of the bed and Alex settled into a chair. He intended to watch over Skye to be sure she didn't overdo. Skye didn't even look in his direction. She intended to overdo until she passed out. She did look at Barclay, who had been staring at her.

"Looking, ah, good, Skye." Barclay stood planted where he'd been since entering the room. He was very uncomfortable. Skye actually didn't look that good at all. Her face and eye were still a little swollen and she didn't sound like she was breathing all that great. And what was with that coughing? Should she even be getting visitors? Shouldn't she be in intensive care or something?

"Are those for me?" Skye asked.

Barclay had what looked like daisies clutched in his hand. He bought them at the airport when he saw that Linda had a package for Skye. He didn't know you were supposed to take presents to someone who had been beaten up during a hijacking. He looked around at the magnificent bouquets in the room. His daisies looked pretty stupid, but not as stupid as he felt.

"Um..."

"Do you know that I just love daisies?"

"Um..."

"Oh good grief," she said under her breath and Linda almost laughed out loud. "Come over here Barclay and tell me everything." When he still held back, she threw the ultimate bait. "I heard you took Sloane a couple of times and beat her down."

She found his 'on' button and he came to life. "Oh yeah. She has a gift, but there are times when I can get in under her." He started talking and before he knew it, he was sitting in a chair next to the bed and giving her a blow-by-blow of their journey through cyber-space. Skye held her wilted daisies as if they were made of precious metal.

Alex watched Skye as she appeared to hang on every word Barclay said. There was a time when he never said anything, but Skye had brought him out of his shell. Not everyone thanked her for that. Alex thought he would have been in a coma after Barclay's explanation of how he got through the seventh level of codes, but Skye looked at him like he was reciting poetry. Alex knew there were over 16 more levels to go, so he decided to implement his role as Skye's intrepid protector and interrupt.

"Hey Barclay, you want to go for a swim in the ocean?"

"Huh?" Barclay turned and blinked at Alex. "Why would I want to do that?"

He had such a look of confusion on his face that Skye almost laughed. Almost. She turned her dancing eyes to Alex. She knew exactly what he was doing.

"We thought you might like to treat this like a day off. Relax, enjoy yourself."

"Well. All right. You got high band internet connections, right?"

"Sure." He picked up one of the books Sloane had left the night before when she sat by Skye's bed to watch her sleep. She'd read it and probably had it memorized in a few hours. "And I have here *An Elegant and Learned Discourse of the Light of Nature* by Nathaniel Culverwell if you'd like to read something."

"Excellent. Just the kind of light reading you want on a day off," said Linda.

"Yeah," said Barclay enthusiastically, missing completely Linda's not too subtle sarcasm. Alex rolled his eyes at Skye when Barclay turned to Linda. "You tell her the rest, okay, Linda?"

She nodded and Barclay and Saint Alex went out to enjoy the day off.

Skye rubbed her hands together in anticipation. "Okay, Linda. Fill me in on everything. Sloane has told me some, but with Hazel hovering, it is difficult to get a complete blow-by-blow account…and you can leave out the next 16 levels of the cyberspace adventure."

"That I'll do, but Skye, can I first do a little girlfriend oohing and ahing over the rock on your finger?"

Skye had nearly forgotten. She pulled out her talent for performing a role and smiled her pleasure. "Of course. And when I get better, we can graduate to the squealing and celebrating."

"And the planning and the shopping."

"Operation Matrimony."

She took Skye's left hand and looked at it. "It is beautiful, Skye. Have you set a date?"

"Not yet." Skye needed to drop it before her perceptive friend saw any hesitation. Linda felt it, but chalked it up to the usual Skye problem with being injured and less than 100%. "Now tell me everything before Barclay returns with part two of 'The Coded Affair.'"

Linda laughed and then started at the very beginning of the hijacking from their perspective. In her usual efficient manner she gave Skye a complete report. Skye returned the favor with her side of the operation. They laughed through the Sloane and Barclay competitions and Fisher's virtuoso performance on the plane.

Then Skye's eyes filled and tears slid down her cheeks when she heard of Sloane's brilliant battle with the dissolving data.

"She's an incredible young woman, Skye. She was positively heroic and I think we can safely say irreplaceable." Linda looked at her with haunted eyes. She had just recently lost a man that she loved and couldn't imagine what it would have been like to lose Skye, too.

"Oh, Skye, I heard how close it was." Now Linda's eyes teared up and she threw her arms around her dear friend. When Alex popped in to tell them there would be lunch on the terrace in half an hour, he found them weeping in each other's arms. He frowned. Hadn't he heard them laughing a few minutes before? Women. He shook his head. But now the timeless question. Did he interrupt this bonding moment? His momentary hesitation took the decision out of his hands.

"You can come in, Alex," said Skye as she pulled out tissues from her huge supply near her side of the bed and handed some to Linda. "We're almost finished with our therapeutic crying session."

"Absolutely mandatory after getting hijacked, beaten, and nearly blown up," sniffed Linda dabbing at the corner of her eyes. She giggled. Skye giggled. Alex frowned. What was this all about? Drugs would explain Skye's schizophrenia, but what about Linda? He completely forgot what he wanted to tell them, shrugged, and turned back to go play with Barclay. At least he was consistently goofy.

They had a wonderful time at lunch. Sloane and Barclay were talking computer speak, so no one really paid much attention to them. Hazel was playing find the doctor and he was, in turn, playing his unique version of hide and seek.

Barclay had something for Sloane, too. He handed her a rumpled bag from a discount store. "Payoff for the last race."

Sloane opened it. "Hey radical. A day's supply of Bubbliscious." She pulled out 12 packages. "And you found watermelon. Sweet." It made Skye's jaw ache just looking at the stuff. Sloane ran off, asking Barclay to stay put.

When she returned, she was hiding something behind her back. "I got a payoff for you, too." She brought her arm around and it held a fluffy brown teddy bear. Barclay just stared at it.

"It's a teddy bear," prompted Sloane, grinning.

"Hey, thanks." Barclay took it and continued to stare at it. He was thinking he really liked it. He wasn't sure at first what to do with something like this, but as he turned it over, he realized it felt good. It had no purpose, but he could live with that.

"What's its name, in case I ever have to send you a coded message?" teased Sloane.

"Doesn't it come with a name?"

"No. Did you come with a name?"

"Not exactly, I guess. Barclay is kind of a traditional family name."

"Then think of a traditional family name for the bear."

"Well, Teddy, I guess. His name is Teddy." He just wasn't good with creativity.

Sloane nearly slapped her forehead, but she showed remarkable restraint. Skye was proud. When Alex and Linda snorted, she gave them a disapproving stare. Barclay didn't notice, however. He was retying the bow around the teddy bear's neck so that the ends were exactly equal.

"We have to get back to D.C.," said Linda when she noticed Skye flagging. Skye had been pushing it and could feel herself sweating with the effort to breathe. She could no longer ignore the fatigue that pounded her fragile energy supply. Alex had been frowning at her for over a half-hour and the doctor came out of his hiding place in the pantry to start his usual scold. Skye hugged Linda and Barclay came over close to her personal space and gave her the softest little punch on the upper arm. Skye could translate that just fine. She loved him, too.

The following afternoon, Skye was resting on the terrace recovering from the visits and enjoying the sun. Hazel had momentarily abandoned her favorite pastime of laying in wait to pounce on the doctor. She discovered a red hat group on the island with a collection of ladies as wacky and fun loving as she and joined them on a trip to Savannah. Sloane was playing chess for the first time with Alex who had suggested a game and had given her an hour to study.

Skye could hear the surf. She loved the steady pulse...it gave her comfort. She tried to read some of the reports on the hijacking, but her eyes would blur, so she gave up and listened to the banter.

"And you got shot rescuing her. God, does it get any more romantic?" said Sloane wistfully.

Alex frowned at her. "How romantic is pain and an ugly scar? Your move."

She moved her piece with no thought. Just wham. Picked it up and plunked it down. "Oh, as romantic as the hottest romance novel Amanda owns. Hot as the steamiest movie imaginable. Hot as the original sin."

"Then you get shot next time." Alex carefully moved his piece. He was working on a strategy and was about ten moves into it. Four more and he would have her.

"Sure. Maybe with a camera. You're always leaving me behind. How the heck am I ever going to get shot if I'm continually grounded?" She plunked down another piece. "Checkmate."

Frowning, Alex eyed Sloane with suspicion. He never saw it coming. "Didn't you just learn this game?"

"Yeah. Read the book this afternoon. But don't worry. I skipped every other chapter. Let's shimmy on over to the mall and spend a few Benjamins."

"You can't go to the mall. You're grounded because of the illegal software you have on your computer," said Skye.

"It was a boost to get Alex the information he needed."

"That's why you're only grounded and not arrested," said Skye, trying unsuccessfully to be the stern responsible adult.

"Same thing."

"Skye is worried that one day you'll cross one line too many." said Alex reasonably, staring down at the chess board, wondering just how he got into checkmate.

Good thing she doesn't know about the hacking I did in the CIA files, Sloane thought.

"Like hacking into the CIA files," said Skye.

Sloane sat very still. God...how did she do that? Just read her mind like that. "Want another game?" she asked Alex, hopefully.

"Not a chance," said Alex. He would step back from this one.

"Sloane," Skye began.

"I needed to know," said Sloane.

"Don't do it again. Amanda is feeling charitable now because she has her grandson back. But you will never do that again," said Skye. "I can't even count how many laws you broke."

"You're marrying a lawyer. He can spring me."

"He's corporate. You're criminal."

"But I'm a minor."

"Not when the crime's a major."

"I won't do it again. I won't need to...probably." She looked into Alex's smiling face. He was inclined to agree that it was the ends rather than the means if it meant saving Skye but it was between the three ladies. Sloane continued, "Amanda is one powerful lady, Alex. I imagine she just saved me from a long stretch in the big house."

"Then there's the matter of you charging cheesecakes and pizzas to my account." He thought he would do her a favor and change the subject.

Sloane snorted and winked. Good one, Alex. "Sorry. I didn't think you'd notice and I knew you wouldn't wig. I've seen you look at your financial stuff. You just make a pass."

"Just because I don't find it as interesting as your companionship and this game I now can't play with you anymore, doesn't mean I don't know what's going on. And it isn't the pizzas. It's the fact that you downloaded all my financial data."

"You're marrying my sister. I have to make sure you're solvent."

"Am I?"

"You'll get by. Did you know that a man named Salsberi is skimming five to eight percent from the reserved revenue accounts you're setting aside for expansion and has been doing so for the last 8 months? He's been sending the money to an account on the Caymans number 2098011079780."

Alex frowned, not allowing his jaw to drop. "I guess I'd better look into that. Thanks."

"Uh huh. And a lady in your law firm downloads nude pictures of models and attaches heads of world figures to them...they aren't actually the real bodies. Just the person's head on a model." She smiled at him. She had him now. He wasn't going to bust her for a few pizzas. "She has one of you. I think it's phony, but I'm not sure. Do you have a cute little birthmark just to the left of your...um."

"No."

"Skye? Does he have..."

"I'll neither confirm nor deny," answered Skye.

"Okay. Whatever. The body isn't too great anyway. Plus it won't have that really awesome scar. Let's play another game. Maybe you can get closer than four moves to checkmate. I tell you what. I'll give you my queen and one knight."

"All right." He wasn't too proud to take the advantage. They set up the board and Alex made his first move.

"So, are you going to tell me her name?" he asked.

"Confidential." Sloane moved her remaining knight.

"Sloane." Alex had never seen the move and chalked it up to her lack of experience. Big mistake.

"Unlimited pizzas and whatever Barclay needs to keep him smiling and cool?"

"Deal." He smiled as he captured another pawn. He would have her this time.

"Okay. Her initials are MDR." Sloane shoved her bishop in a random move.

"Oh God."

"What?"

"She's my top field negotiator."

"Maybe that's because she has inspiration. Are you sure you don't have a little mole…"

"Your move."

"Checkmate."

"That does it. Go to your room and don't come out until I tell you to."

Sloane went around the table and sat in Alex's lap and gave him a hug. "Wouldn't you rather trip on over to Mickey D's with me? I'm jonesing for a Big Mac."

Alex hugged her back. Still a kid.

Later, after they'd returned from a spin to the golden arches, it was just Skye and Sloane sitting together enjoying the sun.

"There's someone I want you to meet," said Skye.

"Look. I had to escape Amanda on that deal, too. I'll meet the booger-picking moron who couldn't spell semi-automatic, but that's it. I don't date boys because boys my age are idiots."

"Sweetheart, that isn't nice. Not everyone has your IQ," said Skye gently. Because Sloane was a beautiful girl she had boys around her all of the time, friends only according to her. Skye was sure Sloane was prominent in a lot of young men's daydreams, but she didn't seem in a hurry to experiment. And that fact, she had to admit, was a relief.

"I'm not talking about their IQ's. I'm not an insufferable intellectual snob. I know how to talk kid talk. It's easier than Shakanwa, let me tell you. I'm talking about their voices changing, their need for making farting noises under their armpits, their obsession for talking with pizza falling out of their mouths. God, Skye. The guys I like are all going to be a lot older. More mature. And I'm complete and utter jailbait to them. Until I turn eighteen and am legal fodder for the male population over twenty-five, I'm going to spend my time just reading about Anatomy and Physiology."

"You have a major in that?"

"No. Gave that up when I decided against medical school. If you think it's like being a zoo animal in a cage sitting in my doctoral seminars, you should have seen it when I took a few classes at the medical school. Those future doctors really know how to eyeball you like a specimen."

"I'm sorry, honey," said Skye.

"Oh, I'm not. Really Skye. Don't cry for me Argentina. As long as you let me just sit and look at Alex for long afternoons, I can be completely happy. Of course it would be better if you'd tell me everything. Let me live the fantasy."

They turned as the topic of their discussion walked into the room. He had on a t-shirt that stretched tight over his broad chest and cutoffs. Skye's eye went, as it had for the last week, to the obvious bandage on his shoulder.

"Hello. How are my two favorite ladies?"

"I'm wicked, but you have to put in a dial to Peaches Galore to find out how she is," said Sloane in a sassy voice. She got a pillow in the head for her trouble.

"Did you hear from all the Coopers, Deltons, and Springfields?" Skye asked smiling.

"Yup. They've all checked in. They'll be descending on Saturday. It looks like they might be able to swing two weeks."

"Excellent!" said Skye and she meant it sincerely. She'd met them all at Alex's little brother's graduation from the Police Academy the month before.

"Who's coming?" asked Sloane.

"There will be Alex's little brother, Tank. Although little refers to chronological age only."

"Yeah. They had trouble finding a uniform to fit him at the academy," smiled Alex. He was wild about his kid brother. Tank was open and fun loving. Loud and brash. A perfect foil for his more reserved older brother.

"Where did the 'Tank' come from?" asked Sloane.

"When he was about four or five, he found this old hot water tank out in a junkyard near our house. Rolled it all the way home. Whenever you wanted to find him, he would be out there rolling this tank around like some big puppy. Just look for the tank, people would say. When he was about seven, he started lifting it over his head. Then when we was thirteen, he grew to the size of a tank and the name stuck." He was also strikingly handsome and the keeper of a whole collection of female hearts. His life's ambition was to follow in his mother's footsteps. First a beat cop, then a detective, then a lieutenant. Maybe even a captain,

"Then there are Alex's parents, District Attorney Blake Springfield, you've heard of him, and Captain Wyatt Cooper."

"The nail'em and jail'em team."

"That's right."

Sloane looked over at Alex, who decided to sit and watch Skye for a while. He had to get to the office, but he needed his fix.

"Where did she get the name Wyatt?" she asked.

"Well, let's see. My Grandpa was a cop. He married a dispatcher and they had three kids," responded Alex. He loved to tell the story.

"Is this going to be like the three bears or something?"

"Not really...more like Adams family meets NYPD Blue. Anyway, my grandfather was himself the only child of a cop and he named his three scary little bears Bat Masterson Cooper, Elliot Ness Cooper, and Wyatt Earp Cooper."

"Your mom's name is Wyatt Earp Cooper?"

"It's a name she's had to live with her whole life, yes," answered Alex.

"What if her folks would have kept going? Would there have been a Serpico Cooper?"

"That would be their really tough cat."

"Cagney and Lacy?"

"Their two police dogs."

"Startsky and Hutch?"

"Their birds. And Columbo is the name of their scruffy cat that had the mange when he was a kitten and never grew back all of his fur."

"So are Elliot and Bat coming too?"

"Sure are, and their wives."

"Are Elliot and Bat cops too?"

"They are. Bat is an Illinois State Trooper and Elliot is..." Alex raised his eyebrows and smiled.

"Don't tell me he is FBI?"

Alex grinned and nodded. "I'm afraid it was his destiny from the moment he was named."

Sloane and Skye loved this, drinking in the flavor of a real family. They never had anyone but each other and Hazel. Both their parents were only children and Hazel was their father's only aunt.

"Then there's David and the kids. You know them." Sloane had met David, Alex's brother-in-law, and his two kids at the aborted party for Skye. That seemed like a long time ago. David was a New York City cop and married to Alex's sister Rita. She was with the NYPD too when she was killed in the line of duty. Rita's kids were like his own. He loved them and helped care for them over the years. He and David were best friends and they shared the special bond of loving Rita. David was a devoted father and a fantastic cop.

Sloane looked over at Alex, who still hadn't taken his eyes off of Skye.

"So the fiction is that you chose a life outside of law enforcement."

"That's right. Actually I did until the day Rita was killed." It was her death that had triggered Alex's interest in working covert operations for the Justice Department. Before that he had contented himself with corporate law and real estate investment. When she was killed, his life cried out for purpose. The need to join his family's fight against the bad guys overwhelmed him and, heartbroken but determined, he went to see Jim Stryker about working behind the scenes...doing it his way. "My role is concealed as much as it can be from a family of really savvy cops so I expect you to honor your oath."

"What oath?" Skye asked staring at Sloane.

"Amanda's idea. Sloane has Level Seven clearance. Our background check didn't reveal anything too horrible, but you may want to read it."

"I don't need to," Skye snorted. "I lived it."

CHAPTER 14

Content that Skye was on the road to recovery, Sloane and Hazel left a few days later. They promised to return soon and talk on the phone every day. Sloane was due to give a report to a high-level Justice Committee on Computer Intelligence on her new software design and she had schoolwork piling up. There were tearful, but gentle hugs and lots of kissing. Hazel even took down the doctor for a major lip lock before she left. Love was in the air.

As soon as they left, Skye's mood shifted. She tried to keep things light and Alex believed Cynthia, Duncan, and the doctor felt she was doing very well. But he could see into her core and her soul wasn't at rest. Her façade was flawless, but her torment was in the layer just under the surface and Alex had access to it.

Her soul was in pain. He could see the agony in her eyes during unguarded moments. Her body was taking a physical beating as well. She barely slept at night anymore, preferring to catch daytime naps, and her weight was dropping. Even though she tried to conceal it, her eyes were sitting in deep shadows and her cheekbones were becoming more prominent. Emotionally she was moving more and more back into herself. The steel that he had melted a few months before was being re-forged and set again around her heart.

When he asked her what was wrong, she would say it was the drugs, or she was still recovering from her injuries. She would shake herself, kiss him until he forgot the questions, and put on a sunny front. But it was just a front and he knew it. He was not only a trained observer of human nature, he had a connection to her that went straight from heart to heart. She was hurting inside and it wasn't the ribs.

Everything should have been over. Been okay. But Alex could see in the night a restlessness and disquiet that was breaking his heart. It was after the sun went down that Skye went alone into the battlefield and her adversary was merciless. She wouldn't allow him in to help...wouldn't even acknowledge the struggle. She would roam or lie awake in the dark and he would worry.

Alex started spending long days at an office he rented in town. It felt good to be back making deals and writing contracts. Normal things. Things he could control. He was merging everything into a single large corporation under one umbrella. Those properties that didn't fit needed to be sold. Contracts had to be negotiated and drafted. He was in his element in the office as much as he was standing with a SIG-552 assault rifle in the doorway of a Boeing 767. Both roles were deeply a part of him.

Alex came home late one night to find Skye asleep on the lounge on the terrace outside their bedroom. She liked the sight and smell of the ocean and seemed to be soothed by the sound of the endless surf. There was a tray beside her and nothing had been eaten. He had dinner at the office that evening and made a mental note not to do that again. She would actually put something in her mouth and chew if he was around.

Skye never went to bed unless he was there with her. She would sit down, but she hated to lie down. It reminded her too much of her weakened status. He studied her, his favorite pastime of late. She was so beautiful and right now she seemed to be resting peacefully. Smiling, he squatted down and picked up the hand that had fallen over the side of the lounge chair. Raising it to his lips to kiss, his blood ran cold as ice, and just as quickly turned as hot as fire. His ring was not on her finger.

He looked at her hands, her fingers were bare. All of them. His smile faded like a shadow in the night. She'd taken the ring off. His ring. He almost lost his patience. This really hurt. Up to this point he was still hoping she was holding herself from him because of her physical injuries. She still winced several times as she pushed herself throughout the day. But this was proof of something else. Something far more serious.

Since Sloane and Hazel had just left a few days before, he wondered if there was a correlation. Of course there was...one didn't need to be a special agent to figure that out. Sloane was always fussing over the ring like it was her idea, wanting to see it and putting on her sunglasses when Skye was sitting in the sun, sniping about the glare. Skye wouldn't want to hurt her sister by taking it off. But what about him? He was hurt and angry. And tonight, angry won.

"Skye?" he whispered.

Frowning, Skye sifted and moaned. Her eyes fluttered open slowly. Blinking, but not waking, she sighed, closed her eyes again and went back to sleep. Blowing out a breath, he swallowed his anger. It caused a grinding pain in his stomach but now was not the time. Picking her up, he put her to bed, then slowly undressed. Tomorrow morning they would talk. The doctor would be there at 8 a.m. She had a habit lately of opening her eyes to the sunrise. They could get in some quality shouting before the doctor arrived. He was actually looking forward to it. Maybe she would reveal what was eating away at *his* Skye...the Skye who smiled that unforgettable smile when he put the ring on her finger.

The next morning, Alex awoke just before sunrise knowing she was wakeful too by the stillness around her. She was waiting, silently and expectantly. He tried to catch her with her eyes open, but he must have telegraphed his movement because when he looked at her, her eyes were closed. He wondered if she slept at all in the night.

"Skye?" he whispered.

No response. All right darling, he thought. Play possum for now, but we are going to talk. He got up to shower and get ready for battle. He flipped the switch on the coffee maker on the way to the bathroom. Resist me, maybe. Resist the smell of coffee, never.

A half-hour later, Alex was ready and dressed for the day. Tossing his jacket on a chair he finished tying his tie. Impeccable and perfect. He looked good and felt lousy...in control, yet close to snapping...he was an excellent player.

The dawn was casting a yellow light into the room. It was going to be a beautiful day. The sky was blue and the air was fresh. Too bad his mood didn't fit the promise of the nice day. He could hear Skye's shower running. She could have joined him in his. Would have a few weeks ago, but now she seemed to want to separate herself from him...both physically and emotionally.

Fifteen minutes later, she emerged from the bathroom, the smell of her shower floated out with her, making Alex's mouth water. Smiling at him, she went over to help herself to coffee. She was moving slowly, but less painfully now. The pain she felt was due to the fact she was determined to get off the drugs, prematurely in the doctor's opinion.

Alex looked at his own mug of coffee, poured but untouched. He didn't want any more acid in his stomach this morning.

"It looks like it's going to be a beautiful day," she said as she took the first sip. She coughed and winced. Alex noticed the sound wasn't so desperately tight anymore, but she obviously was still having trouble taking a deep breath. He wasn't going to let the little tug of concern distract him from his intended course. He confirmed the fact that her left hand was bare. For a while that morning he hoped she'd just taken it off the night before while preparing for bed or something. She hadn't had it off since she got back from the island, but there was always that possibility. It was starting to slide on her finger due to the weight she was losing

Bloody hell. He could feel his anger and frustration bubbling up. Maybe if he channeled all this fury to a seduction. No, maybe not. Too much heat to channel right now. He tensed, trying to locate his control. Looking desperately inside himself for a ton of concrete to patch the crack that was running through the center of his chest.

He'd planned to approach her slowly. With finesse, patience, and persistence. Like a really well strategized business deal. He would start by bringing up her promise to him then enlist her love and need for him to help bring down the wall from the inside. He was sure that love and need were still in there. Well, almost sure. Unless everything the last few months had been a lie, an illusion. No. He wasn't going to go there.

His preference was to push her hard. His noble self, checking in with an opinion, reminded him that she might still be too fragile. Then his angry and frustrated self wanted to register an observation. If she could walk across the room, she could take a little verbal flack, right? He watched her reading the headlines and drinking coffee. She was looking pretty steady.

Putting down her cup, she walked to the French doors, opened them up and went out onto the terrace, flexing her muscles and checking how far she could push herself today. He watched her body tense and relax as she stretched out.

Right now, she elicited more lust than sympathy. His randy animal self decided to make a pitch. He wanted her. All of her. He stood immobile, staring at her, then shook himself. It seemed he could get side tracked so easily these days. And the trio of voices inside his head were in a full-blown debate. They all agreed that taking off the ring changed the rules. Then they came to a consensus. Go get her.

"You, ah, forget something?" he asked in a deceptively calm voice as he leaned against the door jam, watching her stretch.

She looked at him with puzzlement then down at her body. She was dressed in an old t-shirt and baggy sweat pants. She'd put on a skintight jersey earlier, but thought it made her look nearly emaciated. She didn't want Alex's attention to go right to her weight knowing he was worried about her and wanting to minimize his concern. Alex noticed, however. Alex noticed everything when it came to her.

"I'm talking about your talisman." She never called it an engagement ring. When anyone called it an engagement ring and asked about the wedding, she would skillfully deflect every question. Always smiling, always pleasant. But always very firm. She never referred to him as her future husband or her fiancé any more. When he told her he loved her, she would smile and thank him or give him a kiss. And even the kisses were getting more and more chaste.

Now...in the sunshine...she just stared at him, saying nothing.

"It must mean that you no longer feel threatened," he said when she didn't respond. Or no longer feel engaged, he thought.

"Well, there was that drive to the airport with Duncan, Sloane, and Hazel." she said, smiling. "He's really quite an enthusiastic driver and Hazel's directions were a bit vague. She wanted him to make several stops, and never gave him much warning."

She said it so matter-of-factly. Like removing an engagement ring was nothing. Didn't she know she was shooting chips out of his heart?

Alex straightened. He had on his 'no nonsense-take no prisoners' face. His blue eyes were blazing. Well, enough of this. He was going to confront her. If she was well enough to be stretching out, she was well enough for 'the talk.'

She saw it coming...knew it was just a matter of time. Alex was a good and patient man, but he was also strong willed and determined. He'd been so gentle since their return, both physically and emotionally. When he opened his mouth, she braced herself. Now was the time.

"Where is it?" demanded Alex.

"I put it in the safe. I wouldn't want it just lying around."

"It wouldn't be lying around if it was on your finger, damn it!" he shouted. Oh yes, today anger and frustration definitely were winning the battle.

"Yes, you're right," she said, continuing her stretching and ignoring his tone. No explanation. No elaboration.

"What?" he shouted again. This used to work. He yelled, then she yelled. Why wasn't she shouting back at him? He threw up his hands. "Are you waiting for a more appropriate time and place for me to put it on your finger? To ask you again for the commitment? To seal your promise to be my wife?" There! It was out and it felt good.

"No."

"No, what? You tell me what is going on in your head." He was so frustrated now he felt like his own head was going to explode. "Is it the ring? Was it the timing?"

She stopped moving and stood very still. Her eyes never left his face. But she didn't respond so Alex continued.

"I love you. I want you to marry me. Am I wrong in assuming you want the same thing?" He waited. He felt like his heart had stopped and was as still as she was. She was like a statue. A tragic, despondent statue. Still he refused to let his compassion rule his head. He was going to get answers.

"I have no answers for you," she said softly. "I think I'll go take a nap."

"A nap!" Alex completely snapped. "You can't sleep through this one, Skye. Do I have to take you to hell to melt the ice? Because that's where I've been since last night."

She tried to walk by him, but he grabbed her arms. He didn't squeeze, but his grip was immovable. "Answer me. Or is your heart as cold and unmoving as your body? You tell me right now if you've changed your mind again. Don't make me go day after day wondering. I can't take this frigid air, it's killing me."

"I'm sorry," she whispered and her chest hitched. "I'm sorry."

"I don't want you to be sorry, goddamn it Skye. I want you to love me," he shouted. He couldn't believe she was just passively taking his anger. Did it mean she didn't care anymore? Before she would have taken him apart. Her physical ability to do so was diminished, but where was her splendid ability to slaughter him with her sharp, sarcastic tongue. He wanted that. He longed for it.

"Look at me and tell me what's wrong," he demanded, looking at Skye's impassive face through a red haze of rage. "When I bought the ring, I thought of you. Multi-faceted, brilliant, filled with light. Now all I can see is ice. Ice suits you, Skye. You're freezing me out."

She shook her head and suddenly she couldn't get her breath. Short, desperate gasps were barely making it through her tight throat. She was shaking with the effort to loosen the grip on her chest. It took a moment for her difficulty to register with Alex. He still had her by the arms and was angrily glaring down at her.

"What do you think you're doing?" shouted the doctor. Rushing over, he put his hand on Alex's arm. Alex didn't even feel it. But the sound of her breathing did get through. Her chest was heaving and she was under considerable distress. Her face was starting to get flushed and she felt herself start to fade.

"Shit, Skye. God. I'm sorry." What was he doing? Shouting at a woman whom less than two weeks before broke ribs and took a beating. What was he thinking? He hadn't been thinking, that was the problem. He'd been reacting. The doctor still had a tight grip on his arm and he finally felt it through his shirt. He looked down at him with a fierce glare.

"Get the hell out of here," Alex growled as he helped Skye to a chair. The doctor let go, but he stuck. She was his patient. Actually they both were and he knew them pretty well by now. All emotions and messy passion. It was stimulating on one level and completely frightening on another. And a mystery on all levels. He was an old bachelor, for pity sake. What did he know?

"I'm okay, doctor," Skye managed to get out. "Really. All right. Please. I just need to sit down." She took a shallow breath between each word. Her eyes started to water with the effort.

"I'll be back in a half-hour. Resolve this, young man, then leave her be. I'll not have you initiating a relapse."

Neither one of them heard the doctor leave. Sitting down, she stared up into his raging blue eyes. She'd seen skies this color and with this kind of turbulence she would fly for safety. He was still furious, but was exercising his iron will to suppress the intense emotions at war inside him. He couldn't hurt her and yet she was hurting him practically beyond his endurance.

"Tell me," he whispered capturing her eyes with his. "Do you love me? Skye. Sweetheart. Can we start there?"

"Please...I..." It seemed like a lifetime between those two words. How was she going to finish this? Was she going to send him out today with hope or was she going to crush him completely? Suddenly she started to weep, violently and painfully. The emotion was too much for her still healing frame. The torment was too deep and the agony was too intense. His temper faded, giving in to his compassion and he knelt down beside her chair.

"Don't...don't go. Don't leave me." Her voice shook and penetrated his heart.

"Darling. That's okay. I'm not going anywhere. I just need something. Give me something," he asked.

"Oh, Alex," she gasped between sobs. "I'm so sorry. Time. Give me time."

"You can have anything I have to give. I love you, Skye. You're my heart." He grabbed a handful of tissues and handed them to her. She was beginning to breathe easier. He helped her up, sat down, then put her on his lap. He cradled her in his arms, holding her gently to his chest. She sniffed and wiped her eyes.

"I'm wrinkling your shirt."

"I'll keep my jacket on all day."

"I'm creasing your pants."

"I won't stand up all day."

"I love you, Alex," she gasped between hitching breaths. "I do."

"Now I'll make it through my day." His arms folded her closer to his heart.

"Don't sell the ring, okay?" She sniffed and nuzzled against his neck.

"I won't. It's not worth much anyway."

"Glass?"

"I'm afraid so."

"You won't give it to someone else?"

"I have two more back at the office."

"That's a relief." She sniffed, then turned her teary eyes up to his. He stared at her.

"Why did you take it off, Skye?" he asked gently brushing hair off her wet and flushed cheeks. A serious question. It deserved a serious answer.

"I was going to talk to you about it. I fell asleep waiting for you last night. Then I thought maybe…tonight…" her voice trailed off, then she coughed and straightened…she needed to look at him.

"I don't know if I can explain it…Alex…it was…was too heavy," she began, trying to pick her words for maximum understanding and minimum hurt. "Its expectations, its promises, its meaning. I had to lighten my load somewhere. I chose the ring. Does that make any kind of sense?"

"No. But I guess on some level I'm glad you decided on the ring and not me. Will you tell me why you have to lighten your load, darling? Will you tell me what's in your mind, your heart?"

"Let me get well first. I feel so unable to surround all that I'm feeling while I can hardly breathe. I can't even shout back at you when you're going off like a maniac. I can't take a deep breath."

"Sorry I grabbed you."

"I'm not a fragile flower. You left yourself wide open…held me too loosely. I would have had you pinned in two moves if I were in fighting form."

"Give me warning when you feel yourself come close."

"Your family is coming in a few days. It'll be wonderful. I want people around."

So she doesn't have to deal with me alone, he thought. "Is that why you took it off now?"

"They would know what it symbolized. All of them would start to ask questions I have no answers for."

"Like dates, times, invitations, dresses, honeymoon plans," Alex said. Another kick to the gut. Even though she was opening up a bit and trying to keep her words gentle, they were slicing through him.

"And that's just Tank's interrogation in the first five minutes. And then I would have to see the…" she said, tears flowing again. "To see the confusion, the hurt I see in your eyes…multiplied. I can't. I'm not strong enough yet."

Her lips sought out his, her arms going around his waist. She wanted comfort and he was willing to give it without reservation. He could be frustrated as hell, but his need to be there for her was deeper, truer.

The position they were in was painful, but she didn't care. She hadn't felt a full embrace since she got back and she wanted one now. His hands moved over her, up her back, along her good side, circling her waist. She responded, deepening the kiss and his anger turned to heat. His hands went gently under her sweatshirt and explored the unbruised places. Alex forced himself to pull back when he heard her breathing become labored.

"Alex," she whispered and she moved her hand over his chest. "What if I just threw my leg over your lap, like this?" She placed one long leg on either side his lap, straddling him. "And then we get naked and with minimum movement," she rose a bit on her toes, "you and I…"

An incredibly sharp pain rocketed through her chest when she came back slowly on his eager lap, answering her question. She leaned into him, trying to find relief, while they both moaned in frustration. "Can we go back to that damn island, dig up the remains of that dickless asshole, stomp on his ashes, and kill him again?"

Alex smiled into her hair. That was his Skye. "This isn't going to work."

He could feel her tremble with both desire and severe pain. She smelled so good. He sniffed her hair and had to firmly suppress his urge to try going for that naked idea. She was kissing his neck and working her way around his ear, trying to ignore the increasingly intense throbbing in her side for just a few more seconds. When he felt the cold sweat on her skin, he repositioned her and when she sighed, decided to prolong the moment. Taking advantage of her elevated need for comfort and reassurance he continued the really fine kissing and touching.

When the doctor returned he just stared. His patients were necking in a chair on the terrace. He was glad he was a bachelor. This was all too much for him. He cleared his throat, being clueless to the importance of the moment and wanting to keep his key patient on her medication schedule. They slowly came apart and smiled at each other. A truce.

"She's all yours," said Alex. Then got up and gently put Skye back in the chair. He looked down at his wrinkled shirt, wet with her tears. Dabbing at her eyes, she smiled and shrugged. She noticed shrugging was less painful today. That was a good omen.

Alex went and changed his shirt. She'd said she loved him. And he was quite certain she was still really hot for him. Her body sure jumped to his touch. That was enough…for now. He would get that ring back on her finger because it belonged there. And she belonged here. He smiled. Plus he had another card to play.

CHAPTER 15

Skye stopped brushing her hair, looking at herself in the mirror. The bruises were nearly invisible under the makeup she'd applied. Turning her face to the left and right, she decided she looked pretty good on the outside. Then she tried to take a deep breath. Ouch. Not so good on the inside. Today she was determined to go the whole day without painkillers, but it wasn't going to be easy. Tough shit. She didn't need easy. It was time for her to start backing off from her dependence on them.

The windows were all open and she enjoyed the smell of the ocean. She tried to take a deep breath of fresh air, but her attempt ended in a spasm of coughing. Her eyes watered from the pain in her side, even though she held herself tightly. She was glad Alex wasn't in the room. He would be freaking out and pumping pills down her throat. He was far too concerned with her health. Bastard wouldn't even let her go for a walk without a fight.

Then she sighed and looked sullenly around the room. Felt like a damn velvet prison. She knew she was in a funky mood. Alex wasn't really a bastard. He loved her, just wanted her to be comfortable, to be well. He'd left early that morning while she'd played possum and pretended to still be sleeping.

In the distance, she heard a car door slam. Duncan was probably back. Maybe she could talk him into taking her for a ride. He wasn't inclined to do anything if he thought Alex wouldn't approve, but if Alex hadn't left explicit instructions, maybe she could break down Duncan's defenses. Bribe him with a big bag of carrots.

Her face set with determination. She was getting such cabin fever; she was going to go bonkers if she didn't find a diversion. Jim called every day. And Hazel and Sloane, but it wasn't like having something to do. She wasn't good with inactivity. Made her cranky. She sighed and even that gave her a twinge. Which moved her from cranky to pissed. Look out Duncan, I'll not be denied. Getting to her feet, she steadied herself. Damn, she was weak. Well she wasn't going to let anyone know that. She'd be grounded for sure.

Just then, Alex came striding into the room. He was dressed in a business suit and looked professional and efficient. The commando was completely buried under Armani. He looked wonderful.

"Did you forget something?" Skye asked, confused. It seemed too early for him to be knocking off for the day. Then she frowned. "Are you feeling okay? Is your shoulder bothering you?" The rush of concern swept though her and echoed in her voice. It should have made her understand his anxiety for her a little better, but she wasn't in the mood to let that sink in. "Maybe you shouldn't be putting in such long days."

He came over, took her face in his hands and gave her a deep, lingering kiss. "Other than the fact that I'm as horny as hell, I am feeling 100 percent," he said in a low voice, liking the worry he saw in her eyes, heard in her voice. He didn't want her to be troubled, but what the hell. It meant she cared and that was good to know. He tucked it away in his heart to savor later. "I brought you a present…"

"A present? Really, Alex, you…" she cut off her protest when she heard the familiar voice.

"Skye!"

She turned and grinned, all pain forgotten for the moment. She would recognize that voice anywhere. Standing in the doorway of the bedroom was her dear, dear friend. Glory hallelujah, she was saved.

"Connie! You didn't tell me you were coming." Grinning with absolute delight Skye opened her arms and moved forward. Connie gave her friend a gentle but enthusiastic hug, hiding her shock at Skye's appearance. Alex had prepared her, but the reality was alarming. Skye could hide the bruises, but Connie could see the pain, the weight loss and the subtle changes in her manner. Alex had transformed Skye over the last few months and Connie was afraid she was sliding back into the more reserved Skye she'd flown with, shopped with, laughed with for years. Well, that wasn't going to happen. Even though she and Skye talked every day, she could keep a secret. Alex and she had been plotting.

"Have you arrived in the nick of time! I was contemplating taking up crocheting."

"Oh good grief, Skye. That's desperate. Although I'm thoroughly enjoying the crocheted toilet paper cover Hazel made for me last President's Day." Hazel celebrated all the holidays. They laughed. It felt so good. Skye narrowed her eyes. She was good at uncovering secrets and to her eye, Connie's smooth dark face was as transparent as glass.

"You flew the Gulfstream down!" Skye guessed. When she saw the merry light bopping in Connie's dark eyes, she knew this was going to be a great day. She turned to Alex, who was enjoying the pleasure dance over Skye's features. "Oh Alex, I want to go see it. Where is it? Can we go for a ride?"

"Hey, I come on down here to see how you're doing and pay you a visit and all you can say is 'where is the Gulfstream'?" protested Connie, although she too was enjoying seeing the light of anticipation in Skye's eyes.

"At least I have my priorities in order."

"You'll see it soon enough, I imagine. Wow! Look at this room! And look at the view. You snagged not only a complete 10 plus, plus, plus, but a rich one, too. Shagging. Does it get any better? Didn't I say he was the man for you?" Connie kept up the chatter as she walked out on to the terrace. Skye followed, laughing and enjoying the moment. Alex grinned at Connie. A strong and powerful ally. Plus, plus plus? Take that Skye, he thought.

Connie spun around on the terrace. "Since I'm the one who got the two of you together, I think maybe you should buy me one of these views, Alex. Not that I am complaining about the generous salary and benefits. Honestly Skye. Life couldn't get any better."

Connie had recently resigned her position as head flight attendant to be the cabin crew for the Skyward Corporation's jet. She was a beautiful woman, as dark and petite as Skye was fair and tall. Connie's rich mahogany colored skin was flawless and her brilliant smile filled a room with its carefree energy.

Connie had spotted Alex at an airport in Washington D.C. She didn't know that he'd been assigned to follow Skye and his incredible good looks had been his downfall. Connie had rated him on the Connie Scale as a perfect 10 and pointed him out to Skye, thinking they would make great looking babies. It was a fluke that Skye saw him when he was supposed to be covert, an ironic twist of fate that started a chain of events leading to Skye and Alex getting together, both personally and professionally. Connie wasn't privy to Skye's shadow career, so she just knew about the personal part. And was well satisfied with her role in their engagement.

The cover story was that she and Alex had met in the hotel in London and an immediate and powerful magnetic attraction pulled them together. It was close enough to the truth.

"So where is the fabulous diamond?" She looked at Skye's bare hand. Then she looked at how much weight Skye had dropped and came to the wrong conclusion. "Having it sized? You know you're going to gain the weight back...or at least you should. Your frame can support another 20 pounds at least. You lose it, I find it." Connie kept up the Connie banter and Skye didn't even have to make up a story, although having it sized was a good one if pressed. "I expect to see it soon enough. And when you are well we can get down to the serious business of shopping for the wedding and spending a big chuck of hunk's money."

"Connie, it's so great to see you. Really. You're a better painkiller than all the pills Alex and the doctor have been pushing at me..." Skye smiled and both Connie and Alex knew there was a 'but' coming. She had something on her mind and she wouldn't be deterred. She didn't disappoint. "But can we go see the plane? Where is it? Is it at the airport?"

Connie smiled broadly up at Alex, then turned north to look into the cloudless sky. "To answer your question..."

Skye understood her meaning instantly and turned to where Connie was looking. "Oh my God. How?"

"Alex got special clearance, don't ask me how," said Connie, more than a little impressed with her new employer.

It was a glorious sight. It started out as a speck in the sky, but quickly became a craft with wings. Skye's heart and soul soared at the sight of her new plane materializing out of the clear blue sky.

Coming up behind her, Alex slid his arm around her waist. She no longer needed the physical support, but he wanted to share the moment with her. Their plane, their new life. He was thrilled when she put her arm around him and squeezed as the magnificent plane roared past, only 500 feet above the ocean and just off shore. Bill was at the controls and did an impressive wing waggle.

"Show off," Skye said under her breath and felt like clapping her hands in delight. Oh what the hell. She did clap. She'd seen the plans and the pictures, but it was nothing like the reality of seeing it grace the air. It was painted in several different shades of blue with the corporate logo and name emblazed on the side in a rich, luscious gold. Skyward Corporation. Alex was the CEO and she was the corporate pilot. A perfect union of skills and interests. A perfect cover.

She automatically put her arm back around Alex and he liked that just fine. There was still some work to be done on the plane, not everything was complete on the modifications, but what the hell. If you couldn't order your new corporate plane to fly by, what was the sense of owning the whole damn company?

"Who's in the copilot's seat?" asked Skye, although she suspected the answer.

"Carter, of course."

Skye looked up at Alex, her eyes pouring out anticipation and warmth…and did he see love? Yes. It was definitely love. For him or the Gulfstream? Well she was looking at him now. Could have been residual lust for the plane, but he would take it, anyway. It was his plane.

"Can we go take a closer look? Please don't just tease me like this. Please. Please."

"Well,…" said Alex, looking down at the lawn a story below. Duncan came around the corner of the house, as if on cue, Skye thought. Did Alex choreograph everything? She looked up at him. He was grinning. Yes, he did. Somehow that didn't annoy her today.

"Holy heart throb, Captain, get me a resuscitator. Who might he be?" asked Connie. "Talk about the perfect 10!" Connie wiggled her butt. "And just the right shade."

"That's Duncan, Alex's driver, friend and all around mechanical magician."

"Damn, you should have told me you were harboring a gorgeous planet of manhood like him. I would've brought that nasty little red bikini we bought at Harrods last spring. It has those really wicked underwires that can really do something with these bountiful breasts. You said he's a driver? Then I'd say he could park his limo in my garage any day of the week. Do you know if he has a steady? Of course he has…probably several. That's okay. I'm not afraid of a little competition. Does he always dress like that? God those muscles. Looks like he lifts cars, not drives them. And he works for Alex? That's excellent because now so do I. Oh Skye, is life just perfect? I would say. Call him over here will you? Not too obvious, though. Oh what the heck, make it obvious. That's my style."

Skye learned a long time ago she didn't have to answer any of Connie's questions. All she had to do was smile and nod and Connie would carry on an entire conversation with herself. No one could figure out why the two of them were such good friends. Connie was as open and uninhibited as Skye was enigmatic and controlled. It just worked.

"Hey Duncan," Skye called. He looked up and waved and came over to stand just below them. He was in jeans, a black muscle shirt and sandals.

"Good to see you up and out, Captain. I…whoa…who is that?" His eyes locked on to Connie. Skye was practically knocked off her feet by the electricity passing between them. She was delighted. She wasn't sure Duncan even heard her response.

"Duncan, this is Connie Monroe. She's our cabin crew for the new Gulfstream."

"You work for the captain?"

Connie looked at Skye, then leaned over the terrace wall making sure Duncan could get an eyeful. "Now that's a tricky question. I actually work for the Skyward Corporation, so I guess Alex writes the paycheck. But I've worked for the captain for years and when we're on board, she's in complete charge."

"Hey, Brown Sugar, I am here to tell you, she's in complete charge down here, too." Duncan threw Alex a glance. He liked seeing him and the captain all entwined like that. "The Bossman is completely and thoroughly under her command."

"As it should be," said Connie. "Or at least completely and thoroughly under her."

Duncan snorted and gave Skye an exaggerated wink.

"When did we begin losing the authority," asked Skye looking up at Alex.

"And command," he asked, enjoying the moment. "Think we can get it back?"

Skye looked over at Duncan and Connie making eyes at each other. "Think they would notice?"

"So, Duncan...who signs *your* paychecks?" asked Alex causally.

"Damn if I know. The pocket change I get for working around here is deposited directly into my account."

"It was part of the terms of your probation, as I recall."

"Now, why do you have to bring something like that up?" asked Duncan grinning and winking at Connie.

"I can't imagine why I would want to malign your reputation," said Alex wryly.

He turned to Skye, thinking a change of subject was in order. "I came to see if you wanted to burn the road to the airport to get a closer slant at that big bird."

"I would love to," she looked up at Alex. She didn't need his permission, but she didn't want to fight him, either. Alex leaned over to give her forehead a kiss.

"No temperature today, I think we can have an outing. As long as we sneak out the side door. I think Dr. Lacy..."

"I heard my name, young man. You're not taking my patient anywhere. She's been all together too active these last few days. Goodness, all these people."

"But Doctor, my recovery depends on these people. Think of them as medicine." She worked her way out of Alex's arms, but still had hold of his hand. She was inching toward the door.

Dr. Lacy narrowed his eyes. He knew he'd lost the battle, but he still had a little fight left in him.

"Let me go get my jacket and medical bag. Where you go, I go."

"Fair enough," said Skye. "God, an outing." She squeezed Alex's hand with pure joy running though her, intoxicated by its impact. "When did my life get so simple?"

Connie opted for the front seat next to Duncan. By the time they arrived at the airport there wasn't enough space between them to slide a paper through.

Bill and Carter were waiting in the terminal for them, both as handsome as film stars and completely devoted to Skye. There was a great deal of hugging and kissing and touching. Duncan hung back respectfully, but eventually got caught up in the wash of excitement. Alex and Carter talked about their golf games and Skye and Bill talked about the instruments and Duncan and Connie talked about getting together later. The doctor just listened, enjoying the people noises and how his patient was perking up under its onslaught. Maybe these people were good medicine, after all. It would have exhausted him, but she seemed to be getting stronger with each new bend of the conversation. It was loud, fun, and invigorating to the soul.

As beautiful as the Gulfstream was in the air, it was magnificent up close. Skye went into the cockpit and lovingly touched every instrument, running her hands over the throttles and the soft leather seats.

"Oh, to be a throttle," chuckled Duncan, winking at Alex. Bill thought that was hilarious. He laughed with delight, then went up and put his arm around Skye leading her into the communications alcove off the cockpit. Alex had arranged for everything to be state-of-the-art. Skye absentmindedly put her arm around Bill, as well.

"Man's got a lot of hand on your baby doll, Bossman," said Duncan. Connie was busy in the galley, getting refreshments for everyone.

"First of all, don't ever let the captain hear you call her my baby doll, secondly, it's okay. Bill and Carter are..."

"I know. A couple."

"How did you know."

"It's obvious, Bossman." Not to everyone, thought Alex, a little put out. Alex remembered when he met Bill and Carter. They had their hands all over her then, too. At least that was what it looked like through the jealous haze he had in his eye when he saw Carter hugging and kissing her. He didn't think the fact they were a couple was so obvious. Took him time to tumble. He just saw two good-looking men being very cozy with his then newly minted lover. The memory was a good one, however, and he decided to share it with Duncan. He loved the story and soon they were all reliving the moment. Even the doctor had a laugh. A strange, dry sound, but to Skye's mind, delightful.

After her tour and a quick flight to Atlanta for lunch, they talked and Skye told them in person all that had happened on the island...a revised version, but exciting, all the same.

"Must have been horrible for you, Alex. I hope you got all of our messages," said Carter.

"I did, thanks." He had his arm casually around Skye's shoulder. They were sitting in the lounge area inside the craft and Alex and Skye took the sofa. It had been beautifully appointed in the same hues of blue as the exterior. Skye had chosen the colors. The different shades of Alex's eyes, she had told him.

"And it was really great of you to call as soon as you heard from the state department that Skye was coming home. I loved being on the inside track. I knew before anyone at the company and certainly the media. All three networks were still talking about the tragedy and how the plane was missing and presumed in the ocean. It was surreal to be watching the solemn talking heads discussing the dire possibilities when I knew you were on your way home. I can't tell you how proud I was just to say I knew you," said Carter sincerely. Bill was no longer with International Airlines, but Carter was and his relationship with Skye was well known.

"Stop. You'll make me blush."

"You never blush. Not even when Carter was taking your measurements," said Bill. That made Alex frown, so they moved on quickly.

"Speaking of which. Now to the really important stuff." Carter went to the closet and pulled out a uniform. He routinely had Skye's International Airline's uniforms altered by the tailor who did his and now he'd taken charge of designing the uniforms for Skyward Air, the division of Skyward Corporation operating the Gulfstream.

"Unless Bill is wearing skirts in public now, that must be mine," she quipped. The uniform was stylish and a beautiful deep rich berry color that Carter specifically selected to go with Skye's coloring. She exclaimed over the buttons. They were brass with the corporate logo stamped on them.

"All I need now is my captain's wings," she said, running her hands over the soft material. A little cough escaped her throat, but she managed to swallow the one following it.

"You're a far cry from that," said the doctor. He noticed her breathing was becoming shallower and that her cheeks were flushed. "You will not be cleared for flight until your lungs have cleared and you can breathe normally."

"If I can't try on my plane, at least let me try on my uniform. Connie, help me?" Carter went in too. Alex tensed for a moment, then smiled. If Carter decided to go straight and lust after Skye, he would just threaten to mess up his face. Carter needed that terrific face for his television work.

When she came back out a few moments later, Skye was grinning. She looked stunning and very, very capable. The ten pounds she'd lost were obvious, but Carter told her they wouldn't alter the fit since Alex was determined she would gain it all back when she was fully recovered.

When Skye returned to the bedroom suite, the doctor went in with her to check her vital signs.

"A lot of guys seeing the captain unclothed today," said Duncan under his breath. "Can I be next?"

Alex shot him a dangerous look. The commando look. Duncan's expression never changed, never wavered. He knew his boss was the man on the island and he was impressed as hell. He was also the keeper of secrets and he was as steadfast as a mountain. Big as one, too.

Carter sipped on his iced tea. "Damn, she's bruised, Alex. Is she doing all right? I'm no doctor, but she doesn't seem to be breathing all that well."

"She's healing nicely. When you consider where she started, she's miles better."

"She didn't let on the seriousness of her condition when we talked on the phone. I had no idea. We've been reporting her well, no serious injury. Damn. I assumed we didn't hear from her in the first few days because the two of you were, well. Celebrating."

I wish, thought Alex. "Everything will heal. It's just going to take time."

"When are we going to be able to start planning the showers and bachelor party?"

Alex grinned at Skye's friends, now his. "Let's get her completely well, then we'll let you know." Alex was determined to push through the wall Skye had constructed and get to an answer to that question himself...soon.

Connie, Skye, and the doctor came out and to Skye's annoyance, the doctor gave a small 'time to go' signal to Alex.

"It's been a great day everyone, but we should be getting back," he said before Skye could pitch a fit.

"Just one more bit of business before we call this party over and Skye can go get some rest." Carter reached into his inside jacket pocket. Bill beamed in anticipation. He knew what was in the envelope. Carter hadn't been able to keep a secret from him in all years they'd been together.

Carter handed the envelope to Skye who looked at it, confused. It looked official. It was from the insurance carrier of the aircraft. Some kind of notice? She sat down next to Alex and ripped it open. It was a check. She turned it over and gasped.

"What the hell is this for?" she managed to ask through a throat that had constricted in shock.

Carter transformed in front of them. He was all business, now. "Skye, other than a few radios, the phones, and a transponder, the plane was completely unharmed and intact. It's a hugely valuable asset. It's still impounded, but should be released for service within the month. We'll be putting a special logo on the captain's side of the cockpit and will make a big media splash when we put it back in service. If I can slide into my role as the Vice President of Marketing and Corporate spokesperson for a moment, you handed us a gold mine, Captain."

"What about the passengers, their things, the terror they were put through?"

"Except for a small handful, they all signed off on the liability. The company was very generous and cut settlement checks for their losses and recompense for their fear and inconvenience nearly on the spot, no questions asked. Plus, we're picking up the tab on fabulous vacations, free first class tickets and life long elite boarding passes. There was some extremely valuable medical cargo in the hold and we were carrying a full load of mail. The insurance on all that would have pushed the liability into the stratosphere. You did well, Captain Madison. You not only performed your moral obligation, you saved the company hundreds and hundreds of millions of dollars. You saved everyone, Skye. Every human soul in your care. No one can put a price tag on that, but," he grinned.

"Our insurance carrier did just that. This simply is compensation for the quantitative assessment. It's a small percentage of the total. Darling, it's routine."

"But seven million?" Skye could see from Connie's expression that she knew too. Alex, Duncan, and the doctor did not. The doctor gaped and Alex smiled proudly. The money was nothing to him, but he thought the gesture as both dramatic and deserved.

"Hey, Captain. Great payday!" said Duncan whistling. He was impressed. "Mind if I take a look at that?" He was extremely well paid and considered himself the luckiest man alive, but he just wanted to touch a check with six zeros on it.

She handed it to him as if it were just another piece of paper. Her mind was spinning. Then the spinning stopped and she looked at Alex. He could see she had a plan and he smiled his approval. She smiled back.

"Do you have a pen, darling?" Alex drew out his gold Montblanc and handed it to her. She had said 'darling.' Automatically and naturally. His heart rolled over. It felt unbelievably good...better than seven million. She looked at the rich gold pen. "What, you can't have a pen with a hotel logo on it like everyone else?" she teased looking up into his bright blue eyes. He cocked an eyebrow and gave her his millionaire CEO look.

"Darling," he thought he would return the favor. "When you're endorsing a seven million dollar check while sitting in a Gulfstream, you need a gold pen."

"Show off," she said softly.

Skye turned the check over and endorsed it with a flourish. Captain Skyler Madison. Then she put it back in the envelope and gave it to Carter. "First, I want you to peal off one million and send it to a Washington D.C. firefighter. Alex will give you his name and address." Alex was already taking out his pocket computer. "Except for the handful of passengers who didn't sign off, I want you to divide the rest into equal shares for every man, woman, and child on the flight, including the crew. Take a share for me, and you and Bill use that to fund the biggest, baddest celebration reunion party you can manage."

Carter beamed at her. "May I publicize this fact?" He already knew the answer, but the VP in him had to ask.

"No, Mr. Vice President, you may not."

Carter conceded quickly, pleased with both their pilot and his friend.

Duncan whistled again. Now he was even more impressed. Connie gave him a proprietary look and winked. Skye was her friend and if you were judged by the friends you kept, well, she had the seven million dollar genuine article.

"Wow," squeaked Dr. Lacy. He was a general practitioner. When he was in practice, he got paid in baked goods and happy handshakes. He had no real savings. Maybe he could swing that condo on the beach after all. He was getting very fond of the beach. He had no way of knowing that Alex had already placed a quarter of a million in his account. Alex was a generous tipper.

There were hugs and kisses and even Skye had to admit, she needed to fold her tent and get moving. She didn't have much energy left and the pain in her side was killing her. She'd refused any medication all day and the wimpy side of her was beginning to wish the plucky side of her was a little less mulish.

Alex knew she was in trouble when she passively let him help her into the back of the limo. The doctor took the opportunity during the ride home to listen to Skye's lungs, take her temperature and blood pressure again, and try to force some medication down her.

"I don't want to take the painkillers any more," she said petulantly...fueled by the fact that she knew she was having some trouble. She coughed, the sound echoing deep in her chest. Alex looked at the doctor. It didn't sound good to him and he could tell from the doctor's expression he didn't like it either. "I don't like being high. I've had too many shots and pills this last year and my system is getting all whacked out. I can take a little pain."

"I know you can, but you can't take deep breaths when the pain gives you grief. That means your lungs begin to fill again and your coughing will get worse. You cough, it irritates the ribs and slows their healing. Here, take this cough medicine, at least." He handed her a small vial.

"No," said Skye shoving his hand away and giving him her evil eye.

"No?"

"That damn cough medicine has codeine in it."

"Yum. That makes it good."

"Hey, Captain," called Duncan from the front seat. "You don't want that medicine, I'm sure that Ms. Macloruny down the street will take it."

"Is she the one who weighs about 18 pounds and drives the lawn mower down the center of the street."

"That's the one."

Skye turned accusing eyes back to the doctor. "See what happens when you take that shit?"

Exasperated, Dr. Lacy turned to Alex. "Young man, I can see now why you shouted in her face yesterday. Not that I condone that sort of thing, but my goodness she's an aggravator."

"You don't know the half of it," said Alex, enjoying the show.

"Well you're a prune faced, pill pushing nag," said Skye, shifting again, trying to get comfortable. "And I am old enough to know what's good for me."

"See?" laughed Alex, earning a glare of his own.

"I'm a *Doctor* prune faced, pill pushing nag and you're my patient. If you don't take this medication, I get out the needle and enlist that commando who accompanied you back from the island to hold you down."

"You even try and you'll be singing soprano in the hallelujah choir." Skye was in true snapping form and it felt good. Her chest was tight, but her tongue was loose and limber.

"Oh my goodness you're scaring me half to death," said the doctor as he got out a syringe. He got a spine when one of his patients was in trouble.

Skye's flashing eyes went from the needle to the doctor's face. Her hand automatically balled into a fist.

"If you get scared half to death twice, does that mean you die?" Her voice was as cold and sharp as a scalpel.

Duncan exploded with laughter in the front seat. Alex was closer to the action, so he remained silent. The doctor reached in his bag for a vial of clear liquid. Looked like morphine to Skye.

"Doctor, back off. Alex, quit smirking. Duncan, you're fired." Yes, there was nothing wrong with Skye's mouth.

She shifted to get farther away from the doctor, but the movement caused an intense blast of pain to shoot through her side. She winced and coughed again, causing her even more discomfort. Alex already decided he wasn't going to let her make the decision this time and was waiting for a signal to make his move.

The doctor calmly brought the needle up to the rubber covering the mouth of the small bottle.

"Well?" he asked. He saw the pain in her eyes and he was going to have his way. "You want it in the vein or in the mouth."

"I said no," Skye snapped. "I don't need the goddamn medicine."

"And when did you get your medical degree, Dr. Madison?" asked the doctor calmly. He was rather enjoying himself.

"At least I didn't get a medical degree from Whatsamatta U. before Florida was a goddamn state. You put that thing in me and you're going to need to start seriously treating yourself."

There was the briefest of glances between the doctor and Alex. In a flash, Alex executed Operation Injection. While the doctor smoothly and quickly filled the syringe, Alex grabbed Skye's arm, pushed up the sleeve of her shirt and exposed the veins on the inside of her elbow. At the same time, he gently, but firmly pressed his shoulder against her to hold her in place and wrapped a leg around the two of hers. He knew they could be lethal and wanted to immobilize them. In perfect synchronization, the doctor swabbed the skin, inserted the needle and pushed the plunger. In just a few seconds, they had effectively carried out the entire op.

Skye was furious, but she couldn't get a deep enough breath to scream or shout and she certainly didn't have the strength to take Alex down. Duncan was still laughing his head off adding fuel to the fire. Alex decided he could most effectively negotiate for his life if he made a preemptive move on Skye so he turned and covered her mouth with his. His lips were demanding, working to distract her by letting her feel his desire and while he was at it, he reached in and pulled her physical need for him into the mix. He wasn't just giving, he was taking.

The doctor wasn't sure what all that kissing was going to accomplish besides making his patient short of breath, but he thought he would leave it to Alex. He was, after all, engaged to the lovely, but at the moment dangerous, creature. Just in case, he moved to the far side of the limousine. He'd seen her on the island and knew her capacity for inflicting damage to the human form.

The combination of the drug screaming through her system and Alex's breath stealing kiss made Skye's head spin. When Alex finally pulled out of the kiss, he found she was gasping for breath but smiling seductively. Her eyes went dark as a midnight sky as her pupils began to dilate. He thought it was a good sign and cupped her face in his hands. He wanted more, glad that she was falling under his spell. He touched her lips lightly, giving her an opportunity to get her breath back.

It wasn't often Alex underestimated the danger of any situation, but his mind was clouded by her heated response to his kiss. He should have been immediately suspicious of her apparent capitulation. Skye leaned into him, then without warning, took the opportunity for a counter offensive. She bit his lip hard and fast and brought her knee up when he jerked back. There wasn't a lot of power in her leg, but enough to have him letting go with an oath. She shoved away from him, her eyes flashing.

"Got anything in that bag for bitch bites, doctor?" she asked in a voice going husky.

Duncan was barely able to stay on the road he was laughing so hard. He thought this was better than the Pay for View fights. He kept that to himself, however, and even tried to keep his laughter as silent as possible.

The doctor just shrugged and closed his bag. This was all very entertaining, he thought. Then he froze when her dark eyes pinned him and narrowed with anger.

"You shouldn't have done that, you drug peddling, pill plunking, bag man. I'm going to give Hazel your address and tell her you wanted to know her ring size."

The doctor immediately stopped what he was doing and gaped at her.

"And Duncan, if you don't desist right now, I am going to tell Connie you're on probation for sniffing woman's dirty underwear in the Laundromat."

"Hey, Captain. I already told her it was for stealing cars."

"She's my friend. Who do you think she is going to believe? Me or a juvenile, ex-car thief with an addiction to goddamn romaine lettuce for Christ's sake." Skye's snarl was getting fuzzier and fuzzier. And Duncan's laughter didn't seem to diminish at all.

Alex was licking his bruised lip. It was swelling up. He didn't taste blood, but it hurt like hell. He gave Skye a wicked smile. It also turned him on. He felt himself getting hot. Must be some latent pain-loving, masochistic hormone in him, he thought. Skye stared at him through a haze and recognized the signs.

"Well, that backfired," he said softly, caressing her exposed arm and letting his tongue slowly, sensually run over his lip. His eyes smoldered with desire and Skye could feel the tug of heat in her own body as his fingers played with her skin. "You want to do that again?"

She shook her head slowly, frowning. It pissed her off that she was unable to hang on to the anger. The drug was making her mellow. She could feel his touch and it felt like heaven. Her eyes went down to his mouth. She wanted that mouth, not to bite this time, but to devour. The drug and her general exhaustion prevented her from taking action though. She felt tired. So tired.

"Alex?"

"Yes, darling?"

"I think I won't kill you until morning."

"All right. Before or after breakfast?"

"Oh after. I want coffee first. Put it on the calendar." She slurred the word calendar and her eyes closed before she could get out another breath. Alex took her in his arms and held her against him. Her head went for a familiar spot on his shoulder, her face snuggling into his neck. Within seconds she was completely under.

The doctor came back over, braver now that she was down for the count. He lifted her eyelid and studied her pupils.

"She will be out for at least 12 hours."

"I guess I don't have to worry about dying early, then."

"And she won't remember any of that last stuff, right?" asked Duncan from the front seat, still snickering.

"I sincerely hope not, young man," said the good doctor, wondering how difficult it would be to move to a new town and arrange for an unlisted number.

Alex was just enjoying the feel of her warm and compliant body nestled in his arms. Tonight she would get some sleep. He didn't feel at all guilty that it was drug induced.

CHAPTER 16

By Saturday, Skye had forgiven the trio of men for Operation Injection. Mostly because she had to admit the long night's sleep did her a world of good. Now for the really wonderful medicine. This was the day Alex's family was arriving and she would have a distraction. She considered it better than any drug.

David arrived first from New York with Al and Jason, who tore through the yard to find Skye. She was sitting on a lounge chair, enjoying the sun, and anxiously awaiting their arrival. She loved Alex's nephews and she thought David was a wonderful man and a great father.

Al was in the lead until he tripped over his own feet and went skidding over the lawn. He was one big grass stain with teeth when he picked himself up and continued to run toward Skye. Jason was a little older and he tried to be a bit more mature, but when he saw her sitting there, he started running too. David waved. Skye could actually raise an arm today so she did. Alex positioned himself beside his convalescing captain to protect her from the two projectiles who had made it to the steps but he wasn't needed as they skidded to a halt right in front of her chair. David must have already talked with them about not jumping on her.

"I lost a tooth. I don't wet my bed at night any more...not once. And I can spell cranberry and Ms. Lutz's cat had babies," said seven year old Al, wanting to get out all the important stuff right off the bat. The approval of the magnificent Skye was all a little boy could want. Well, that and a scooter, a new video game, and now maybe a baby cat.

"Kittens, stupid," said Jason, showing off his superior knowledge to Skye.

"Oh yeah. Anyway Dad said you're very sensible and we shouldn't rocket into you and that we should be very, very careful when we trade kisses for stuff...only to touch your lips." Since that was Al's favorite part anyway, he didn't mind.

"Sensible?" asked Skye as David caught up and bent down to give her a kiss.

"I think I said sensitive." David didn't want to scare his kids too much by telling them that their Aunt Skye had a serious injury. They always carried anxiety around with them about losing people they loved. That was especially true of Jason, who still remembered the day his Mom went to heaven and he never saw her again. He was just standing at the edge of her lounge chair and staring at her with a look of trepidation in his eyes. Skye understood immediately and completely. Jason was still standing back. Still assessing. Still anxious. It hurt her heart.

"I brought back something for you from London," said Skye. "Jason, would you help me up? My ribs, the bones right here, were hurt" she poked Al in the ribs who giggled, sending spit flying through the gap in his teeth. "And I could use a strong guy to lean on." Jason nodded solemnly and helped her up with great ceremony. She looked okay, he thought. And if stupid Al had ribs and if it was sort of just the tickle bone, well he guessed it was going to be all right.

Then Skye lowered her sunglasses. "How do you like my black eye?"

Jason looked up and saw the best black eye he guessed he had ever seen. "Wow, Aunt Skye. That's awesome." His face lit up. A black eye was definitely cool. He knew about them and he knew they healed just fine. Actually had one himself once when a kid at school was coming out a door just at the same time he was going in.

He took Skye's hand and she leaned on his thin shoulders. He had his dad's slender frame. Al was all Rita. Red curly hair, stocky build. He wanted to help too and they got into a battle over who was going to open the door. They ran into Duncan as they entered and he turned around to go in with them. The kids loved Duncan and the feeling was mutual.

Alex and David heard Skye's laughter as they disappeared into the house. "Hey, Duncan. Al lost a tooth, he doesn't wet his bed at night any more not once, he can spell cranberry and Ms. Lutz's cat had babies."

"Kittens!" shouted Jason and giggled when Skye got his ribs, too.

David went to shake his brother-in-law and best friend's hand. Looking after them he smiled fondly.

"Now there's one sensible lady."

"Sensitive, too." Alex put a beer in David's hand. It was Miller time.

"Seriously, though, Alex. She doing okay?"

"I think so. She's still in a great deal of pain. She has a real thing about drugs and she's been weaning herself off the good stuff. And she's doing light exercise that the doctor thinks is excessive."

"You had quite an adventure."

"Quite." That ended the conversation. Alex's family never went beyond a casual inquiry. It went against the grain since they all were instinctive investigators and interrogators, but they respected Alex's secrets. He was on the side of the angels and that was all that mattered. Conversation went to sports, headlines, Jason's report card, and other less secretive subjects.

Ten minutes later the boys came tearing back again to show their dad the Scotland Yard t-shirts she had salvaged from her flight bag. Their dad had told them they couldn't ask about them. But they didn't have to. Was there anything in the world their Aunt Skye couldn't do? They were anxious for the others to arrive so they could show them off.

When Skye sat back down, they traded kisses for chores all morning. Skye was feeling quite pampered and the boys were feeling secure again.

That afternoon, Skye was watching the boys play in the surf while Alex and David were busy building the biggest sand castle ever constructed. The fact they used several empty beer bottles in the construction gave it a rather tilted, but unique attitude.

She knew the minute the Cooper/Springfield clan arrived. The air exploded with voices and laughter. They had arranged vacation time and personal leave, clearing their calendars so they could enjoy being together while assuring themselves that all was well. They hadn't heard much from Alex for days before the stunning return of the airliner. The media said he was in seclusion but the family of cops suspected something else. As usual, they wouldn't mention it.

They'd followed the media accounts with both interest and dread. Alex filled them in periodically so they knew the plane was down and that Skye was alive even though the media still reported the plane as missing. Then he was gone. Passengers told of a brave commando, deadly, scary, and hard. A soldier with black hair, brown eyes, tall, scar, eagle tattoo. The description didn't fit exactly, but they suspected whom it was standing behind the captain.

And they heard about their Skye. Her valor, her constancy, her courage. International Airlines put out a brief statement and a biography so stories of her parents resurfaced. Her picture was everywhere and because she was so camera friendly and beautiful, the media always wanted to incorporate her face into all of its accounts. It sold magazines, newspapers and video news accounts. Jim worked behind the scenes to squelch most of it, but the interest was huge. Skye's close friends understood her need for privacy, so personal accounts were rare.

Since returning, Alex had filled them in on her condition, but someone from the medical center had leaked that she had been close to death when they brought her in. Since no one in the media had talked with her, there was a great deal of speculation on her health. The fact that no one had seen her since the plane landed fueled the speculation. Was she hovering near death? Was she alive? The family was here to see for themselves.

The Coopers were all stocky, red haired, and robust. Wyatt's rusty hair was streaked with gray, a fact she attributed to her youngest son Tank, and cut in a short, functional style. She had a confident manner, but a warm and wonderful approach to people around her. Her brothers Bat and Elliot, were also going gray, but their stocky frames were well maintained and spoke of the hours they invested in conditioning and the active life they had outside their jobs. They were strong, fun loving, and demonstrative. They brought their wives, the saintly Sue Ann and the sweet Stacy. Sue Ann was a social worker in a large hospital in Chicago and Stacy was an attorney for a local legal aid consortium. These women loved their husbands, were proud of their accomplishments, and formed a sisterhood that kept them happy and content with their lives. Skye thought they were wonderful.

A tall man came around the corner hefting luggage. Skye smiled. Alex favored his father. Blake Springfield was more reserved than his outgoing wife, but just as affectionate. He was a lion in the courtroom and a pussycat at home. He was slightly shorter and leaner than Alex, but his thick curly hair and sharp blue eyes were the same. Gray flecked his temples as well, and his laugh lines were deep, but his long body was trim and well toned.

The man responsible for all the gray hair was the most delightful combination of charm, deadly good looks, and irreverence Skye had ever met. While she was still partial to Tank's big brother, she was completely gone over him as a younger sibling. He was the little brother she never had. Always laughing, teasing, and talking. He had the Cooper build and his youthful, stocky body was all muscle. His hair was more auburn than red and he tamed it when he needed to in order the get it to the regulation length and style.

They all surrounded Skye who beamed at them. Alex stood close. He wanted to be sure their enthusiasm was not painful, but they restrained themselves from their usual hugging and stayed with just the kissing. They admired her black eye and all asked questions at once. The volume only increased as they volleyed for dominance. David and the boys came up to greet everyone and pandemonium broke out.

Alex did step in when Skye started laughing and it spiraled into an uncontrollable and painful fit of coughing. When she started gasping, he knelt down beside her and took her hand. She finally caught her breath and wiped the tears from her eyes. There was a momentary silence, then they all started to talk to each other, scolding and censuring. Alex looked at her shining eyes, shrugged his shoulders, and made a face. She nodded and smiled, still trying to get her breath.

"Let me show you all to your rooms," he said to his concerned family. She looked so good, thin, but good, that they had momentarily forgotten she was recovering from serious injuries. "Mom. Stay with Skye, will you? I'm going to send down the doctor." He gave her a quick kiss and stood.

"Of course." Wyatt sat down next to Skye, holding her hand and brushing some of the thick wavy hair off of Skye's forehead.

"Are you all right, sweetheart?" she asked, her concern as obvious as her love.

Skye couldn't get enough air to speak so she just nodded and smiled. Her wheezing was winding down and her ribs were responding to her tight hold on them.

"Don't say anything right now, honey. Let me just look at you. We were all so worried, but it doesn't surprise me that you brought all your passengers back."

"I had help," Skye rasped.

"I realize that." Wyatt waited for a heartbeat, then asked. "Would you like me to change the subject?"

Skye nodded. She would like that very much. Alex's family was far too perceptive.

So Wyatt entertained her with stories of the family, Tank's first month on the force, and the latest case Blake was working on.

One by one the family reassembled around the pool area. They were far more civilized when they arrived one by one.

Cynthia and one of the young women she hired to help her in the kitchen put out a spread of wonderful salads, sandwiches, snacks, and desserts. Tank thanked her and asked her what she had prepared for the rest of the family. David took bar duties and soon everyone was splashing in the pool, enjoying the sun, listening to music, and discussing their favorite topic of late, which was the hijacking and miraculous return of Flight 127.

Later, things quieted down as the family lounged around. Skye had been checked out by the doctor and was sitting in the shade. He didn't like her elevated temperature, but she vetoed a nap. She was just too happy to see everyone and insisted that this was far better for her convalescence than a few hours in bed. She looked over at Alex and saw the doctor standing near the doorway talking with him and gesturing wildly. She heard 'excitement' and 'overdo' and 'relapse.' Alex nodded politely and then said something that seemed to appease the little man.

Alex came over to where Skye was sitting and pulled up a chair beside her. He took her hand in his and leaned over. "The doctor is upset with you, darling."

"Me? But I'm the model of cooperation," she said, batting her eyelashes and looking innocent. In her white shorts, black tank top and pretty little gold sandals, she sure didn't look innocent, he thought. Her hair was pulled back and piled high on her head with a gold clip, but enough of her curls escaped so that she looked sensual and hot. Alex had to hold himself on a short leash to keep from taking her upstairs for that nap and a bit of necking.

"Are you really okay, sweetheart? You look delicious, but I can still hear your breath in your chest. We don't have to entertain them, you know. They're family."

"I really want to be here," she said and he was shocked to see tears in her eyes. "I may not be able to participate fully in all the activities, but I feel so alive here, with all of them around us. Please. I don't want to be alone."

"All right, darling, but I told the doctor that if you sounded any worse, I would have the Hulk over there," he indicated Tank, "carry you up to your room." She nodded and sniffed.

"All right, but I get to decide."

Her tone was sweet, such a contrast to the sexy picture she made, Alex found her irresistible. Leaning over, he kissed her so gently, everyone in the pool said, 'awhhh.' She liked it and kissed him back. Another 'awhhh' from the appreciative audience. Blake and Wyatt looked at each other. Their oldest son appeared to be completely under the spell of the stunning woman in white shorts. It was wonderful. A mother's dream come true. A father's pride in his son's exquisite taste.

Alex and Skye turned to the grinning faces.

"Just taking her temperature," said Alex.

"Is it elevated?" asked Stacy.

"It is now," said Skye giving Alex another quick peck. He looked into her eyes for a few more seconds to see if she had the pain under control. They looked clear and her breathing sounded less like a broken steam engine.

Wyatt continued to look at the two of them sitting with their heads together and sighed to her husband of nearly 35 years. "They're a splendid couple, aren't they? I didn't think he was ever going to find a soul mate. I was so afraid he was going to make his way alone."

"There was always that possibility, darling," he said, unconsciously playing with the rings on her finger as he held her hand. "He needed someone who was his equal and I think he's found her. She's quite a package. We did well, Wyatt." He looked in the direction of Tank, who had both their grandsons on his broad shoulders, then back to Alex. "We did very, very well."

Wyatt sighed again. "If they had only chosen accounting."

"I know, but they didn't."

She snorted, "That's for sure."

After some of the group decided to go to town for ice cream, Tank, Wyatt, David, Skye, and Alex were enjoying the setting sun on the south terrace. Skye sat beside Alex in a doublewide lounge chair. It felt like heaven to Skye to have the family around. Enjoying the display of pastel colors on the horizon, she moved further into Alex's side. He felt it, liked it, and shifted so she had more room.

Skye could feel his laughter. He was always looser when he was around his little brother. More relaxed. More fun loving. Skye liked that.

They'd been laughing over a remembered exploit that started when their mom was part of a squad of officers assigned to keep order during a circus parade in downtown Chicago. Apparently the elephants were considerably rude when it came to their bathroom habits, making walking pretty treacherous for the formation of politicians and high-level police commissioners set to be the grand finale of the parade. Skye was wheezing again by the time they were finished with the story, so they decided to talk about more serious topics.

"According to CNN, there was a pretty scary desperado working with you to get everyone out," Tank said to Skye, smiling. "A lot of the passengers felt he was either from a special operations branch of the military or one of the hijackers who turned on the evil forces because he saw you and couldn't resist your charms. You'd better watch out, Alex. He sounds like someone the ladies could really go for. Skye may change her mind and throw over the suave lawyer for the soldier. You know how some ladies get turned on by action heroes."

"Yes," said Wyatt. "Although I recall you saying you fell in love with the sky blue of his eyes. I know the feeling." She looked into the eyes of her own husband. "And this man apparently was very dark with dark eyes...not your type...huh, Skye?"

"Not at all," said Skye. She closed her eyes and leaned her head back against Alex's shoulder. "I like them soft and safe." She felt him give her a little bump with his hip.

"The account said he was injured. They saw blood on his shirt," said David.

"Maybe it wasn't his," said Skye, logically. "He was pretty much a one-man army."

"Sounded like he got help from the captain," said Blake.

"They took my plane and I was pissed," she said shrugging. Skye then began to answer their questions, filling in the details from her perspective. She left out what she felt she had to, elaborated on what they were curious about. Even Tank was subdued when she finished.

"Not to change the subject," said Blake, casually. "But you look like you have been favoring your right shoulder, son. You fall down again?"

"Clumsy oaf. Never could keep on his feet. As bad as a six-week-old puppy," said Tank. "You better reconsider that action hero, Skye. The way you get into trouble, you need someone like him watching your back. Hey!" He perked up. "Maybe I could apply."

"I'll keep that in mind," smiled Skye.

"Back off," said Alex, good-naturedly. He'd kept his shirt on around them that day, but he figured his family of cops would recognize a bullet scar when they saw it, so he improvised. "Actually," he said cryptically. "I fell over a gun this time. Went off. Scared the shit out of me."

"And the bullet hit your shoulder?" asked Wyatt without a hint of skepticism.

"Went right through it. Bled like a bitch, too."

"Was this while you were in seclusion, keeping vigil by the phone for word of Skye?"

Skye sat very still. This was getting close to the line. She felt Alex tense up a bit. She knew what it was costing him to keep things from his family. They were not business people and teachers. They were as committed to law enforcement and justice as he. Yet, he had to keep a part of himself hidden from them. It was to their credit that they allowed him to do so. Never asking one question too many. Knowing when to stop. It was an interesting dance and a touching one.

"Well, actually it was."

"You can take your shirt off now, dear. I won't give you a time out for foolishness," said Wyatt, although Alex didn't move to comply. It was one thing to refer to it in general terms. It was quite another to let his mother see it. It was healing nicely, but his mom didn't need to see a fresh bullet wound in one of her children.

"Do you remember when we were at your mom's precinct softball game?" said Blake to Tank. Subject discussed. Subject closed. "She was pitching and she wanted to talk to the shortstop. She yelled 'time out' and you jumped a mile, thinking you were being punished for copping her stash of potato chips while she was at the pitcher's mound. You plopped your pudgy little butt on the ground and wailed for five minutes. You must have been three or four. Alex and Rita told you she had special powers and knew exactly what you were doing every minute."

"I was so spooked I shaped up for a week," laughed Tank.

"A record, as I recall," said Blake. The discussion of Alex and his injury had been noted and now passed. They were not going back there. Wyatt looked at Alex's shoulder, breathed a mother's sigh of relief and moved on, too.

"I do have special powers," said Wyatt. "I know what you're thinking right now."

"What?" asked Tank.

"You're thinking 'please don't say things like pudgy little butt' in front of Skye," said Wyatt.

"Jeesh, Mom. That was exactly what I was thinking. It's embarrassing."

"No more than your display at the dinner table tonight."

Tank and the brothers Cooper, Bat, and Elliot, had a lobster-eating contest. Tank disappeared under a mound of lobster carcasses, pausing only to wash down the meat with gallons of beer. Both Bat and Elliot had conceded a full half-hour before Tank had nearly collapsed under the table.

They talked until the stars came out, catching up on what they'd been doing since Tank's graduation. Everyone else came out at different times to say good night.

"So, Skye," asked Wyatt. "Any plans for the wedding? Should we save a date?"

Alex held his breath. She'd said this was what was going to happen. When people asked in the past, she always cleverly, but deftly, changed the subject. It would be extremely difficult to do with his mom.

"Skye?" said Alex, when she didn't respond. Her head had been leaning against his shoulder on and off since they got on the lounge chair and it was currently resting on it. He looked over at Wyatt, who was gazing at Skye's face and smiling with both affection and compassion. She looked up into her son's eyes.

"I do believe we have put your lovely fiancée to sleep."

"Speak for yourself," said Tank. "It wasn't my electrifying stories that put her under. She was fascinated until David started talking about Al's tooth. Can't blame her for wanting to escape into sleep."

"Skye?" said Alex again. "Sweetheart, wake up. Let's go to bed." His arm was stretched over the back of the lounger, but now came down to wrap around her.

"Poor thing. I think we've exhausted her," said Wyatt with a mother's compassion.

"No, she does that to herself," said Alex. "She doesn't know when to quit." He was a bit awkward because of his shoulder when he moved to position himself to pick her up. Tank stood up quickly and scooped Skye up effortlessly.

"Allow me the honors," he said. "God, she's really light for someone so tall. You've got to feed her, Alex."

"I tried, but she sat next to you at dinner and the food was flying by her so fast, I'm not sure she got anything at all."

Tank laughed and Wyatt was right beside him, wrapping a big fluffy towel around her as they walked. Blake and David stayed by the pool and finished their beers. They saw Alex flex his shoulder when he went to open the door for Tank.

"He's gotten a bit more accident-prone over the last few years," said Blake.

"I've noticed that," responded David.

"Want another beer?" asked Blake.

"Nope. I promised Jason I would come in and play Firewalkers with him."

"Is that the new game Alex bought him?"

"Yup...and it's just the kind of game Alex likes. Lots of shooting, hidden secret weapons, nothing out in the open, clues cleverly hidden, mysterious and clandestine operations. It's a game of wit and strategy as well as all out action. You want to watch?"

"No. I think I'll wait and see if Wyatt comes back out."

"Good night, Blake," said David.

"Good night, son." He watched as his son-in-law walked across the terrace to the game room. Rita's husband. The father of his grandchildren. A fine man. Then he sat back and waited for his wife. He knew she would want to talk. He looked at the stars and thought of his children. So his oldest boy had a bullet wound. Just as he thought. He allowed himself one shudder then calmed himself with a rush of pride. Just couldn't help himself. He was alone. It was dark. He didn't have to play along right now. Then he heard the familiar footsteps and made room next to him for the mother of his children.

Skye never woke up. Tank laid her gently on the chaise and Alex covered her with a soft blanket. They looked down at her and Tank cleared his throat.

"How close was it this time?" asked Tank.

"Too close," said Alex. Tank put his arm around his older brother, careful not to bump his sore shoulder.

"She has you and I would say that makes her well protected now."

Alex smiled. He felt his brother's arm on his shoulder and the contact made him feel connected to something bigger, stronger than just himself. It was a very good feeling.

"I'm glad you're all here," he said.

"Me too." Then they looked at each other and smiled brother smiles. "Are we going to get really mushy here?"

"It's possible. Or I could get Skye to bed and we could go down and join Jason and David in the game room and do manly things."

"Or I could get Skye to bed while you could go down and join Jason and David."

Alex stared.

"Or, I could stop in the kitchen and get the cold lobster and meet you down there." Tank bent down and kissed Skye's cheek. "We won't wait for you. You may change your mind."

"No. By the time I get her all cozy and covered, I'll be in the mood to blast some Firewalkers and take out squads of deadly invaders."

"Ah. Okay." Tank looked down at Skye and caught the sound of air going in and out of her lungs. He guessed that meant no physical activity tonight. "I get it. No heavy breathing. Well. See you in a while."

Alex loved getting Skye out of her clothes and into bed. The doctor would be checking on her, so he grabbed a nightgown out of her drawer that was relatively modest and brought it over to put it on her. He treated himself for a minute and looked at her naked body. It was a warm night and she looked comfortable enough. The rib bruises were fading, but the ribs themselves were too prominent. He couldn't control his hands and he found himself running them up her sides and over her breasts. He leaned down and kissed them and then her neck. When he heard her moan, he wasn't sure if it was pleasure or pain. It fanned the embers and fueled the fire. He was losing control now; he wanted her so badly. Needed her. His lips came down on hers again. Maybe…maybe tonight he could…but a cough, starting deep in her chest, cooled him right off. No. She was still so sick.

Another cough woke her up. Still very groggy, she opened her eyes and blinked.

"Alex. Alex?" Her voice was very raspy and dry.

"Would you like a glass of water darling?"

"No," she said and drifted back down into sleep.

She still called for him, he thought. Even when she didn't really want anything, she wanted to know he was there. He sighed. He could wait. This would be enough for now. He swore that when she got better they would get married as quickly as possible and not get out of bed for a week. He would make love to her all night, then have breakfast in bed and make love to her all day.

Whoa. He had to stop that train of thought before he jumped the track. She was still naked. Better cover her before temptation overpowered his more righteous self.

The doctor came in just as Alex covered her up to her chin with a sheet. Her deep cough would have been tolerable, but not in combination with her sore ribs. She winced every time she coughed. She would sleep soundly only because of the powerful drugs the doctor administered with Alex's consent. Skye would just have to rag on him later for allowing it. He spent the rest of the evening working out his frustration in game after game of Firewalkers. He blasted a bit of his sexual tension every time he pushed a button and the enemy went down.

It was just before dawn that Skye started shaking. Alex woke up immediately. He looked over and saw she was awake.

"Skye? Are you cold?"

"No," she whispered. He came over to her, to hold her, but she pulled the blanket around her and turned from him. Blasted by the cold shoulder, he put his hand out to touch her. When he heard her moan, he nearly snapped.

"Sweetheart, let me hold you." He felt the bed shudder again. The drugs should have kept her under for hours yet. She coughed and he turned her, put his arm around her shaking shoulders and held her rigid, tense body. He knew her eyes were open.

"Darling. Do you need something?" In the pale night light he always had on, he could see the tears on her cheeks. Drugs sometimes did that to her. Brought out volatile emotions, vivid dreams. That was one reason she hated them so much. She didn't pull away, though, and that was a plus. He held her until the sun came up. He knew she would be better then.

And she was. As matter of fact, she was ticked off at everyone for agreeing with the doctor that she needed to stay in bed the next day and have her visitors a few at a time. She hated missing anything. So she made everyone solemnly promise not to have any fun until she got well enough to join them again. Everyone agreed. Skye sat in bed and once in a while thought she heard laughter or the boys' loud voices above the surf. She frowned. No fair.

Alex kept a close eye on her over the next few days. Skye's ribs were healing fast, but she wasn't getting better. She was still losing weight, despite Cynthia's best efforts to get her to eat. Skye always smiled, thanked her, and picked at what was on her plate. She never slept more than a few hours. Alex would wake to find her sitting in a chair by the window, or out on the terrace.

He would watch her and his heart would clutch at the expression of pain on her face. At first he tried to convince himself that it was her injuries. But after three weeks, he had to admit the truth. It was not physical torment he saw, but anguish deep in the soul. She never showed it in her waking hours. She was always in good spirits, laughing and talking with her family or his. Swimming slowly, tentatively in the surf, or going for long walks in the sun. She even engaged in mild exercise and had her Tae Kwon Do instructor design routines that would protect her healing ribs.

Everything should have been restful. Tranquil. All the debriefings were done, the reports written. If an official needed to talk with her, he or she flew down. Terrin hadn't been apprehended, but that was only a matter of time. Amanda kept them informed on her investigation. It seemed she had reactivated herself temporarily and since she had trained half the state department and Joint Chiefs of Staff and called the President Andy, she got her way. She was due to come down at the end of the week for a verbal report.

He sheltered her from the media and they frequently enjoyed watching various passengers interviewed on CNN or Oprah singing the praises of the courageous captain. She took calls from her crew and found they were all doing well and enjoying the spotlight. Most of them had returned to a full work schedule. Bill and Carter were busy planning a huge party at the end of the month. They rented a hangar and invited all the passengers and families from International Airlines Flight 127. It would be quite a reunion. Already the networks were asking to be on the inside. Alex politely and firmly foiled all their efforts. No media.

A very persistent and resourceful news crew finally located Skye. The source at the medical center traced the address where a doctor had sent supplies the day the plane landed. The media grabbed it and were camped out on the lawn for a few days. They didn't even get a glimpse of her. The boys loved to watch the news reports broadcasted live in front of their gate. They would fly a kite to see if they could see it on the afternoon news. It amused them for days. Alex didn't like it that Skye's location had been made public. He wasn't too keen on anyone knowing where she was, but didn't feel like moving everyone, either. After a couple of days, the news crews left.

As soon as she was cleared by the doctor, Skye started mingling with everyone again. Once among them, however, it was nearly impossible for any of them to convince her to take a nap. If Alex thought she needed the rest, he would pick her up bodily and because she didn't want to hurt his sore shoulder, she didn't resist. Whatever worked, thought Alex.

Alex reached over and, as expected, he was alone in the big bed. He squinted at the clock. It was nearly dawn. She'd been very restless again. Ever since they got back, Alex would sleep with her in the big bed, watching over her while his own wound healed. He wanted to be close those first days. She wasn't critical, but she was very, very ill. He would hear her labored breathing and she seemed to respond to his touch, his voice in the night. When she coughed, a sound that chilled him, he would hold her to his chest to minimize the movement of her painful ribs. When he kissed her fevered forehead, she would move into his arms. Now, she kept herself as far from him as possible. It was ironic that the healthier she became, the more she withdrew.

She never came to him in the night anymore. It was hurting him badly, but he gave her the space she needed. He longed to touch her, but his instincts told him to give her time. She'd asked him for time and he would give it to her. His heart told him to move through her defenses before they became too strong, but there was a part of him that knew she would have to come to him before their relationship could re-establish itself. Permanently. He was willing to take a beating in the short run, if the payoff was sufficiently high in the long run. He was, after all, a seasoned and successful businessperson and in this case the payoff was beyond what his mind could measure. He would wait.

She wasn't in bed. She rarely was now. Getting up, he walked soundlessly to the double doors leading to the terrace. The door was open and he could hear the surf. Then he heard the sound that ripped a hole in his gut. She was crying. Not just shedding tears, but weeping as if she would never stop. He just didn't know what to do. Should he go out there and try to help, or was this something she needed to work out herself?

Bloody hell. Never one just to leave things to fate, he decided to try to do something for her. He went out on the deck.

She knew he was there. She always did. She quickly wiped the tears off her cheeks and rubbed the ache in her chest. As he came up behind her, she took a deep shuddering breath.

"Skye. Honey, is it something you want to talk about? Can I help you?"

She just shook her head and turned to him. The look in her eyes was so sad. So haunted.

"No. There's nothing you can do. I'm afraid this is a solitary journey." She turned back to the ocean. She could see what this was doing to him and it added to her torment. "I've been thinking about going away. Taking some time alone. Some time after the family leaves."

Oh no, he thought. Unacceptable. "You can do that here. I'll give you all the space you need." It was killing him to say this, but he didn't want her to leave. "Would you feel more comfortable if I slept in one of the other rooms?"

She just stared for a while. "Yes." Then, when she felt the immediate blow of that idea slam into her, knew Alex had felt the same horrible impact, she quickly said. "No. No. Please." She put her face in her hands. She couldn't get herself around the hurt. And Alex had felt it. His chest was burning with the shock.

"Oh God," she said. "Alex I'm so sorry. I can usually sort things out better than this." Her voice hitched and she started to cry again.

"Can I hold you?" he asked gently, his arms aching to draw her against him, but standing back.

"Oh please...please," she said and almost collapsed into him. He went to her and held her tenderly, not wanting to press her painful ribs, but wanting to absorb her into him. When she swayed, he picked her up and carried her back to bed. She curled up and he covered them with the sheet. Her eyes were closed but her breathing was still ragged. He had heard the term heartsick, now he saw clearly what it meant. As exhaustion took over, she slipped into a restless sleep.

It tore a piece of his soul to move away from her, but he had to do something with the hurt. He got out of bed and looked down at her. At least she was getting some sleep. Turning, he left the room. It was almost dawn, so he went to the gym and pushed himself through a punishing series of repetitions with the weights. He ran full out on the beach as the sun came up. Alone. Solitary. In as much pain as his sleeping angel.

Skye looked down at Alex running on the beach. He was flying, like he was trying to outrun something. But she knew it would still be there when he stopped. Another tear leaked out of her eye. She was hurting him. And she felt powerless to stop it.

Just as daylight was breaking though, Skye came to the gym. He was still there, listening to the morning market reports, talking on the phone, and going through reps. She smiled at him. "Multi-tasking?" she asked when he finished his conversation.

"Indeed." He smiled up at her.

"And how many millions did you just make?"

"Two or three, I guess. Why, you want to go shopping again?"

She laughed. She could do that in the daylight.

She picked up some light free weights and began working with them, wanting to find her limits. Alex stopped completely and just watched her.

"I was thinking, Alex," she began, and she really had been thinking about this a lot. "After everyone leaves, I want to go home for a little while."

"To the townhouse?" he asked casually. It was all right with him. She probably wanted to see all her friends in Washington D.C.

"No. To Stafford." Alex's face went to stone. That was where she grew up. That shouldn't have been what she considered home any longer. Her home was with him, where they lived together. She continued a few reps, unaware of his reaction.

"The media is mostly gone, according to Sloane and Hazel. I would like…"

She never got to finish her sentence. Alex interrupted her. "Could you tell me two things?"

She looked up at him. He looked so angry. "What?"

"First of all, why are you so anxious to leave me and secondly, when did the house in Virginia get to be your home again? I thought you lived with me…here, or the townhouse or the house we're renovating in Virginia. You remember, the house you picked out? The one we're going to live in after we're married? When did you start thinking of this living arrangement as temporary, again?" He was shouting and he didn't care any more. She had completely destroyed him with this and he was going to get answers. His irritation and temper momentarily greater than his hurt.

Skye sat very still. Then started to finish her reps, ignoring him. He lost it completely. Grabbing the weight from her hand, he threw it hard out the closed window. The sound of the glass shattering was perfect, he thought. It punctuated his feelings and mirrored his mood exactly.

"I love you. I want you. I want you to be my wife. I want you to only truly be home when you're with me. I want you to wear my ring." He grabbed another weight and threw that out another window. Fury raged inside him. She wasn't even reacting. "Ignore that, you ice queen."

Slowly standing up, she turned to him. She looked calm and in control, but her nerves were raw underneath. Her injuries were nothing compared to the beating her psychological well-being was taking. Since her return, she'd been in a nightly battle with her personal demons. She didn't know if she could beat them, but she did know she couldn't wage war on that front and then have enough energy left to face Alex's frustration, hurt, and now fury. She blinked a few times.

"I'm sorry, Alex. I think I did a bit too much with the weights. I'm going upstairs to take a nap." She turned and coolly left the room. Her knees were shaking and her palms were sweating, but she managed to walk out of the room. She cringed when she heard the sound of more glass shattering. She was so very, very sorry and tears rolled down her cheeks as she slowly climbed the stairs.

Alex threw the twenty-pound weight that had the misfortune to be within arm's length. It hit the opposite wall with such force it shattered the entire mirrored panel. He watched as it hit, then stood stunned as the whole wall collapsed into a pile of shiny, jagged debris. A tiny shard shot out across the wood floor. He stared at the triangular piece that had skidded to a stop at his feet.

Shit, that's exactly how I feel, he thought. Shattered, in pieces, a pile of sharp, splintered glass. She'd completely ignored him. He would rather she fight him. He needed to get through the perimeter she had again built around herself. Through that steel wall to her heart and soul. It was in there. He saw it. Or was that an illusion, too? Why the hell wasn't she reacting?

"Wow, man," said Tank as he came running into the room. "Remodeling?"

When he had heard shattering glass, he came on the run. Terrin was still out there and even though there was excellent security and no one thought he would be foolish enough or stupid enough to choose revenge over safety, everyone was on the alert. Alex noticed Tank discreetly tuck his Glock back into his waistband. Then they both turned as Wyatt and Blake came charging into the room, with David close behind. All guns were drawn, all eyes alert.

They looked around at the destruction. Quickly assessing. Standing down when they saw no danger. "What happened here, son? You okay?" asked Blake. Alex looked okay. Well sort of. He looked like he could do more serious damage.

"What?" asked David. "The exterminators missed a few cockroaches? They got so big you got to start chucking weights at them?" He too repositioned the safety on his gun and slipped it in his waistband.

"Can't a guy throw a tantrum around here without an audience?" asked Alex irritably.

"And an appreciative one. You really did a job on that wall." Wyatt was in a swimsuit and had nowhere to tuck her gun, so she handed it to David.

Sometimes his family was too damn diligent. Actually it was one of the reasons he had invited them all to come, then to stay. He trusted his security system, but he trusted his family more. "All we need are the Uncles Bat and Elliot and this party is complete."

"You rang?" asked Bat, as he and Elliot strolled into the room. They had taken the perimeter and since no bad guys came flying out of the room, they assumed all was well. Elliot had two weights in his hand. He put them on the rack. "Interesting lawn art, but they would play havoc with the mower blades."

Bat turned slowly in a circle and whistled. "Those windows do open, Alex. Of course someone as soft as you may not have strength to turn that little crank there on the ledge."

"Someone say little crank?" asked Sue Ann, as she entered through the garden door. "I thought we left him in the playroom with Jason. Holy shit, Alex. Did you get a little cranky yourself?"

"Where is Stacy? Why don't we all go find her so we can make this party complete?" said Alex through clenched teeth. He loved them all, but right now he was in a funk and he didn't want them around.

"Party? Did someone say party?" asked Stacy as she, too, entered the room. She stared at the shattered wall mirror on the floor. "Wow! Now that has got to be good for more than seven years bad luck. No one take Alex's financial advice for the next decade."

"Like anyone would take it in the first place. I seriously question his stability," said Elliot.

"Seriously questioning anything is Mom's job," said Tank. He was nosing around in the refrigerator. It was an ongoing joke in the family that the way you capture a tank is to put a refrigerator in its path, then slam the door when it had its armaments in the meat drawer. "You got anything besides fruit juice and mineral water in here?"

"No. We're in the gym. If you want to party, I suggest sticking your nose in the refrigerator in the bar. Better yet, why don't you stick your lard ass on the floor near the refrigerator in the kitchen and we can have Bat and Elliot shovel all the contents into your big fat mouth?" There wasn't an ounce of fat on Tank, but he got the idea. He also thought it was hilarious and laughed.

"Good strategy, oh guru of business," he said. "Cut out the middle man...ah...woman." Getting Alex mad was one thing. Getting his Mom mad with a chauvinistic remark was quite another.

"Good strategies are my department, son," said Elliot. "FBI. And I think since the danger appears to be localized to glass only, we should move this shindig to the bar and pool area. I do believe our gracious host here is buying?"

He grabbed a 50-pound weight as if it was a Q-Tip and tossed it to Alex. He was as strong as an ox, but Alex always teased him about his cushy desk job. "Carry on, boy. If you need us, we'll be the drunks out by the pool."

Alex caught the weight but it took all of his strength to casually put it aside. The anger helped.

Tank was the last to leave the room. "If you're this frustrated, big brother, I could loan you my collection of Playboys and stand guard at the bathroom door."

"Did I ever tell you that you were adopted?" he glared at his brother. How did Tank always get so close to the mark? He was going to make a great cop. "The circus came to town one day and just left without you."

Tank walked out of the patio door, laughing and making monkey noises. Alex took a deep breath and tried to get his temper under control.

"That was as distracting as hell," he muttered. But the upside was that the back-up security system was tested and passed. He could hear Tank still making monkey noises. Then his uncles were joining in with animal sounds of their own. What a team. On the other hand, his home was safer and better protected than the White House. Turning, he looked at Duncan standing in the doorway.

"What!" shouted Alex.

"Just thought I would see what all the noise was about. I'll get someone to clean up, Bossman. Ah. Your family sure is one well armed posse."

"Shit. No intruder is safe with them around. They don't even have to use their guns. They can just annoy them to death."

Leaving Duncan to deal with the destruction, he followed Skye up to their room. Back to his mission. He was going to go get that ring and make her either accept it again and all that it symbolized, or tell him she changed her mind. He was determined to have it out with her. He wasn't going through what he just went through and wind up with no results.

Skye was lying down, completely exhausted. She had slept little the night before and not at all the night before that. The short session with the weights had sapped her of all her reserves. She hadn't the energy to work out in the first place. It was just an excuse. She wanted to be next to Alex. To see him. To know that he was all right. Oh Alex. She tucked her hands under her cheek as she lay on her good side. She studied the unadorned fourth finger of her left hand. She hadn't meant to hurt him. Another tear slid down her cheek and on to the back of her hand.

Her eyes were so heavy, so in need of relief. Closing them, she sighed as she started drifting. Her ribs felt okay. She could take a deep breath. Well, hell. All that meant was that her sighs were more heartfelt and successful and her weeping was less physically painful.

Alex came storming into the room and stopped cold. He watched her as she slept. Her hands were tucked under her cheek in a very innocent, childlike pose. His heart was wrenched by the sight, then squeezed some more when he noticed the dried tear on her cheek. He wanted to hold her, to kiss away whatever was upsetting her so much. But instead, he pulled up a chair and sat. Watching her sleep, thinking about his next move. Skye was frowning in her sleep now.

"What's going on, my darling?" he whispered. "What's going on in there?"

CHAPTER 17

There were two of them now. Hanging in the closet side by side. Beautiful. Chosen with care and eager anticipation. Long, white, elegant. Oh God! No! Please. She reached for them. They were both drenched with blood. Two wedding dresses. So much blood. She stood, staring at them, knowing what it meant.

Then she was in the piazza. She saw her parent's car blow up and the bodies inside burn. They hadn't died right away. Her heart was screaming, then she looked down…her heart was in her hands. It was bleeding. The blood running into the river that she knew would merge with the blood dripping off the dresses. She couldn't stop the bleeding and she was dying. Then she put it away. Put her still heart in a magic box and somehow she got stronger. She had no heart, but she could breathe…and fly. She was flying. Flying and she could breathe again.

Then she saw a man. A handsome man, laughing and loving her. He was in a uniform. Waving, smiling, and she was so happy. Her heart was back in her chest…beating. Strong.

But why he was naked. Jeff. Not laughing any more. Not alive any more. On a slab, a sheet covering him. She pushed the sheet away. Open your eyes. Marry me. The face. Familiar, but not. Pale, cold…so cold. As white as the dress hanging in her closet.

This time she looked down and her heart was completely broken. It was in pieces and she tried to find them all. She went from room to room, searching for all the pieces. It was her home in Virginia. She found them and put them all in the box. There was blood everywhere. Opening the closet, she saw her wedding dress, blood flowing from it. She moaned at the sight. It was hideous.

Alex. Her prince charming. Her valiant guardian. There was a ring, a talisman. He knelt before her and presented it to her on a pillow. It glimmered and it was filled with warmth. She was so warm, so filled with light. It was an amulet and she put it on. Going to the box, she placed the ring on the lock. It opened and she saw a lovely, white gardenia where the pieces of her heart used to be. She sighed.

She was in her wedding dress. She must have taken it out of her closet. No. It was a different dress...a different man. Then she saw him lying still. On a slab, with a sheet covering his body. As she watched in horror, the front of her dress became drenched in blood, Alex's blood. She turned to ice and something hit her from behind. She cracked into tiny pieces. The pain was excruciating. She couldn't breathe; she was drowning in blood. So much blood. Now there are two wedding dresses hanging side by side. Spinning, she walked toward two men and her parents lying on slabs of marble, hideously burned, horribly mutilated. Nearly unrecognizable. Now the blood was hers, gushing from her chest, her own heart. She was drowning. Drowning. She couldn't breathe. Someone was trying to save her, to pull her out. No...no. Let me drown, let me die. Let me go.

Alex watched as Skye slept deeply, peacefully. Maybe now she would get some of the rest she needed. Then perhaps this would all resolve itself. Maybe he was reading too much into her lack of response to him. Maybe it was just her injuries. Damn, why had he allowed himself to lose control like that?

Abruptly her face changed. Alex sat up and watched as she started murmuring. He thought she was saying blood, then he distinctly heard her cry his name. There was such a forlorn and heartbreaking tone in her voice that his chest ached. What was it she was going through? When her defenses were down, what was she seeing in her mind, in her dreams? Whatever it was, he could see it was bad, very bad. This must be when she usually got up and left his bed. She must have still been half in it when he saw her sobbing on the terrace. This fearless woman was battling and she was losing. The demons were too strong for her while she was asleep. She was crying now, hard. He jumped up, no longer able to take the sound of her heartbreak. Chilled by her words. "Let me drown. Let me die. Let me go."

"Darling...baby," he whispered, gathering her up in his strong, steady arms. "Shhhh. It's all right. I'm here. I'll protect you. Shhh. Darling, wake up." He got into bed with her and held her.

"Alex...Alex," she murmured, still not fully awake, but completely out of breath. "Alex." She couldn't stop saying his name. She seemed to be looking for him. She was sobbing so hard, Alex was afraid she might reinjure herself, but he simply couldn't get her calmed down. He wished he knew what to do, thought about getting his mother, then decided to let instinct be his guide. He just held her tighter; shifting until he was sitting braced up against the back of the bed with his arms around her thin, shaking body. He held her gently, but firmly so her violent shuddering wouldn't rack her healing ribs and continued to whisper to her in a soft, tender voice. "Darling I'm here. I'm here. You have to wake up. Come to me and we'll talk. We'll fight this together. You aren't alone. Darling, please."

Slowly she came out of the deep, dark hole, opening her eyes. She was so groggy, so bleary. She couldn't get the sight of the two blood soaked wedding dresses out of her mind. They were right there. Her eyes were open, but they were still in the room. Feeling Alex, she clung to him with the desperation of a drowning woman.

Sobbing, she mumbled in Italian. He couldn't understand all the words, but he felt the emotion. It was raw and it was terrible. Wave after wave of extremes...fear, sadness, anger, grief, hopelessness, betrayal, despair. It was pouring out of her and he worked hard to keep the contact so she would feel his presence, know his love, lean on his strength. He was finding it hard to breathe with the effort to absorb her anguish. Her trembling became less vicious the more she came to consciousness. Finally she blinked and sighed hugely. She had her arms around Alex's waist and lay against him, very still. If he hadn't felt her racing heart and heard her ragged breathing, he would have thought she went under again.

Skye was in his arms. Alex was here and he was alive. She lay very still so she could hear his steady heart beat. His tender words had penetrated the fog of her nightmare.

"Skye?" he said, finally. He wanted to assure himself that she was conscious and awake.

"Shhh," she said softly. "I want to hear your heart beating for a while longer." She sniffed and wiped her face, then went very still again. "I just want to hear your heart," she whispered and the words were like a knife through it. He found himself more conscious of the rhythm of his heart than he ever had been in his life. He willed it to beat strong and true. He willed it for her. If it brought her comfort, he could sit like this for hours.

As it happened, he did. Listening to the comforting beat of his heart, the steady pulse, she went to sleep. Right between heartbeats, she fell into a deep, undisturbed sleep. Alex shifted to get more comfortable and held her tightly. He kissed the top of her head. She was sleeping, and if his arms, legs, and feet also fell asleep with inactivity, it was a small price to pay.

She was walking down the aisle. Alex was smiling at her. Standing there, handsome in his tuxedo and he had that look he got when he was observing her. She caught the look sometimes and it was the most wonderful wash of love imaginable. Her heart was beating again. In her chest again. She could hear it. Then she reached for him and he was gone. There was no one there. She looked down and her dress was soaked with blood, his blood. The gardenias were wilted and brown and blew away as she watched them turn to dust. He was dead. Alex. Standing at the alter with a coffin now…she took the hand of the man inside…and wrenched awake, a sob in her throat.

Alex felt the jolt when she awoke. She'd been asleep for a solid five hours. She never moved and he knew from her steady breathing that it was a dreamless and healing sleep. Then suddenly she gave a little cry. He'd been drifting a bit himself. She just felt so good that he didn't want to move. It had been a long time since they lay fused on his bed. The fact that they were fully clothed was incidental.

Alex loosened his stiff arms and she moved to a sitting position. She sat for a moment, getting reoriented. Her hair was in its usual disarray, all curls and tangles. As much as he loved the sleek and polished look of her, he thought this was when he cherished her the most.

She saw the sun over the ocean and stared at it confused. "Alex?"

"I'm right here."

She lay back down and nuzzled into his chest. "What time is it?"

He moved his wrist around. "Almost noon."

She sighed heavily. "And I suppose I was laying right on top of you all this time?"

"Indeed."

"Good grief, Alex. Sometimes I'm in awe of your ability to withstand physical punishment." She shook her head again and was rewarded with some cognizant thoughts. Pushing the hair out of her eyes she looked at him. "So how numb are your arms and legs?"

He stared at her. A few hours before she was nearly paralyzed with misery, coming up at her from wherever she buried it during the day. Now she had it caged and her natural good humor was in control.

"Just don't ask me to move right now. If we were invaded, I would have to just lie here and pretend I was in a coma…half of me is already." He could feel the pins and needles of returning circulation.

"Great, then I can use the bathroom first." She snickered and jumped off the bed, walking a bit stiffly, but swiftly toward the bathroom.

When she returned, she was fresh and well groomed. Her hair was back in its ponytail and there was a smile on her face. Alex hadn't moved an inch. Coming over to the bed, she stared at him.

"Need a hand?"

"No. What I need is some incentive to move. I'm trying to send mental signals to my extremities and they're ignoring my desperate messages."

"All your extremities?" She smiled playfully. That sleep must have given her outer self a great shot of energy. If he hadn't seen her and felt her five hours before, he would have believed she didn't have a care in the world.

"Why? What do you have to offer?" He was grinning. She was definitely acting flirty. A very good sign.

"A sail on your boat, the warm sun on our scantily clothed bodies, a bottle of wine, a loaf of bread." She was right over him now and brushed her lips on his. "And me."

"Whoa. That worked. I just heard from the front lines. There's a definite consensus. We're very enthusiastic about the idea."

"Great! I'll give you fifteen minutes. I'm going to talk to Cynthia about the food portion of the enticement."

"The feet and ankles have just checked in. They want chicken. Cynthia's fried chicken."

He heard her chuckle as she walked out the door.

Alex sat up and stared for a while at the doorway where she had disappeared. Then a smile spread over his face, giving the sun some competition. Between him and this Skye, they would overpower the other Skye and get to the problem. Once exposed, they would fight it together. He debated taking the ring out of the safe, but decided that was going to have to be her decision. She locked it away; she held the key; she would open the door and take that step herself. Then he would know it was her decision. Her choice. No pressure. Well, not much.

Today, she would have to take on both Cynthia's chicken and his wit...okay, Cynthia's chicken and his hands all over her body. Provided they ever checked in. He got up with renewed vigor, shaking his hands, flexing his fingers. His body ached for her and he hoped he would be able to be patient. He was sure his body would want to jump her the minute they got beyond the horizon, but he could handle that.

Alex took the helm of his 98-foot Jongert sailing yacht. He was an excellent sailor. The sun was warm and the ocean was calm and as blue as Alex's eyes. The spray coming up from their wake had the wonderful smell of the sea. Salty, clean, and fresh.

Sky loved the motion of the boat beneath her...it made her feel like she was in the air. This was exactly what she needed. She had a vague recollection of her morning, knowing instinctively that she had reached the end of her rope and had just let go. She had a blurred impression of falling, falling. Then of being caught and held. But she wasn't going to think about that now. She needed a break and was going to take one. Alex needed a break and she was going to give it to him.

They spoke little. Mostly just sailing talk. On board, Alex was the captain and he would give her instructions. She would cheerfully say "Aye, Aye." He grinned at her, a roguish look on his face. He decided not to shave and looked like a modern day pirate. Jimmy Buffett's high-energy lyrics provided just the right mood for the moment.

"I sure could use a beer, mate," he said.

She got him a Corona and snagged a glass of wine for herself. Alex thought she looked delicious. She had on a one-piece tie-dyed Speedo with a matching skirt. Sitting on the bow of the boat, she looked like an elegant wooden masthead on one of the old sailing ships. She thought it was a conservative look, something more modest for the occasion and the one-piece suit covered both her bruises and her fading scars. The fact that it left nothing to the imagination and the slight chill of the spray made her nipples erect, was lost on her.

It was not lost on Alex or his extremities. His hands itched to stroke her warm, soft skin. His arms longed to hold her. His legs and feet where impatient to get him to her side. And the other extremity? Well, he was turned on and ready to get naked. Down boy, he thought. Let's take this slowly. Let's not spoil the mood with a premature mashing. He trimmed the sails and lashed the wheel.

"I think we'll float awhile," he said, and went to sit on the bow next to her. She drew up her knees, wrapping her arms around her long, long legs. Those long shapely, muscular, tanned legs. He looked at them out of the corner of his eye. It had been a relatively long dry spell. He blew out a breath. She turned and smiled. He chugged the rest of the bottle of beer. He needed some anesthesia to desensitize his jumping nerves.

Skye sighed. "This is nice." Laying back, she closed her eyes and stretched out her long, long body. Her shapely, muscular, tanned body. She was far too thin, but she still had curves. Fabulous curves. The boat was gently rocking. It was like the sea was simulating the motion of two bodies making love.

"Gotta get another beer," mumbled Alex. Did she have any idea what a torture chamber she was turning this boat into? He thought it was a good idea to come out here with her. Now, remembering her morning and her vulnerability, he felt that if he made a move it would be like taking advantage of her and abusing her trust. When he returned, he was sweating and it wasn't that warm. The cool breeze helped, but he knew he would have to be somewhere on an Alaskan glacier in order for there to be a more permanent solution to his frustration.

Skye heard a splash and sat up, startled. Alex was swimming around the boat. She smiled, then laughed.

"Did you fall off the boat?"

"No. Just cooling off."

"It isn't that hot out here." She had even considered grabbing a cover-up when she found that if she stretched out in the sun, her body warmed up a bit. Getting up, she looked over the edge.

"That's easy for you to say."

"But you still have your clothes on." She was laughing, her hair coming out of its clip and flying around her face in the ocean breezes. Her back was arched; her hip was cocked provocatively. She was loosely hanging on to the lanyards. She was such a picture of raw sexuality and uninhibited amusement, Alex decided not to come out of the ocean until dark.

She sat down on the edge of the boat, dangling her legs, sipping her wine and licking the liquid off her lips. She decided to just look at him for a while.

Moaning, Alex ducked under the waves. This was turning into a nightmare. Nightmare. Suddenly, he remembered one of the primary reasons he wanted to have her out here alone. He came back up out of the water to try to catch her at an unguarded moment, but he saw her expression hadn't changed. It was actually becoming more amused. It was beginning to dawn on her why Alex was so hot.

"Come on up. I'll put on a thick terry cloth robe and we can nibble on some chicken."

Alex nodded. He really was cooled down nicely and thought he could survive a few hours on the surface. Provided the robe was very thick.

When he heaved himself up the ladder, she greeted him with a towel. A woman of her word, she'd donned a long, bright yellow robe.

"You look like a giant banana," said Alex. Skye laughed and looked down at herself. Looking back at him, she gave him a welcoming, sensual smile. Was she playing with him? He decided to test the waters, so to speak.

He came over, all wet and chilled and gave her a big good-natured hug. He shook his head and cool ocean water flew off his thick hair and got her all wet. His wet clothes got the rest of her damp through her robe. She was appreciating the way the wet t-shirt clung to his marvelous chest and arms and thought it really was getting warmer. Must be the robe.

"Can I peel you?" he asked, smiling down at her. Her arms had automatically snaked around his waist, as if they had a mind of their own. Their eyes met, hers were sparkling and open. They were miles from pain and nightmares and reality. Everything was fresh and bright. They were alone in the universe. One man. One woman. Mutual affection. Mutual need. They came together. There was nothing to complicate it, nothing that could withstand the combined force of their shared passion.

His hands went up to her shoulders and pushed the robe down. Meeting with no resistance, he smiled. He kissed her. She tasted like coconut oil.

She thought he tasted like the first sip of a margarita, all salty and sweet and intoxicating.

"Mmmm. You taste salty." She licked her lips, then lit up with a good idea. "We got any margarita mix?" she asked. She looked up at him and he saw a welcoming glint in her sparkling eyes. Hot damn. This was good. But it could just be a temporary reaction to all the heat pouring out of him. He figured the heat would probably sustain itself through the mixing of a few drinks. Not wanting to risk it, however, he took her hand as he started toward the galley.

"You get the tequila and the mix, I'll get the limes and salt." They blended a huge pitcher of margaritas and were back up on deck in short order. Alex sat down on the comfortable lounge and pulled her down on his lap. Skye poured the margaritas into two chilled plastic glasses rimmed with salt.

They drank and necked and drank some more. He got bolder and she got more responsive as the pitcher emptied. His fingers trailed along the armholes of her suit, and moved in to stoke her bare breasts. They were both breathing heavily as his lips trailed down the curve of her neck and her hands moved over his body.

"You really should get out of these wet clothes," she said when she came up for air after a long, passionate, hungry kiss. "You get pneumonia, you're in bed for a week."

"Will you be there with me?" he asked, his eyes flashing like the sun off the ocean behind them.

"No, but I know where you can get some good antibiotics."

"I would rather have another pitcher of margaritas."

"That would do the trick, too. You'd still be sick, but you wouldn't care." She tugged at his damp shirt. "But why risk it?"

She put down her drink and stood up, grabbing his hand and pulling him to his feet. She slowly drew his shirt over his head. Her hands moved up his sides and over his chest, enjoying the reaction she got as his skin shimmered and got hot under her touch. As his arms went over his head, she pressed her body to his. When the shirt was peeled off, he threw it on the lounge and brought his arms down around her. She wiggled around, much to his delight, until she snatched the pitcher. She emptied it in their glasses, singing and swaying.

Jimmy Buffet moved to another classic, *Brown Eyed Girl,* and Alex felt fate took a hand in expressing the perfect theme...as he smiled at his own brown-eyed girl.

She handed him his drink with exaggerated ceremony. He grabbed her around the waist and brought her up against his body so he could take advantage of some of that swaying. "My brown-eyed girl," he said in her ear and while he was there, decided to nibble a bit of it.

Skye rarely drank and when she did it was a glass of wine or one celebratory margarita. She was a controlled person and she didn't like the feeling of slipping away from herself. Also, being a pilot, she couldn't have any alcohol in her system eight hours before a flight. She liked being ready, always prepared for flight. And she liked to fly whenever she could. Didn't leave a very large window of opportunity in her day for drinking.

But what the hell, she thought as she took another sip of the frosty drink. They were going down good today. Besides, she was grounded until she passed her medical anyway. Suddenly, Jimmy Buffett cranked up another perfect theme suggesting, *"why don't we get drunk and screw."*

They looked at each other and for a moment neither one of them moved, then Skye erupted in delighted laughter and Alex joined her.

"What really great advice," he said and drew her closer. He was intoxicated, completely drunk, but it had little to do with the tequila. For just this moment, he had his Skye back. And he thought Jimmy Buffett was a goddamn genius.

"Well, as long as we're halfway there...why not just go all the way?" she suggested with a mischievous sparkle in her eye. Dancing, laughing, singing along, she chugged the rest of her drink, threw the plastic glass over her shoulder, and wound her arms around his neck. Executing a little jump, she wrapped her long, strong legs around his waist.

"That takes care of the drunk part," she laughed. "Ready for the screw part?"

Alex drained his glass, tossed it in the corner with hers then spread his hands under her lovely bottom. Kissing her all the way, he took them down to the spacious stateroom, periodically bumping into dressers, chests, accessories, pictures on the wall, and other assorted furniture.

"Are you sure you're ready for this?" breathed Alex, as he laid her gently back on the soft king sized pillows.

"Are you?" Skye countered with a sigh and a smile. Her hands moved down his back...slowly, sensually...then around his waist to his flat, lean stomach and down some more. "It's been a long time and I've banked a lot of heat."

He smoothed her hair back from her face. He wanted a clear view of her eyes. They were a deep simmering brown...melted chocolate. There was no pain there...or none that she let him see. Reassured, he moved onto the bed kissing her, touching her, feeling the fire through her skin.

"I can feel the heat, Captain. Scorch me." He eased himself over her as she fisted her hands in his hair and brought him down to her. Passion flowed from his lips to hers and back again. The connection was combustible and it fueled their pent up passion.

His hands moved up her arms and he laced his fingers through the straps of her swimsuit. Slowly he pulled them over her lovely, well muscled shoulders, kissing each spot that he exposed as he pulled the suit down and off her body.

"Oh. Yes. Right there. That was never bruised." She sighed her pleasure and every flame he lit stoked his own smoldering desire.

Her strong, capable hands returned the favor as she ran her fingers around his waist band and pulled down the only barrier between him and her already throbbing body.

"You know I have a throttle fetish," she smiled as she took him in her powerful grip.

"Ah...well, my love," he chuckled. "I appreciate that very much, but you better throttle back or be prepared for a premature landing."

What started as a laugh ended in a deep throaty moan as his fingers explored the landing site.

"Pain?"

"No...I can't feel a thing," she gasped.

"Nothing?"

Her breath caught in her throat as his lips and tongue teased her highly sensitized skin. "Let me rephrase that. Oh God. Yes." Her body bucked, then shivered. "I felt that...darling don't stop. I need you...I need this."

Another moan escaped her lips as her breath came in ragged pants.

"Are you sure you're all right?" he asked, bracing himself on his elbows and looking down at her flushed face.

"Oh yeah...all parts operational and ready for take off."

"I don't want to hurt you." Alex's husky voice reflected both deep concern and adolescent anticipation.

"And what would happen right now if I asked you to stop?"

"I would start stuttering for sure and perhaps go mad...I've heard it can happen."

Wrapping her arms around his neck, she rolled him over. Looking down, she grinned roguishly. "I wouldn't want you to lose your mind."

"Too late for that," he moaned as she nibbled at the under side of his jaw...his 'on' button as she recalled. "So this is going to be playful sex?" His body hummed as her naked breasts skimmed his bare chest and his breath nearly exploded from his chest.

"You have our sex labeled?"

"Oh yeah...there's playful sex, fast and primal sex, traditional sex, experimental sex, spontaneous sex, stand her up and..." He never finished his sentence as her mouth swooped down on his and otherwise occupied his tongue. And when she blew right through one of his favorites and beyond, he decided to add another...extreme sex.

They rolled around the huge bed, touching, kissing, laughing, finding familiar places, and discovering new delights. Their bodies kept perfect rhythm to the music and the rocking of the boat. The waves lapping up against the sides accompanied their breathing.

They were hungry. Starving for each other. Thrilling shivers of lust rocketed through her as his hands touched all the places they had longed to feel for weeks. His eyes took in her body, her face, and his hands followed.

When he slid into her, he found not only heat, but home. Her craving for pleasure after the weeks of pain took her over and her reaction was frenzied, enthusiastic, hot. Their sexual dance was perfectly timed, their bodies wonderfully matched.

When he took the last plunge with her, they lay for a moment sated. But it was only the eye of the storm, the sea of calm before another surge of passion. Skye sighed with release then felt her need build again. Everything felt so good, so perfect. Fueled by love and lust, their hands continued to move, their bodies continued to ride the waves until they came together again. And again.

"Je vous aime, mon chéri," whispered Skye, completely overwhelmed with the man, his body, his compassion, his desire.

The words softly stroked Alex's soul. The heat of his body cooled to a subtle sensual warmth by its perfect place between them.

"I love you too...with all my heart. I always will."

Finally, when they felt both full and drained, Skye lay quietly in Alex's arms. Safe, secure, loved. She sighed. The margaritas were beginning to wear off but she still felt high. She ran little kisses along his chest and up his neck. Then, leaning on her elbow, she looked blearily around the stateroom. The bed was a complete tangle of sheets and blankets and pillows littered the floor. Both of them were so tall, they would occasionally knock something off one of the low dressers beside the bed with their hands or feet when they were lost in the intensity of their desire for more...for each other. Their path into the stateroom was obvious, a table and chair near the door couldn't withstand the storm. The curtain over the large porthole had been pulled off the wall. The mirror over the dresser was listing a bit to the left.

"Christ, Alex," she snorted. "Did we go through the Bermuda triangle?"

"No, from what I can remember, I think we just survived Hurricane Skyler."

"Very funny. Just for that, you have to serve me...I'm starving," she yawned and lay back down, using his chest as a pillow. A very hard pillow, but nice. She felt herself slip from the 'being tipsy' stage to the 'being sleepy' stage.

Alex smiled. She hadn't had an appetite since they got back from the island. This was another good sign.

"Want a picnic in bed?"

"Mmmm. Yes." She sighed hugely and laid her arm over his waist. "Eat me."

"Did that...I'm talking about food."

"Yeah. Food. Good."

"Well, you have to let me go, I have long arms, but the galley is a bit out of my reach."

"Okay." She blinked twice, then closed her eyes. She fell instantly asleep.

Reaching down, he snatched one of the pillows off the floor and slowly, gently, extricated himself from her grip, replacing his chest with the pillow and sliding out of the bed. He gabbed a pair of jeans and pulled them on. Then he stood for a long, long time looking down at her.

He could still see the bruises along her right side. He was careful during their lovemaking to protect that side, just as she was aware of his sore shoulder. He brushed the tangle of hair from her face and kissed her warm cheek.

"We're quite a pair, aren't we, my darling? And we are a pair." He ran his finger over the fourth finger of her left hand. Her hand looked bare without the ring. "I'm never going to let you go."

He covered her with a comforter and set about to get everything picked up. Hurricane Skyler. That was a storm to remember.

Dressed in jeans and a light sweater, he sat on the deck, watching the sun getting low in the sky, his feet propped up on the rail. He'd brewed some coffee to ward off the slight chill in the air. Jimmy Buffett was replaced by soft jazz. His contentment was a wonderful feeling after weeks of anxiety and apprehension. But he knew he couldn't lose himself in the pleasure. He had to be vigilant.

Sipping, tapping his bare feet to the music, he was thinking about his next move. Everything that had happened during the afternoon was spontaneous. No thought. No strategy. Just two people doing what came naturally. A breathtaking interlude. Something they both desperately needed. And wanted. But he also knew that it was only a reprieve. Soon there was going to have to be a showdown.

He took another sip of coffee. She'd mentioned going away. Well, that was not going to happen. Away from his presence, she might not want to fight for afternoons like this one. He strongly felt that his being there, real and compelling, was a critical foil for whatever was bothering her. He wanted to be her guardian. He couldn't help her with the burden of whatever was weighing on her heart if she went away. She would be alone.

Alex got up and stretched. God, he felt good. He had to fight the primitive urge to pound his chest and howl. Everything she did to him, he could still feel inside and out. He wondered if she was still sleeping and just couldn't resist going back down to check it out.

Skye woke up slowly, feeling the movement of the boat and letting it sway her into wakefulness. This must be what it's like in the womb, she thought. Warm, gently rocking, sheltered from the world. She didn't want to get up, but she smelled coffee. She wondered if her mind was powerful enough to send a mental signal to Alex to fetch her a cup so she wouldn't have to move.

She knew she would have to get up…eventually. Her brain was kicking in and warming up. Rolling over on her back, she stretched like a cat. She felt wonderful.

"Thanks for the suggestion, Jimmy Buffett. Getting drunk and getting screwed was perfect advice," she mumbled to herself. Or she thought she was mumbling to herself, until she heard a distinctive, deep chuckle. Damn. Maybe if she didn't open her eyes, he would go away and forget she said that.

She lay still for a moment, but he knew how to trap a possum. She could feel him coming toward the bed...and she could smell the coffee.

"Mmmm...," she groaned. "Coffee. I surrender." She reluctantly opened her eyes and sat up. Noticing the pillows were all back on the bed, she took advantage of their presence and stacked them behind her. Propped up, she covered herself discreetly with a sheet, and reached for the cup that was in his hand.

"Are you ready for an audience your majesty?" teased Alex as he handed it to her.

"Yes indeed," she said looking at Alex from the top of his wind-ruffled hair to his bare feet. Perfect. "Are you one of my subjects?"

Alex sat down on the edge of the bed. He ran his fingers through her riotous hair. Enthusiastic sex really did a number on it. "I'm one of your slaves. For a lock of your hair, I'll lay down my life."

Skye sipped her coffee and tried to finger comb the tangles out. "Then get the scissors, slave. I'm about ready to hack it all off." As far as Alex could tell, she was making it worse...and the effect was extremely provocative. "Our sex has got to get more civilized. Maybe if we just..."

That did it. Alex leaned over and kissed the air right out of her lungs. She was breathless when he pulled back. "Did we bring any oxygen? I think my lung sprung another leak."

"I would be glad to give CPR."

"Which part, the lip lock, or the chest work?" She raised her eyebrows and took another sip.

His eyes went from her full, smiling lips to her chest. The comforter had fallen to her waist and her lush and tantalizing chest was campaigning for his vote.

"That's the kind of choice that can freeze a man's brain and do serious damage to his circuits." He kissed her lips, then kissed each breast.

She kissed the top of his head. "Checking out the choices?"

He went back to her lips. He knew this wasn't going to last, that reality would settle in soon, so he intended to take what he could before the curtain came down.

"Do you want to get up and get something to eat and go in, or would you rather just spend the night out here?"

"Hmmm, this is kind of like the lips or chest decision." She tried to

265

make it light, but the alcohol was leaving her system and the sun was setting. She felt it was near the end of her reprieve.

Alex saw the cloud pass over her face as she sipped her coffee. He waited.

Then she chased the cloud away. She decided to extend this wonderful afternoon for as long as she could.

"Are you serious about staying on the boat tonight?" Maybe she wouldn't have the nightmare tonight if she were here. Maybe the shore and real life were far enough away. Maybe she could escape its grasp for tonight.

"I'm perfectly serious. We're out of all shipping lines, we have running lights, and the seas are forecasted to be calm tonight. Unless." He kissed her lips. Then deepened it until they were both breathless. "You want to rock the boat some more and kick up the surf."

She smiled and kissed him back. "I don't know…they may have to change the forecast."

"Heavy seas caused by Hurricane Skyler."

"Why don't you get the food out while I get cleaned up? This hair shouldn't take more than four hours to untangle. Then I'll come up and we can decide if we want to stay out here."

Alex smiled as he left her. He'd already decided. If she was out here on the boat, there was nowhere for her to go. She couldn't ignore him. She couldn't escape him. They were going to talk.

They ate the crispy fried chicken legs and a tangy pasta salad that Cynthia had prepared. Skye warmed the bread in the microwave and poured the chilled wine.

"I didn't know you cooked," said Alex as he took a piece of the steaming bread.

"Hey, if you can nuke it and it comes with explicit instructions, I can figure it out. I'm an aeronautical engineer, after all. I guess if I can calculate the compressible mass flow rate and use it to determine the thrust of a jet engine, pushing buttons on a microwave is within the parameters of my cognitive skill level." Alex shook his head and smiled. He had to admit, he was impressed.

"You cook?" she asked taking another bite of a big, fat, juicy orange Alex had peeled for her. It tasted good. Fresh air, fresh sex, fresh fruit. Damn she felt great, the strain and stress were melting away. Nothing could get her here.

"Nope. Rita always took on that duty. Mom had strange hours so we were pretty independent in the kitchen. Unfortunately, I never got the whole picture...Rita was bossy as hell, like a drill sergeant...delegated like a maniac. I got into the chopping and cutting and opening jars and things like that. You know, sharp instruments and muscle. Manly things."

"Ah, yes." She was enjoying herself. The sunset was going to be a stunner this evening. The colors were already reflecting off the clouds on the horizon. Like the sea gods were smiling down on them...or up at them. She relaxed. Let her guard down even more. Reality was miles away. The boat was gently rocking and she felt tranquil. It was what she needed, what her heart had been longing for. Uncomplicated. No threat, no terror, no enemy.

"How much older was she than you?"

Alex paused. Swallowed. Then licked the chicken oil off his fingers. Postponing the moment. "Three minutes and a few seconds," he said softly. Sadly.

In total shock, Skye put down the wine she'd been about to drink. "She was your twin?" The distress shot right through her. Somehow this made Rita's death far more heartbreaking. "Oh, Alex. I didn't know that. How awful for you. How awful."

"It's been like half of me has been missing." He looked at her and smiled the sweetest most melancholy smile she'd ever seen. It broke her heart. "Until I met you. Now I'm whole again. You have made me whole."

Then she felt it coming. Not miles away. It was right there with her. Her nightmare. Oh my God! The demons were screaming in her head. Her defenses were gone. She threw up her wall, but not soon enough.

Alex frowned. He saw the attack. Witnessed the assault. He saw it in her eyes, saw it on her face. Alarm rippled through him and grew into full blown dread as the piece of orange she had been nibbling on dropped from her limp hand and she started to sway. The shock was rocking her, changing her.

She felt ill. All of her nightmares plowed into her at once. They didn't even give her a chance to prepare. She stood up abruptly, her hand flew to her throat, and tears sprung into her eyes.

"Don't. Don't. Please. I can't. I can't. I can't make you whole. Don't do this." She backed up and moved to the rail, trying desperately not to be sick. Turning her back on his alarmed face. Suddenly she couldn't get her breath. She was gasping for air. The weight of her dread crushed her. Reality wasn't on shore. It was right here and she was drowning in it.

Alex came up behind her and spun her around. He took her arms and gently shook her. "No. No, sweetheart. Don't fight it. Let it come out. I want to see it. I want to see what's been tormenting you. You can't do this alone. I won't let you. Tell me. You tell me. What has hurt you? Why can't you sleep? Why can't you eat? Why can't you marry me? Why can't you love me? Tell me, Skye. What is killing you?"

"You." She shuddered violently. "You are." And she collapsed into his arms.

Alex caught her. He was surprised he could still react. Nothing in his life prepared him for this. Nothing. She was completely limp. Sweeping her up, he carried her into the stateroom. Brandy. He knew he had some. He just couldn't get his mind to work. Had he heard her right? Did she just tell him that it was he who was causing this horrible suffering?

He went into the galley and started pushing things out of his way until he found the brandy. The margarita glasses were in the sink. His eyes fixed on them like a homing beacon. Skye. His mind flashed like a fanatical photo album. Picture after picture of Skye. Laughing, sleeping, running, working out, dancing, attacking, running across a lawn with a gun out in front of her, lying in a hospital bed, showing off a new pair of shoes...three inch heels because he was so tall, eating pancakes and smacking her lips, naked and pliant.

He had to put down the bottle and glass. Putting both hands on the counter he leaned into them, taking deep breaths and regaining his balance. God help him. He had to know. He had to force it out of her. He let the genie out of the bottle. Now what? How the hell was he going to fight himself?

Then he heard her scream his name and the chill that went through him was ice cold and terrifying. He grabbed the bottle and glass again and ran into the stateroom. She was sitting up in bed, her hands over her face, weeping and saying his name over and over.

"I'm here, darling. I'm here. I just went to get you a brandy." He poured it with unsteady hands and put the bottle on the bedside table. Sitting down next to her, he put his arm around her shaking shoulders. "Sweetheart. Here, drink this. Please."

"Alex?" She lowered her hands and looked at him with a mixture of relief and regret. "Oh my God, Alex." All the strength went out of her. He drew her to him as she took the glass and obediently sipped. She felt the burn, all the way down her throat and into her belly. Coughing painfully she took another sip. Both the pain and the brandy helped.

"I'm so sorry. I didn't know that was going to happen. I'm so sorry." Her head rested on his shoulder.

"Don't. You have nothing to be sorry about." He kissed the top of her head. "But darling, you have to tell me. You have to tell me now."

She sat very still in his arms for a minute, then nodded. "I guess so. I guess it's pretty obvious that I'm royally screwed up. Man, what a show. Psycho-woman, my secret identity." She took the brandy out of his hand and chugged the rest of it. "You may want a bracer yourself."

He was way ahead of her. He'd already snagged the brandy bottle and was on his third big swallow.

"Okay. Consider me braced." He gently cupped her chin with his hand and forced her to look at him. "Now, how do you want to do this?"

"Over the phone?"

He just stared at her.

She took a shaky breath. "Okay. How about we turn down the lights, fluff up the pillows and you can hold me? I'll have to tell you all at once."

"Works for me. Can I get you anything?"

"The name of a good shrink?"

"Darling, you tell me, then we'll decide together whether you need to talk to anyone else. Didn't work for you too well in the past, as I recall." Skye had seen counselors and psychologists after the death of her parents. She managed to get them to declare her well adjusted and coping admirably. What they didn't know was that she was acting, role-playing. At the time, she'd completely suppressed the memories of the event and the aftermath.

He put the pillows against the headboard, turned down the lights and got into the big bed beside her. Coming to him, she rested her head against his chest. She wanted to hear his heart when she told him everything. She needed to hear his heart.

"Comfortable?" he asked, knowing it was important she feel protected and safe.

"Mmmm, yes," she sighed. "This is so difficult. I'm not used to sharing my inner thoughts, my hidden feelings, my secrets. I wanted to do this myself. I'm used to standing alone."

"I know," he said simply.

She looked up at him then and tilted her head. A look of wonder came over her face. It had just dawned on her. "You really do, don't you?"

He just smiled, and nodded slowly. Something passed between them then. Not love or passion or lust. It was a simple, uncomplicated, basic connection. He knew. He knew exactly. He was used to standing alone, too. As she continued to stare into his understanding eyes, she knew she could tell him anything. Everything. He saw her trust return and it gave him hope.

Nodding, she took her position over his heart again.

"I don't know if I should start at the beginning, the end, or the middle. It always gets so jumbled up in my dreams...my nightmares, actually...I'm never sure where I am." She sighed again and stopped. The silence lengthened. The brandy was making her feel a little woozy. Or maybe it was the motion of the boat.

"Newton's Law," he said, giving her a little shake.

"Huh?"

"Newton's Law. A body in motion tends to stay in motion. A body at rest will just sit there. Just start anywhere, honey, and inertia will get you to where you need to go."

"Did Newton put that honey in there?"

"That would be my spin."

"Ah." It helped. A bit of light chatter before the heavy stuff. "Okay. The beginning. We were doing well. You and I. You and I." She repeated. "No. That's not where I want to start. Sounds like some kind of epic novel." She heaved another sigh. She swallowed. She fidgeted.

"Skye?"

"I've never put this into words. I don't know if I can."

"Why do you leave me at night, darling? Why do you weep out on the terrace?" Maybe a few questions to get her started. He knew how to get information from a reluctant source. Maybe it wasn't fair to use it on Skye, but he had to know.

"It's the dream...the nightmare, really. Every night now." Then she told him about her nightmare. The details, the blood, the bodies, the horrible pain. By the time she got to the end, she was sobbing and he was frozen with sympathy and sadness. He had no idea. This bold and courageous woman had been battling very nasty, very ugly personal demons and at a horrific cost to her both physically and emotionally. The fact that she could continue to function at any level was a miracle and a testament to her inner strength and resilience.

"What triggered it?" he asked gently. He knew that she didn't used to have these nightmares. He knew she had trauma, but this was different.

He felt her shudder. He felt the hot tears soaking through his sweater. She was crying and she was in pain. She shook her head, resisting the final secret. It was a necessary revelation but it was stuck in her chest. She could get it out, or she could continue to fight it on her own.

"Skye?"

"This is the worst," she said. "The worst."

How could it get worse? He thought. He held her tighter and it seemed to release the words.

"I…I was watching. I was watching from the window. I saw it. It was like when my Mom and Dad…when I saw them…" She couldn't finish the sentence. "And I couldn't do anything. I saw you go down."

She was sobbing again. Her body was wracked with the force of her sobs, but she continued. "I saw. I saw. I knew there were too many of them. I knew you were going down. And you did. And you didn't move. And there was your blood. I thought you were dead. Right in front of me. I see it again every time I close my eyes. I see it. I see it. Every time."

Now the words came tumbling out of her. She couldn't stop them. She didn't have the strength to stop them. For Alex, every word was like a physical blow. He had no idea. He saw it now, but it never occurred to him how his actions must have affected her as they were happening.

"You talked me into loving you. You said I could open my heart. You thawed the ice, you melted the steel, you got me to say yes to you. I loved you. I trusted you to guard my heart. I said I wouldn't love another cop. After Jeff, I had to protect my heart. It bleeds. It bleeds so easily. But you wouldn't let me just live. You wanted me to love. You didn't want me to just go through the motions. You wanted more. You wanted more for me. I wanted more. I was never so happy and I didn't even know there could be so much joy, so much love. Then you brought me the ring and it was perfect. At that moment everything I was or would ever be was connected to you." The words continued to pour out. Alex listened, each word hammered at him. He vowed to protect her and he had instead hurt her terribly.

"I saw my parents die horribly. They were burning up in front of my eyes and the people wouldn't let me go to them. I survived. I got through it by burying it. Then Jeff made me open up. He was my friend, my first lover. Then he came home to me in a box. In that box was my heart. Where did all the laughter go? Where did all the happiness go? I made up a new, simple rule for survival. No love, no pain. My rule. Straightforward." Skye held on to him tighter, the tears soaking through were like acid on his skin.

"Then you were there. Now, you're my air. My survival depends on you. My very existence. With you it was so much more wonderful, so perfectly right…and it was so much worse. Oh, my God, Alex. I could control this before I met you. When I opened my heart to love you, I exposed it to all the pain. Then I saw you die. I saw death coming for you. I couldn't stop it. You were killed, horribly, so I closed down again. Everything shut off. That night I wanted to die."

Her breath was coming in gasps. "If I hadn't had all those people counting on me, I would have died. I was absolutely hollow; like there was nothing inside. Nothing. A void. Empty. Then you were there, alive. You did the right thing. I know that. You had to play dead. It was perfectly done, but you didn't know. You didn't know I was watching. I took out two of the men coming at you and one at your back and still it wasn't enough. It wasn't enough. They hit me, stopped me from taking out the one that shot you. I couldn't breathe and I saw your blood on the hangar wall. Then I didn't want to breathe. You came back and you were alive, but it was too late. I'd already reconstructed the wall. I closed down. Don't let love in. I have to go away. You're like a fire. Warm from a distance, but deadly when you're too close. If I let you back in I'll be consumed by the fire. I have to go. I can't go through that again. Two wedding dresses drenched with blood. Two. Two."

She knew she was getting hysterical, but she couldn't control it. "I'm drowning in my conflicting emotions. I see you going down, I see the actual bullets fly through the air into you. I see you die. I'm dead, too. But then I'm in your arms and I'm alive. I'm whole. I'm home. I love you. I love you but I can't let you have my heart. I have to lock it up in the magic box. The box only the ring can open. My talisman. I want you, but I'll die. I did die. I was still breathing but there was nothing inside."

Alex was buffeted by wave after wave of raw emotion, coming from her, coming from inside him. He could hardly breathe under its onslaught.

"Oh Alex...who can live without a heart? *Vous ne pouvez pas habiter sans un Coeur?* Who can live without a heart? When I thought you were dead I was hollow, void of anything that makes a human being alive. I was going to stay on the island, Alex. Put Stuart in the left seat and stay on the island. I was going to find you and be with you and let the explosion end the pain. My life was already ended. The blast would have been a relief. I have to go. I have to run. Don't stop me. I love you." Her words came out slower and slower and she was beginning to slur them. "I love you but I have to go." She was running out of steam. "Please...let me go." She was completely spent, she had nothing left. Sleep was the only place she could go. Escaping the pain, she tumbled into a deep sleep.

Alex couldn't say anything. He was numb. It was him, he kept saying to himself. It was he who was her tormentor. The sea gulls outside were screaming as if they were accusing him. Guilt paid a visit, as did remorse, but they were quickly cast off. He simply couldn't regret anything when it came to her.

Everything she said was true. He pushed her. He made promises to her. Pursued her until she made the same promises to him. As night came and the boat was surrounded by darkness, he searched his heart and his inner being. Could he let her go? No. The answer to that was never.

He knew how she felt. At least partially. His sister had died in the line of duty. His twin. He never really stopped feeling the emptiness inside him, that vacant place beside him. The grief was horrible and the fear that Skye could meet the same fate was something he had come to terms with. He lived with the terror of losing her by surrounding it with his limitless love. He sat by her hospital bed less than three months before when she was hovering between life and death. He'd seen her lying in a pool of her own blood. He'd seen her in pain…paid a huge price for loving her and he never once thought it was too much.

Alex was raised by cops and he knew the risks. He knew that to love someone who was in harm's way could be very, very difficult. He also knew that Skye had lost her heart to him before she knew he was a special agent…a man with a gun. Flying in under her radar, he got through before she could put up her defenses. Fairly or unfairly he hadn't regretted it for a minute…until now.

Alex looked down at the woman who defined his happiness. Her hands were in fists. She didn't even stir when he straightened her fingers and placed them in a more relaxed position. Even in her sleep she was ready to fight.

He ran his fingers lightly over her cheek. He understood everything now. He thought it would help him help her. It didn't. He didn't have a clue. He just knew he wasn't going to give her up. He couldn't. She'd said it. You couldn't live without a heart. She was now his heart.

Alex replayed the day on the island. Why hadn't he done this before? He knew someone was behind him. Someone covering his back. It registered at the time, but he hadn't really thought about it since. Now it was clear. Someone up and over his left shoulder. The two men in front of him and the one behind. They went down, but not by his hand. The slam against the hangar wall kind of knocked it out of him. But now he remembered.

It was Skye. She saved his life. One of those three men would have taken a head shot. He kissed her and felt her sigh. How could he love anything more than this sleeping woman? His jaw tensed when he thought of how much they must have punished her after she took those shots. He thought she'd been a lot worse the morning he found her. He attributed it to the deterioration of the original injury. God. She was going to stay with him on the island. Be blown to bits because she thought he was dead. Someone who loved life as much as she. Someone as vital and loving as Skye chose to stay on an island with a dead man.

Then another thought shot through him. Could he live with the possibility that if he died, she would die with him? He saw her staying behind. The explosion ripping through her. It chilled him. To the bone.

Alex should have told her he had on a vest. If she'd been able to hold him earlier that day, she would have felt it. He never realized she was watching...would be witness to his clever dead man act. He rested his head back on the pillows. His throat was tight, his chest hurt.

He wondered how she managed to put this incredible nightmare away when the sun came up. Pushing it aside, she laughed, loved, and brought magic to everyone around her. Skye had been carrying this emotional agony around with her since the morning they flew off the island. No wonder her nightmares were so violent. When she let her guard down in sleep, it grabbed her and shook her. Combined with her physical condition and the increased vividness caused by the drugs, he marveled at her ability to function on any level. He looked down at his sleeping warrior. She fought it and fought it hard. But it was wearing her down. He held her tighter and kissed her lips.

"But that was because you were fighting it alone. Trying to protect me from this. You're not fighting alone any more, my darling champion. We're going into this battle as a team."

Alex was exhausted. He also had little sleep the last few weeks. When she was not beside him, he found it difficult to be restful. The last few days were such a roller coaster, he wasn't sure he was still on track. On the other hand, they were on the ocean, just the two of them, together despite some rough seas. He had her in his arms and he knew more now than he knew yesterday. Even though he wasn't sure what to do with the information, he knew he had her for now. Alex drifted off listening to the gulls, feeling the subtle movements of the boat, hearing the lapping of the waves, holding his life in his arms.

Alex came awake in the predawn light. It was chilly and Skye kept close throughout the night. He had covered them up with the comforter, but it was mostly body heat keeping them warm. They were still in their clothes, neither one of them having the energy to strip.

Alex went over everything again, and started to work on a plan. His beloved decided to get nearer to the fire she talked about the night before and snuggled closer, her arm going around his waist and her head resting on his chest. Her hair was tickling his nose and he had to resist the urge to sneeze. God, what a package she was.

Then his mind was pulled from a study of her body to a lesson of its own. Oh boy. Her hand was running over his stomach. Just a little lower, my darling, he thought, and we'll start this day off right. As if by telepathy, her hand moved downward. He could feel the familiar tingle as his whole body started to quiver inside.

"Cold?" she asked, sleepily. He hadn't known she was awake. So the progress of her hand was not just random movement.

"Freezing...would you mind stoking the fire?"

She laughed. "Let me get my bearings first." She moved and moaned. "Tell me you're as stiff as I am."

He moved around just a little to test his muscles. "Yes. I think I can accurately say that with one obvious exception, my entire body is stiff."

"Hmmm. I think I can rectify that." And she did. Masterfully. And before the sun popped up completely from the ocean, they were both naked and had found that friction was an excellent producer of heat.

As they lay under the comforter, he decided not talking about what happened the night before was like trying to ignore a 300-pound pink gorilla in a tutu. It was impossible.

"Sweetheart?"

"Hmmm?"

"Can we talk about last night?"

"Yes. We need to although I'm afraid I don't have it all clear in my head." She kissed his neck and it sent little fingers of pleasure all the way down his spine and back up again. "I do know I got very wacky there at the end. I have a feeling I told you everything, just not necessarily in the right order. How about we get cleaned up and dressed and we can have coffee on the deck while we talk?"

"Good plan. I'm sure the gulls have carried off every bit of food we left up there last night."

"Yes, that's what woke me up. It sounded like a gull convention. They must have found the wine, too. They sounded very excited."

While she made the coffee, he took a shower. All in all, he was feeling pretty good. She hadn't moved away from him in the night, it seemed she had a good night's sleep and she still wanted him to make love to her this morning. Maybe talking it out last night was all she needed.

When he got out, she handed him a cup of steaming coffee and got in.

Alex went on deck and cleaned up the mess from the night before. The gulls had indeed helped themselves to everything. He found orange juice in the refrigerator and some granola bars in the cupboard. The cheese and bread from the picnic basket were still intact. When Skye came topside a half-hour later, he was quite proud of the spread he presented her.

She rewarded him with a dazzling smile. "Lovely," she said and took some of the bread and cheese.

"I live to serve."

"Is that in our oath?"

"I don't know. I wasn't really paying any attention. Just sort of repeated what they said. Kind of like a groom at a wedding...you know the minister says a line, you say a line. And speaking of weddings..."

"Not yet, please."

"Just thought I might bring it up and get it into the conversation early."

"You're a very clever man."

"Majored in it."

"Must have been summa cum laude."

"No...I was too busy applying my major to football, beer kegs and...well...women of the co-ed variety." He almost said bimbos. It was what his less enlightened teammates used to say...not that he ever would use such a pejorative term. His sister and his mother were both armed and would have used him for target practice if they even saw him nodding and laughing. He looked over to Skye. And now he was madly in love with another woman with a gun. Christ, he was doomed.

"This is nice." She looked over the ocean and breathed in the fresh morning air. It was even nippier up on deck and she was glad she had on a thick cotton sweater. It was one she found in Alex's drawer and it had the faint scent of him all over it. She found comfort in that this morning, like his presence surrounded her.

"Did you call anyone last night to let them know we were staying out here?"

"Yes. Tank answered the phone. He wanted you to know there was a wet t-shirt contest in Fort Lauderdale at one p.m."

"And what did you tell him?"

"I didn't say anything. Mom answered the extension. She gave him a time out for being a pig."

Skye smiled, but it was a bit too reserved, too false, and Alex could feel her slipping back into her steel cased shell. He decided to dive after her before she got all the way in.

"Darling, about last night. I want you to get leaving me out of your head." Alex's inner voice told him to take the fast, direct approach. For a smart man, someone who majored in clever in college, someone successful in business and fearless in covert operations, he sometimes took really bad advice from his inner voice. "You belong with me. That's not negotiable."

That got her back up right away. She put up her hand facing him when he started toward her and gave him the 'I can't believe you said that' look. Followed closely with the 'you moron' chaser.

Undaunted, but no smarter, he dug himself in deeper. "And you can't walk away from me, ignore me, or blow me off because I'm not taking you ashore until we talk this out and you agree with me."

Turning her back to him, she looked toward shore. It must be there just over the horizon. She looked down at the little dingy with the outboard motor and decided she had an out if she needed one.

Alex followed her gaze. "I'll shoot a hole in it before you get two feet away from the boat."

Using herself as bait, Skye stood still and calm near the edge of the boat. She didn't respond. She knew exactly how Alex was going to react to that…and he didn't disappoint her. He always wanted physical contact when he felt a less than enthusiastic response from her. He came over and put a hand on her shoulder.

"Skye. Talk to me. What are you thinking?"

She glanced up at him and he saw the look far too late. He was in the water in one easy, smooth, leveraged pivot.

"You want to know what I was thinking? I'll tell you what I was thinking," she shouted at Alex. "I make my own decisions, you moronic Neanderthal, and I'm not going to let you back on this boat until you agree with me."

Then she turned, grabbed her right side and slid down the side of the boat onto the deck. The pivot and projection was brilliantly executed and she got him right over the rail and into the water, but shit…shit…shit. Her ribs were not ready for the physical strain. The pain shot through her so viciously that she couldn't get her breath. She was so angry, she didn't feel it right away. But now, it was excruciating. Damn Alex. This was his fault.

She wished she had the strength to get up, start the engine, and leave him out here. Well, maybe start the engine, cut the rope to the dingy, and then leave him out here. Right now that plan was so far out of reach, she might have wished for a ride out of here on the space shuttle.

"Skye? Skye?" She heard him calling and cussing, but couldn't get a deep enough breath to answer. *Come hold me,* her mind whispered. *I need you.* Tears sprang into her eyes. She closed them, concentrating on breathing and containing the pain. Her medical was the day after tomorrow and she wanted to be clear to fly...if not jets, then something. Almost three weeks without being in the sky was making it difficult for her to find her center, to get to a state of harmony where she could sort things out. She needed to get in the air to reflect on her options. It was where she did her best thinking. And contrary to what the idiot in the water thought, she did have options.

Right now, she would settle for one deep breath. The pain wasn't diminishing. It was throbbing and admonishing her. Who's the idiot? She wanted Alex. *Alex. Come embrace me. Kiss me. Make the pain go away.*

Alex was mad as hell. Where did she go? Was she rummaging through the stateroom for keys? It would be just like her to start the engines and go in under power. He looked at the ladder, half expecting her to remove it from the side and throw it in behind him.

He was also mad at himself realizing now his approach wasn't a good one. It's difficult not to realize it when you're flying over the rail of your boat into the cold water. Goddamn it. Why did he have to fall in love with a freaking Amazon? That petite, sweet receptionist in his building was crazy about him. She was probably the type who would greet him warmly, fetch his slippers, and have dinner ready for him when he returned from a long day at the office. And she would never, ever sling him over her shoulder or think his ideas were anything but brilliant. Shit, he was describing the best attributes of a good and loyal pet. He didn't want a pet for a wife...well most of him didn't.

Then he felt her calling him again. In his head. In his heart. Man that was strange. That hadn't happened since...suddenly it was very important for him to get on the boat. He swam quickly over to the ladder. He was shivering when he hauled himself back onto the deck.

His plans for retaliation dissolved when he saw her. She was sitting on the deck, holding her ribs, with tears sliding down her face. Her eyes were closed and there was a line of concentration between her brows. He'd seen her do this before...surrounding the pain with her mind and disengaging it. From the look and sound of her ragged breathing, it wasn't working very well. Damn her for playing around with her health. She must have re-injured something inside.

He was kneeling beside her before his next heartbeat.

"Skye. Honey. What happened? What can I do?"

"Hold me," she whispered through clenched teeth.

"But I'm all wet."

Her eyes opened and a flash of humor showed through the pain. "That you are. Ever stop to think, and forget to start again?"

She laughed and another wave of pain shot through her. Moaning, she closed her eyes again. Alex ran down to the stateroom and grabbed the comforter off the bed, then came back up and used it as a barrier between his wet clothes and her. He wrapped it around her, then pulled her into his arms. They sat on the deck of the boat, being rocked by the gentle motion of the ocean.

Alex kissed her face, and could taste the tears. She moved her mouth to his and he tasted like the sea. It was like déjà vu. She was beginning to get her breathing under control and the pain was definitely going into the tolerable range now. She liked just where she was, however, and decided not to move quite yet.

"Sweetheart, what happened?"

"Let's see," she said in a soft, breathy voice. "We got up, it was a beautiful sunrise, we had coffee, you acted like a caveman with about six brain cells, you somehow went over the side, and my ribs started hurting again."

"Ah ha. In other words, I screwed up, you got pissed, you chucked me overboard with the intention of leaving me out here to tread water and Neptune punished you for your foolishness by zapping you with his powerful trident."

She opened her eyes and looked into his. He kissed her gently. "How bad?"

"Bad enough but getting better. I guess I wasn't ready for a full body over the shoulder slam."

"No, I think I heard your Tae Kwon Do instructor specifically mention the danger of doing that."

"Oh, yeah. I guess I was going more on instinct than good sense."

"Considering I wound up in the ocean, I would say that was a definite."

"If you hadn't been such a bonehead in the first place, I would still be enjoying the sunrise, drinking my coffee."

This time, Alex played a smart card and said nothing. He just lifted her chin and sucked some of the pain out through her mouth. He knew from past experience, that there could be temporary relief when the blood rushed from her ribs to her brain, throat, and inner thighs...and this time, he didn't think her moan was entirely the result of pain. There was a distinct tone of pleasure in her sigh as well. He decided to keep the pressure on for a bit longer. And caressed the back and side of her neck as he continued to kiss her in a very primitive, Neanderthal kind of way.

When she finally pulled back, he knew that it worked. Dr. Alex knew his basic holistic medicine. Lots of touching, lots of contact, lots of love.

"Can you stand?"

"I think so."

"Would you like to lie down?"

"No. I think I would rather sit up here on the deck." She really wanted to avoid the stateroom and the sights and smells of recent sex. It was going to be hard enough to keep a clear head. Especially since she so recently only wanted Alex when she was in pain. Her mind went immediately to him. Her inner voice instantly called to him. Her heart longed for him. Was this a test? If so, Alex was the answer.

Gently, he helped her up and assisted her to the lounge chair. When she eased herself into it another pain knifed through her chest and she let out a sharp intake of breath.

"That does it," insisted Alex. "We're going in and I'm calling Dr. Lacy to meet us at the dock."

"No, please Alex. I'm sure it will be all right. It doesn't feel like it did before, just a tightness. The pain is already much better than it was." That actually was the truth. It really had passed from mind numbing agony to a throbbing ache. The fact that the ache was only this side of tolerable was relative.

Give him something to do, her mind suggested. "Darling, could you get me a couple of Tylenol and a glass of water?"

He hesitated for a minute then nodded. "Okay, but if you're not better in a half-hour, the doctor gets to take a look."

She smiled weakly. "Deal."

Alex was solicitous for the next half-hour, making sure she was comfortable, fetching her another cup of coffee. The Tylenol was taking the edge off and she was feeling better.

"If I promise not to make any more stupid comments, will you promise to listen to my case?" he asked, sitting across from her and leaning forward.

"Are we going to stay out here until I agree with you, counselor?" she quipped taking another sip of coffee.

"I'm not even going to answer that question. It's a trap."

Skye nodded. "Smart man."

"An early morning swim can be quite an eye opener."

"It helps lay the ground rules."

"All right."

"And don't put on that reasonable, but wily negotiator face...this isn't a corporate merger."

"No it's a far more important merger I want to discuss. Tell me. You've seen a lot of my faces. Which one would you prefer?"

Skye shrugged. "I liked the face you made at Al the other day quite a lot."

"We were playing animals of Africa."

"Oh...I thought you were showing him how to pick up girls at day care."

"Always worked for me."

"No doubt."

"Skye, darling. You're stalling."

"Yes. Yes, I am."

"Last night was pretty intense," he prodded softly. "Can I begin with thanking you for saving my life?"

Skye said nothing, then slowly nodded.

"Darling, I want you to be my wife. I know you have issues and I understand their genesis, but I think my love...our love...is a much stronger force. I think we need to face them and fight them together." When she didn't respond, he prodded her again. "Talk to me, Skye. Please."

"All right. It's fairly simple, actually. A part of me, a part that is growing in intensity, is terrified that your heroic style...your fearlessness will someday test your mortality and I'll be left without a heart." She said it softly, calmly, but Alex saw the sadness in her eyes, and the inevitability of it written on her face.

"I could say the same about you, my love," he said, never breaking eye contact.

Seconds ticked off as they stared at each other. They both knew their constant flights into danger were a part of not only what they did, but also who they were. It was built into their essence. It defined them.

"I can't change that style darling. And I've accepted the fact that you can't either," he said as he continued to stare into her deep brown eyes. They had arrived at the core of the dilemma. There was nowhere else for him to go. He was totally exposed. Either she took the step forward, or their relationship was not viable. More time ticked off and Alex could feel the tension in his body.

"Oh Alex. It's one of the reasons I love you so much," she whispered, finally. Then sighed. "I think I can live with the terror, but I know I can't live without you." Her eyes filled with tears and Alex's heart clutched in his chest. "I can't live without you even though the possibility of losing you is ripping my soul to shreds. I know you can't make any promises, any guarantees. I know that in my head. But please, please, lie to my heart." She was crying now, and hurting horribly, both physically and emotionally. "Hold me and lie to my soul. Tell me you'll never leave me. That you'll always come back to me. That we'll grow old together. Tell me a fairy tale. But tell me. Say the words."

Alex got up, then knelt down on one knee, actually looking like a prince out of that fairy tale. He took her hands and his penetrating blue eyes captured hers. "Darling I love you. I'll always find you. I'll always be with you. I'll never, ever leave you alone."

Then he gathered her up in his arms and carried her to the big bed in the stateroom. He laid her down and got in with her. He wanted desperately to make love to her, but he knew she was not in any condition to exert herself. Instead he soothed her with words and light kisses, whispering to her the words she needed to hear. He held her and calmed her. Touching her soul, he eased the pain.

She clung to him. She only knew he was the source of her life force. Without him she was like a lamp that wasn't plugged in. Just a piece of equipment, well-designed, with a purpose, but totally unable to function. No light, just an object. She needed him to give her energy, to fulfill her purpose, to bring her light. And if he ceased to exist? She shuddered. On a very basic level if he ceased to exist, then so did she. She knew she would die with him. Did she have the courage to live with him?

There was no real choice. The risk was huge, but so was the potential for happiness and joy. She wanted that pleasure, that delight, that heat. She needed it. She needed him. Despite the pain, she wrapped her arms around his waist. Lifting her mouth to his, they came together. One deep, passionate, desperate kiss that went on forever. That promised forever.

"Skye," Alex whispered when they came up for air. He had her face in his hands and was looking into her eyes, the window into her soul. "I have never loved you more than I do at this moment. Please marry me. Spend your life with me. Let's face this together. Our love is a miracle. I'll never be able to breathe without you. I'll never see the sun again without you. I'll never be content without you. I've been a solitary man. Alone. Please come to me and stand beside me and love me. We'll grow old together. I'll never leave you."

Skye's heart both ached with longing and hummed with enchantment. She was so moved, so affected that she released the doubt clouding her mind. Staring into his loving blue eyes, she knew what he said was true.

She kissed him with all the love in her heart. "Make love to me," she whispered. "Make this moment perfect." Gently, so gently she barely felt his touch, he did. And they slipped into sleep in each other's arms. Skye's dreams filled with white clouds, deep blue sky, and a weightlessness that made it easy to fly.

They awoke a few hours later to the sound of the cell phone ringing. Alex reached over and picked it up. He saw that it was from his VP of Operations-International Division. Hell. He must have had a meeting. "Dishelm?"

"You two ever coming in?"

"Where are you?"

"Standing on your dock with binoculars. If you're naked out there, you better get dressed before you come up on deck."

Alex snorted. "We had a meeting?"

"You scheduled it. I have a PowerPoint and everything. If you want to unschedule it, that's your choice."

Alex and Jessica Dishelm had known each other for years and had a great working relationship. Alex had hired her, provided her with resources, and left her alone. Jessica was the VP of one of the most profitable ventures in the industry. Periodically, however, she reported to Alex. This morning they were to have a meeting.

"Hmmm...the sea, bright blue sky, a beautiful woman...or a presentation on operations. You're making this decision difficult."

"Seriously, Alex. I can come back."

"No. No. Give us an hour. Have Tank fix you some breakfast." Cynthia was at a quilting convention with her sister Edna and taking a well-deserved break. Tank took over the kitchen in her absence.

"He already has things going. Do I trust an omelet from a guy named Tank?"

"Let's just say you can be sure the eggs are well beaten."

"There's that."

"See you soon."

Alex rang off and shook Skye slightly.

"I heard," she moaned and turned over.

"How are the ribs? Did I hurt you?"

"They're doing okay and no. You didn't."

"Look...um...we have to go in." He looked into her still bleary eyes.

"Did we get anything settled here?"

She smiled sweetly, lovingly. "Reach over and snag my bag, will you?"

"Can you answer my question before you start repairing your make-up?"

"No."

Alex was feeling his frustration mount and Skye could feel the tension in his arms and chest.

"Please. I think we're still in the post passion 'you can't deny me anything' stage," she said with a seductive smile.

He roughly grabbed her bag off the side table and handed it to her. Alex still felt he was on a roller coaster and it was stretching his patience. She was the most irritating, exasperating person he'd ever met. He watched as she rummaged through her underwear and other girly things. And he loved her more than life. Must be mentally ill, he thought. Connecting himself to the source of all his aggravation.

Completely vexed, he snapped. "Goddamn it, Skye. I'm talking about my life here and you're mining for just the right color lip gloss."

"A lot you know," she said and she continued to dig and pull out things that Alex couldn't begin to identify. When she pulled out her gun, he growled. "Why don't you use that thing and just put me out of my misery?"

"Too loud," she giggled.

She was giggling, he thought. Giggling. She was driving him mad. Yup, he was going to have to commit himself to an institution. Wrap up this case and then go away. For a long, long time. She found what she was looking for and let out a little 'gotchya.'

"Christ, Skye. What did you find? A long lost pair of perfect earrings?" he asked sarcastically. That tone would have made his associates cringe and hide, but she just giggled again. Had she snapped? Maybe they could share a room at the No Hope Home for the Permanently Insane.

"Close," she said as she looked up at him with dancing eyes. Her fist was closed and she moved to sit in front of him. She just couldn't resist. He was sitting there, scowling like a petulant child. She'd seen the same face on little Al. She laughed out loud. It hurt her ribs, but she didn't care. At this moment she was as close to carefree as she had been in...well...forever, she guessed. "If you take that stick of dynamite out of your ass, I might just share my secret."

Just when his temper was about to erupt, she decided to end the suspense. She slowly opened her hand. Lying in her palm was the ring.

Surly and ready to explode he followed her eyes. The fuse was yanked from the stick of dynamite up his ass and he felt instead a steady, warm sensation spread throughout his body.

"Your talisman," he whispered. He felt his body completely dissolve into the sheets. His shock, his surprise, his absolute elation all flashed through him and showed on his face.

"No," she said as she took his hand and placed it in his palm. "This time when you put it on my finger it's an engagement ring."

His hand shook a bit as he took her left hand and placed it on her finger. "I have no words," he said with a ragged voice. He looked into her shimmering eyes and found he didn't need any.

She came to him and he held her. Then he took her hand and held it out. "You have no idea," he said with such emotion, Skye couldn't swallow.

"Oh yes," she said softly. "I think I do." She smiled up at him. "This isn't going to be easy."

"Nothing worthwhile ever is."

"When we get back on shore, I may start slipping."

"I'll catch you."

"Probably scream in the middle of the night."

"I'll hold you."

"I may never be at peace."

"I'll be there to keep a safe place for you."

"I may have something deeply wrong with me. I may be horribly flawed."

"As Aunt Hazel says...a diamond with a flaw is many times more valuable than a brick without one."

"Are you saying my diamond has a flaw?" she asked, smiling.

"No. Don't be so literal. I love you, my darling. And we belong together."

"It's our miracle...our destiny" Their lips barely touched, but it sealed their fate. They were one.

They took their time getting ready. Skye was still moving gingerly, but she was convinced nothing was damaged. She just pushed through the limits and had to pay the consequences. That was something she did routinely, so she ignored the ache as best she could and stood on the deck as Alex expertly sailed them back to the dock.

His eyes would go to her hand frequently. He knew she had some ground to cover before she completely released the demons to the dark, but they would face it as a team. Together for as long as they lived. He had told her once that they must love intensely...cherish with extreme passion...because if the time together was going to be short, it would at least be powerful. If they were blessed and life was long and rich, that was a bonus. He would work hard to get her to believe this. And he had a plan.

CHAPTER 18

After his meeting, Alex found the man he was looking for leaning on the railing, gazing out over the ocean, and smiling at a private thought.

"Where are your progeny?"

"Gosh, Alex. I'm not sure. I think maybe if you'd quit showing off your superior vocabulary, I would have a better chance of providing you with the information." David had a master's degree in Criminal Justice, but he always downplayed his intelligence. Came from hanging with the criminal element. He always wanted the street to underestimate him. David was a great looking man with a kind face and a hard body. It made for a surprising package and it was the reason he was both a good cop and a great father. "But, if you're referring to the two little creatures that claim they're mine and keep showing up at my dinner table, Saint Skyler has zoo duty this afternoon. For some strange reason, she seems to like really loud, really messy aliens."

"Yeah, she does. But she's been able to domesticate them pretty effectively. They actually come in at below 60 decibels when they're around her. She even seems to know where the 'sit still and eat your peas' button is."

"Yeah and they've kept that hidden since birth. The fact they would actually eat peas shows the depth of their devotion." He smiled when he remembered them overcoming their aversion to vegetables and all things green to try and impress her at the dinner table a couple of nights before. She would trade kisses for obedience. Tank kept wanting in on the deal, but she strictly enforced the age requirement. Under 12 and over 85. "They would probably eat dead jelly fish off the beach if she asked them to."

"Doesn't everybody?"

"She sure seems to have you domesticated, too. Of course you're just a larger version of Al."

"What do you mean? I haven't refused to take a bath in years."

"That was some battle Tuesday night, wasn't it? What did you have to promise him?"

"Other than Disney World, space camp, and some dinosaur videos?" asked Alex.

"Man. I told him to hold out for the Porsche. Shit, I was really looking forward to driving him around in it. So what worked? Nothing on that list seems compelling enough. I noticed the shouting and screaming halted pretty abruptly."

"Well, Skye did pop in and mention she was getting her medical tomorrow and she might be cleared to fly. She promised him a ride in the new Gulfstream. Then she distracted him with a rubber snake and I was out completely."

"Oh yeah, that would work. God, how do I get her to pop into my bath? My snake isn't rubber, but it sure is impressive."

"Watch it, pal. She's all mine."

"Selfish bastard."

"Live with it. And keep your snake buttoned up."

"You're a brutal selfish bastard," laughed David.

"That's me." Then, he turned serious. He thought the world of David and didn't want to hurt him, but he needed his advice. He needed to talk to someone whom he both trusted and would be able to give him some insight. "Can I ask you a personal question?"

"Why not? I can always prevaricate if I don't want to answer it."

"Would you ever consider dating a cop again?"

David didn't hide the shock. "Where the hell did that question come from, a parallel universe?"

Alex smiled grimly. "Answer the question and I'll tell you."

"Okay." David looked back over the ocean. He could see it was important to his friend and brother-in-law. "Why do you suppose I haven't dated in six years?"

"Other than the fact that you're ugly, have no personality, eat peas with a spoon, and are straddled with two of the most diabolical monsters ever to escape a Disney movie?"

"Yeah, other than that."

"Well, I guess I assumed you were never ready. Or that you thought Rita would come back and kick your ass across Central Park."

"Well you're right about that. For the first few years she was both too much with me and too much gone. There was so much pain…so much loneliness…there were times I shouldn't have been carrying a gun. If I didn't have those two monsters at home waiting for me…."

He didn't finish the sentence, but they both knew what he meant. David shook his head, his face flashing the haunted look Alex had seen before, both on the face of his friend and now on the face of his lover. "Well. Anyway, to answer your question, for the last year or so, I've been thinking it would be nice to have someone around who didn't talk about boogers and Nintendo and eat Lucky Charms for breakfast. You know, someone other than you."

"And why haven't you?"

"Because most of the single women I know are cops," David said quietly and took another sip of his coffee. Alex nodded. He got his answer and it hit him like punch to the gut. David was one of most courageous men he knew, and one of the strongest. If he couldn't face the idea of getting involved with another cop, how could anyone? How could Skye?

"I can't open myself up for another blow like that. I'm just not brave enough. I loved Rita so completely, that when she was killed I couldn't function on an important physical and emotional level. I was a shell, going through the motions and doing my job, but I wasn't really living and that's the most agonizing existence imaginable." He tensed, then shook off the memories. He was beyond that now. "I assume there's a good reason you asked." And when he saw the troubled look on Alex's face, he added. "And that the answer I gave you, while honest, was not the answer you wanted. I'm very sorry about that. Can you answer my question?"

"Sure. I can always prevaricate if I don't want to answer it."

"Why did you ask me and why is my answer so important to you?"

"Actually, it's because I'm trying to understand Skye."

"I have noticed her weight is dropping and there are times when she thinks no one is watching that she looks so...not sad, really...but conflicted."

"Christ, David. I really need to talk about this. She's been rethinking our relationship and she's in agony over it."

David looked at his brother-in-law, his normally unflappable friend and saw the pain.

"But she's totally gone over you. If I thought I had a chance with her, I would take you out in your boat and turn you into shark bait." He hesitated a moment. "Is she ill?"

"No...not exactly." Alex hesitated. He was under a vow of secrecy and even though he suspected everyone in his family wasn't fooled by their shadow life, he couldn't get the actual words out.

David saw his hesitation. They weren't officially supposed to know about Alex and Skye being in the law enforcement business. Oh, what the hell, he wasn't an idiot. He didn't know what they called themselves, but no one consistently got into this much trouble by being a millionaire and a pilot. "You having a problem facing the danger she's constantly in?" He guessed.

Alex flinched then shook his head. Skye's danger was one thing he managed to suppress. And if he answered David's question, it would implicitly confirm his and Skye's status with Justice. It wasn't that he didn't trust David. He did. With his life. It was just having to overcome the wall of silence they built around themselves, the need to stay in the shadows that kept him from immediately replying. He was trying to formulate his words and, as usual, David helped him out.

"You could always lie. But then I'm a trained and perceptive interrogator. You have my permission to be appropriately cryptic and enigmatic."

"Okay. Let's just say that my business puts me into situations I need to have special training for. Skye has the same tendency to get involved in these incidents."

"And there's a bullet wound in your shoulder and Skye has spent more time in a bed these last few months than a Las Vegas call girl. Are you having difficulty with her extraordinary tendency of finding herself in the middle of trouble?"

"No, actually, I've learned to deal with it. I would rather be with her, covering her back, than have a relationship with a nice safe attorney or something." He looked again at his friend's compassionate eyes. He had on his dad's eyes today. He must have left his cops eyes in the closet. It made it easier to confide in him. "It's the other way around."

That really surprised David and he showed it with a puzzled expression. "I don't understand."

Alex told him. About Skye seeing her parents blown up when she was fifteen and how she blocked it out and locked her heart in a steel box. How she had opened it and let herself fall in love. With a Washington D.C. cop and how two weeks before the wedding, his captain and the chaplain had made the visit that all friends and family of cops dread. David knew. He knew the precise feeling. David had to take a few deep breaths during Alex's explanation.

"Sorry David," said Alex softly. "I don't mean to stir up your own bad memories. I shouldn't have brought this up."

"It's okay, Alex. You have to talk to someone. I remember all of our late nights when you helped me chase the demons from my front door. Go on."

"She buried him one week before they were to be married and she vowed she would never open herself up to that kind of pain again."

David nodded. He had already told his friend that he was not brave enough to do that, and he was beginning to see where this was going. It chilled him and made his admiration for Skye go up another notch.

"When we first met, she didn't know I was, um, well, that I was anything but a suave, debonair millionaire lawyer."

"Then she got to know you better," said David.

"Indeed."

"And there was more there than was immediately apparent. I hope that someday you will be able to tell me the whole story. It should be very entertaining. So she discovered the truth."

"Yes."

"That you were a relentless, ruthless capitalist pig."

"You could say that."

"Just did. It must have been interesting, though."

"That it was."

"So she didn't want to continue the relationship when she found out about the pig part."

"Exactly," said Alex, relieved that David was following his thoughts perfectly.

"And you wore her down with physical incursions and enlisted her impressionable sister in the assault."

"I'm merciless."

"But she agreed to marry you. She must have decided a life with you had the lesser potential for pain. With you, possible loss. Without you, constant never ending heartache and unthinkable loneliness."

"I convinced her of that, yes."

"You always were a superb negotiator."

"Rarely lost one with Rita."

"Yeah, that's what she let you think."

"Anyway, she opened herself up completely to me. I…ah…oh hell…" They knew he was the commando, for God's sake and he needed to get this out. He had the power to make field decisions on whom to bring into his confidence and there was no one more trustworthy than his family. "She…um…saw me go down. She didn't realize I was wearing a vest. It was quite a gruesome show. Five guys came out of a bunker behind me.

291

I turned, actually thought I got four of them. The fifth one caught me. I remember at the time thinking it wasn't me that took them all. She was actually covering me from a window…saw the whole thing. Took two of them out herself and one at my back. Couldn't get the fifth one because Terrin incapacitated her." David's reaction was both shock and anger. There are the cop's eyes, thought Alex. "I flew through the air pretty good. I really was knocked out for a while, and of course there was a convincing amount of blood, but when I came to, I played dead. Skye didn't know I was acting."

"For how long?"

"I really don't know…through the evening almost until daybreak."

"Oh my God." All color and humor dissolved from David's face and was replaced by distress and sadness. He rubbed his face with hands that shook, trying to reduce the horror of what he just heard. "Christ, Alex. For years, I saw it in my mind. I saw her face, the moment of impact, the blood. It was all in my mind, but it was horrifying. I can't even imagine what it would have been like to actually see her fall. To see her…" There were tears in his eyes. He couldn't finish. He never looked at any of the crime scene photos or heard any of the official accounts. He had to protect himself from the reality of it. His imagination was hard enough to deal with.

Alex was shook. David's reaction was powerful, his pain excruciating. "Goddamn it, David. I'm sorry. I should never have brought this up. Let's go back to the shark bait." He had a lump in his throat, too. He missed his sister terribly. He couldn't imagine David's pain.

"No. No, it's okay," said David smiling shakily and taking a deep breath to clear out the images. "It's been a long time since the sorrow hit like that." He took another breath and blew it out. He was going to hurt his friend, but he believed in honesty "I'm sorry, Alex. I can see the problem through Skye's eyes. It must be killing her to love you. To have had this happen to her before, then to see it happen again right in front of her like that. She must be struggling with whether or not she can open herself up again. I can see now that she's making herself sick over it. Damn it, tell me you aren't pressuring her."

Alex was silent. Was he pressuring her?

"I tried to give her space. To give her time to come to her own decision. It's been very…difficult."

"So that was the reason for the glass shower yesterday?"

"Yeah. Pretty juvenile of me, but the strain got a bit cosmic. I only found out last night that she thought that I'd been killed. I guess I assumed she knew about the vest or...I don't know. I was living it from a totally different point of view. I wasn't thinking, only reacting."

David was dying to ask him more details. Later, he thought. First things first.

"How did you get her to agree to marry you in the first place?"

"It took me a long time to melt the steel wall around her," said Alex.

"Used all the Springfield charm?"

"And a bit of hand to hand."

"Ah. I want you to tell me more about that later. Turns me on."

"Anyway, she's reconstructing the wall, stronger and more impenetrable than before. I'm not sure I have enough in my arsenal for titanium."

David thought for a moment. "You sure you'll be doing right by her if you break through again? You sure you're the right man for her? Her instincts are telling her no more risk."

"I'm the only man for her," Alex said more sharply than he'd intended. Imagining Skye with anyone else was unthinkable and if that made him a selfish bastard, so be it. "On most levels, she knows that."

David stared at him for a heartbeat, then nodded. "I agree, otherwise she wouldn't be so troubled. I see her love, it shines in her eyes. I see two possible solutions to your problem."

"They are?"

"Give her up like a noble, but foolish hero in an old Greek tragedy."

"I'm not that noble."

"No, I didn't think so."

"The other?"

"Send in something stronger than titanium." David looked over at his mother-in-law sleeping on a lounge chair near the pool.

"Mom?" Alex brightened. Why hadn't he thought of that? He smiled at David. He was brilliant.

"Exactly!" They looked at each other like conspirators. Victory was assured.

David finished his drink and pushed away from the railing. "And, ah...as long as we're talking about this. There's a woman at the day care center I would like to approach. How would you feel about that?"

"I think it would be great," Alex said sincerely, wanting nothing but the best for Rita's man.

Then David sighed. "She is a real nice person, but I think she might be too familiar with my children to consider dating their dad."

"You could just sell them."

"I've thought of that. But who would buy them?"

"You have a point." Both men loved the two boys more than life. They smiled and moved toward the bar near the pool. "And while we're having this man time filled with shared secrets and confidences, tell me more about this little adventure of yours. Your cursory and superficially official account was not very satisfying."

"Sorry. If I told you I would have to imprison you for life."

"But then you'd inherit my kids."

"Hmmm. Okay. Raise your right hand." David raised his left. "Close enough. Do you solemnly promise to never reveal what I'm about to tell you under penalty of breaking the National Security Act of 1994?"

"Yeah, sure."

"The hijackers had my Palm Pilot and I had to go in after it. No self respecting millionaire corporate attorney can take a meeting without his Palm Pilot." He grinned. David grinned.

You went in after your pilot, all right, David thought, but not of the palm variety. He knew all of Alex's secrets started right after the death of his wife. A drive that was latent inside Alex was triggered by Rita's murder. Another reason he was connected to this guy. So David did the connected guy thing. He wrapped his arm around Alex's shoulder, punched him in the ribs, not too hard, and suggested they pop a few brewskies.

Early the next morning, Skye walked slowly along the shore of the ocean, trying to absorb its serenity into her soul. She thought the nightmare that had plagued her every night wouldn't come back. She didn't remember having it on the boat. But last night was over the top. She woke up screaming and shook in Alex's arms for over an hour before she could get the image of the bloody wedding dresses out of her mind's eye.

She looked at her ring and twisted it in the sun. She wanted Alex so badly. She would just have to live with the consequences. Probably look like a weathered old hag by the time she was forty if she couldn't get a good night's sleep. With a pissy personality, too. Then he would leave her. Problem solved.

Skye was still thinking of going away for a while. When she mentioned it in the night, Alex stiffened and said no. She was too exhausted to fight him. Too exhausted to fight anything. She needed help and she knew it. But who? Alex was wonderful, but every time she shared her fears, it hurt him so badly. Wiping a tear off her cheek she continued to walk the beach.

Alex looked down at the woman he loved more than life. She was being tortured and he was her tormentor. He turned and smiled at his mother, looking tanned and robust in her casual clothes. She would be returning to duty in Chicago soon and now was the time to enlist her help. Coming up beside him, she looked out to see what he was watching.

"She is a picture, isn't she?" said Wyatt with appreciation for the woman who had captured her son's heart. She was absolutely in love with her new child and looked out the window with affection and compassion. "Why is she so sad? It breaks my heart."

Alex put his arm around his mother. "And she thinks she hides it so well. It's me, Mom. I'm the reason she's so unhappy."

Wyatt frowned. This was the last thing she expected to hear.

"Don't look so fierce, Captain, it's nothing you'd arrest me for."

Alex explained to his mother what he knew about Skye's nightmare. Her parents, Jeffrey, him being attacked and injured right in front of her. Her thinking he'd been killed. Wyatt listened without comment, but when he finished, there were tears sliding down her cheeks.

"Oh Alex. That poor child. Not only does she have to face the trauma and horrible heartache, she carries the guilt of survival. If she hadn't asked her parents to stop, she would have perished with them. She couldn't save them. Then she opens up her heart again and finds happiness and her man goes down just before the wedding. Then seeing you…well…and thinking you were dead. That she couldn't get just one more man before he got you. I certainly can identify with that, even though I can't imagine what it would have been like to actually experience it…the effect must have been devastating. As well adjusted as she is. As optimistic as I have found her to be. There's something deep in her heart that must feel doomed. Maybe even a voice inside her that whispers she's responsible."

Alex stared at his mother. In just a few short minutes, she'd identified the problem, then put it simply and concisely into words. Skye must feel doomed. His heart ached for her. Then he remembered another death, very recently experienced. In their business it was always a possibility, always just outside the door.

"There was, ah…also a friend. An associate she was very close to who was killed by someone she trusted."

"That situation this spring?"

"Yeah. She never says much, but I know she always felt she should have been quicker to recognize the danger. Not that anyone ever saw the signs, felt the threat. She always thinks she needs to be just a bit better. I don't know how she can improve on near perfection." When he saw his mom smile, he added. "Did that sound like a love sick boy-child?"

"It did. But it's lovely and I'm very proud of how my boy-child turned out. And in his choice of mates."

"I can't give her up. I realize I'm causing her this torment, but just I can't give her up."

"I know. Nor should you."

"And I can't make her any guarantees."

"I know that, too." They never talked about his job at Justice. It was after all, a secret. But Wyatt was a trained and perceptive detective. And she understood her son through and through. She knew.

"And she can make none to you."

Alex smiled. "No."

"How is your heart with that?"

"It terrifies me."

She nodded and touched his cheek. He really was a good man.

Looking back at Skye, Alex knew he was going to have to put a little pain into their discussion, but he needed her and he knew she would understand.

"Mom, did you ever try to talk Rita out of becoming a cop?"

"No, dear. That would have been a little hypocritical of me."

"But she was your child. And you lost her." They had all lost her. Vital, vibrant, always laughing Rita. The hole was forever there.

"Yes," Wyatt whispered. "We did. And for a long time, I blamed myself."

Alex looked at her, stunned. "You what?"

"She was a cop because that was what she grew up with. I felt responsible. David is still in the business. Now there's Tank…and you. It scares me. But you learn to live with it. Live through it." She looked at him out of the corner of her eye. "Not that I don't believe that you're a lawyer and financier. Just one that always seems to find himself in the middle of trouble."

"Life is like that."

"Indeed. Anyway, I've come to terms with all of that. The fear, the dread, the guilt. Your wonderful Skyler has just had it more directly. Right in front of her eyes. It makes for more vivid nightmares, more direct suffering. I can't believe she's still standing. Still living. Still loving. She's remarkable, your woman."

"Yes." And in that one word Wyatt heard all the love of the ages. "What can I do?" He was grateful for her. To be able to talk about it reduced the ache in his heart, the burden from his shoulders. "What can I say to her?"

"Nothing."

He looked at her sadly. "But I need to help."

"But you're the cause of her pain. "

"That hurt." And it did. He wanted to be her protector, not her tormentor.

"But it's true. That poor courageous woman wants to marry you. Her love is stronger than her need for self-preservation. That's an incredible display of fearlessness. How many more battles can she fight? How many more nights can she go without sleep? How much more weight can she lose? Her body must be close to shutting down and yet she still loves and laughs and lives."

He nodded. "I feel so helpless."

"I think she needs a mother." Alex turned to her, nodded slowly, then grinned. He hadn't been able to articulate it, but that was exactly what she needed. What she lacked. Aunt Hazel was a wonderful woman and Skye got a lot of her good humor from her, but Hazel was not maternal.

"Got any one in particular in mind?" asked Alex.

She patted her oldest son on the cheek.

"I think I've done a pretty good job, so far. Of course Tank is still a work in progress." She looked back to the melancholy scene of the solitary figure by the ocean. "Let me try."

Wyatt gave Alex's arm a reassuring squeeze and went to spread her mantle of maternal love over her son's future wife.

Skye turned, put the veil of happy anticipation back on her face and smiled at the woman who bore and raised the love of her life.

Not quite quick enough, thought Wyatt as she approached. A valiant attempt that pulled at her soul.

Skye's smile was genuine, however. Even if Wyatt hadn't been Alex's mom, she would have loved her. She was an excellent detective, an intelligent and witty woman and a great mom. The motherless child inside her had been attracted to the kind, gentle side of this woman, even as the two of them shared stories of blood, murder, and mayhem.

Wyatt approached her future daughter-in-law with a loving look on her face. The mother who had lost a daughter in a vicious world opened up her heart to this vision her son had fallen in love with. Even if Skye hadn't been the chosen one, the one perfect for her son, she would have liked and admired her. Loved her. It made her throat constrict when she realized it was love. A mother's love. She wanted this daughter. She wanted her for her son, but she wanted Skye for herself, as well.

As Wyatt came nearer, Skye felt a connection that was both powerful and poignant. It was like Wyatt was throwing her a lifeline and Skye decided to grab for it with all the strength of a drowning soul. The hole in her motherless heart was aching to be filled. Wyatt stared into Skye's longing eyes and felt it too, so she reopened the wound in her own heart and stood in front of Skye, vulnerable and exposed.

"Alex told you," Skye whispered.

"Yes," said Wyatt simply.

The child inside of Skye stepped into the aching core of Wyatt's soul. Heart spoke to heart. The tears started to fall as Wyatt folded Skye into her arms. They cried and held onto each other and their tears flowed together as their hearts became whole again. A mother for a daughter. A daughter for a mother. Their sorrow and feeling of loss were shattered by their shared bond. They let in the relief of love…pure, natural, familial.

Alex felt his father come up beside him and put his arm around his shoulder. Both men watched as their women wept. And both men wiped their eyes as well.

"Well, shit, son. If that isn't exactly what she's needed all these years," said Blake with such tender feeling that Alex could only nod. "Good move, boy, sending your mom in after her. Wyatt will not only do the job, she'll be healed by it."

"Skye is now in Rita's spot," whispered Alex, realizing how perfect that sounded. How right.

"And it's been a powerfully large hole that I've never been able to fix." Blake's throat was tight and he had to stop for a moment. "She had it covered up, but never filled. She was never whole after Rita was killed. I think she may be close right now. Complete. God bless that young woman."

Alex nodded, captivated by the thought, and touched beyond measure. He knew that his decision to keep Skye in his life was not only his destiny, but also hers.

Blake blew out a deep breath. "Now before we start clutching and weeping, too, how about leaving them alone and making them some breakfast. After all that tear letting out there, they'll both be ravenous. Cynthia is still at her sister's on Singer Island, so I think we're it."

"Sure, Dad." And for the first time in weeks he felt lighthearted, hopeful. Maybe they could get on with their plans for the wedding. "How about you fry the bacon and I'll make the pancakes."

"No son. You make the flattest, hardest, grossest pancakes this side of Texas. Every time you make them, we have to register them as lethal weapons. Too much paperwork. How about you fry the bacon and we wake up Tank? He can handle himself in the kitchen."

"Yeah, but who's going to wake up Tank?"

"Whose turn is it?"

"Yours, I think."

"Damn. You lock up his gun when the two of you got home last night?"

"Sure did."

"Okay, I'll do it. If I'm not back in five, go get your mom."

"Deal."

Skye's nightmare, fears, and personal torment came pouring out of her like poison pouring from an unhealed wound. She talked and shared secrets from her heart that she didn't even know were there. Wyatt told her of her own feelings of grief and guilt. They were sitting in a pretty sun filled room off the atrium. They had endured Tank's breakfast and his crankiness and sent the boys out fishing. They wanted to be alone.

The men, picking up on the peculiar female vibes coming in waves off the two women couldn't wait to get their bloody chum, six packs, chips, subs, and poles on the boat and put out to sea. They weren't sure what was up, but it was definitely girly and they wanted no part of it.

Wyatt needed a daughter to confide in her, a daughter who would share her thoughts, her troubles, her joys, her happiness...and Wyatt was convinced that as soon as they vanquished the troubles, they would definitely get to the joy. She saw years of birthdays and babies, celebrations and confidences. She loved her boys to distraction, but she missed her daughter and their relationship so much.

Skye didn't even know how much she needed a mother. An older, wiser, nonjudgmental woman who would love her unconditionally and share both her triumphs and her disappointments. To have someone to confide in. She loved her Aunt Hazel and her sister, but they weren't women in love and wouldn't understand her fears. Plus this surrogate mother had the added bonus of knowing how to shoot a gun and take down a suspect. She understood her life as well as her heart.

They talked all morning, then decided it was time for aerobic shopping. They spent the afternoon in Jacksonville laughing, enjoying the hunt for just the right pair of earrings to match the perfect blouse bought for half price from the designer shop they both had seen on one of their trips into town. They discovered a mutual passion for silk teddies and couldn't walk by a shoe store without stopping in for a pair or two. By the time they took a break for ice cream, they were giving off such intense female pheromones they would have flattened the boat the men were skuzzing up nicely with empty beer bottles, chip bags, cookie crumbs, and very few fish.

It was a wonderful day for everyone.

CHAPTER 19

The next day, Alex dressed for a series of business meetings in town. He watched Skye in the reflection of the mirror as he tied his tie. She was sleeping and he was thankful. Skye's nightmare had come early and she'd just gone back to sleep. He picked up his jacket, went over and kissed her cheek. He knew there was something more peaceful about her, more settled and at rest. He knew his mother was responsible and he would forever be grateful to her. They didn't say much when the men and women merged last night for dinner, but there was a lot of touching and knowing looks as the men were forced to admire the incredible bargains the ladies found in the shoe stores across the city.

He ran his fingers over the bronze colored silk teddy Skye had on under her casual jeans and t-shirt. When she took off the outer layer last night before they went to bed, his mouth started watering immediately. And that was just the looking part. He couldn't believe it when she told him his own mother bought one in red. He wondered if the cops at Chicago Central knew what lurked under the tailored dark suits she favored for work.

He took one last look at her as he pulled on his jacket. Her ring flashed brightly on the hand that she had tucked sweetly under her cheek. The symbol of his commitment, of her pledge. This was how he intended to spend the rest of his life. Long or short, it was his idea of perfection. His family all went wild when they saw the ring. He warded off all specific questions himself, protecting her from the majority of the onslaught. Taking one last look to get him through the day, he left the room.

Skye's eyes came open when she heard the door close. He wanted her to sleep so badly. So she tried. She just couldn't turn off her brain. She liked having her hand tucked right there so she saw the ring when she woke up. She intended to keep it on this time. No flagging, no turning away from her happiness because of the potential for despair. If the nightmares were the price tag...so be it. What she got in return was worth it. She just wished she could get the sight of Alex slamming against the side of the hangar, bullets pounding into him, then falling that endless fall to the ground out of her mind. A single tear slid down her cheek and onto the ring.

Her medical exam was today. The one that would clear her for flight. God, how she needed to get airborne again. Up there, soaring, where there were no bullets and bad guys.

She stretched. Her ribs seemed okay. Not 100 percent, but okay. She wondered if Cynthia would make her some pancakes this morning. She had returned from her sister's home last night clucking about the condition of her kitchen. It seemed Tank's philosophy of doing dishes was based on necessity. You didn't wash something unless you needed it. And since Cynthia's kitchen was stocked with every utensil, appliance, pot and cooking device manufactured, the counters were stacked high and long.

Skye smiled and actually felt lighter as she looked out into the cloudless sky. If she got her wings back, she was going to rent a plane and fly all morning. Jumping out of bed, she went to shower. She grabbed the extension in the bathroom while she was putting on her makeup and pushed the kitchen intercom.

"Good morning," came Cynthia's cheery voice. She had enjoyed her time with her sister, but it was good to be back where she belonged.

"Good morning, Cynthia."

"What are you doing up? Mr. Springfield told me you were sleeping. I was to wake you, very gently I think he said, in an hour."

"I couldn't sleep." Before she could start clucking again, Skye hurried on. "I'm too excited. I think I'm going to get cleared today for take off. I was wondering…" she didn't even have to finish the sentence.

"Pancakes?"

"Would you mind?"

"Honey, they'll be on a plate and ready by the time you get down here. Want to eat on the terrace?"

"Yes, I would love to eat on the terrace. Anybody out there, yet?"

"Only Mr. Springfield Senior and Captain Cooper. I've banished Tank forever from my kitchen, so he may be eating Cocoa Puffs in his room or maybe he stayed down in Lauderdale. Ginny will tell me later if his bed's been slept in, although I'm not sure how anyone could tell. His room is always a declared disaster area. Mr. Delton took Al and Jason down to Cape Canaveral. The brothers Cooper and their wives aren't back from the Keys yet."

"I'll be down in five."

She put on a simple lightweight linen suit in magenta and a matching pair of shoes. The shade was excellent with her coloring and the lines complemented her long neck and even longer legs. The suit wasn't tailored so it wouldn't hang on her frame and make her look sick when she went into the doctor. She was going to eat as many pancakes as she could stomach. This scrawny look was getting annoying.

Taking a deep breath, she stuck out her chest. Even though her frame was by nature tall and thin, she inherited generous breasts from her Italian mother. It seemed she might have lost an inch there, too. Bastards. They were going to burn in hell for sure. She carefully applied her makeup to hide the tiniest shadow of discoloration around her eye, sprayed a light scent on her wrist and neck, and declared herself alive and well.

When she came out on the terrace, she saw Tank wolfing down a stack of pancakes. Blake and Wyatt were working on the crossword puzzle together. Skye went over and gave them both a quick peck on the cheek. They looked at each other and smiled. Such a natural daughter thing to do. It felt so good.

"Hey, where's mine?" Tank asked with an exaggerated wink.

"You just get in?" she asked sweetly giving the top of his head a little peck. Tank caught a whiff of her and tried to keep his eyes from sliding down to her lovely cleavage when she reached over him to grab a piece of melon. What the hell, she wasn't his sister-in-law, yet. He completely stopped chewing and just stared at her.

"Tank?"

"Huh? Oh...yeah. About five minutes ago. I would tell you where I was, but Mom is sitting within earshot."

"I see Cynthia forgave you."

"She had to. Springfield charm. We turn it on the ladies and zap...we're forgiven just about anything. Right Mom?"

"What is an eight letter word for gibberish?" asked Wyatt.

"Huh?"

"Starts with a 'b' and ends with shit."

"Bullshit? Oh. I get it. Good one Mom." He rolled his eyes at Skye.

"I saw that, Tank," Wyatt said automatically, never looking up from the paper.

Tank stared at Skye. "You look, well. Ah. Well...different."

"The Springfield charm at work," observed his father.

"I mean, well, you have grown up clothes on."

"Tank," said Blake as he came to refill his coffee cup. "The fact that you get anyone to ever go out with you is a source of mystery to your Mom and I."

"I can't help it. She *is* kind of blinding." Skye turned and gave Tank one of her best smiles. "Whoa. That one was lethal," he said touching his heart. "Mom, if I kill Alex and take his girl, will you arrest me?"

"No dear, you're my son. But if you say girl again, I'll shoot you in the kneecaps. What is a four letter word for unenlightened chauvinist?"

"Hurt?"

"Exactly."

"Skye, here's one you'll know…what is a pilot's 'H'," asked Blake, his pen poised.

"Hotel," she said automatically, helping herself to a mug of coffee.

"Doesn't fit," said Blake, frowning.

"Oh yes it does, dear," said Wyatt. "You need to change that f to a t."

"A four letter word ending in k that means intercourse."

"That would be talk. This is the New York Times, not Playboy."

"What?" said Tank, swallowing. "Pilots have a different alphabet?"

"No, the alphabet is the same, just how we say it different…prevents any confusion…like A is Alpha, B is Bravo, C is Charlie, D is Delta…and so on," said Skye, thinking she would be using the letters today.

"And H is for Hotel? That doesn't seem like it has much panache," said Tank, attacking another stack.

"Depends on whom you're with."

"Panache. That's it! A seven letter word meaning flamboyance," said Blake. He looked up at his son. Eating pancakes in stacks instead of servings. He hadn't changed much since he was thirteen. Just got bigger. "Your vocabulary has improved since you have been emailing Sloane."

"She is one intelligent girl. But she doesn't make you feel stupid," said Tank, making a stupid face.

"I always thought you were gifted," said Wyatt.

"Of course he was gifted. Who would pay for him?" asked Blake.

Cynthia came out just then and presented Skye with an enormous plate of pancakes. "There you are, dear. Now see if you can eat every bite. And Mr. Springfield left you this. Told me to give it to you at breakfast."

"Need help with those?" asked Tank softly in a conspiratorial voice.

"I heard that, young Mr. Springfield," said Cynthia. "You leave hers alone. You had your share."

Skye just nodded and winked. Together they finished every crumb.

When Cynthia came back out and beamed at the empty plate, Skye pulled back and patted her flat, fit stomach. "It's lucky your pancakes are so light or I would never get off the ground today."

"Going flying?"

"If I get cleared through medical."

"You look good."

"I feel good. They just have to be sure that my lungs are okay. The air can get pretty thin up there."

"Your lungs look okay from where I'm sitting," said Tank, looking around for something more to eat.

"Theodore Ambrose Springfield," scolded Wyatt. "Knock it off. You're talking to your future sister-in-law."

"Consider it knocked off, Mother Superior," he snorted under his breath.

Skye mouthed "Theodore Ambrose?" to him as she pushed over the bowl of melon.

He rolled his eyes again and mouthed "grandfathers."

"I heard that," said Wyatt.

Suddenly the house alarm went off, a loud clanging noise. Tank sprang out of his chair, his reflexes incredibly fast and agile. The humor went out of him instantly and he was all cop. Big, commanding, and in control. He pulled his gun out of the holster he had strapped on his side. His face and body transformed into a serious, alert, prepared protector. It was fascinating.

"Mom, you carrying?" he asked, his eyes already taking in the area around the terrace. No imminent danger that he could see. No movement, nothing out of the ordinary.

"No. Everything is locked in upstairs." Wyatt had the same quick reflexes. She was already up and on her way inside.

"Skye?"

She already had her small .40 caliber Glock out of her purse and was scanning the beach side.

"Okay, you go up and then take the house. Skye and I'll take a look around the perimeter. It's probably nothing, but the call will go right in to central dispatch."

Cynthia came running out of the kitchen. "The police are on their way."

"The police are already here," said Tank. "Cynthia, find Ginny and stay in the house. Get in a room and lock the door."

He looked at Skye. "I'll take the north path," she said, "you take the south and we'll meet at the foyer. That should pretty much cover the outside. If you see anything, shout. Back-up should be here in less than five."

Tank had grown up with women who were equal in the field. As much as he teased and tormented his mom and any other woman in his immediate area, he never underestimated their skill or ability. It was a given that they stood ready and they stood together. He just nodded and started out along the south path, cautiously, carefully, checking everything.

Skye saw the breach point about fifteen feet from the shore. Someone had jumped the high fence. The scrubs were trampled and there were distinctive footprints. Not boots. Sneakers. One pair. Didn't look too threatening, but she didn't want to take it lightly. She turned and studied the footprints. They disappeared when they reached the stone steps to the side terrace.

"Tank!" she shouted when she saw a movement behind two large columns in the garden to her right. "Tank! He's coming toward you!" She ran, chasing the intruder in Tank's direction. He had something in his hand. Was it a weapon? She flipped the safety off her gun as she ran. Then she saw what he had and almost laughed. She let up, no sense in getting all sweaty. Tank would take him easy enough. When she saw him round the corner of the building, she shouted again. "Camera, Tank. Camera! No gun."

Tank lowered his weapon, holstered it, and easily ran down the man with the camera. He reached out, took the man's collar, and yanked him right off the ground at a run. By the time Skye reached them, she was feeling a bit sorry for the guy. He was breathing heavily and looked scared out of his wits. He was only about 5'4" and his bony little knees were knocking. Looking up at the large man who held his arm in a vise-like grip, he nearly fainted.

"Shall we throw him back and let him grow some more?" asked Tank, a little ironic grin on his face. Now that the danger was passed, he was back to the familiar laid back routine. "He's what I'd call trespasser lite."

Skye was impressed. She smiled at the man she thought of as a fun-loving little brother. When he transformed into a cop, he was damn impressive.

Later, Tank was eating more pancakes fixed by Cynthia who cooed over him now for his bravery.

"It sure pays to be a hero," he said smacking his lips and grinning like a kid.

"Yeah. Good collar," said Wyatt holding her stomach and laughing so hard she could hardly stand up. The local police had taken their statements and hauled away the tourist from Topeka. He was hoping to sell photos to his local newspaper...just like they do in the National Enquirer, he told them. Was minding his own business and this big guy, Mafia for sure, picks him off the ground and exposes his entire roll of film...not that he got any good pictures of that tall girl pilot, but he'd been to the track the day before and was sure he got a photo of Burt Reynolds. At least it looked like Burt Reynolds, or was it Burt Parks? Anyway this big guy, didn't look Italian (pronounced eye-talian), but Mafia for sure, pulled his film out. Who was going to pay him for his film?

"Mom," said Tank, laughing more at his mom's reaction than at the original circus that had played out on the front lawn. "If you tell the guys back at the precinct that I took out a tourist from Topeka armed with a deadly Kodak Instamatic, I'll tell everyone in your precinct about your silk underwear."

"Have you been in my underwear drawer again, son?" she said, wiping tears from her eyes and laughing harder.

"No," said Tank. "As a matter of fact something even more hideous. A couple of months ago I was at Mirror Lake with some of the other rookies and I grab that black FBI t-shirt Uncle Elliot gave me last Christmas. I put it on in the dark, cause we got to get out there before dawn to get the damn fish while they're still groggy or something. When the sun comes up, Crackers says...what is that bump there under your arm? I look at it. I can't figure it out. So I reach under the shirt and I pull out this really sexy dark green one-piece silk thing. Well the only one that does laundry with me is my dear old mom. But I can't tell the guys that. It would be too wacked. I would never, ever make detective with that on my record, so I did what any self-respecting son would do. I lied to protect your reputation. I told them it belonged to a dish from Northwestern who came in with it and left without it."

Wyatt's laughter was out of control now and Skye and Blake joined in. It felt so good to laugh and have a moment to just enjoy being alive.

Suddenly, Skye remembered the package that Cynthia had given her with her pancakes.

"Tank, did you eat that little box Cynthia gave me from Alex?"

"Thought about it. But no...there it is."

Skye picked it up and rested a hip on the low wall of the terrace. She looked at the anticipation on the faces of Alex's family. "Any idea what's in here?"

They all denied it in one voice, shaking their heads and making 'no' noises.

"He showed it to you?" said Skye, the Special Agent, knowing b.s. when she smelled it.

"Actually Tank peeked and he can't keep a secret," confessed Wyatt.

Laughing easily, Skye opened the box. In a field of blue paper was a pair of wings. In the center was the company logo. They looked like solid gold and sparkled in the sun. It was a symbol of her new life. Her next step. Corporate pilot. Captain of her own plane. She stood very still, wanting this moment to just wash over her. Wanting to prolong the feeling of anticipation, pleasure, pride. Her life had been transformed since she met Alex. She'd always had happy moments, but this overwhelming feeling of contentment was new. Standing among the Springfields, she was holding her wings given to her by the man she would love and cherish until she died.

Skye smiled up at them, her eyes filled with delight and pleasure. "Aren't they spectacular?"

They'd been watching her. The play of emotion on her face. The love. The excitement. The enchantment. She was a show and they loved the happy ending.

Skye quickly checked her watch. "Whoops. I'm running late. Wish me luck. If I pass my medical, watch the skies. I'm going to rent the little Cessna with the red wing tips."

"No, I don't think so," said Tank. Skye didn't think his smile could get any broader. But it did. "Alex wanted to be here himself, but he has to go out and make the millions so we can sit on our asses around here and soak up the sun. He told me to give you these." He gave her a set of keys. She recognized the key ring. It was her father's. It was about the only thing besides the compass and logbook that could be salvaged from his old plane...his old Cessna. The plane she learned in and then lost a few months before.

"And this." Blake handed her a paper. It was a title to a Cessna 182. Same make, same model, same year. "He said he'll meet you at the Graystone terminal."

Skye was too stunned to react. Too overwhelmed to laugh or to cry or to show her excitement. They were all beaming at her and she was like a statue. Completely staggered by the man. She couldn't move. She just stood there, blinking, looking up at the faces of Alex's family.

"Wow," she said simply. Then repeated it with more feeling. "Wow!"

"And one more thing," said Tank. Gathering her up in his strong arms, he gave her a lovely, but chaste, kiss. For a moment she could feel his heart beat and then he smiled and pulled away.

"That was an improvisation, right?" She beamed at her soon to be brother-in-law

"Yeah. Just taking advantage of the situation. The kiss was my idea."

"Great lips." She hugged him again, then hugged Blake and Wyatt and went skipping down the steps with a little whoop. Out to her car for the short trip to the doctor and then on to the airfield. There was no doubt in her mind that she would be flying within the hour.

Tank watched her, a smile on his lips and a wistful look on his naturally good-natured face. "I've never in my life ever envied my brother anything. Until now," he said softly.

Wyatt came up beside him. She was hurting a little for her baby. "Yours is out there, darling. She's out there and she's looking for you."

Tank shook himself and put his usual easy smile back on. He hugged his mom back. "I don't know. You've set the standard and it isn't going to be easy to find someone like my dear old mom."

"Well you already have the underwear and the fantasy. Now all you have to do is find the woman to fit them."

"I'm hungry."

"I know dear."

Laughing, they went in to beg some donuts from Cynthia's kitchen.

CHAPTER 20

Skye went right from the doctor's office to the small general aviation airport terminal. She had her papers in her hand, clearing her for flight. She felt free. She felt wonderful. And she was going to see the man who made these sensations possible.

There he was…standing with his arms crossed leaning up against his battered old truck looking out over the field at the planes coming and going. What a picture. A strikingly handsome man in a $2,000 suit, tie tightly tied, hair perfectly groomed, sunglasses protecting his eyes. God, he was gorgeous. Then there was his first vehicle, a rusted out Ford pickup. She wasn't sure exactly what you'd call the color. It really had no color anymore. Duncan kept it running like a dream, but it was, well, a real eyesore. Gentlemen's Quarterly meets Hillbilly Yearly. But he loved that old truck. Go figure. Men were unfathomable creatures.

She felt her eyes tear up. Where did that come from? She swallowed hard. Damn. Damn. Damn. The image of him falling, bleeding, ripped apart flashed in her mind. One of the happiest moments in her life, the most beautiful site imaginable, and that old dread intruded. That really pissed her off.

Suddenly it disconnected. It was like something just stopped. She remembered Hazel saying that sometimes you get too busy mopping up the floor to go turn off the faucet. It was like she decided to turn off the tap.

Enough! She wasn't a child. She was a full-grown woman. Capable and strong and smart. Not another minute was she going to give those bastards and that frightful sight. Not another minute or another tear or another moment of fear. Done!

She was going to plan a wedding, build a life with the most wonderful, patient man alive and maybe even have a few babies…well, maybe later on the babies. What she put Alex through since she met him...it really was a miracle. A miracle he hadn't just strangled her, or thrown her over the terrace, or just left her. He stayed with her, constant and true. Well it was about time she gave him something back. Maybe a few days of peace. Maybe a lifetime of her devotion, love, and gratitude. And, of course, as much passionate, tender, zealous, scorching, kinky sex as he could stand. Planned, spontaneous, standing, lying down, in every room of the house.

Whoa. She was getting all jittery inside just thinking about it. Mentally, emotionally, spiritually, she turned the page, locked the door, slammed the lid, and bid the surly dread farewell. Goodbye. Releasing the painful hold of the burning past, she took the final step into the full light. Feeling unfettered, she felt herself fly toward her future.

Alex turned and saw her. He didn't move and for a moment he looked like a statue. It took all of her considerable personal strength not to just run over and jump him, rip his clothes off, and bounce on him for a week. Right there, right in the front seat of the eyesore. She couldn't see his beautiful blue eyes behind the sunglasses, but she saw the flash of his smile. Then she just couldn't help herself. She ran. Ran to him with a heart that was light and a love that was glowing all over her face.

Alex turned. Skye was looking at him. Standing there in a bright-colored, spectacular suit...her cultured, refined look. His breath caught in his throat. Would he ever be able to convince his heart that this vision was his? That she was wearing his ring and that she had promised herself to him. Only him. Her eyes were bright, her smile was endless, and she looked, well...more than happy. It was a look of complete joyfulness. She was wearing her love on the outside and it shone. She shone. He opened his arms when she started running to him. He would let her come to him this time. And he would drink in the feeling that he was her target. He was her destiny.

They came together and merged. She nearly knocked him over with her enthusiasm. He was rock hard and strong as a mountain or he might have toppled. Her lips locked on his for a dazzling, searing kiss.

"You're definitely getting your strength back," he ginned when he regained a few of his senses.

She laughed out loud, a fantastic accompaniment to his elevated heartbeat...and elevated body heat. "Didn't mean to practically knock you off your feet."

"Darling, you did that the first minute I saw you."

She laughed again and Alex looked at her more closely. Unless she was acting, there was a change in her. Nothing dramatic, it was subtle. Something he felt only he could see. She had knocked something over all right. It actually looked like the gleam of victory in her eye.

"What?" she asked when he continued to stare.

"You win the lottery or something?"

"Yup. The jackpot." She kissed him again. "Hello, jackpot." And again.

Alex was totally senseless by the time her lips released their hold on his. His brain was unplugged and his body was running on instinct alone.

"Is there any way I can convince you to forget flying and check in with me at the…" He looked around the airport and rested his eyes on a small rather run down motel. "Fly-Inn?"

Skye looked at the airstrip and saw the little Cessna 182 sitting out and ready. He must have ordered that. Bless him. What a guy. Her guy. She looked into the perfectly blue sky and ignored the pull of the air. Then turned to him and removed his sunglasses to look at the matching blue in his eyes.

"Hop on into your pick-em-up truck, cowboy, and put the pedal to the metal. Your woman is hot and hungry," she said with an affected Texas accent.

"Serious?"

She shoved her body into his for full body contact. "Do I feel serious, cowboy? I'll only make this offer once. Then I go on down the road apiece and pick up the next available man. I'm in the mood for a ride." Still with that accent. Alex thought it was about the hottest voice he had ever heard her use.

She looked serious, all right. He felt the heat pouring off her. Or was it coming from him? Didn't matter. His entire body was panting.

He couldn't believe she could restrain herself from jumping right into the plane. To jump him instead. He hadn't really thought she would come with him. It was just a playful suggestion…he thought more rhetorical than literal. He knew how long she'd been looking forward to this day. Not a man to look a gift horse in the mouth, however, he put his hand on the handle of his pick-em-up-truck, and yanked open the door for his hot and hardy woman.

"Then crawl into my ride, honey bun and let me take you for a spin."

They felt like a couple on a clandestine tryst. The Fly-Inn must have been used to horny couples meeting in the afternoon, because the desk clerk didn't even blink when Alex pulled bills out his pocket. He didn't want to wait for a credit card to clear. He had a hottie in the front seat and he was up and ready to go. He wondered if he would be able to get the key in the lock. She chose him over the sky. Hot damn. Just when he thought he had life figured out, he went around another bend. Just when he thought he had her figured out, she chucked him a curve ball.

He jumped back into the truck and was immediately attacked by his woman. "What room, cowboy?"

He frowned. He really had gone brain-dead. Was there an answer to this question? What was the question? Skye just laughed and took the key with one hand while the other was playing with the little cowboy in his lap.

"It's room 7." When he just sat there, she laughed. "Can you drive?"

He put the truck into gear. "Yeah." He gasped as she found just the right spot. "But I seriously think I won't be able to walk once I get there."

"Lean on me, then, mister, 'cause your legs seem to be the only thing below your waist that isn't working right now." She laughed gaily as the tires sprayed gravel and the truck leaped forward and parked in front of room 7.

They hopped out of the truck and Alex found he could walk. Their lips were locked as they made their way to the chipped and peeling blue door. Skye was already loosening his tie and unbuttoning his shirt. She had the key and she momentarily took her lips from his. His mouth remained busy, however as he traced the curve of her neck with passionate kisses. Trained pilot that she was, her hand was steady as she placed the key in the lock and turned. The door flew open and banged against the wall. Alex scooped her up, carried her in, and kicked the door closed with his foot.

The desk clerk readjusted the blinds, fanned herself, and called her husband. "Honey, I'm coming home for lunch. How about you meet me for a little salami samba?" Her husband, ever grateful for the opportunity, agreed with enthusiasm.

It had never been sweeter, hotter, or more eager. They were a couple exploring for the first time, seasoned lovers knowing the places to touch, primeval animals needing to couple. Deep in the cave of the Fly-Inn, they became one heart, one soul, one life.

When they surfaced, the sun was low in the sky. Skye lay in a tangle of sheets in the arms of her cowboy.

"I think it's a good thing it's dusk," she said, surprised she could still talk through her puffy lips. "I'm not sure we could have faced this room in the full light of day."

She heard the chuckle deep in his chest. "What...you don't like orange naugahyde?"

"It isn't that, darling. I'm not a snob. It's the duct tape holding it together. The aqua shag carpeting is nice. It hides stains so well."

"That it does, along with critters up to the size of a small dog."

Skye gave a mock shudder. "I don't even remember crossing it."

"I was carrying you."

"Oh yeah." She rolled over so her naked breasts pressed against his chest. She kissed his neck, just where it met his broad, beautiful shoulders. He tasted a bit salty and all male.

"More?" he asked.

"I don't think I have the energy," she sighed looking up at him.

"Thank God."

Laughing, she laid her head back down on his chest. Her hair had long since been released from any restraint and was slipping out around her face.

"You want to risk a shower?" she asked, yawning and stretching.

"I don't know if I have enough guts for that," he said looking into the bathroom with its pretty pink tiles and its green plastic shower curtain with palm trees, shells, and coconuts.

"This from a man who drives that abomination out there."

"Excuse me?" he said with indignation. "That truck is a classic."

"That truck is a pile of metal debris with an engine."

"Your Aunt Hazel loves it."

"I rest my case counselor."

"Okay. You got me. You win. I surrender."

She sighed. "At least we know for a fact no one will find us here."

"That's a plus." He tightened his arms around her, then took her hand...her hand with the ring and kissed it, remembering the pleasure that hand had given him this afternoon. "Sorry you had to change your plans."

"Are you?" Skye asked with a twinkle in her eye.

"Okay. So I'm not the least bit sorry. But I know how much you wanted to fly today."

"You mean I wasn't flying a few minutes ago? I could have sworn I was airborne."

"I love you, Skye. I can't begin to tell you what this afternoon meant to me." He kissed the top of her head and ran his hands over her bare back. "I know how much flying means to you. How much a part of you it is. When you came to me, came with me..." He stopped. He didn't know how to thank her for the gift of herself.

"Several times, I think." Skye knew. Her cheek was resting on his chest over his heart. She knew.

He chuckled. "I guess. I was beginning to lose count. Anyway, thanks."

"My pleasure," she purred. "And I mean that sincerely."

She rolled off him, sat up, and sighed. "As much as I have enjoyed our afternoon rendezvous here at the No-tell Motel, I think maybe we should get dressed and move on down the road, Jack. Shall we see what lies behind that artful creation in the bathroom?"

"Okay." He gave her one last gentle kiss, then jumped off the bed. "If I get in there first, I get the towel."

As it turned out, the bathroom was clean and fresh. They shared a tiny bar of Cashmere Bouquet soap and two child sized towels that had Property of Fly-Inn printed on them in green letters. Everything was funny to them. They laughed their way through the shower and getting dressed.

"I know I came in with underwear," said Skye as she flipped the sheets and spread to find them.

"Ah...darling?" She looked over to Alex, who opted for just his shirt and slacks and looked all put together already. He was pointing at the lamp in the corner. Adorning the shade was a pair of pretty silk panties.

"Oh good grief," she said and snatched them. "How did they get there...and how did they get ripped?"

"Um...I think I remember that they were between me and what I wanted. I wasn't my usual cool-headed self."

Skye snorted. "I'll say." She inspected the underwear, declared them a lost cause and threw them in the trashcan shaped like a seashell. She was puzzled by the sea theme since the motel was located by the airport, but such were the mysteries of life. Must have been on sale.

"That will give the cleaning person something to talk about." She smiled at him wickedly, "And you're going to have to think of me without underwear all the way home."

Alex's stomach actually took a little leap. Man. Sometimes his hormones were so juvenile. He had to clear his throat before he could get the words out. "You're coming home with me?"

"Yes. I'm going to leave my car at the airport. Then tomorrow you can drop me off there on your way to the office. I have a plane to try out." She walked over to him and put her arms around his waist. "A plane my future husband bought for me. And one I have yet to thank him for." She gave him a long, slow, passionate kiss. All he heard was future husband echoing through his brain. It was so sweet.

"That should do it," he said when she pulled away. "What else can I buy you?" He really liked the thank you part.

"I don't need anything else," she said as she pecked him once more on the lips. "I have everything I ever wanted or ever needed. Except underwear. Now where is my skirt...ah...how the hell did it get over there?"

Alex just stood there watching her dress, trying to process it all. She had no idea how her simple words were washing over him and bringing with it waves of pleasure and contentment.

"Do we have to go straight home?" he asked when she was as dressed as she was going to be.

"Why? What did you have in mind?"

"I thought maybe we could stop by the park overlooking the ocean, get some ice cream, and I could feel up your skirt."

"I beg your pardon?"

"Every boy's fantasy. A woman in the front seat with no panties. Gives me chills just thinking about it."

"And the ice cream?"

"Women use their tongues to lick the cone...slow, long strokes with the tongue, up the side of the cone, around the cone, sometimes flicking ice cream off the top."

"And this is every boy's fantasy too?"

"Guaranteed." He came closer until her breasts barely touched his chest. He looked down into her chocolate brown eyes. "And if the woman is beautiful and has a great body and long, long legs. And if she has to bend her knees just a bit to fit in the front seat. And if she slides over to sit right next to me and the way is clear to move up her thighs with the hand that isn't on the wheel...." He swallowed. He realized he was physically reacting to the sound of his own voice and that she was smiling at him in that sensual, teasing way she had. Damn. It was like verbal masturbation and she knew it.

"Shit. We had better get out of here now or they won't be able to re-rent the room for the night."

"Okay, darling." One last look around the room. Everything added to the surreal atmosphere. The orange chairs, the aqua carpet, the snappy seashell accessories. So out of their element here. On the other hand, it was a perfect adventure. She looked up at her cowboy and grinned. "I like strawberry."

The next morning Alex dropped her off and she had the chance to try out her little plane. It was a beauty. A bit more upscale than her last one. Alex had ordered every modern radio and positioning devise available for this model. She loved it. She loved Alex.

When she flew out over the ocean, she nearly burst with the rapture of flight. Her mind went to the other form of ecstasy still so clearly on her mind. She could feel his hands on her skin, his mouth on her body. She was free. Free and yet bound forever to another. She smiled. And that was as perfect as life could get. The little plane was great and as she put it through its paces, she felt her father beside her. His compass was in the small shelf near her seat. He was with her up here and she shared her joy with him. Another thing she had to thank Alex for. Later. The best part about thanking him for anything was the extra-added bonus she got out of it for herself.

Alex was watching her from the ground. He and Duncan stood next to the limo and watched as the Cessna lifted off.

"That ever make you nervous, Bossman?"

"Every time," said Alex smiling.

"From what I hear, though, she's the best."

"That she is." When she disappeared out over the ocean Alex reluctantly uncrossed his arms. "Let's get me to my meeting, Duncan. I have to go make some money to pay for the lady's gas."

Duncan opened the door and Alex stepped into the luxurious back seat.

"Privacy, Bossman?" asked Duncan.

"Please." The privacy window went up, creating a cool, nearly soundless environment. Alex liked to work back here. He liked to think. Opening his briefcase he made a pretense of reading contracts.

Duncan smiled when he glanced in the rearview mirror. The Bossman hadn't turned a page in fifteen miles and it didn't look like he was going to. He just sat there with this shit-eating grin on his face, staring at a spot just to the left of the small TV. The spot where Alex had placed a picture of Skye standing next to the new Gulfstream she would be flying by this time next month.

Alex's mind was definitely not on work. He and Skye had stopped for ice cream on the way home the night before and parked near the ocean. The waves of pleasure he saw on her face and felt in her body when he lived every boy's fantasy kept perfect time to the sound of the ocean surf breaking on the sand. His fingers walked up her thighs and found their target easily. She was writhing under his skillful hand and it gave him a rush of power. When she told him breathlessly she couldn't stand it anymore, she begged him to take her home, to their own bed.

When he heard her say home, not *your* home, he knew the changes in her were not imagined but real. She was his. Without reservation. Their lovemaking last night was sweet and gentle. A consummation of a promise. They would make it official soon enough, but they didn't need the ceremony to know they belonged to each other forever.

Duncan smirked when he neared the office. Alex still hadn't turned a page and his eyes were glazed over. He had that kind of satisfied morning-after look...actually he looked like someone who was watching a movie in his mind.

He had waited a long time to see that look in his boss's eye. Driven a lot of bimbos, beauties, and businesswomen around in the back seat. Always ask a driver and he will tell you if a lady has a chance. It isn't what happens when the lady is in the car...Alex was always attentive and a fabulous companion. It's what happens when the lady isn't there. The look of anticipation before the meeting or the musing and daydreaming after the evening or the morning after. No one spun for the boss. There was never any of that. He would always be working right up to time he picked up a date and almost immediately be on the phone to whatever time zone was still awake after she was out of the car or he had left her bed. No one seemed to stay with him for long, either in his mind or by his side. He was a solitary man.

Not any longer, was Duncan's guess. As a matter of fact, the Bossman was going to have to dig up some more discipline if he was ever going to get any work done at all. The Captain. Well she could make a man forget his name. He thought she was just about as beautiful as they come...inside and out. Although he wasn't partial to skinny women and she was a bit too white for his tastes. But she was someone with style, class, and compassion. Ask a driver. He will tell you and this driver knew love when he saw it.

Alex hadn't realized they stopped. He looked out of the open door surprised to see Duncan standing there, patiently waiting for him to button up his briefcase and grab his jacket. When he stepped out a moment later, the picture of a powerful tycoon on his way to build another empire, he saw the knowing smirk on Duncan's face.

"Must have been a very complicated single-page document, sir."

"Erase the face, Duncan."

"Erased, sir."

Skye's smiling image was tacked to the wall of the small room overlooking the rugged hills of northern Columbia. Several cuts had been made in the likeness...the one that had graced Newsweek, Time, and Aviation Quarterly a few weeks before.

Terrin paced and sweated. The generator in this god-forsaken hovel was broken again. This was a nightmare...why wasn't he waking up? He kicked at the moldy chair feeling a satisfying crunch of splintered wood. Junk. Everything here was falling apart and symbolized his life the last few weeks. He hadn't maintained the place, thinking he wouldn't need it any longer, but it was about the only safe haven right now. He was being hunted and hounded. And worse. His own people were beginning to desert him and question his invincibility.

He'd led a charmed life...until that she bitch devil from the fires of hell was put into his path by the powers of fate. He couldn't believe how everything fell apart so quickly. Years in the planning, months in the execution. Execution. He didn't even get to enjoy the feeling of seeing Moreno die. When his men returned saying he had escaped, he didn't waste time searching. He figured the execution would be carried out through fire rather than a bullet to the head. Now the fucking moronic people in his country were on the verge of electing that aberration President.

"You. You," he said to Skye's likeness. "I had you...I touched you...I could have had you begging for me...panting for release...or I could have slit your throat and gutted you. It proves I am stronger...more powerful. Did you offer yourself to the guards? How many did you fuck to get back on the plane? Damn, I was surrounded by traitors and idiots."

When he took off from the island, he knew things were not going as planned...he heard the sustained gunfire and assumed some of the passengers had grown some balls and decided to make an effort to fight. He wasn't even concerned at the time. He still had his last card to play.

When his pilot informed him he was at a safe distance from ground zero, he pushed the button to detonate the explosives. Overkill his munitions expert said with manic satisfaction. Enough plastic to blow up a small country, more than enough to vaporize the evidence ten times over, but he was determined to leave nothing. After he felt the slight rock of the shockwave, he ordered his pilot to turn toward the island so he could see the fireball rise into the air. Beautiful. Finished. Now for his triumphant return to his vulnerable island. His. All his. It was time to begin the rest of his life. What a feeling. The explosion was like a celebration of his victory.

319

His smile faded when his eyes traveled to a silver flash in the distance.

"What is that? What is that?" Dread caused a knot to form in his stomach...huge pulsating waves of alarm and anger emanated from it and worked its shock through to the shaking hands raking his hair.

"Sir," said one of his elite from the back of the large Blackhawk S-70A-9 chopper. "It looks like the plane...from the island."

Terrin turned, drew his weapon and blew the man's brains out the back of his head...as if that would erase the possibility of truth. No one else spoke.

"Chase it...chase it down," he screamed and even though it was both irrational and impossible, the pilot moved in the direction of the Boeing 767...fast becoming a mere speck in the bright blue sky. Terrin slid open the cockpit window, leaned out and emptied his revolver into the screaming air-stream, his own blood howling with frustration. It was a week before his ranting subsided and his mind cooled enough to think.

He looked at the picture of Captain Skyler Madison. One of his operatives in Miami had secured the magazine for him along with all the news reports and the inside intelligence he needed for the next phase of his new campaign.

Bitch. It was her fault this whole operation had turned into a fiasco...she was the reason. His nemesis. To think he once had her...had his hands between her legs. Well, she wouldn't escape again. Once he had her, he could take the first step back to greatness...regain his power among his followers. They needed to see him as their leader...someone who was invincible. When he publicly tortured her, then killed her, his men would see that it was he, Terrin, who was the chosen one. Maybe he would allow each of his men to have her before he took slices out of her skin. His fingers and palms remembered the feel of her warm, soft flesh. Before he destroyed her beauty he would have her.

Grabbing the knife from his desk he viciously pounded it into the picture. "Soon it will be my cock slicing into you, whore, slut, bitch. Soon you will beg for mercy and all you will get is the feel of steel."

Throwing open the door, he shouted out into the camp. "Get me a fucking whore." He needed relief from the throbbing ache in his crotch.

"Soon," he snarled at the ravaged picture. "Soon you will be ripped apart by my savage dogs."

CHAPTER 21

Jim was waiting on the dock as Skye and Alex pulled into the dock after a very pleasant afternoon sail. Standing with him was a tall, stately woman with gray hair and a big smile. Her sunglasses hid her eyes, but her body language was competent and poised. Skye remembered her from months before when she sat next to Alex during a flight from London. This woman looked less like the benevolent grandma she thought she remembered and more like an elderly monarch. She couldn't wait to meet her again, now that she knew her background and credentials.

"Ahoy, land!" shouted Alex. "Grab a line and let's get this thing tied down."

Jim was a powerfully built man who had no trouble tying down the craft while Skye automatically began to gather up their debris. She couldn't bend over very well and she was sweating with the little ticks of pain that were still reminding her of her adventure. Looking at her armload of baskets, towels, blankets and bags Alex grabbed everything from her and frowned. She wasn't to carry stuff. He threw everything but her bag down the stairs into the stateroom.

He looked around the deck. "Clean," he said.

In answer to her horrified stare, he shrugged. "I'll send someone for everything later. Duncan has little on his schedule this weekend. He loves any excuse to come down to the docks," Alex smiled wickedly. "He loves to scare the rich people."

Alex pulled the gangplank to the dock and turned to help Skye up and over. Amanda was watching from behind her sunglasses. The last time she saw Skye, she'd been in uniform. In her role as captain of the craft. Professional and in command. Now she was wind blown and casual. A different look, but just as compelling. Judging from the electricity that was passing between her and Alex and the flash of that ring on her finger, their relationship had survived yet another test. She nodded slowly. She'd seen them come and go. Agents of all kinds. Covert and military.

This was going to be an interesting afternoon.

Amanda also noticed Skye's overly thin body and the rigid posture indicating her recent painful injury. Her heart bled for the younger woman but she figured if they would have had a few more like Skye in the old days, the Berlin Wall may never have been constructed.

Skye's smile was both friendly and respectful when she was introduced. Amanda liked that. The handshake was firm and authoritative, just what she would expect. And the voice was the one she remembered. Amanda removed her sunglasses. Now that she had made her personal and up close assessment, she figured Skye deserved to see her eyes as well.

As Skye shook Amanda's hand, she saw a woman of age and maturity. Now that she knew Amanda's history, she tried to see the clandestine and concealed woman behind Fisher's grandmother. She couldn't detect a thing that would indicate a woman of intrigue and mystery. Then Amanda removed her sunglasses and took down the shield. Ah. There she was. Skye's smile went dazzling and the two women looked knowingly into each other's secret places.

Amanda glanced around, an automatic response. She needed to be sure they were alone. "Special Agent Madison, I have you to thank for the life of my grandson. Nothing made me feel more helpless or more frustrated than to stand down and work only behind the scenes. Knowing you were there, knowing precisely what your actions cost you, I felt closer to the action. Not only did you bring my grandchild back to me without a scratch, I might add, you gave me peace of mind throughout the entire operation. Because I knew you. Right here." Amanda pointed to her heart. "I knew there was no doubt he would be safe."

Skye felt herself blush. She never blushed. Alex stared at her. "You're blushing!" he said with a bit of awe in his voice.

"Don't be silly, boy," said Amanda as she pushed Alex aside and gently put her arm around Skye's waist. As she guided Skye to the waiting car, she said over her shoulder. "It's the sun." Jim and Alex looked at the backs of the two women. Straight, proud, in charge. Amanda was only slightly shorter than Skye and heads turned as they walked by.

"Now there's a picture," said Jim.

"They could pop out a few armies," said Alex.

"Should they be in the same car?"

"I don't know, we have to drive through populated areas."

"Let's risk it. I wouldn't want to be the one to separate them."

"Good point."

They joined Skye and Amanda in the limo. Duncan closed the door, grinning, as usual. "Back home, Bossman?"

"Please and take us the long way. Make it about 45 minutes."

"I know the drill."

"Would you mind coming back and cleaning up the boat after you drop us off at home?"

"Can I take it out for a spin?"

"Be my guest. Take it out for the rest of the day. Enjoy," said Alex.

"Oh. I will, Bossman. I will. You leave the Jimmy Buffett on board?"

"All hot and ready to go."

"That makes two of us then, mate."

Then he put the car in gear and pressed the button for the security window. Like everyone associated with Alex, discretion was everything. And so was excellence. Duncan was not in conventional chauffeur wear, he wore a leather vest with Born to Ride across the back and cut off jeans, but he could maneuver the car though any kind of traffic. It allowed Alex to completely relax in the back. He trusted his people and they trusted him back. It was how he built his empire. And how he lived his life.

Amanda removed an instrument from her purse and held it in the palm of her hand, studying the gauges on the face of it. Recognizing it Alex opened the small compartment on the side and took out his model. The debugging device was state of the art and soon he and Amanda were smiling like a couple of kids showing off their toys. She 'oohed' and 'aahed' over his and he was suitably impressed with the fact that hers was a souvenir from a KGB office in Moscow, modified of course, to detect more modern bugging devices. Skye and Jim watched them in amused silence.

"God, I love this business," said Skye as both Amanda and Alex turned to her, then to each other, and grinned some more.

"We're clean, wouldn't you say so super spook Mitchell?"

"I would say that was an affirmative junior spook in training Springfield." Skye actually clapped her hands when she laughed, she was so delighted. She immediately regretted it when she felt the tug of her injured ribs. She reached into a small compartment and reluctantly popped a few tablets into her mouth. It looked like she needed to be ready for some action.

Amanda went immediately serious. "It seems you're still paying the price for your heroism."

Skye dismissed it with a slight rub across her sore chest and a shrug.

"A very small price to pay for 117 people." She looked over at Alex. "118."

"You didn't lose one, Skye," said Amanda proudly.

"I had help," she said. "Including Fisher. Where is he? Is he back at the house?"

"Yes, he is. He didn't get a chance to talk with you at the airport when you returned…the only thing that made it palatable was the fact that he got to ride in a B2. The pilot saw the Captain's wings you gave him and he got to sit in the cockpit for a while. He's talking about flying lessons and jets. At first I thought it was just that he was smitten with a certain pilot, but I think he's serious."

"I was doing cross country solos at his age. This is the time it will bite you."

"Anyway, he's anxious to show you his material on a flight school but I wanted to talk with you two alone as soon as possible. Fisher discovered the game room and a couple of lively little chaps called Jason and Al," she laughed. "There are more people at your home than there are at the Hilton."

"Yes." Skye smiled. "Family. But they're nearly all cops, so Alex calls them our backup security system."

"Well, as it turns out, I think this is an excellent idea. At least until you consider a more secure arrangement."

"We have excellent security," said Alex, suddenly serious and all business.

"You're located on the ocean, Alex. You can't secure the entire ocean. You're terrifically vulnerable from that side."

"I guess you're not talking about the possibility of CNN renting a boat and coming ashore."

"No I'm not." She reached in and handed them a folder. "One copy, your eyes only, it doesn't leave my sight. There are names of five deep cover agents in there."

"How did you get this?"

"I trained them."

"Ah."

Skye and Alex read swiftly and efficiently. Jim had already been briefed.

The first paragraph made Skye and Alex gasp, then laugh out loud. They looked up at Amanda for confirmation and she nodded. "Emilio Moreno is a remarkable man. He realized his vulnerability. He wanted to be sure the assets were safe. He was afraid he had a possible leak in his inner circle and as it happened, he did. So he shipped the gold and other valuables by a private cargo carrier a week before his own journey. Only a few of his closest advisors knew," explained Amanda.

"So the big media splash was a diversion?" asked Alex.

"Exactly."

"Sounds like he'll make a fine President," commented Skye

"All my sources think so. That's the good news. Keep reading." Alex and Skye read in silence. They could both feel Alex's temperature rising.

"My goodness. We sure pissed him off," said Skye.

"No Skye. *You* pissed him off. They know about Alex...see here." She indicated a highlighted section that talked about Alex. "But they're unaware of his status either as your..." She looked down at the ring. "Your fiancé, or as an agent of the United States government. Alex's picture has appeared nowhere in the accounts of the hijacking. Descriptions of him have been consistent and totally unlike Alexander Springfield. Well done, Alex. When we put you on that helicopter, I knew you'd be able to pull it off. The passengers were drugged most of the time and when they referred to you it was as a commando or soldier. They have described you as rough, dangerous, threatening, intimidating, and tough. Also older, shorter, heavier with black hair, dark eyes and a heavy accent. And it appears as though you have a scar and an eagle tattoo. Well done, Jim."

She looked at Alex in his casual clothes, ruffled by the wind, clean-shaven and smiling. "They won't make the connection. He is still thought of as a traitor from the ranks of the Serpent and the Spear." She looked down at Alex's arm. The temporary tattoo was gone. "From this report, they assumed you died in the battle over turf. Terrin told the followers of Faneta that you had been shot and killed by Lomar's men. You must have died very convincingly."

Alex's eyes slid to Skye. Skye took a deep breath and smiled weakly.

"Apparently," he said.

Never missing anything in her range of perception, Amanda took in the look and drew the correct conclusion. "Oh, my dear. You thought he had been killed, too?"

"Yes, at least for several hours."

"You saw it happen?"

"I did."

"And you didn't know he was wearing a vest?"

"I didn't at the time, no."

Alex recognized her impersonal reporting mode. He was about to cut off the discussion, but Skye squeezed his hand. She didn't step back from anything.

"Christ, Skye. That wasn't in your report," said Jim, in shock. He knew what that would do to her, what she had gone through in the past. Amanda knew too, but held back her reaction better. She'd read all there was on Skye. Every word ever written. She felt no guilt about breaching all of Jim's files and getting to Skye's highly confidential psychological profile. It was her grandson's life at stake and she needed to know. So she too knew how this would have affected Skye and her heart bled some more.

"Alex is alive. It wasn't relevant," said Skye.

"But...," started Jim.

"She's right Jim. It isn't relevant. It's her call. She ran this op," said Amanda. She worked with her own husband on several occasions and had experienced something similar. She'd seen his boat blown up and had assumed he was on it. He hadn't come back to her for days. It was the worst kind of torment. To see it happen. Then to force yourself to immediately proceed with the mission because lives were depending on it. The shell that was left having to do more than just go through the motions. Having to think, act, remain steady. All the time suppressing the horror, the grief, the need to just curl up and die. Amanda looked Skye right in the eye and in the few seconds they stared at each other, Skye saw perfect understanding. The empathetic charge was message enough. The women knew, no other words were necessary. Amanda tore her eyes away from the impassive face she saw, knowing the price Skye was paying for keeping on the mask.

"I want you to continue with your impressions of this transcript," ordered Amanda, back to business at hand.

"They're coming," said Skye simply.

"My thoughts exactly. And they're coming after you. Terrin lost face, internationally, no less. Moreno's election is imminent. People are turning on the Serpent and the Spear. They've lost their power because a woman took them on and escaped with over 100 men, women, and children right from under their noses. Terrin in particular sees you as symbolic. If he can take you down, he may get some of that power base back. From my notes here, however, you'll see that the tacticians at Langley feel he's delusional. The Serpent and the Spear ruled through intimidation and the people are just not intimidated any more. Your actions have put a crack in their organization and it's self-destructing on the inside and imploding from the pressure on the outside."

"It looks like the man is making this personal," observed Alex.

"Oh there is no doubt. Agents have heard that Terrin continuously rants about you...specifically. You have become to him an impediment, a millstone...I think the exact word was albatross."

"Good," she said. "I want him to feel me around his neck. Me...personally."

"Christ, Skye," said Alex angrily. "Turn it down."

Skye stared back at him and Alex saw agent eyes. "Let me revise that...every single minute of every single day."

Alex turned on his own agent eyes and looked back at Amanda. "Then let's go get him...do your agents know where he is?"

"We raided his compound last night...he was gone," she looked over at Skye. "He's on the move. There was a picture of Skye hanging in his office...at least what was left of one. As you can see from these," she handed them another file. "He was quite angry at the captain."

Alex saw the mutilated magazine bearing Skye's picture. Knowing it could have been the real thing if Terrin hadn't been stopped, he felt his jaw tense. Amanda felt his reaction, ignored it, and went on.

"My five agents are good, perceptive people and excellent forecasters. They're unanimous. When Terrin comes after you, he will do so personally and will try to make it big, ugly, and sensational."

Skye nodded, dismissing the sight of the knife cuts on her picture. No concern, no affected behavior, no fear. Just a cool head and a steady hand. "I'll prepare to move out of the house. We can't have the lives of the people there endangered."

"Oh no," said Alex. "You aren't going anywhere."

"I disagree, Alex," said Jim. He and Amanda fought over this all the way down to Amelia Island. "I would like to put her in a safe house for a few months until we get these guys. As Amanda said, the ocean makes it nearly impossible to protect the perimeter. We have to move her."

"Yes, I'll move," said Skye. "But not to a safe house. What good is having bait if you can't use it? We can use the media. Make my move public. Wherever it is, we need to be sure it's secluded and away from any civilian population. How much time do you think we have?"

"The elections are three weeks from tomorrow. We believe he'll make a move before then."

"You'll go to a safe place. We'll plant false accounts in the media, but you'll be buttoned up until after the election," said Alex firmly.

"I'm with Skye on this one," said Amanda. "She has to be seen. To goad Terrin. To mock him. That way we're assured he'll come himself. His psychological profile assures us of that."

"I don't need a psychological profile," said Skye. "I looked into his eyes. He'll come. His plans for me were interrupted by his discovery of the gravel and sand in the crates. He had his gruesome, revolting hands on me...expecting me to respond. I didn't. He will want to do the actual deed himself."

"I agree. He follows type..." said Amanda.

Looking sharply at Skye, Alex interrupted. "Back up a minute. He had his hands on you?"

"He did. In addition to being a fanatic, a killer, a sadist, and an assassin...this man has a monumental ego. He thinks he's irresistible. Needless to say, he wasn't my type. He didn't take the rejection very well." She rubbed her ribs absent-mindedly.

"And why haven't you told me about this before?" asked Alex. He was furious...beyond furious. "How come I keep getting little pieces of this adventure that are news to me?"

Both Skye and Amanda looked at him. In perfect unison they said, "Not relevant."

Suddenly the back of the limo erupted. The privacy screen soundproofed the back, but Duncan, stopped at a red light, noticed angry faces, flying hands and four people shouting all at once. He shook his head. He never could understand the business world. Probably negotiating for a mall in Boise or something. Oh well, none of his concern. He was thinking about his afternoon...probably could push it into the evening. Bossman wouldn't care. Floating on the boat, rocking to reggae, and going on down to Lauderdale to see a few sweet flowers he knew. It was time to party and pollinate. He turned up the music in his impeccable front section and started the party early. He was feeling good and sassy.

As they moved slowly through traffic, Jim called a halt to the debate. "Wrap this up, we need to have a plan. Skye, brief Alex later if you have to. Alex, cool off and clear your head. We need you to stay focused on the next step."

Jim was satisfied when both his agents turned off the shouting and looked at him with respect and anticipation. Amanda was impressed. Jim went on. "Skye and Alex, this is your op. You will both take the role of Special Agent in Charge. This is your chance to work together as a team. Skye, you take care of strategy. Alex, you're in charge of execution. Also, same as before, you're to secure her and protect her. Work on that. Amanda, please provide her with any intelligence you can. I'm going back to Washington to coordinate with the State Department. They're working with the United Nations to send observers down to Soteras. That should discourage any overt action to take down Moreno again. He returned in triumph last month. He's a shoo-in. Now we just have to keep him alive and well. From these reports we see that he's the real deal. He'll bring about reform. He's the country's best hope and he'll be our friend in the middle of the drug wars down there."

Skye smiled and looked at Alex. Their first official op together. Something inside her was thrilled and she could see it in his eyes, too. As dire as this situation was, this was a special moment. Still, there was no time to enjoy it. There was a great deal to do. She looked at Amanda. "You will stay with us a few days?"

"Certainly."

"I want to get the children out right away. Let's get Cynthia, Sue Ann, and Stacy to take Fisher, Jason, and Al to Disney World for an overnight trip."

"That's an excellent idea," agreed Alex.

"I appreciate that," said Amanda. She wanted to bring Fisher because he was so anxious to see Skye, but having him out of the way would be a load off her mind.

"I'd like to get everyone else out of the house tomorrow. Do you think they'll be offended if we ask them to leave?"

Alex grinned. "Heck no. We'll just tell them we ran out of food and beer and they'll be packed and out of the house by noon."

Skye laughed. "Seriously. How much should we tell them?" She looked at Jim for advice.

"I think a DA, two cops, a state trooper, a regional director for the FBI, and their respective spouses, who have lived with discretion and law enforcement their whole lives, can be trusted with the relevant information. Sources, true motives, and level of threat will be withheld." He looked at Amanda, who nodded.

"I must be getting soft in my old age," Amanda smiled. "We can tell them that Terrin is after Skye for reasons of some macho code of retribution and revenge. I think they can draw their own conclusions. From what I've read in your family member's dossiers," she grinned at Alex's surprised expression, "they're competent, savvy professionals who will understand the importance of getting everyone out of harm's way. I expect a lot of movement in the next few days."

"You have dossiers on my family?" asked Alex, more than a little irritated with her.

"Yes. Anyone who has come in contact with Skye for the last few weeks has been thoroughly scrutinized. Would you like to know who your brother Tank spent the night with last night?"

"I think that was unnecessary," said Alex though clenched teeth.

"I would like to know," said Skye, trying to keep things from heating up again. She didn't need the distraction of an internal feud right now. Alex fixed an angry gaze on her. He wasn't finished being irritated and offended.

"It was a rhetorical question, my dear," said Amanda. "I'm sorry if this upsets you, Alex, but I'm methodical and thorough. It's why I lasted in this business for nearly five decades. Now, let's not get distracted." She looked back at Skye. "What have you decided?"

"I'll leave publicly." She felt Alex stiffen. Too bad. He would protect her and he was good. "And move with a lot of fanfare to another location. These people will have no idea we know they're coming. I'll call a press conference and refer to him in, shall we say, less than complimentary terms. I'll specifically call his manhood to question. I'll laugh at everything from his operation to his choice of ties. I'll mock him. He'll come for me all right." There was a gleam in her eye. "I'd like to get your ideas on that, Amanda."

Amanda smiled. "I think you have him pegged perfectly, but I'd be happy to help you fine tune it."

Skye turned to Jim and Alex. "Jim, you'll work with the FBI, the Army Special Ops, and the local authorities to secure personnel. I would say from this report that Terrin is down to about two or three dozen secure followers. He had seven specially trained bodyguards." She looked at Alex. "He only has two of them left. I don't see how he can transport more than a dozen men for this mission, especially since I'll be in the United States. That will mean a maximum of fifteen men. Alex you'll lead the advance team to the secure site. Maybe if we can locate three or four possibles you can assess them and select the one you think has the greatest chance of sucking them in, then trapping them. You know the criteria and protocol."

Alex hesitated, then nodded.

"Then I," said Skye sitting back and crossing her lovely legs, "will sit around, do my nails, and watch you all scramble."

Amanda chuckled. She really loved this new breed. She'd been a pioneer. This young woman was the whole damn wagon train.

Alex was still seething, but he agreed. This was business. His business. He had to remember that at this moment, Skye was his colleague and not his lover.

They pulled up to the front of the mansion, anxious to get things moving. Jim wanted to spend the rest of the day on the phone coordinating the various players so Duncan was going to drop him back off at the airport.

"Have fun," said Skye to Duncan as he opened the door for them. She was suddenly feeling a bit self-conscious. She and Alex had spent some their time that morning, well, celebrating the rite of the sunrise. She couldn't remember if she'd made up the bed afterward.

"Oh I intend to set the boat a'rocking," said Duncan. "Those puny little ripples you two kick up will be nothing compared to the beach eroding waves I intend to make. Kids will get their surfboards out and the lifeguards will put up the red flags. Mammas will grab their babies off the sand and run for higher ground." He gave her an exaggerated wink as he got in the front seat.

"We get the picture," she muttered, no longer self-conscious in the least. Alex had the most unusual staff.

Amanda wanted Alex to give her a tour of the grounds and brief her on the security system. She would be spending a few days on the premises and she never slept in a house she wasn't intimately familiar with. Old habits. And one of the major reasons she was still alive and well at 70. Skye wanted to get the family together and move the children out of the house.

She heard the kids the minute she walked into the foyer. They were in the game room enthusiastically engaged in mortal combat. Fisher had a control in his hand and from what Skye could gather, he was playing solo against Al and Jason. They were all whooping and hollering and jumping on the furniture. Skye let them play until there was some break in the action, then she walked into the room.

The boys all dropped their controls and greeted her with the same enthusiasm they showed toward the little creatures on the oversized TV screen.

"Skye!" they shouted. "Fish got to Level Twelve in Firewalkers. He is so chilled! Iced!" They were both talking at once. There was a new hero in town and his name was Fisher Taylor Stanaslov Mitchell.

"Hi Fisher!" grinned Skye.

He just stared. The last time he saw her, she was bruised, her face was swollen, and there was an air of pain around her. Now, in this great house, with her face back to normal, a sparkle in her eye…well, Fisher fell in love all over again. He was speechless and for him, that was a red-letter event. Swallowing hard, he managed to find his voice. The fact that it cracked was one of the tortures of adolescence.

"Whoa. You look…great," he said realizing how lame it sounded, but not being able to do anything about it. He simply lost his whole file of adjectives. He suspected they were in his brain somewhere, but right now they were dusted.

"Why thank you," said Skye. "I see you found something to do."

Al and Jason, who had adjusted to Skye's incredible charisma months before and were more comfortable in her magnificent presence, both started talking at once, explaining what an incredible feat it was to attain Level Twelve. Skye had no idea what they were talking about, but displayed a suitable amount of wonder and awe.

She took pity on Fisher, who was still gaping and couldn't get his tongue untied. "I hear you brought information on flight schools." Giving him a topic to discuss, especially one that had captured him so completely, was all it took for a full recovery.

He proudly showed Skye all of his catalogs on ground school and flight lessons and charmed a promise for a ride in the Cessna. Tank, Wyatt, and Blake came in, introduced themselves and looked over his shoulder at the information. They knew who he was and the part he played in the rescue. Their impression of him fit the reality and they bonded immediately.

"Will you let me take the controls?" asked Fisher.

"Will you be my sister's date for the wedding?" asked Skye. She wanted to get the two kids together. Sloane was a wonderfully adjusted young woman, but the boys she knew were just not able to handle her and her incredible brain. She thought Fisher would be able to handle anything. He may not have had Sloane's genius, but he had style and wit and…well…something. Also, he got to Level Twelve. Sloane was a video game junky too, and this could be the basis for a solid relationship…a teenage one.

"What wedding?"

"My wedding." She waggled her left hand in front of his face. Fisher stared. He wondered if the guy she was marrying knew about the la-de-da that was going on between her and the Special Forces guy. He would keep her secret but he sure hoped that soldier didn't get it in his head to come after her.

"Who are you marrying?" teased Fisher, looking over at Tank. "He looks pretty cool."

"That he is, but he's too young for me." Tank made a face, crossed his eyes, and stuck out his tongue.

"Well, I guess that completely takes me out of the running," said Fisher with a grin.

"And who said you were ever in it?" asked Alex as he strode into the room with Amanda and the rest of the clan. He looked so completely different from the last time Fisher saw him, it didn't register.

"Fisher. I would like you to meet the only man in the running, Alex Springfield," said Skye.

Grinning, Fisher automatically offered his hand. When Alex took it, Fisher looked into his face and eyes and did a slow, intuitive double take. Alex's eyes revealed nothing but a friendly welcome.

"Wicked. Ah...well now I guess I can see why you chose him over me." Fisher frowned, looked at his grandma, then back at Alex. He could keep a secret. The blue eyes threw him off for just a moment, but he got the total picture now. His grin got broader. He looked at Alex's shoulder, then back up to the smiling blue eyes. "Think you can *shoulder* the responsibility, sir?" Fisher asked, his tone teasing, his bright green eyes conveying insight.

Alex just nodded slowly. Damn the kid was good. It was in the genes for sure. He had Amanda's eyes and he had her savvy. Interesting.

"Back to the issue of being my sister's date for the wedding," said Skye, turning the attention back to other, less sensitive areas.

"What? She's so revolting she can't snag her own side dope?"

"No. She's actually quite lovely. I just think you two are completely compatible. And since you'll be coming, anyway..."

"Tell you what," said Alex, rubbing his hands. "If I beat you in a game of Firewalkers, you take the sister. If you beat me, you can have her." He pointed at Skye.

"Deal." Fisher grinned wickedly and winked at Skye. He hadn't lost a game in nearly two years and he only lost then because he was playing with two broken fingers. He had no doubt he would be able to beat this old guy real easy.

They all gathered around the big screen as the two combatants took their places. It was close. And it was brutal. Their fingers were flying and their bodies moved with the motion of their action figures. They sailed right by Level Twelve and were still battling for supremacy on Level Seventeen. Then it happened. Alex earned another weapon and used it to edge out Fisher. The game was over in a flash.

Fisher was so thrilled, so pumped, he didn't even care. He and Alex had bonded during the clash and would forever be friends. They were pounding each other on the back and Al and Jason were jumping on the furniture. David gave up disciplining them when Tank started pounding on the back of a chair and stomping on a fallen cushion. There was pandemonium at the end of the game and Fisher got as much congratulations as Alex. They stood pumping each other's hand, grinning like idiots, and replaying every move.

"There's so much testosterone in this room," mumbled Wyatt to Skye. "I feel myself growing a beard."

Alex came over and actually picked up Skye and swung her around. "Mine!" he said to Fisher.

"Watch out," said Fisher. "I've seen her take out a platoon. Maybe you better ask her if it's all right."

Alex looked at Skye, who was laughing, then put her on her feet with a flourish. "I ask your permission to claim my prize," he said.

She presented her hand and just as he was going to put it to his lips in victory, she spun, caught the back of his leg with her toe, flipped him onto the couch and placed her sneaker under his chin. She was standing over him, tall, beautiful, and triumphant. "Mine!" she said to the applauding audience.

Al and Jason gave each other a high five. Fisher raised his glass to Alex and grinned. Amanda raised an eyebrow with approval and Tank started fanning himself.

"Damn, that was hot," he said falling into the chair he'd been pounding on. "Big brother...just give up now."

Alex captured Skye's eyes and smiled. Slowly she lowered her leg and he got up. He stood up next to her, put his arm around her waist, drew her to him, and kissed her thoroughly.

All three boys had the exact same reaction. Their faces registered horror. "Oh, gross. Yuck. Go back to the fighting stuff." All the flying monster parts on the screen were not nearly as disgusting as the display of lip lock before them. It was almost too nasty to bear.

Skye turned to them, but kept her arm around Alex's waist. She liked the hard, lean feel of it. "Well, boys. If you want to escape this den of horror, how would you like to go to Disney World for a few days?"

"Me too?" asked Fisher, looking at his grandma, about five years sliding from his youthful face.

"You, too," said Amanda matter-of-factly. "We thought you might like a break. Sue Ann, Stacy, and Cynthia said they would drive you over. Fisher, why don't you take Al and Jason up to their room and pack...say for three days?"

"Three days!" they all said and whooped some more. The last the adults saw of them, they were tearing out the door and pounding up the stairs.

As soon as the Disney-bound contingent was in the big van and on their way, the rest of the family gathered in the great room. Several secrets stood behind the words, but as expected, there was little pressure by the family to reveal them. They operated on trust. When Alex had come to them and told them they needed to get the kids out of the house, everyone fell into the plan and took the tasks assigned. Sue Ann and Stacy were solid and true. Cynthia never questioned Alex on anything and the boys...well, all they could see was three days with Mickey.

When Skye and Alex, looking at each other and sending nonverbal signals, thought it was time, they stood and asked for the attention of the group. The large, fun-loving family turned immediately serious and professional.

Alex told them what he could. Outlining the risks, he asked that they all pack up and move to the Hilton the next day. He'd made reservations for them and was picking up the tab.

"So you're moving out tomorrow, too, Skye?" asked Wyatt hopefully. She didn't like the idea of her newest child in such jeopardy.

"Not quite so soon. I'd like to have you all out of here by noon. Then, when I know you're safe, we can begin the public campaign to move me and draw out Terrin."

Everyone nodded grimly. None of them liked it, but they knew that risk was part of the price one paid for bringing people into the circle of justice.

"You couldn't just politely ask us to leave?" complained Tank as he went to the bar and opened a bottle of mineral water. "You have to invite an international terrorist to the party?" Everyone could see the strain around his eyes and Alex didn't think he had ever seen Tank drink mineral water. Not by choice, anyway. "What if we just all stay here until you can get into a safe house? You need protection and it's our duty to serve and protect. I, for one, would like to be where you are when this all goes down."

"No. You're here as our guests. I know you never really leave the cop behind, I saw that the other day, but you're not my personal guard." Skye noted his concerned look and tried to get him to understand.

"You're our best man and my future brother-in-law. You'll have plenty to do to assure my future health and happiness." Her words were soothing, but strong. "You'll serve us best by going back to Chicago and make the streets safe for children and little old ladies."

Tank stared at her, saw her resolve, then shrugged. "I guess after I witnessed my big brother's humiliating take down, I should know better than to argue."

Skye smiled and nodded and answered the few remaining questions.

They had a wonderful time that night despite the threat that hung over them. Amanda put her little old lady face on and entertained them with fictional stories of her exploits as a private detective. The cover worked once before when she sat next to Alex from London to Washington D.C. and she loved taking the character out again. Over the years she got attached to certain roles and this was one of them.

Alex grilled every possible meat he could find in the well-stocked freezer and they raided Alex's bar. His family was leaving in the morning and they were going to party hardy. Alex and Skye both noticed, however, that they all switched to soda and lemonade after the first two drinks. This family wasn't going to stand down until they were out the door the next day.

Alex looked out over the ocean. Skye could see him mentally assessing his position, his mind seeing the face of their enemy and preparing for battle. Coming up behind him, she wrapped her arms around his waist and laid her cheek against his broad, stiff back.

"How come you didn't tell me?" he asked, his voice calm but wrapped in ice.

"Tell you what?"

"Don't pretend you don't know what I'm talking about Skye."

She sighed. She hadn't mentioned it because she knew what his reaction would have been then...what it would be now. "Darling it wasn't important."

He spun around so quickly it startled her. Taking her shoulders in his hands, he held her at arm's length and looked into her eyes. His were storming and nearly gray with suppressed rage. "You tell me the fucking bastard had his hands on you and it isn't important?"

"Yes."

Skye could feel his grip tighten. "Did he...did he..."

"No. You and the circumstances of the long night before we flew off the island didn't give him a chance. I believe it was his intent but things deteriorated so rapidly, he lost interest. I think my diminished capacity at that point to fight him off also contributed to his lack of follow through." She needed to cool him off, defuse his rage or he might go after Terrin before they could set the trap.

"Don't you dare turn on your cool, calm report mode, Skye."

"All right, how about this. His cruelty required an unwilling partner and after I saw you shot, I didn't give a shit. He touched me and I didn't move, didn't struggle, didn't care. I was empty…without feeling. So you could say, you saved me that night without realizing it. He couldn't hurt me because I was beyond his reach and that probably meant he couldn't perform. He didn't get beyond groping because I was a corpse." Alex could feel her vibrate and loosened his grip.

"I want him. When the time comes, I want him."

"No!" Skye's voice was strong, her eyes flashed with anger and determination. "He took my plane, endangered my crew, and I nearly lost all the souls placed in my personal care."

"He had his hands on you…touched you."

"It was my body he touched, my life he nearly ended by starting the chain of events that almost had you killed. Oh Alex, for that one night…that one night when I thought you were dead." Tears started to flow down her cheeks and her chest heaved in gulping sobs. When she moaned, Alex gathered her up and held her close. "For that one night, please. If you have to make the choice, let me…let me."

Holding her, he hoped he would be strong enough to let her if the time came…let her take him.

"All right, baby. Don't cry. Shhh. The man is toast either way." Skye lifted her face to him and he tasted the salty tears and lost himself in the desire to erase the picture of Terrin from her mind…from his.

"Touch me…Alex…make me feel alive. I need you," she whispered between sobs. Alex scooped her up and carried her into their bedroom where his gentle caresses and words of love made her forget everything.

Terrin put down the picture he kept close. Captain Skyler Madison in her uniform, her hat pulled down low over her forehead. "Tonight bitch," he said softly. "Tonight your lover will be dead and I will have you."

Everything was in place. They had no idea he was coming…that he was so bold and daring. As soon as he got her, he would take her back to his compound…parade her before his followers. Then when they had spilled her blood and pounded her flesh into the dust, they would go back to Soteras…his island. His people. The Serpent and the Spear would rise up again…stronger. He could still rule. There were plenty of people loyal to him who were waiting for a sign. Tonight he would take his first step back into his rightful place. Raising his binoculars again, he waited for the lights of the house to go out and tell him it was time.

CHAPTER 22

At 3:17 a.m. the digital clocks and night-lights blinked off throughout the mansion. The steady hum of the refrigerators and central air ceased. The ceiling fans slowed, then stopped. The house was dark and silent. Eight men dressed all in black, faces covered, and equipped with night vision goggles, made their way stealthily through the four French doors at the back of the house. Their landing craft was secured on the beach with one man at guard.

Noiselessly, they let themselves into the house, knowing the alarm system had been disengaged. They had secured the blueprints for the house from a source at the town hall. A pitiful man, who was tonight lying in a pool of blood in an alley near the downtown district. Just another victim of random violence. They knew where the master bedroom was and that was where their targets would be. It was painfully simple to land their inflatable watercraft on the moonless night. Anxious to get their quarry, but patient and professional, they'd come ashore silently, using the tide and the surf to propel their rubber raft onto the sandy beach.

Cautiously they swept each room with their goggles, their guns up and ready. They climbed the stairs in a well practiced, precise formation...two point men, two on each side of the staircase, and two covering the rear. They were seasoned experts here to do a job and leave.

On the second floor, they moved quickly to the tall double doors at the end of the hallway. The leader of the group tried the handle and nodded. Six of them would go in. Three high, three low. Two would remain in the hall, although they expected no resistance.

The tall man in the front turned the handle and pushed the door open slowly. The six men rushed into the room and spread out. The goggles revealed a large bedroom with a terrace beyond. Their orders were to kill the man and take the woman. This they would do efficiently and without conscience. No shooting, yet. They needed to be sure of their targets. The

E.K. BARBER

leader grinned. This was child's play. They approached the bed, positioning themselves around it.

Suddenly they were completely blinded. Night vision goggles are designed for night vision. Very, very low illumination. Light, especially abrupt light when the pupils were fully dilated and the goggles on the highest setting, stunned the eyes into temporary blindness. The men shouted with alarm and their quick reflexes went to remove that disability fast. As one, they reached for their faces to remove the offending goggles.

Then they heard it. The sound of multiple pistols being cocked and bullets being chambered, one after another. The sound was deafening in the quiet room and they knew they were facing death. Nothing they could see...yet...but chilling and convincing.

A commanding voice came out of the brilliant light. "Put down your weapons very, very slowly. Any sudden move and your faces are gone." As the terrorits' vision cleared, they saw the threat. They were literally surrounded. Four men and two women armed and angry, had guns aimed at each of their faces. Alex had two pistols aimed at the leader. The safeties were off and they each held their weapons with confidence and competence.

"Slowly," Alex ordered in a voice none of his family had heard before. Menacing, furious, dangerous. "I wouldn't want to ruin this rug with your brain matter. What there is of it."

They stood for a moment, unable to comprehend their predicament. As their sight returned, there was confusion and disbelief. None of them doubted, however, that they were dead if they didn't obey. These people were not just civilians with guns purchased at the local discount store. They held formidable weapons with well-trained hands. The terrorists assessed their predicament and made the only decision available to them. The leader nodded and they put down their weapons.

Bat and Elliot grabbed the guns while Skye and Wyatt kept theirs trained on the intruders. David brought his two in and a drenched Tank came up a few minutes later with a very wet catch.

"He tried to swim for it," he explained. "Didn't get very far."

"The long arm of the law," said Elliot.

Never taking his eyes off the leader, Alex walked toward him and reached for his mask. Was it Terrin? Suddenly the man reached around and brought a pistol out from behind his back. As much as Alex wanted to blow the man's brains all over the wall, he restrained himself and struck out with the butt of his Beretta. In one lightening quick move, he knocked the man out cold.

"Ouch," said Tank. "That hurt."

Amanda came though the door then, as calm as if she were taking a stroll in the park. She looked around the room. "More guests?" She smiled at Alex. "Flipping on the light switches was a great move."

"I figured the power would be back on in minutes and I suspected these intruders would be in goggles since it was a moonless night."

"Good thing you had a backup generator," said Bat, assuming Alex had one and that it was programmed to activate soon after there was a power failure.

"Good thing I had backup," said Alex with a discreet wink at Amanda. Alex didn't have a generator...he had a spook.

Reaching down, he pulled off the mask on the leader. Skye already knew it wasn't Terrin from the moment the lights came back on. He wasn't the same body shape. The rest of the gang was unmasked and Terrin wasn't among the lot. Maybe they were wrong about this being personal, Skye thought, looking over at Alex. Okay, then. They would continue with their original plan to draw him out through public ridicule.

Alex called Jim, who was shocked by the invasion, but both pleased and relieved they had taken prisoners. He would be sending people to the house immediately to take possession of the men and get statements from everyone. The mood in the room was almost celebratory as Tank and Elliot lined up the prisoners.

"Um...I like your pajamas, Elliot," said Tank. Elliot looked down. His shorts had little guns all over them.

"Oh, hell." He knew Tank would never let this one rest.

"Where do you keep your ammunition?"

"At least I wear them," he said and raised his eyebrows and lowered his eyes. Tank slept naked and had quickly pulled on a pair of old gym shorts. He still looked pretty naked, all wet from his jump into the ocean. The shorts were clinging to his tightly muscled bottom and his other attributes were pretty evident as well.

"How about you get some clothes on Tank?" said his mother with a chuckle deep in her throat. She knew he was her baby and all...and that she was biased, but there was no statue in all the world as beautiful as her Tank.

"And miss the fun?" He went to Alex's dresser and took out a sweat suit. It was tight across the chest, but managed to cover the important parts.

Skye and Alex put their guns down with relief. They had been roused immediately to the deafening sound of silence. When they saw all the electrical out in their room, they knew they had been invaded.

Skye's natural instinct was to grab the gun she kept near her side of the bed and go out looking for the source of the trouble. Alex had a cooler head. He whispered in her ear to wait for them to come to her, then eased himself out of the bed and armed himself with the guns he kept within reach. He pulled on a pair of sweatpants and she put her nightgown back on.

Alex had flipped the switch trusting that Amanda was awake and taking care of restoring the power to the house. He knew the rest of his family would be in soon to back him up. They would sense the danger. And they didn't disappoint. Within a few minutes, the family had assembled, formulated a plan, and laid out their trap. Then the bedroom contingent positioned themselves on either side of the door and waited.

When the men had come through the door, it still was a shock. It was an insult. Invaders had assaulted their home. It was both offensive and infuriating. But the intruders were now in custody and they would pay. The whole operation was spontaneous, but well executed. Skye and Alex were proud, relieved, and grateful.

Jim was coordinating the small team of investigators from Justice and the representatives from the local FBI office. Elliot was proving to be invaluable coordinating the transportation of the prisoners to a federal facility. He was having the time of his life, certainly the time of his career. He was a well-respected regional director, but this case had national and international implications. He missed the field and this very substantial dose of it had him so pumped up he thought it might sustain him until retirement.

Leaning against the wall, Tank sipped his first cup of coffee. The sun would be up in a half-hour and he needed the extra zip of caffeine. He had supervised the transfer of all the prisoners to the unmarked cars lined up along the drive. Everything was quiet and subdued. He doubted if the neighbors even woke up. And if they did, they probably thought Alex was entertaining again.

He watched Alex and Skye discussing the results of their preliminary questioning. There wasn't much. The initial shock caused some of the terrorists to reveal a few choice thoughts, but since then, there was nothing. Terrin was not among the group, which meant he was still at large and this was just the forward team. There were more out there and they would be coming.

As Tank walked over to them, Skye and Alex looked up expectantly. They saw Tank, the cop. He was serious, focused, and alert.

"I've been thinking about something I heard one of them say. It didn't seem too important at the time, but in the morning afterglow, I'm hearing it again in my mind. When something continues to rattle around in there, I can't stand the noise and have to suck it out and take a look at it."

He was all cop now. His eyes flashing, his face expressive. "You have already figured out that they didn't come in to shoot and kill. Their purpose was to capture and secure." His eyes went to Skye. "At least one of you."

Both Skye and Alex nodded. The rest of the group had stopped and were listening as well. It was agreed that this was not an assassination. The gunmen had come in to seize someone, probably Skye, and had not been concerned with others in the house. They hadn't entered the bedroom shooting.

Tank went on. "I'm thinking out loud, but let me get this out and we can see if it means anything. One of the gunmen mumbled something like 'they're alone' or 'they will be alone.' I definitely heard the word 'alone.' Well, anyone casing the house would know that you haven't been alone since you arrived here. As a family, we're kind of hard to miss." Tank stopped and let the rest give that some thought.

"So they didn't do a visual," said Alex, intrigued. Wyatt, Blake, David, and Bat were listening now. They were nodding in agreement.

"Exactly. That leaves getting information from some other source. But here's the kicker. They had the wrong information. I think someone told these assholes that you were alone here. It's the only thing that explains why these men, professional and well trained, didn't secure the rest of the house. I think that this same someone knew we were here and took the calculated risk that your dear family of personal bodyguards would be alert enough to protect, defend, and potentially capture the intruders. These guys had the layout of the house. We found the rendering on one of them and it came from the city hall source they found dead tonight. But they didn't have knowledge of the people present."

Jim had checked with the local police and a city records clerk was found in an alley earlier that evening. Tank went on. "I think someone fed them information. Inaccurate information. The person deliberately sent them into a house full of cops. The terrorists didn't even fan out to check the other rooms because they thought you two were here alone."

"Who? Who would know about all of you?" Alex looked around, then got a sick feeling in the pit of his stomach. He remembered the morning everyone had rushed into the gym, guns drawn. Duncan had seen his family react to trouble. He'd even commented on it. "Duncan," he said, his voice filled with apprehension.

"Didn't you say it was unusual for him to stay out this long?" asked Blake.

"It makes sense," said Skye, dread flowing through her knowing that if Tank had figured it right, Duncan was in mortal danger, maybe even dead. From the expression she saw on Alex's face, she knew he'd drawn the same conclusion. It made her angry and frustrated and very anxious for Alex's driver and friend. "Oh my God, Alex. They must have had someone on an advance team gathering intelligence...they saw Duncan take the boat out."

"Maybe they were there in the boat waiting for him. Could be they're still out there. These guys came from somewhere. The raft is very sea worthy, but it's unlikely it came from any great distance," said Blake.

"Also, did you notice how many of our intruders tonight had bruises and abrasions? I thought it was just from training, but Duncan would have put up quite a fight," said Elliot.

"That would mean that the boat is out there, relatively near shore," said Wyatt. "And that Terrin is waiting for a signal."

"If they're watching, they would assume the lights were turned on by their team. There were no flashing police lights and no indication of trouble here. All the activity was out front. And it was dark outside until a few moments ago. If Terrin is out there, he could still assume everything is going well. But not for long. If they had a specific signal worked out, and I'm assuming they did, he'll be watching for it."

Skye nodded, feeling her blood heat up. "Terrin is staying out in the boat until the house is secure. He'll be out there waiting for that signal before he comes in and exposes himself. Spineless, gutless, coward. He wants to come in and do the actual dirty work, but only after things are secured and protected." She reigned in her temper and got it under control. It wasn't helping.

"We need a plan," she continued. She looked at Jim, who had caught some of the conversation and was impressed with the teamwork, skill, and coordination of this family. "We can't wait for federal backup or a special ops unit and we can't use local law enforcement. The boat may be beyond their jurisdiction."

"You have your special ops team right here," said David looking right at Jim. There was an edge to his voice and a flicker of impatience in his eyes. It gave his words a special punch because it was unusual for David to be impatient with anything. "Let's stop the charade, or maybe just suspend it for a while. This evening has been very interesting to say the least. I know the whole thing didn't play out like you thought. Your mark moved up his timetable and the family got caught up in the tidal wave. This isn't a complaint. We comported ourselves according to our training and our passion for our duty to the law. We did well. Hell, we did brilliantly. This evening was just an extension of our work. Our duty. Our mission. Our lives. I know we don't have any federal clearances. But we're smart and we're well-trained observers, interrogators, and detectives. You don't have to confirm or deny anything, but we all know that Skye and Alex are not just a pilot and a lawyer."

David was just getting started and since he was only articulating what everyone else was thinking, no one else spoke. "Ever since Rita's death, Alex has been pursuing a different, more important mission than making money. We all know that. We respect that. And we've always given him the space to do his job and implicit permission to lie to us. And Skye." His eyes went to her and registered both fondness and admiration. "Well we know that she's special, but she's also just a bit too accident prone. We'll not breach your security. We'll not betray your secrets. But what we'll do right now is get this fucker. His men invaded the home where my children would have been if this had played out a day earlier. This terrorist has assaulted our family's home. You can't expect us to stand down. We won't. You may think this Terrin is your problem. Well move over. He tried to do mortal harm to people very dear to us. He's after my best friend's future wife. Now it appears as though they've captured and injured a man we think of as one of our own. Well, the bastard's messed with the wrong family. And we'll not stay out of it. When this is over, we can get real ignorant again. Pretend this never happened. Go back to your covert movements and top-secret assignments. We won't ask questions. We won't pry. We'll believe the lies. But right now, let's get a workable plan together and get moving before there's another tragedy!"

No one said anything. They just stared at David, then back again at Jim. This was the longest string of words they'd ever heard from him. And he was angry...furious in fact and David rarely got hot.

Jim looked at Skye, then at Alex. His two best agents. Like his own children. Destined to be the finest husband and wife team ever in the intelligence community. He was obligated to keep them safe from outside discovery. He looked at their family. For the rest of their lives

Skye and Alex would have to lie to them. These people weren't stupid. Quite the opposite. Hell, he'd already brought in Skye's sister. He never before had this much trouble containing departmental secrets.

"Let me consult with...other agencies. I'll be back in five minutes. Until then, I would suggest you work on a contingency plan...just in case this isn't all cleared."

When Jim returned with Amanda, there were some shocked faces. Why the nice old lady? Only Skye and Alex weren't surprised to see her.

"I would like you all to accept this one on faith and not ask any questions." They nodded. Then there were some smiles as they saw the subtle, but very real differences in Amanda's bearing and certainly in her eyes. Shrewd, extremely intelligent, and just slightly amused.

"I've found the best way to give advice to my team is to find out what they want to do and then advise them to do it. Skye, this is your op. For as long as it takes to get Terrin into custody, you'll come out of the shadows."

He looked at the family assembled in the room. "After that goal has been reached, no reminiscing, no mention of any of this. Ever. We go back into the shadows and you all get complete amnesia."

They all nodded their agreement and since David appeared as though he was the spokesperson, he said it out loud. "Agreed."

"Man, does that mean the pajamas too?" complained Tank.

"Complete amnesia," insisted Elliot, grinning.

"Amanda will give us any assistance she can. She is still capable in the field and will procure for us resources, intelligence, and clearance." No one asked how she would go about doing that or what was in her background that gave her the contacts and the power. Assumptions were made but were never confirmed. Not that day, not any time in the future.

Skye was in her element. Strategic planning and leadership were natural to her.

"First we have to locate the boat. Alex, posing as a friend of Duncan's, just tried to raise the boat on the radio. No response. Duncan would have answered the call. He's very meticulous on that...never out of touch." Her eyes slid to Alex. "Comes from working for a demanding boss."

Alex took up the narrative. "We can assume he is unable to respond. I think this confirms Tank's observation that someone has given the terrorists information...false information. Duncan is smart and he is tough. But he's not invincible. Somehow Terrin and his men took him. They're out there. Hopefully they see some benefit to keeping Duncan alive. We need to find the boat, discover Duncan's status, and if he is...," Alex swallowed hard and went on. "If he is alive, mount a rescue."

Nodding, Skye continued where Alex left off. "We're also assuming Terrin and some of his men are still on board our boat. The ocean is large, but the area they would need to be in to make a quick landing is limited...probably just over the horizon. We assume they have a craft they used to board the boat and overpower Duncan and they will use that to transport themselves to our section of the beach when they get the signal. None of the men who trespassed tonight are talking. So we don't know the signal. That means we can't lure him in here. We have to go to them."

Alex's family had never seen this side of either Skye or Alex before. They were working in tandem, a perfect team. They were confident and concise, and both seasoned in tactical planning and execution.

Skye continued. "I'll be able to cover far more area from the air. Blake, you and I will take the plane up. I'll fly a search pattern and Blake, you'll do the spotting. This shouldn't take long once we're in the air. We'll direct the rescue craft. No radios. Secured cell phones only. Amanda, I'll need three sets. One for the boat, one for the plane, and one for Jim. They're not foolproof, but there will be no casual eavesdropping on the operation. Then I can direct you to the location using your global positioning unit."

"Our cover story will be that drug runners overpowered Duncan," said Alex. When they all smiled, Alex elaborated. "Okay, an army of really big, mean, heavily armed drug runners overpowered Duncan and we were able to get him back. Jim will be standing by at the Coast Guard facility in Jacksonville. It's a secured location."

Skye nodded. "Once we have recaptured the boat, rescued Duncan, and arrested Terrin, we'll bring the boat back to the facility to drop off the revolting cargo. Hopefully at the same time, we'll be able to transport Duncan to a medical center for care. We assume he didn't tell these people anything until it would sound convincing. That perhaps he had to take some punishment." Skye took a deep breath as she unconsciously took Alex's hand. "He knew exactly what he was doing. He sent those men into a trap. It was a calculated risk on his part, but it was a good one."

"We'll need a diversion. Amanda," continued Skye. "I don't wish to offend, but you're the least...ah...least likely looking person in this room to be perceived as someone dangerous."

"You don't offend me. It's how I get just about anywhere I want to go.

There are advantages of being a little old lady." The fact that she was in marvelous shape and could still kick her leg over her head was beside the point. "You want me to be the diversion I take it?"

"You read my mind."

Tank stood to protest and both Skye and Amanda, in identical moves, held up a hand, palm out.

They looked at each other, then at Tank, who sat back down and said, "Whoa! Never mind."

The laughter felt good. Skye and Alex continued to give everyone their assignments. When the plan was analyzed, discussed, and refined, they were all ready to move with confidence.

Terrin was enraged. He had yet to get the signal from his advance team and the fury was causing his vision to blur as he stared unblinking at the horizon. One small flare from the raft. That was all he was waiting for...all he needed to see to complete this mission. That captain was going to pay. He wasn't just going to kill her. He was going to rape her, cut her, torture her. Then allow his men to use her. It was going to be long, painful, and degrading.

He couldn't wait to get her back to his compound. His reputation would take a huge surge...he would become a legend. The bold Terrin snatching the national heroine from her own home in the invincible United States.

Everything was in place. A huge seaplane was waiting at the secluded dock of an elderly couple currently on a cruise in the Bahamas. Rich old imperialists who had no idea their property was being used to give aid and comfort to a band of so-called terrorists. Well, today's terrorists were tomorrow's duly elected officials. The world would write a different tune when he was elected President.

The dock where the plane was moored was secluded and secure and located on the intracoastal waterway. After they had the woman on board the boat, they would leave the ocean, come around the south end of the island and bring her to the plane. He had a little trouble recruiting a pilot, but managed to find one who loved his wife and five sweet daughters. The family was under surveillance on Soteras assuring the man's cooperation. They would fly to Nassau where a rented jet was waiting to take them to Columbia. The arrangements drained his already depleted accounts. That was another thing the bitch was going to pay for...this venture cost Terrin nearly everything he had put away.

Then another thought flashed into his mind. Damn them. If his men were looting and using the woman before he got there, he would have their hearts for breakfast. He would give them only a few more minutes, and then he would take action.

The sun was just coming up, making everything transform from black to gray to subdued colors. Alex walked Skye to the door while Blake went to bring the car around. They were on their way to the airport and the rest of the team was gathering what they needed. Alex had secured a large cruiser for the rescue and they would be leaving within the next few minutes.

"Okay," said Alex, giving her a quick peck. They were in their operational mode and were all business. He gave her another quick peck. Well, almost all business. "No unnecessary chances. This is a search and report for you. Not a search and rescue. You will fly and you will call."

She nodded as she checked the chamber of her Glock, slipped off the safety and stuck it in the flight bag. Her fingers were as efficient and competent handling the gun as they were on the throttle of her plane, or, Alex thought, stroking him into waves of desire.

"I know you wanted to get your hands on him, but darling, we need you to be our eyes."

She looked up at him and nodded. "I'll subjugate my own preferences for the good of the mission. For Duncan. He's more important than my wishes. However, be sure you don't kill the son-of-a-bitch before I have an opportunity to gloat and see him squirm."

"I'll bring him in," said Alex, thinking of ways to hurt the man and still have him conscious and breathing.

"You be careful out there," she said looking into his eyes and knowing he would be going back into peril. She searched her heart and found anxiety, but not mind-numbing terror. Normal. Nothing paralyzing. She was ready, her mind was ready, and since this was their first real op together as a team, her heart was ready. It felt good. Exciting and right. He felt it too.

"We'll celebrate tonight, darling," she said and gave him a proper kiss goodbye. She figured some of the protocol would have to be rewritten for a husband and wife team anyway.

The dark moody man stood on the wheelhouse deck, his legs slightly apart, his arms folded pompously. Dressed in black with sunglasses covering his eyes he looked out of place in the Florida sunrise. This wasn't where he'd planned to spend the morning. They were supposed to be in the plane and on their way back to Columbia. Staring at the cruiser making its way toward him, he ordered the men to take arms and stand ready. When he saw the older woman at the helm, he snorted and rescinded the order. No danger there.

"Young man! Young man!" shouted Amanda in her best little old lady voice. "Do you have any Metamucil on board? My husband isn't feeling well."

She was steering the boat crazily, covering the bubbles coming up from Alex, Tank, and David's scuba gear. They'd slipped over the side just before Amanda had blasted her horn and waved an embroidered silk hanky. Alex grinned when he saw her pull it out of her cleavage. The little details. A hanky, for God's sake.

Amanda looked like a woman having a very tough time keeping her craft under control. The fact that she was expertly maneuvering it ever closer to Alex's boat was obvious only to Wyatt, Bat, and Elliot. They had a great view looking through the portholes. Checking their weapons, they stood ready.

"How many?" asked Wyatt in a low voice.

"I can see only five...no six," answered Amanda. "They're all topside. I don't see Duncan. There's probably another one with him. They still haven't shown any guns. They're pretty sure they can handle one little old lady. I don't see Terrin. Ah. There he is. The man in black. What an arrogant son-of-a-bitch. Looks like he's playing for a crowd. That would make seven for sure. Maybe eight. Good odds. We should be home for lunch."

They heard a plane overhead. "That would be Skye again," Wyatt said. "She's making another pass."

Skye and Blake had immediately spotted the boat just over the horizon and nearly parallel with the mansion a half-hour before and directed the rented cruiser right to the location. They didn't want to make too many passes and arouse the suspicion of the men on board. No one looked up, however. They were too interested in what Amanda was doing.

"Hey lady!" someone shouted from Alex's boat. "Don't come any closer."

"Oh please, young man," she begged in a quavering voice, coming closer anyway.

"We can't help you."

"They're talking," said Amanda softly, still waving her hanky with one hand and steering with the other. "They know now they have to get rid of me. I've seen them, their boat, and their location. They'll change their minds in a minute and ask me to come up close or send someone over."

Amanda knew how to read a situation. After conferring with the tall man in charge, the man turned back. "Okay, lady. We'll send someone over with what you need."

"And a very big gun," murmured Amanda as she came closer still. Judging from the bubbles she tracked using her peripheral vision, their guys were very near Alex's boat. She would wait until she was sure they were on the other side, then cut her engines and disappear. She needed Terrin's men to come on board and she didn't want to give them a convenient target.

Skye returned from another broad sweep, wishing she could be down on the surface participating instead of flying safely overhead. Staying high to keep from appearing too obvious, she had an excellent perspective of Amelia Island and the intracoastal water beyond. There was a great deal of boat traffic out already and it was getting more crowded by the minute. It was a good thing Alex's boat was large, distinctive, and already identified.

Blake noticed her staring toward the intracoastal waterway on the other side of the narrow island.

"What...you see something?"

Skye turned back to him and smiled sheepishly. "Sorry...I saw a Grumman amphibian down there...it's a beauty."

"A fish? You saw a fish?"

"No it's a seaplane and a very nice one. I haven't noticed it before. I'm kind of a nut for aircraft."

Blake smiled back. "Are you saying my son is going to marry a woman who's more attracted to propellers and jet fuel than diamonds and Gucci?"

Skye's eyes narrowed good-naturedly. "You have a problem with that?"

"Hey, I'm married to a woman who thinks there's nothing more beautiful than a gun exhibit and prefers dress blues to Vera Wang. I see no problem with your interest in big metal bodies."

"Show time," said Skye, suddenly serious and nodding at the two boats converging. Blake raised his powerful binoculars and started giving her a running commentary on what he saw. It looked like it was all going smoothly. Exactly as planned.

"The boys just went over the side," said Blake. "Well done, Amanda! She's all over the place. Damn if she doesn't look like an ineffectual old lady completely overwhelmed by what she's trying to do. She's waving that little hanky…having a conversation with the terrorists. Still no sign of Duncan, I'm afraid. But then, he's most likely in the stateroom. Ah! There's a bit of interesting activity."

Skye glanced at the boats and watched as two men from Alex's boat lowered the dingy from the side.

"Looks like they're going to go over and drown one helpless old lady," said Blake, smiling confidently.

"Right. They'll need more than two little men and one big ocean," said Skye, snorting.

"CIA?" asked Blake surreptitiously, his expression not changing as he kept his eyes on the dingy.

Skye laughed. "Can't confirm that, Blake. Let's just say Amanda is one woman neither of us wants to mess with."

"Can you take a quick peek here and give me a positive ID on the man standing like a pompous ass on the deck?"

"Let me take a look."

She brought her knees up to control the yoke and kept it steady while she took the binoculars from Blake and looked at the man's face through the powerful lenses.

"Oh hell, Blake…I don't know. It looks like him. He has the same features, but the cap is pulled down low…and there's something…I don't know…different." Frowning, she handed him the binoculars and put her hands back on the yoke.

"What do you mean?"

"I don't know," she repeated. "It's just that my brain is clicking and when it does that, I have to take the picture, develop it, look at it again and give it some thought. It may be nothing…just my frustration that I can't be down there looking him in the eye."

"I suspect it wouldn't remain eye-to-eye for long."

"No…more like foot to face."

"The boys are up. I can see their heads." Blake turned to Skye. "How about we go on down and cause a distraction? That'll give them a real nice opportunity to board."

She put aside the nagging feeling and grinned at her future father-in-law. "Great idea. Hang on!"

Skye performed a stomach-sinking maneuver, turning the plane and reducing altitude at the same time. Going down to 500 feet, she headed right for the boats.

As the five men topside looked up Alex, David, and Tank were over the side in easy, silent, agile moves. They crouched along the wall of the wheelhouse, hidden from view.

The two well-armed men in the dingy were calling to the old bitch. Annoyed, they took hold of the side ladder and went up, looking forward to popping the wacky old broad and feeding her and her ailing husband to the fish. They dropped down on the deserted deck. No one in sight.

Suddenly a plane came swooping right over them. Looking up, they wondered if they should put a few bullets in its fuselage. This whole operation was going south fast, the men thought derisively. Then it went even further south. The mercenaries went down into the stateroom to take care of one little old lady and found three very seasoned cops instead. Wyatt Earp Cooper, Elliot Ness Cooper and Bat Masterson Cooper were there waiting. That was a hell of a lot of cop. And they were holding a hell of a lot of firepower. The intruders didn't even have time to raise their guns.

Skye's diversion had provided the perfect cover. It was both a compelling visual distraction and a loud disturbance. Amanda smiled wickedly at the two men. "Hello fellows. Just one word of advice. Never underestimate a senior citizen." In a flash of motion, Amanda produced two hypos out of her pocket, stuck one in each man's jugular and pushed down the plunger. Swift, perfect aim, no hesitation. The men fell like a couple of trees under a lumberjack's ax.

"Wow! That would come in handy in the streets," said Wyatt.

"I'm not sure it's completely legal," said Amanda calmly. "I didn't even read them their rights. Oh well, this will be a messy extradition issue anyway. We'll need to secure them, then our job is done. Two down, five to go. We can sit back and wait for the show to begin on the other boat."

The operation was going very well, indeed.

The five men on Alex's boat looked up again. Damn plane. What the hell did it want? Was it some kind of border patrol? Didn't look like an official plane. They started to bring up their weapons, but before they could get them waist high, three men in wet suits stepped out from behind the wheelhouse.

"Throw down your weapons...now!" shouted Alex a gun resting easily in each hand. They were trained menacingly on the two men directly in front of him. Tank's was pointed at Terrin and David had the two men to the left. Alex could see first the surprise, then the calculation of the terrorists closest to him.

These were not run-of-the-mill lackeys or ideologues. Terrin had kept his best around him...highly trained, highly paid mercenaries. They didn't particularly care for Terrin, Moreno, or politics. They cared about their money and the man paying them had issued orders.

They were used to working together as a team and they were fearless. One that David was covering shouted something in another language and all four of them spun at once, bringing their guns up, fingers already pulling the trigger. If Alex or David had hesitated, been a split second slower, or less skilled with weapons, one or both of them would have taken a bullet. As it was, it was the terrorists who made the miscalculation and paid for it.

"Head shots!" shouted Alex and took out his two simultaneously, each one with a neat hole between the eyes. The terrorists went down, bullets pounding out of their guns and ripping through the hull harmlessly away from any of them. David got one man in the shoulder and neck and Alex spun and took out the other in a fluid well-practiced motion that had David gaping. Where the hell had this Alex come from? He certainly didn't learn to shoot like that in his class on corporate law.

Tank didn't move, didn't shoot, but stood his ground leveling the gun at Terrin knowing his family had everything covered. Bullets were whizzing around, but his hand and eye were steady. Terrin didn't move either. Let his men risk their lives, he would let the dust settle before he made a decision. The big man in the rubber suit looked competent and dangerous. His men on the other boat and the one in the hold would take care of these three from the water.

"All clear on deck," shouted Alex as he put one gun back in his belt. David covered him while he checked the pulse of the four men. "Two alive. Two dead," he said. "They're all yours David. You have your man secure, Tank?"

"I have. Go find Duncan."

"Amanda!" called Alex. "Could you and Wyatt come over here? Elliot, you and Bat stay with the other two."

Turning, Alex cautiously made his way down the stairs, gun drawn and ready to fire, but he met no resistance. Duncan was tied up, unconscious, and bleeding on a chair in the stateroom. There was blood on the walls and the floor. Alex checked for a pulse and was relieved to find one. It was strong and steady, just like Duncan.

"Duncan?" he whispered. "We're here. You did well. We got your message." When he went to loosen the ropes, he saw Duncan's hand. The terrorists had broken all of his fingers on his left hand. Alex's stomach pitched and rolled. His friend and driver had let them break his fingers so his capitulation would be convincing. Disinformation...delivered deliberately only after torture and incredible pain. He heard Amanda and Wyatt on the deck above as he got his stomach under control.

"Amanda, come on down here. Wyatt, cover Terrin and send Tank down here too. I need muscle."

"God!" said Tank. "They really worked him over." He and Alex gently lifted the giant to the bed and laid him down. Amanda checked his pulse and his eyes.

"He's drugged. They must have overpowered him, then pumped him with some drugs to bring him down. Unless..." Amanda looked at Alex. "Is he a user?"

Alex shook his head. "No. One thing for sure. They weren't self administered."

"They should wear off soon. Tank go back up and keep Terrin in your sights and send Mom down here. She knows drugs."

"Watch Terrin. Cover your ass. Come down. Lift your driver. Go up. Shit, you're bossy," complained Tank, but a grin was fastened on his face. Duncan was bruised, but he was breathing just fine and the relief and adrenalin rush were feeling pretty good.

"Once we've secured the men topside, we'll need to search this craft to be sure there are no more of them." Alex turned Duncan over to Wyatt. "Amanda, did you bring your phone?"

"I did."

"Why don't you report to Skye and Dad. They've been circling for the last ten minutes. I'm sure they want to know about Duncan."

"From what I can tell," Amanda said as she and Alex started topside. "He'll recover. There's nothing life threatening that I can see or feel. The pain must have been horrible, but they didn't cut him or shoot him. Blood loss was minimal. He's quite a man, Alex. Maybe if he ever decides to give up running you around town, we can recruit him."

"Keep your hands off my staff, Amanda. A spook is a spook...but what Duncan can do to an engine is an art form." Alex started to relax. Duncan would recover, Terrin was in custody, his fiancée was safe. Things were going well.

Tank had his gun on Terrin while Amanda made the call. Blake answered and she gave him just the minimal information. Nothing specific.

Wyatt came up and reported that Duncan was in a deep sleep. "I found the vial. They injected a strong sedative which is probably good right now. He's going to be okay, but he was pretty well worked over."

Tank turned to Amanda to score on her little white hanky when he saw the gun come up out of the lower stateroom where one of Terrin's men had been hiding. In one smooth move, Tank jumped over, pushed Amanda behind the wheelhouse, spun, brought his own gun up and shot the terrorist through the shoulder and forehead.

It was a beautifully executed move and Alex was about to applaud when the whole scene turned completely bad. The terrorist's finger pressed the automatic trigger in the split second before death and a volley of bullets slammed into Tank, propelling him over the side of the boat and into the water.

"Tank!" shouted Alex as he ran and dove into the water after him. Terrin saw his opportunity and slid down the stairs toward the back of the boat, but Wyatt was both quicker and angrier. She crossed the deck, tripped him, turned him over, pinned him, and had her gun to his forehead with the same automatic ease of movement her son displayed only a moment before.

"Alex!" shouted Wyatt. "You tell me Tank is okay or this man gets a fucking third eye!" Her hand was steady and her eyes never wavered. Inside she was screaming, but she never lowered her guard. Then she heard the words that brought life back into her body.

"He's okay!" called Alex, dragging Tank back to the boat. "No holes. He got it in the vest. He's just out."

"Out?" said Wyatt. What the hell. She was the mother. Tank was her child. Bringing her gun back, she hit Terrin hard across the skull. He gave a small cry of pain and then didn't move. "Out!" she said and holstered her gun. Then she got up to assist her sons back into the boat.

After pulling Tank up on deck, they systematically searched the rest of the boat. No one else was on board. Tank came around within a few minutes. Alex gently took off his vest and inspected the angry bruises along his chest. There didn't seem to be any internal damage, but he would call Dr. Lacy when they got back. The poor man sure wasn't getting much of a retirement.

Alex looked up at the plane that was now circling low over the water. Amanda's phone had sailed off the deck and into the water so he relied on visual communication and waved, then made a sign of victory. Clasping his hands over his head and bringing his arms up and down.

Skye waggled her wings and took off. They would meet at the Coast Guard dock.

Tank tried to say something, working to get a full breath into his lungs and not being too successful. Looking around, he found he was lying on a lounge chair in the middle of the deck.

"Just take it easy," said David, kneeling down beside Tank. His hands were shaking and he was having trouble getting a breath himself. Tank. Rita's brother. God. He was freezing inside from the sight of Tank flying through the air and slamming into the ocean. The sound of the bullets thudding into his chest was still ringing in his ears. David had no siblings. Tank and Alex were it for him. Now Skye. Wyatt came over and stood next to him. When she put her hand on David's shoulder and squeezed, he could feel the slight tremor in her hand as well. They shared the moment, then steadied themselves by looking at Tank's face and the grin that was breaking out on it.

As Wyatt looked down at her son, Tank could see the love and concern, but there was more. Much more. He could see the pride and approval in her face. It was a son's dream to see that look. Not just love, you expect that from your mother. This was cop to cop. Her endorsement. Her sanction. He passed and he felt real fine. Time to celebrate!

"Corona time!" croaked Tank.

"Beer," Alex laughed. His brother was back. He looked up into the haunted eyes of his brother-in-law and watched as the fright faded into relief and affection.

"David, you serve his majesty here." His voice still had the edge of Special Agent in Charge. "Amanda, keep working on making Duncan comfortable. There's a first aid kit under the sink in the head."

He leaned over the deck and shouted to the boat along side. "Elliot, you and Bat bring the cruiser in. Bat, you make contact with both Skye and Jim. Amanda's phone is swimming with the fishes. Minimum information. Get an ambulance for Duncan."

"What about Tank?" asked Elliot. He knew his nephew was okay, but wasn't sure if he needed medical attention.

Alex looked over to where Tank was lounging. David was handing him a Corona and Tank asked if there were any pretzels in the galley. "I think he'll be fine. I'm going to have Dr. Lacy make another house call. Unless his condition changes, I'm taking him home." Turning, he looked at Wyatt.

"Mom, you're in charge of keeping the prisoners subdued." Everyone nodded and went about their duties. If anyone thought it was unusual to call a member of an ops team Mom, no one mentioned it.

Alex looked around his boat. There was going to have to be some repairs. Getting the blood off the deck, patching the bullet holes. That was nothing. Right now he took a moment for himself. He too had to shake the visual image of his brother being hit. It made him empathize more with Skye's horror in seeing him get shot right before her eyes. It all seemed to happen in slow motion and his feet felt like they were nailed to the deck. He saw each bullet hit the vest, then Tank flying over the railing and into the water. Even the sound of the splash replayed vividly in his head. His heart had stopped and he didn't think it started beating again until he saw that none of the bullets had hit his brother's flesh. He let the quiver rip through him, then shook it off. Tank was all right. It echoed through his brain like a mantra. Tank was all right.

"I'm going to revive Terrin and we're going to have a little talk."

Wyatt looked up at her oldest son, two guns strapped to his belt, the sound of him yelling 'head shots' and shooting his guns with no hesitation still playing over in her head. There was a wild look about him she'd never seen before. Impressive but untamed. "Jim wants him alive, son," she said softly.

"Oh, his heart will still be beating," Alex said, then turned as Bat shouted up at him.

"The pilot's on the phone. She needs to talk with you."

Alex frowned. It wasn't like Skye to make unnecessary chatter. He leaned over his boat. "Throw it up here." Bat tossed it over the water and Alex neatly caught it one handed.

"Yes?"

"Check the main cargo...I have a feeling you have the wrong package. The people we're dealing with like counterfeits. Be sure we have the genuine article. Call me back."

What the hell? Alex looked over at Terrin. He was still unconscious, the bruise on his temple the only mark on him. His cap and sunglasses were gone exposing the face. It looked like him, but then Alex had only seen him once. How could Skye possibly see any flaw from the air? He could hear her coming back and went over to revive his prisoner.

"What is it?" asked Amanda, coming up from the stateroom after hearing Bat's shout.

"Skye wants me to check for a possible stand in. Do you know if Terrin used them?"

"Oh hell, Alex. I must be getting old. I never gave it a thought. All the demigods and dictators in that part of the world have them and use them regularly. I would think Terrin would be no exception."

Alex went over and none too gently pulled the man in black into a sitting position. Slapping his face and shaking him, he prodded him to open his eyes.

"He looks like the pictures I've seen of him," commented Wyatt over Amanda's shoulder. Amanda was down on one knee beside Alex and looking intently into the eyes.

"What's your name?"

The man rubbed his bound hands over his face and looked at Alex with hatred. "Terrin. And you are a dead man."

The voice sounded the same...same accent with strong British undertones.

"Where is the real Terrin?"

The man said all he was going to say and just glared at the people watching him. Alex made a fist and moved it swiftly toward the man's face. He didn't even flinch. "He's playing a part. His eyes are different. I think the real Terrin would have blinked. This man is a mercenary."

"He's dazed. Maybe..." They all looked up as Skye flew over.

Skye flew low and glanced out the window. Blake had his binoculars trained on Alex.

"It looks like he's managed to revive the man."

Skye dialed the number again, not wanting to wait for Alex to call her back.

"Yes?"

"Measure the catch. This one looks longer...maybe two inches. Our other specimen was five feet ten and a half inches."

Alex yanked the man to his feet. He was easily a half-inch over six feet.

"We have a six footer here."

"Check the time on our guest's watch."

Alex didn't even question her motive; he grabbed the man's wrist.

"Movado?"

"Not even close."

"It's a counterfeit. I'm going hunting." As Alex looked up, he saw Skye bank the plane and climb. She would fly a search grid again and find the man if he was still in the neighborhood.

"He was here," said Amanda when Alex filled in the rest of the team. "He would have come here personally to get her, that I'm sure of. He must have sensed something was wrong when his landing party didn't follow through with their prearranged signal."

"Do you think he started in toward the house when he didn't get that signal?" asked Wyatt.

When they saw Skye headed in the general direction of their compound, they knew she figured the same thing.

"If he was on this boat, I would say it's a distinct possibility. Let's get Bat and Elliot over here to take Duncan in. The cruiser is faster. David, Mom, transfer the prisoners over. They may know something. Amanda...you can see what you can do to get information out of these men. Tank, you want to go to the hospital with Duncan or stay with us...your call."

Tank snorted and stiffly but gamely got up as Alex pushed the fake Terrin toward the side of the boat. "Do we let them ride, or do they get to swim over?"

Blake and Skye flew over the house...all looked quiet. No sign of a boat or intruders anywhere. Skye was agitated knowing that as the minutes ticked by, her quarry was getting farther and farther away.

"He has an escape plan and he's using it. I know it. He's running...going out the back door, Blake. Shit. I'll fly low and slow...see if you can spot a suspicious boat. It would be all men. Several, I would think."

"You're joking...this is an area known for excellent fishing...there are boatloads of men all over the damn place." He trained his binoculars on one boat after another.

"He would be moving."

"Maybe he's already on shore."

"I don't know...we're on an island...it seems like it wouldn't be a good tactical move to place himself on land."

"Well it wasn't a good tactical move to go after you either, and he still did. How far could he go on water if he started out shortly after his men were taken last night?"

"Miles from here...but I think he would have given them some time...that he wouldn't have aborted so soon. I think he's down there, Blake."

"So many boats...maybe he's just going to lay low until dark."

"Yes, or..."

Blake lowered the binoculars and looked over at her...she had stopped in mid-sentence, her mind obviously working something out. Blake remained silent...he was used to being around a woman synthesizing clues and drawing conclusions.

"Or he could take to the air." Smiling, she suddenly banked the plane and increased her speed. "I have you, you bastard. Blake, tune in." Blake listened as she dialed his son's number.

"I know where the big fish is headed. I'm not the albatross...there's a Grumman Albatross seaplane parked on the intracoastal. I'm going after him..."

Blake could hear his son shouting...sounded like he wanted to modify her idea a little.

"We may not have time to set the net. You're too far away...so is the rest of our party. I have a plan...let me get on the ground and I'll fill you in."

Alex voice was cut off as she disengaged and looked around. Blake watched her face as a daredevil smile formed on her lips and a moxie look came into her eye. It was a real show.

"We're going down..."

"Down where?" Blake looked around. They were miles from the airport.

"Down there." Skye nodded to a short pier near an abandoned marina undergoing reconstruction.

"On the pier?"

"Sure...it's flat and it's straight."

"It's also short and narrow and surrounded by water."

"You can swim, can't you?"

He grinned and nodded.

"Do you trust me?"

"Of course, but will you think it unmanly of me if I close my eyes?"

"Hell no...mine will be closed all the way."

"God, if my son wasn't gone over you and my wife wasn't so dear, not to mention armed, I think I would be falling in love all over again." His daring smile matched her own and filled her heart.

"Let me line this beauty up and I'll put her down. It's called pinpoint landing and I am a champ."

Alex, piloting the cruiser at top speed across the water, watched the horizon with the rest of the family as the Cessna did a 180 and started back toward the dock.

"What the hell?" said Tank gaping at what looked like a plane coming in for a landing.

"Jesus Christ...what's she going to do?" asked David.

Amanda grinned her approval. "Damn...I think she's going to land."

361

"On what? The fucking pier?" choked Tank.

"I don't know if I'm going to be able to watch this," said Wyatt even as she grabbed the binoculars from David and focused them on the little plane. Her heart was in her throat or more accurately in the air with her future daughter-in-law. "Alex, tell me she's as good as I think she is."

"Better," said Alex grimly never taking his eyes off the Cessna, willing it to safety.

The plane headed straight for the short wooden pier. Everyone held their breath as if breathing would change the air currents and throw off Skye's precision landing.

And precision it was…as well as thrilling and beautiful. Skye sat the plane down gently and accurately on the end of the pier with an edge of a little over a foot and came to a smooth safe stop near the entrance of the abandoned marina.

Tank and David whooped it up as Alex answered the phone again. They heard him shouting and caught the gist of what Skye intended to do. Then he swore as the phone went dead, turned, and headed toward the Coast Guard station on the mainland. They had a plan and he would have to count on his father to stand in for him at Skye's back.

Skye quickly reached over and grabbed her flight bag, removing her Glock .357. Out of a pocket on the back of her seat she located her spare .40-caliber Glock.

"Blake…I am going after Terrin. I can't reveal how I know this, but albatross was mentioned in reference to me…we thought he was talking *about* me, but that Grumman…"

"Yes, I heard…it's called an Albatross."

"That means I know where he's headed. I have no idea how many men he still has around him, but I'm going to try to take him. I want you to stay here."

"Don't even waste your time or breath." Reaching into his pocket he brought out a small Smith and Wesson .32 caliber pistol. Skye glanced at it and couldn't keep an eyebrow from inching up her forehead. He gave a little laugh. "It's Wyatt's purse piece. Not quite as macho as your pair there, but let me assure you, I know how to use it. I don't intend to stay here while you jump into danger."

"It's my job, Blake."

"I think my son would like me to watch your back. That's my job, Skyler."

"You sound just like him…"

"Why thank you…shall we go?"

362

Skye considered for a moment, then not wanting to waste another minute, nodded. Jumping out of the plane, she raced to the road leading across the island with Blake right behind her.

Terrin finished with his rant and settled in to put his escape plan into action. He didn't have what he came for, but he needed to get out of the country so he could bide his time and make another attempt. Failure wasn't an option. He wasn't sure why all these setbacks seemed so inevitable and for the first time in his adult life he felt the twinge of uncertainty. It was only fleeting, however. For he was the mighty Terrin. His name made men shake, women shrink, and babies cry. And he outwitted the Americans. That was something he could brag about and build on when he reported the mission to his people.

The idiots were out there floating on the ocean with the wrong fucking man. They captured Mandalay Pagotta, a former colonel in the National Guard who he hired years ago to stand in for him on occasion...and Pagotta wouldn't betray him. Terrin had recruited and trained the man...he was fearless and prideful and would play his part until he could humiliate an American judicial system with his true identity. Maybe even create a delightful scandal. They knew how to play the game.

When there had been no signal from shore, he suspected something had gone wrong...fools. His close scrutiny had revealed no movement in the huge house, so he decided to distance himself from the woman's lover's boat and the black giant who just may have sent his men into a trap of some kind. He didn't figure the driver as an agent, but he must have been assigned to the bitch and her trained dog.

Four of his men were left...his best. None of them had said a word since leaving their comrades on the other boat. Following orders was what they got paid for, but Terrin could detect some unease among them. No matter...they would stand. They had no choice. There was nowhere else for them to go. Their names were well known to the self-proclaimed pretty-boy reformer, Moreno. It was in their best interests to stay with him and help overthrow Moreno and eliminate the weak people who had gone over to his side.

They would pay in the end. All of them. First Moreno would die, then he would unleash men like those beside him on the countryside and make an example of all the spineless peasants who dared to defy their fate. For he was the man of destiny and they would soon regret their slide into disloyalty.

The best seaman among his men had made good time over the water and smoothly docked their boat. On the other side of the pier was his ticket back home...the beautiful big seaplane with Island Adventures stenciled along the fuselage. As instructed the doors were standing open. He could see the pilot and copilot in their seats ready for the order to start the engines and take off. The moment he stepped into the dark interior, the engines roared into life. Perfect timing. The last man in slid the doors shut and almost immediately the plane moved away from the pier.

Nodding his approval, Terrin took his place and strapped in. There were ten seats in the passenger area and his men spaced themselves for maximum comfort, removing their weapons and settling in for the ride across the Atlantic. Terrin could read the relief in their eyes, even though they remained silent and stoic. Perhaps he would have them shot when they returned to the camp in Colombia to regroup. If he were going to rewrite this bit of history, he would need to get rid of all the witnesses.

The plane taxied smoothly out into a wide place in the intracoastal waterway between the island and mainland Florida. Terrin watched the terrain with little interest. He had escaped once again through his cunning and careful planning. No one was better at smelling a rat than he. Leaning back, he allowed himself to relax. There was no way they could catch him now...he would disappear and they would be down below him, searching the island and the waters around it while he slipped away...far away.

They popped out of the water, smoothly and swiftly and were climbing fast. Terrin could feel the G force pressing him against the seat. Apparently his pilot was under the mistaken impression that the faster he got them to their destination, the faster he would be finished with his task. But he would never be released from his obligation to serve...not until he was finished living and breathing. Terrin needed a pilot if he was to return someday. Glancing up at the men in the cockpit, he thought about the pilot's five daughters. Maybe he would move them all to his camp...he never took five sisters to his bed...and some of them were still children. He would enjoy that. Very much.

Letting his mind wander, he wondered where the bitch was right now. The stupid people around her had messed up. He was alive, free, and on his way back to Columbia to plot her demise. There was no doubt in his mind that she would eventually fall. As the time passed, he pleasantly marked it by thinking of ways to torture and humiliate the woman.

The Albatross soared, the engines hummed. The pilot looked at the altimeter...10,000 feet, 12,000, 15,000. Everything was working well as the plane banked a little to the right and leveled off. The copilot watched out the side window for familiar landmarks and any sign of other craft. They had no flight plan, so they were flying visually. The pilot checked and rechecked all the instruments. Perfect. As dangerous as the situation was, the thrill of flying such a beautiful bird couldn't be denied.

Terrin took a deep breath. He was feeling euphoric, almost light headed. It was a narrow escape, but a thrilling one and very satisfying. He'd been on U.S. soil and the combined force of the Americans couldn't stop him. A short laugh escaped him and sounded like the giggle of a child. Looking around to see if anyone heard him, he noticed that all of his men had fallen asleep. That was unusual. It was a tacit strategic agreement that a least one man would remain awake and vigilant at all times. He was not happy. Another giggle escaped him. What the hell. Why was this insubordination and negligence so funny? It wasn't.

Snorting with suppressed laughter, he tried to get up, but his legs and arms weren't working. They didn't move. Suddenly, he felt fear mix with a feeling of complete relaxation. This wasn't normal...something was very, very wrong. In a slow motion haze, he looked more closely at his men...they weren't sleeping, they were slumped in their seats...they were unconscious. Suddenly he felt his chest squeeze the air from his lungs...he couldn't breathe.

As he felt the darkness come for him, he looked at the cockpit and tried to hail the pilot...he needed to do something. Oxygen. He tried to reach for the mask near his seat, but his arms seemed too short, the distance too great. Never taking his eyes off the pilot, he felt relief when the man seemed to react to his thoughts. He was moving around in his seat. Soon he would notice something was wrong and take appropriate action...the man was a seasoned aviator and more importantly, he loved his children.

The pilot shifted in the left seat and in slow motion turned to look back at Terrin and the other passengers. Terrin stared as the man took off his hat and shook out waves of long golden hair. What the fuck? He was hallucinating. It looked like...no. No, his mind screamed. No. No. No. Terrin saw the mask on the pilot's face...oxygen. The pilot was breathing in oxygen. Above the mask, brown eyes flashed and he heard his nemesis saying, "It's hypoxia, you son-of-a-bitch. Enjoy your little nap, the next thing you will see are the smiling faces of your worst nightmare."

"You..." he managed before he passed out.

Skye grinned at her copilot. "That should do it Blake. Hypoxia affects people in different ways, but one thing for sure, without oxygen even well-trained highly paid mercenaries are nothing but meat. I'll take it down under 10,000 so we can get these masks off. Call Alex and make sure he and Jim are in place at the Coast Guard pier. Tell them all of our passengers are resting comfortably and should be out for a while. Then while I get this plane on the ground, how about going back there and taking away any dangerous toys you may find. Probably wouldn't hurt to tie them to their seats."

Nodding, Blake settled in to wait for them to descend to a safe altitude. "I think I can handle that, Captain."

"I wish my conscience would allow me to stay up here long enough to give them all brain damage."

"Well, think of it this way…at least they'll understand fully what's happening to them when they are extradited back to their country. I'm no expert in international law, but I think these thugs are in some real nasty trouble."

"Since you put it that way, I think this little caper has ended very well indeed."

She and Blake grinned at each other behind the masks that were pumping oxygen into their lungs.

They had reached the seaplane only minutes before Terrin's boat came speeding down the waterway, out of breath from their two mile jog, guns concealed until they got close enough to make their point. On Skye's signal, they boldly walked arm in arm up the pier, as if they were just enjoying an afternoon stroll. The two men waiting near the plane were pacing nervously, eyes on the water. Clearly not trained in tactical defensive maneuvers, Skye thought. When they got within a few feet of them, Skye drew her two guns, aiming one at each man and had Blake search them. They weren't even armed. That indicated that they were men who were drafted for their ability to fly not fight. The sight of the weapons was convincing enough to subdue them. They didn't put up a fight and were currently tied up and gagged in a small outbuilding near the pier waiting to be picked up by Jim's agents.

Blake still wouldn't stay on the ground and since Skye simply didn't have time to argue, they quickly pealed off the jackets and hats of the cockpit crew and placed themselves in position just as Terrin's boat came around the corner. As they waited for the heavily armed men to board the plane, they realized how vulnerable they were. But the men saw what they expected to see and didn't even think to check the identity of the cockpit crew. A great deal could have gone wrong, but nothing did.

Improvisation was one of Agent Skyler Madison's legendary talents and she worked each opportunity as it presented itself. Blake's trust and ability to adapt made him an effective partner. Together, they won the day for the good guys...hell, they won the whole goddamn shooting match.

For the second time that day, Skye prepared for a landing...this time next to a pier instead of on it.

The rented cruiser was already docked. Alex ran down the pier and yanked open the door to the plane as soon as it stopped. He directed his team of agents as they poured on board the Albatross. A few of the prisoners were already stirring and making dangerous noises.

Alex shook his father's hand as he and Skye stood up and came out of the cockpit then grabbed the Special Agent In Charge and gave her a long, hard kiss.

"I'm not sure that was exactly by the book," said Skye grinning. The agents all pretended not to be watching as they cuffed the terrorists and prodded them awake.

"So we're going to have to rewrite the fucking book. Damn it Skye...sometimes you just go over the top. I can't even cuss you out properly because I don't know where to begin."

"Then don't."

"I could make a few suggestions," said Blake with a wink at his partner and future daughter-in-law.

"Don't be ganging up on me now. We have him, Alex. That's the only important thing."

"It's him?"

"Yes, I'm sure of it. How's Duncan?"

"According to Amanda and Mom, he'll be fine, but they beat him up badly...that makes two of you we owe him for." Alex's anger was obvious as he glanced over at the semi-conscious Terrin. "Bat and Elliot are on their way in with him. Jim has an ambulance waiting."

As Skye stepped out of the plane, she looked over at Jim and waved. He gave her a thumbs up and went back to chatting with Amanda and making calls. David was assisting the agents in getting the prisoners off the cruiser and Wyatt was keeping close to Tank. Arm in arm Alex and Skye walked with Blake toward the rest of the party.

Suddenly a revived Terrin realized where he was and what was happening. He saw Skye standing next to Alex with her arm around his waist and he felt his sanity slip. He tried to lunge at her and nearly got away from the two agents who held him.

"You will not be able to cage me, you bitch. I'll get a lawyer. I was in international waters. You cannot stop the Serpent and the Spear. When you cut the head off, another one grows back. The body still lives. And you will be its first target. You will never be able to rest, you whore bitch. You will never know peace. Keep looking over your shoulder, slut!" He struggled with the agents, strengthened by his anger.

Skye felt Alex tense and she squeezed his waist before she disengaged herself from him. "Allow me, please, Special Agent in Charge Springfield. Since I do believe I was the target, I claim special privilege."

"He's yours, Special Agent in Charge Madison," said Alex, holding himself in check through monumental self-control. Skye knew what it cost him and figured she would make it up to him later.

There was a great deal of eye contact between all the family members as Skye walked over to the ranting man, but no one said anything. They decided to watch the show.

Terrin had never seen her healthy and whole. She was taller than he remembered and she was pissed. Her eyes bore into him, staring him down. And he blinked. Something she expected. He was a coward. When she was less than three feet from him, she looked down from her superior height and just smiled with disdain.

"You want to repeat that?" she asked in a clear, composed voice.

"You bitch. You're a dead woman. I'll put contracts out on you. I'll have your entire family blown up. They will never be safe. I know their names. I know where they live. I'll come back and feed that black bastard's heart to the fish. I broke his fucking fingers. One at a time. And I'll come back to finish the job. On him. On you. And your lover. Anyone you're with. Everyone you are close to. You will never know a moment's peace. You fucking whore. You're just a woman. You're nothing. You spread your legs to the guards. That's how you escaped. You slut. You have no power over me. You haven't won. No fucking female can ever win. They're too stupid. Too weak. Women are only good for one thing. To lie under a man."

Wyatt said softly. "Oh boy. Now he's done it. He can blow her up, but he should never have blown her off. Maybe we should back up."

Skye looked at the two agents standing beside Terrin and smiled. "Take a break," she said. She was still smiling, but the temperature was Alaskan cold.

The agents were reluctant. They knew who Skye was, of course. She was a legend already. But this was a very unorthodox request. Not by the book. They looked over at Jim. Jim looked at Skye, then at Alex. Alex nodded. Jim nodded at the agents and they stepped back. Although they were initially reluctant, they appeared almost eager now.

Terrin stared at Skye. He was assessing his situation. He would put a mark on this arrogant bitch. If he was going into a cage, even temporarily, he would go in with the memory of her bones breaking under his blows, her face crushed, her beauty ruined.

"I think a perverted asshole like you is only good for one thing…target practice." Skye's voice was low and deadly. Her tone was condescending and insulting. Everyone watching was glad it wasn't them on the receiving end of that look, that voice, and as it turned out, that fury.

Terrin was quick. He was military trained and had risen in the ranks of the Serpent and the Spear through both cunning and physical prowess. The fact that he was a very unsound man and basically a coward was covered up by bravado and evil intent. Skye was never fooled. She saw his flaws and smelled his fear. She was also quicker.

As Terrin moved his hand up to strike, Skye countered swiftly and decisively, slapping away the attack easily and slamming the palm of her hand into his chest. He flew back and would have fallen if he hadn't hit the side of the Albatross. She could have ended it right there, but she didn't want to. She wasn't done.

Skye backed up, taunting him, not through words, but though her smile and her actions. Lowering her hands, daring him to come at her bodily. It was an insulting taunt and Terrin felt all his self-control explode. He came at her and she sidestepped, caught his torso with her arm, grabbed his forearm and flipped him over her shoulder. He went flying and landed hard. She spun around to face him. Still smiling, barely breathing heavy. Shaking himself, he still believed he was superior. Let her get in a few lucky shots, he was confident he would be able to tear her apart.

That changed over the next few minutes. Terrin did learn a few tricks in his years of training. Skye was on the ground a couple times, always protecting her side and rolling with the few hits he managed to land, but in the end, her masterful series of kicks and punches wore him down. The fact he stayed standing as long as he did was a testament to his intractable need to win…to come out on top. In the end it only hurt him and gave Skye an even greater sense of victory and satisfaction.

She fought through her rage and took her time. Each satisfying blow purged another ghost. She fought for her passengers, for President Moreno, for Cliff and his family, for the night she thought Alex was dead, for the invasion of her home, for Tank and that moment of terror when he went flying into the ocean, for dear, courageous Duncan. And finally for herself. For the weeks of pain...for the weeks of heartache...for the memory of his hands on her flesh. She was the champion of light. Her flight into terror was at the end of its journey.

Terrin moved with fear, viciousness, and cold-blooded brutality. Skye moved with justice, morality, and finesse. It was an uneven match right from the beginning.

Blake had a hand on Alex's shoulder and felt the restraint his son was exercising. Alex had his arms crossed over his chest, a slight smile on his lips. He watched with intensity, his insides knotting up painfully every time Terrin landed a blow...and yet he looked relaxed and amused. Blake was sometimes amazed that this incredible man was his boy. He was proud. More than that. It was an indescribable combination of love and respect. He squeezed his hand to communicate that fact. It ran through Alex and it helped. He felt some of the tension ease. Not all of it, but enough.

When Terrin went down for the last time, Skye stood over him, breathing heavily and wiping blood from the corner of her mouth. Her shirt was torn, her hair was in complete disarray, her eyes were flashing, and she was grinning. Everyone on the dock, but a few proud family members, was gaping.

"*You* look over your own shoulder, you fucking spineless limp-dicked loser. I have better things to do," she said. She turned to the two agents. "Cuff him and put him in a cage." Then she turned her back, insultingly, dismissively and walked away to the sound of applause. She looked around. She forgot for a moment that she had an audience, but she obliged them and executed a little dainty bow. Amanda walked up and handed her the lacy silk hanky. Accepting it with a smile, Skye wiped the blood from her hands.

Alex took a deep breath to expel the last of the stress, left his dad's side, and went over to inspect his future wife for any damage. There would be a few new bruises, maybe a sore muscle or two, but she had managed to protect her side beautifully and kept Terrin pretty much on the defense the whole time.

As he kissed a tiny cut right to the left of her lips, he had to admit, a bit sheepishly to no one but himself, that he was really, really turned on. Sometimes Skye was a beautiful, ferocious animal and he could feel the heat pour out of her. He hoped to channel some of that energy and heat to...well, other more pleasant physical activities. Later. The fact she could kick the shit out of a man made her willingness and compliance in bed even more titillating. If she was going to make him go insane with her need to mix it up with villains, he was determined to go slowly mad with a smile on his face. Consider it his bonus.

Blake, Wyatt, David, and Tank stood watching them as Alex put his arm around her and casually brushed the dirt from her clothes and inspected her knuckles.

"Just another day at the office," said Blake walking over to his family.

"Should I worry to death now or later?" asked Wyatt.

"Damn. Can you imagine the babies they'll make? That's some gene pool," said David.

"I need another beer," gasped Tank, finding it a bit hard to breathe and chalking it up to the bruises on his chest. Then they all started talking and asking questions at once while Blake filled them in from his perspective.

There were ambulances and dark, nondescript sedans all over the government facility. Jim would keep things low profile and discreet. No media, no inquiries.

Skye and Alex personally supervised the transfer of Duncan when Elliot steered the boat into a slip. The gurney strained under the weight of the battered and beaten Duncan as the EMS team started an IV. Skye looked down at him, making sure he was breathing all right and as if sensing her presence, his eyes opened. He tried to smile, but the effort was hindered by the damage inflicted on his face. His beautiful, wonderful face.

"How did you know?" rasped Duncan out of swollen and bruised lips. "How did you know I was in a little trouble?"

Skye gently took his hand and saw the several broken fingers. She just wanted to hug him and weep, but instead, she smiled down into his bottomless black eyes. "There were no beach eroding waves. Kids didn't get out their surfboards. The green flags were still up on the beach. And mamas weren't grabbing their babies and running for higher ground. Plus nearly every one of the intruders had a bruise, a black eye, or sore balls."

Duncan barked out a laugh, then winced in pain. His hand actually squeezed hers. Leaning over, she kissed his fevered forehead. "I got a few licks in," he said.

"You did well, Duncan." She smoothed some of the loose hair from his face. He looked back into her eyes, then closed his in relief. Her words took a load off his mind. He needed to hear that from her before he could let go. He knew she was the target and he tried to play it smart. He saw respect in her eyes behind the compassion. His heart beat stronger and his mind was at rest.

"I saw your plane," he said before he lost consciousness. "I saw your plane and I knew the good guys were coming over the hill."

She looked down at him. "Just in the nick of time, I think," she whispered as a tear escaped, landing on his broad, heroic chest. Then she kissed him tenderly and nodded to the paramedics who loaded him into the waiting ambulance.

Brushing her face with her hands, she straightened her shoulders. Tank was being assisted to a waiting car by Blake and Wyatt. Blake had seen his son from the plane and had a few bad moments himself. His youngest boy, carrying a bottle of beer and grinning like a conquering hero held his chest and walked gingerly, but under his own power.

"So. Did you enjoy your swim?" Skye smiled as she walked up to him.

"Hey," he said in an indignant tone. "Duncan got a kiss." He wiped another tear from her face. "And a little sympathy."

He looked into her eyes. The lips were smiling but the concern was there and it was deep. He really didn't want her to worry. It was a lark and his only regret was he would never be able to tell anyone about it.

"So. Where's mine?" He puckered up and nearly jumped back into the water when Alex quick as lightening, grabbed his face, kissed him on the lips and made a huge smacking noise.

"That ought to work," said Alex as Skye burst out laughing.

"Worked for me," said Skye, sliding her arm around Alex's waist. Alex adored the look of love he saw in her eyes and gave her a big smacking kiss as well. "Just a little booster shot."

Tank made gagging noises. "Get me another beer, will you. I just had this really scary flashback of Aunt Gertie coming to visit."

Alex and Blake laughed. "Gertie is dad's aunt. She would always go right for Tank. He was her favorite. She would squeeze his pudgy little cheeks, squeal over how much he'd grown, and give him a great big kiss. Dad would have to give him a dollar every time she visited just to get him out from under the bed."

"I could always smell her coming. I still can't stand the smell of lavender." Tank laughed too, but that made his chest hurt, so he had another suggestion. "Let's go back to Alex's little bungalow and get this party started."

The debriefing was loud, raucous, and unlike any that Jim had conducted in his extensive term with the department.

"If we're going to develop amnesia after today, we're going to beat it to death now," said Tank as he opened another Corona. He was enjoying the attention and spirited discussion of his launch into the water. Everyone told the story from his or her point of view.

"A fucking third eye, Mom? You actually said that? Goddamn it if you don't sound like Dirty Harry or something." He laughed uproariously. She laughed too, but at the time, she meant it. He looked over at Skye and Amanda. "This is how she kept us in line when we were kids. All the other kids had moms who went to parenting classes and the PTA. Our mom carried a gun."

"Judging by how you turned out, her formula must have worked," said Amanda. She had already upbraided him for shoving her out of the way.

"What? Loud, obnoxious, and insufferable?" asked David. He had soaked up a lot of suds himself and was feeling no pain. He would have to work to get the image of Tank going over the rail out of his head. Tonight it would be as much beer as he could stomach. Tomorrow he would seek his own unique brand of therapy...he would play with Rita's kids. Hugs, kisses, mock punches, video games, shouting, and pizza. It worked for him.

Then they relived every moment, every click of the gun, every punch, every shot. Blake loved his role as copilot and the pier got shorter with every telling. The scenes were vivid, the stories slightly exaggerated and the affection, admiration, and love flowed as easily and as often as the beer.

"Does this mean we can unpack?" asked Tank. His vision had been blurry for almost an hour.

"Absolutely," said Skye laughing.

"Now that we have this thing all sewn up, can we get to something important?" asked Blake. "Like a wedding date?"

Skye and Alex looked at each other. Skye shrugged. She was mostly sober and the very thought of actually setting a date scared her more than Terrin's threats. Alex could see that. But what the hell. He was mostly drunk.

"How about tomorrow?" he said, quite satisfied with the idea. Then changing his mind almost right away. "No. That won't work. We need to find a tux for Tank. That could take awhile." For some reason all the men in the room thought that was a riot and laughed their heads off.

"Can't be a Saturday in the fall," said Elliot.

"College football," they all shouted in unison.

"Can't be Sunday or a Monday night, either," said Bat.

"NFL!" they shouted.

"How about Halloween?" asked Tank. "With all the spooks and scary people in this room, it seems appropriate."

"Yeah. You could come masquerading as a cop," said Alex.

"Exactly. And you and Skye could disguise yourselves as a pilot and a lawyer. And Amanda, well she could come as a little old lady." Tank laughed himself into a coughing fit and rolled off the couch. He lay there gasping until the little old lady helped him back up.

Tomorrow, there would be secrecy and secrets. Tonight was a time to punch holes in the deceptions.

"So, Amanda," said Tank, taking her hand before she could back away. "CIA? Right? Huh?"

Amanda just smiled. "AARP, young man. That's my only relevant affiliation."

While Tank was going through every other acronym he could think of, Alex took Skye's hand and led her out into the night. Gathering her up in his arms, he kissed her long, slow, and deep. Her lip was a bit tender on one side but he could always make the pain go away. She held on to him as they turned and looked out over the ocean.

"So, what about a date?" he said. He hadn't realized until his dad had asked how important it was to him. It would make it more real. More tangible. More settled. And, he admitted to himself, more difficult for her to back away.

The silence lengthened and Alex's heart started to beat a little faster. Was she going to balk now? She took his ring. That was a promise. A date was only the next step. He held his breath. He was absolutely not going to pressure her.

"How about October 27th?" she asked, looking at him out of the corner of her eye. "That way you'll never forget our anniversary."

"My birthday?" he asked, pleasure running through him like a warm river. "I didn't even know you knew my birth date."

"I know a lot about you. I had you investigated once, remember?"

"Yes."

"And I loved you then."

"You did?"

"I did. I just didn't know what to do with it, so I carried it around rather than let it in."

"So we'll get married on my birthday?"

"Yours and Rita's."

"What a great present!" All of his doubts and fears evaporated. It was official and he knew how to hold someone to a contract.

"All gift wrapped and everything."

"You aren't going to wear a big bow, are you?"

"No. I told Hazel she had no role in selecting the attire."

Alex kissed her until he heard the group wondering out loud where the Special Agents in Charge had gone.

"Merging their notes, no doubt."

"Well of course, they have to provide a united front."

Alex laughed and gave his bride-to-be one last peck. They would be sleeping together tonight and he would be able to finish then what they just started.

"October 27th," he said. "We'll tell them tomorrow at breakfast."

"Make that lunch," she said. "They won't be up much before then if this party continues."

And it did continue. They partied until just before dawn. Jim left at midnight to check on all the prisoners. Amanda kissed them all good night about 2 a.m. At 3:30, Elliot and Bat managed to find their way upstairs. They heard Elliot shouting when he discovered Tank had taken his pajamas and had them flying like a flag from the terrace. Wyatt and Blake decided on a walk on the beach to watch the sun come up. They grabbed a blanket and a bottle of wine and left.

"Major takedowns make Mom really horny," said Tank, laughing. "It's the gun thing. You know, having something hard and long and able to shoot bullets in the palm of your hand. Dad always loves the big raids. Keeps him smiling for a week." Then Alex and Tank looked at each other. Parents having sex. They both shuddered.

Skye and Alex poured Tank into bed just as the eastern sky was giving up the darkness. Grabbing Skye around the neck, he pulled her down for a quick kiss.

"I'm warning you," he said solemnly. "If you ever, ever leave my big brother…" Then he broke out into his award-winning grin. "You can climb right in here with me and stay forever." With that little speech, his arm fell down on the bed and he was out cold.

Leaning over, she kissed his forehead. Alex pulled the blanket over him and ruffled his hair.

"Scared the shit out of me today," said Alex as he blew out a breath. "There's a lot of Rita in him."

"Ever try to talk him out of being a cop?"

"Nah. It's all he ever really wanted to be. And he will be one of the best."

"I think he already is," said Skye.

They left the room arm in arm and turned out the lights.

EPILOGUE

It had been over six weeks since the hijacking. The media had gone on to other things. There were cameras on the perimeter, but none were allowed in the hangar International Airlines had rented outside Washington, D.C. It was the reunion of the passengers and crew of Flight 127 and the mood was upbeat and festive. Bill and Carter took care of everything and were in their element.

The hangar was beautifully decorated and blinked with a thousand lights. Like the stars in the heavens Bill had said. Skye shimmered too, from her eyes to the hem of her long sequined dress.

Nearly all the passengers and their families were in attendance. They all wanted to meet and greet the captain, although few recognized her out of uniform or without a bruised face. Alex stood beside her, the picture of a successful, polished businessman. Beautifully groomed, presenting a well manicured hand and a friendly smile to everyone. It was a testament to his ability to change and blend that not one of the passengers recognized him...with one exception.

"Hello, Mr. Springfield. How's the shoulder?" Alex heard the low, pleasant voice of a man he recognized. Turning, he saw Cliff and his family. Smiling, excited, and eager to shake hands with the captain. Alex looked at him for a second. Then smiled and nodded. Cliff wasn't going to spread it around. He and Skye had decided not to deny it, just not bring it up. Still, he didn't answer the question.

"Cliff," said Alex with sincere pleasure, taking the man's hand. "Good to see you. Please, call me Alex. I know Skye has been anxious to talk with you."

"She has?" said a little girl with curly red hair. "I have her picture on my wall. It was in the paper. My dad was on the plane. So was I, but I threw up. I hit the bag, though. Dad said he was proud."

Skye had come up beside Alex and the children's eyes went wide with awe, then wonder as the famous captain took their dad's hand, called him by his name, and then kissed him on the cheek.

She then shook their mom's hand. "Good to see the two of you again. I'm afraid I was a bit under the weather when we landed in Florida."

"We want to thank you again for the real nice addition to the children's college fund, Captain," said Cliff as his wife nodded her agreement and pleasure. They had called and written several times, but this was their first opportunity to talk with her face-to-face.

"Seconds mattered on the island, Cliff. And you gave us more than a few of those." Then Skye turned to the two children. Neither of them had ever seen such a tall woman. At least they couldn't remember if they did. And certainly not one this beautiful.

"Did your father tell you he was a hero?" she asked the children. They were struck dumb. A condition Cliff later told her was a first. They silently shook their heads but if the blessed captain said it was so, it was so. Cliff beamed. His wife turned and smiled, impressed and more than a little turned on by the image. Cliff beamed some more. He was going to get lucky tonight. Thank you again, Captain.

"Did you get to Disney World?"

They both nodded their heads this time. Still unable to formulate words.

"Did you enjoy yourselves?" Again they nodded. She knew that International Airlines had picked up the tab for all the families. It reduced the trauma, was good for public relations...and it was a nice thing to do, especially for the children.

Skye realized that she was going to have to stop asking yes or no questions or she was only going to get nods and shakes. "What was your favorite part?"

That opened the dam. They both started talking at once and each one had several favorite parts.

"There they are," said Cliff's wife, laughing along with Skye, Cliff, and Alex. "I was beginning to think they were aliens that only looked like my children."

"So where's your uniform?" asked her son. He liked the red sparkly thing okay, but the uniform was the best.

"I have it on under here. I'm like Superman. I only reveal it when there's a plane to fly. Then I rip off the dress and become...The Captain." The children didn't know whether to believe that or not, but since there was still a Santa and a tooth fairy, they were completely captivated by the possibility.

Skye wore a strapless, sparkling, red, skintight dress that had already been on and off once that evening. Alex knew for certain there was no uniform underneath. As a matter of fact, there was very little on underneath. Nothing for children, that was for sure. Earlier that evening, Alex had sent Cynthia with the children and all the family members from both sides on ahead to the party. They were blissfully alone and Alex was tying his tie when Skye walked out of her dressing room, carrying her shoes, totally unaware of the impact she had on her fiancé. He stood watching her with his hand in midair. Completely forgetting what he'd been doing a few moments before, he looked at the ends of his tie with absolute confusion. Where was he? Left over right. Right over left. Shit. He took it off, threw it on the bed and started unbuttoning his shirt.

Skye, sitting on the chaise slipping into her new red sandals, looked up in surprise. As usual when she went to parties, she indulged herself with very high heels. Being engaged to a tall man was a dream come true for her. She could come into a room well over six feet and he still had a good three inches on her. When she saw him pull his unbuttoned shirt out of his pants, she frowned.

"Aren't you going in the wrong direction?" she asked. Then she forgot what she was doing as Alex crossed the room shedding clothes on the way. She stood up and was out of her dress in the blink of an eye. The advantage of a one-piece outfit. A one-piece strapless teddy followed his underwear through the air and they were skin to skin before either of them came to their senses. It didn't take long before they came to all of their senses at once. When their surroundings shimmered back into focus, he was smiling into her laughing eyes. They were standing. He had her pinned to the wall and her legs were still around him.

"Wow! That felt good." She kissed him thoroughly. "And you didn't even muss my hair...much."

"If you weren't the guest of honor," he said. "We could forget the party and I could just muss up everything."

She sighed. "But I really want to wear these shoes."

He gave her one more long kiss, then let her slide down his body. By the time she was back on her feet, she had almost changed her mind.

"Obligations," he said. "What a drag."

"Buck up, darling. We can lock the door in the morning and tell everyone we're indisposed."

"Like that will discourage Jason and Al. They'll probably climb up the side of the building and shoot through the window." His nephews loved to come wake Aunt Skye and drag her downstairs for pancakes. "I'm the one who has to be sure you aren't naked," he grumbled as he managed to get through the tying of his tie this time. "You're always so out of it in the morning, you might just sit up and stunt those kids growth for a decade."

"Such a burden you have to bear," she said and made him wait another half-hour while she got cleaned up and reapplied her makeup.

"I thought I didn't muss up anything," he called from the steps below checking his watch after ten minutes had passed. When she swept down the staircase twenty minutes after that, his impatience vanished. Some women were just worth the wait.

Alex and Skye were making the rounds and found Sloane talking to a group of young people about the latest album by the Restless Pretzels. Alex had taken Sloane and a group of her friends to a concert a few months before and sealed their relationship forever. Skye was glad Sloane could communicate so well with people her own age. 'Age-appropriate social behavior' Sloane called it. Giggling, snorting, gagging, eye rolling, comparing CD collections, and being silly was what Skye's grateful heart saw.

Alex took Sloane for a spin around the dance floor. She chattered the whole time but had a natural grace that had her flawlessly following Alex's expert lead. His head was down, smiling and laughing at what she was saying. Skye's lips turned up with affection and appreciation for the fabulous picture they made. Family. It warmed her. It healed her.

They came back to Skye when the song was over, laughing, arm in arm. "Skye, Alex told me that if I don't have breasts by the time I'm twenty-one, he'll buy some for me." Skye was sure nature would kick in long before that, so she simply smiled, winked at Alex, and nodded.

Just then, Amanda came into the hangar on the arm of a very handsome, distinguished looking man. He was tall and straight and it looked like he'd stayed in shape over the years. There was a commanding set to his broad shoulders. His full head of hair was a thick luxurious silver gray and his matching gray eyes were alert and intelligent. Amanda was obviously smitten with him. Skye noticed the man had a very slight limp. Nothing distracting. As a matter of fact, it gave him a roguish air...like the man of mystery he apparently was.

Skye, Sloane, and Alex turned to greet her, pleasure written all over their faces.

"Skye Madison. Alex Springfield. Sloane Madison. I would like you to meet Cameron Mitchell, my husband," Amanda said with a twinkle in her bright green eyes.

"Your husband?" Skye and Alex both exclaimed in one voice. Sloane was the only one who didn't seem surprised. Amanda looked at her and sent a distinct, unspoken but subtle message. Shame on you, you darling little hacker.

"I didn't know…," began Skye, then looked at Alex.

"We didn't know," confirmed Alex and shook the man's hand with a grin and an assessing stare. "It's a pleasure."

Skye took his hand next. It was firm and communicated great strength. "Yes, a real pleasure." Still completely flabbergasted, she simply couldn't think of anything clever to say.

"I understand it's the three of you we have to thank for the safe return of our grandson." His voice was low and authoritative.

Skye composed herself and smiled. "I hope Amanda didn't leave out the part she played."

"I read the report," he said, looking at his wife fondly. There was pride there, too. Amanda was beautiful in a green one-piece pantsuit. The long lines of the flowing material accentuated her trim figure. Her hair was piled high on her head and deep, richly colored emeralds sparkled at her throat and on her ears. The green of her eyes matched them exactly. Someone had taken great care choosing them for her.

"Forgive me for this really strange question…but where were you during this whole adventure?" asked Skye.

Amanda took Cameron's arm and smiled at them. "Your clearance isn't high enough to know, my dear," she said gently, but firmly.

Sloane knew, but this was one secret she was definitely going to keep to herself. The gray eyes were on her now and she could feel herself vowing to be good as they continued to bore through her. She prayed to the computer gods: *No more hacking. No more hacking. I'll be good. I'll be good.*

When he extended his hand to her, she almost expected there to be handcuffs and a warrant. "May I have this dance? It will give Mandy an opportunity to talk behind my back."

Amanda was right, he thought, as he led the teenager out onto the dance floor. The little genius could keep a secret, even from her family. It was obvious that neither Skye nor Alex knew anything about him. He wouldn't bring it up to her although it was one reason he was in attendance tonight. He needed to assess this young woman and make a judgment. Mandy was tough, but in this case, she might have been too swayed by sentiment. Gratitude aside, in this instance, she was right. He wouldn't pursue the incredibly well executed security breach into the top-secret files any further. He could however make the young lawbreaker sweat…just a little.

"Well, Mandy," said Alex, as Cameron led a shaky, but game Sloane out onto the dance floor. "You really tossed one in from left field with that one."

"So...where was he?" asked Skye. "Do you keep him in a closet and bring him out for dances, or what?"

"Sorry, my dear." Amanda looked at her husband with love and a lifetime of devotion. "As far as I can determine, your classification hasn't changed in the last few minutes." Then she looked at her grandson who was in the corner with Jason and Al showing them the latest electronic game he bought. "I guess Cameron is the only Mitchell to sweep Sloane off her feet this evening." Effectively changing the subject.

"I thought they would be so compatible. I mean, when he told me about the Bubbliscious...well I thought that would be something to build on. Shared passions sometimes are," sighed Skye. It was the only failure of the evening. "When they met, it was more combatable than compatible, I'm afraid. It was instantaneous loathing. You should have seen the sparks. They were snarling at each other just after the hello's and hi's." Because they were strong personalities, their clash had the power of a Jedi battle. "They started with a bit of name calling. He called her a brainiac and she called him an arrogant, conceited, vain, smug, self-important cretin." Skye had felt a flash of pride on the really excellent use of adjectives before she went back to being disappointed.

"Give it time," said Amanda.

"Sure." Then she smiled conspiratorially. "He still has to be her escort at our wedding. He lost the bet fair and square."

Amanda nodded and winked. She noticed the little surreptitious looks and glances they flashed on each other when they thought no one was looking.

"Sloane is a beautiful girl with unbelievable potential; not a buck-toothed, pimply, undernourished, pale faced, skinny-necked bore."

Alex and Skye laughed. "And your tall, brave, intelligent grandson is not a booger eating idiot with mismatched clothes and a fetish for really loud bean farts."

Amanda laughed with them. "Maybe they're too much alike. I think I'll go spring Sloane and tag a dance with my husband," Amanda said.

Alex and Skye watched as Amanda claimed her man and Sloane went off in a hurry to get a glass of punch. She'd been holding her breath for five minutes and needed something to fortify her.

"Do you know how that man Faneta was taken out?"

"No. It was something that Amanda arranged."

"Hmmm. And all those calls she made to Langley. Who was she talking to? How did she get the CIA for God's sake, to completely reprogram the satellites?"

"She never said."

"Hmmm."

"You said that before."

"And the incursion force of special ops personnel that we, thank God, didn't need. Any idea how that got put together so fast? And how did Terrin and his men get extradited to their country without a lot of legal haggling? You're a lawyer. Isn't that unusual and terribly fast?"

"I thought so at the time. But we may never know. On the other hand, if you get to the higher classification before me, darling, you're just going to have to promise here and now to tell me."

"And the same goes for me. Think we should put that in our wedding vows?"

"Sure. Why not?" Skye turned to him.

It was so wonderful. So normal. Parties. Dancing. Wedding vows. It was a magnificent night. Looking around, she nudged Alex and nodded toward the tables in the corner. Alex looked over to where she had indicated. Tank and Amy had their heads together in conversation. He was using his Springfield charm and it was working very well indeed. Looking up, he gave Skye a wink. She winked back and nodded. Amy was a wonderful choice.

Duncan had recovered, mostly. His hand was still in a cast and he had to replace his beautiful gold tooth. Apparently he'd swallowed it and he told Skye he simply didn't have the moral fiber to recover it. He decided to opt for a more mature porcelain crown. Tonight he was in all black leather. Relatively conservative and very hot. He and Connie were dancing in perfect rhythm.

"Our boy is growing up," she sighed. "His leather jacket doesn't have any writing or logos on it."

"Apparently tonight he isn't Born To Ride."

They looked at each other and said in perfect unison. "Unless it's Connie."

One very interesting and wonderful development was that David had asked Linda to dance. Several times. "They make a wonderful pair," said Skye sighing. She truly loved matchmaking.

"A wonderful pair of what?" asked Hazel, coming up on the arm of Dr. Lacy.

"Hi Aunt Hazel." Hazel was in an unusual combination of colors and textures. She wore a hat with stunning aqua blue feathers, obviously from an aqua blue bird. It complimented her party dress of orange sequins. Some had fallen off so she sewed them back on with purple and red thread. One of the shoulder pads was missing, so she looked a bit off kilter. Sometimes she used her shoulder pads to stuff in her bra, but she looked pretty even there. She'd been known to move them throughout the evening, just for a little fun. Skye couldn't imagine where it was. Better it remained a mystery. Her makeup this evening was subdued...more Las Vegas showgirl than Ringling Brother's circus. Skye thought she looked wonderful. "Enjoying yourself?"

"I am. Sure does pay to shake it with a doctor. Don't have to worry about getting overheated and passing out. He can take my pulse and recommend treatment, right on the dance floor, huh Livingston?"

Dr. Livingston Lacy was so enthralled with this woman that he couldn't even think of an appropriate response. So he just smiled.

"And thanks for loaning us your truck. We'll try to get it back to you in one piece...course who's gonna know?" She laughed with abandon. The fact that he loaned her his beloved truck showed just how much he thought of her. "Mind if we try out those reclining seats?" She elbowed the good doctor and he blushed. "We can play find the other shoulder pad."

Ah. Thought Skye. Mystery solved. It was a game. Hazel grabbed the good doctor's hand and led him out for another dance. Alex couldn't stop laughing, so Skye sent him off for more wine.

Stuart had recovered and was flying again. Tonight he was flying with nearly every female passenger in sight. And some of their daughters. He was young and handsome and single and, in the eyes of all the people here, heroic. The role suited him. He'd been promoted to captain on Skye's recommendation. He was wearing his captain's wings this evening and he knew he had her to thank.

"Anyone see Frank Sills?" asked Stuart facetiously when he came over to take a breather.

"Yeah. In court," Alex said and Skye just stared at him. This was the first she heard of this development.

"I've been working with International Airlines, the FAA, and the Justice Department," explained Stuart. "Alex has been invaluable providing legal council and advice. Pro bono. I realize he wants to keep a low profile, so I've been the front man. I was deposed last week by the grand jury. Sills may be facing a whole shitload of federal charges."

Alex looked at Skye and remembered the agony she suffered because of Sills. He and Stuart had pursued the charges with the commitment of a crusade when he got back to his office. Not only had Sills injured Stuart and brought discomfort to Skye, everyone knew that if he would have disrupted the operation of the aircraft even ten more minutes, they all would be dead. Sills was pursuing his own lawsuit, but Alex was determined to bring the man down and put him in prison. Stuart was with him all the way.

"But enough of this law stuff. There are several passengers I haven't had a dance with yet," laughed Stuart as he went off to do his duty.

"Love is in the air," said Skye.

Even Barclay and a young woman were sitting at a table in the corner. They weren't talking and they seemed very interested in the plates of food they had in front of them, but they were at the same table and she had some kind of electronic device sitting next to her, so there was hope.

Just then, the crowd turned and hushed. There seemed to be a great deal of excitement at the entrance to the hangar. Bill and Carter were clearing a path to Skye and the passengers obliged by stepping aside like the parting of the Red Sea. In strode Moreno, the newly elected President of Soteras. He looked wonderful. Tanned, tall, handsome, and well rested. Everyone's image of a reform President.

There was a hush as the band stopped playing for a minute. Then a strain of a folk song from the beautiful island played softly. As President Moreno approached Skye, she extended her hand and smiled. "Mr. President." He took her hand and kissed it lightly. The place erupted in applause.

"Captain Madison," he said in the cultured voice she remembered but loud enough for everyone to hear and share in his presentation. "It's so nice to see you well. You have received my communications, but I wanted to be here in person to say thank you and to present to you this gift from my country." He handed her a velvet box.

She opened it, looked up at him with dancing, bright eyes and smiled a charming, enchanted smile. In it was a simple, lovely multicolored rock.

"No gold can adequately compensate you. No jewel could be as lovely as your eyes. No amount of proclamations can possibly capture our gratitude. No reward could possibly pay our debt to you. This rock represents a part of our island. It's an ancient symbol of hospitality in our culture. This is a part of Soteras. You will be forever an honorary citizen and welcomed in our homes as well as our hearts. There's a stretch of land on one of our beaches where that stone was harvested. It was the home of Terrin. His house has been torn down. The gates have been opened. It is now Madison Park. It is a place of clean sand and warm water. A place where families will come to play and enjoy the sun. Where artists will paint. Where poets will write."

Skye thought she had it under control. She made it through the rock part and the honorary citizen part, and almost all the way through the open gates part. But she just couldn't contain the tears through the artists and poets part. It was just too lovely. She laid her head against Alex's shoulder, clutched her exquisite gift to her heart and let the tears flow.

It started a flood as tissues and handkerchiefs were pulled out of pockets and purses...like some kind of flag waving salute. Bill and Carter decided to keep the theme going and had the band play another Soteras hymn. The President bowed his head to Alex in a gallant gesture of permission. Alex nodded and Moreno took Skye's hand. All eyes were on them as people moved aside. They looked royal as they swept over the dance floor. A frowning Alex had to chant. *She's mine. She's mine. She's mine.*

The President was already making a difference in Soteras. The State Department had extradited Terrin and all of his men to the federal prison on the island. After a very public trial where the dregs of the Serpent and the Spear had tried to assassinate a judge, the will of the people completely turned. Terrin was scheduled for execution at the end of the month as were many of his followers. The newly inaugurated President was busy building schools, hospitals, and roads with the confiscated funds from the faction's accounts. Oil companies were bidding on the rich deposits and the future of the country looked solid.

Skye and Alex had a standing invitation to come to the country for a visit. They were thinking of it as a possible honeymoon site. As Alex stiffly smiled and watched the President's hand move up Skye's back, he decided it was going to be Europe. Or Mexico. Or Alaska. Maybe the fucking moon. Anywhere the President wasn't. Christ, was this jealousy? It was a new experience for him. He never cared enough for any woman in the past to feel this way. He didn't much like it.

Skye laughed at something the President said and Alex could feel the slam of it again. Then she caught Alex's eye and waved her left hand gaily at him. His diamond sparkled and he felt his breath coming back. He was happy. That was his ring. He guessed he could share a small part of her. A very small part.

"Hey, man," said Fisher as he came up beside Alex. "You going to let that guy paw all over your armpiece? Just because he's a freakin

President or something doesn't mean he can have diplomatic relations with your sugar bowl's ass."

"I think you' re right," said Alex. Sometimes being around a fifteen-year-old got you in touch with your more basic instincts. He started toward the dance floor. Amanda had him by the arm before he went two feet. "Don't start an international incident right here," she smiled sweetly. "I'm claiming my dance."

He looked down at her and good sense returned. Sometimes being around a 70-year-old woman brought you back in touch with your more mature, charitable self. He led Amanda out on the dance floor and by the time the music ended, he was back in touch with his good-natured, confident self. Still, he claimed his fiancée the first chance he got.

The party went on and on. No one wanted it to end. The President danced with Skye twice more, but Alex figured she would go home with the guy who brought her, so he was in a good place. Jim came up to him later in the evening. He'd come in with the President's entourage and had escorted him back to a waiting government transport.

"That went well," he said putting his arm around his young agent. "Although he did ask about her marital status. I think he's looking for a first lady."

"She is my lady first."

"That's what I told him." He looked around the room at the people remaining. "Now there's a picture of power," he said, nodding to where Sloane, Amanda and Skye were chatting excitedly over something. Laughing, carefree, completely comfortable with each other.

Alex smiled broadly. "A picture entitled...Past, Present and Future."

Jim nodded, his eyes taking on a thoughtful look. "Indeed."

Printed in the United States
50816LVS00003B/130